The Doctor Stories

RICHARD SELZER

The Doctor Stories

Picador USA ✿ *New York*

Picador® is a U.S. registered trademark and is used by St. Martin's Press under license from Pan Books Limited.

NOTE: "Fetishes," "'The Black Swan' Revisited," "A Worm from My Notebook," and "Tom and Lily" were published in *Taking the World in for Repairs;* "Whither Thou Goest," "Luis," "Poe's Lighthouse," "Pipistrel," and "Imagine a Woman" were published in *Imagine a Woman;* "Imelda," "Brute," "Mercy," "Witness," "Semiprivate, Female," "Chatterbox," and "Impostor" were published in *Letters to a Young Doctor;* "Tillim," "Four Appointments with the Discus Thrower," "Raccoon," "Sarcophagus," "Alexis St. Martin," "Pages from a Wound Dresser's Diary," "The Masked Marvel's Last Toehold," "Tube Feeding," and "The Mirror: A Tale of Aran" were published in *Confessions of a Knife.*

Library of Congress Cataloging-in-Publication Data

Selzer, Richard.
    The Doctor stories / by Richard Selzer.—1st ed.
      p.   cm.
    ISBN 0-312-18687-8
    1. United States—Social life and customs—20th century—Fiction. 2. Physicians—United States—Fiction.
    3. Medicine—United States—Fiction. I. Title.
PS3569.E585D63 1998
813'.54—dc21   97-53233
                                    CIP

First Edition: August 1998

10 9 8 7 6 5 4 3 2 1

To
Daniel Aaron Selzer,
Edward Stanton Selzer,
and
Eleanor Cooper Selzer

Contents

The Doctor Stories

Introduction

An introduction ought by rights to come first, but this one would have served better as the tail of this book. Just as I have taken any number of liberties with grammar and syntax, so have I made free with the term "Introduction." This is none such, as it has not been content to speak only of the stories that follow but has wallowed and floundered and inflated itself into a kind of *apologia pro mea vita.*

First, my name: the only thing I have in common with Shakespeare is the habit of spelling my name in a number of different ways. At age eight I looked at my name—Allen Richard Selzer—and winced. It was as uncomfortable as wearing someone else's shoes. That I'd been called Dickie since the hour of birth further distanced me from my legal name. Well then, I thought. Let the unbecoming unbecome! And right then and there I performed my first editorial act. I disimpacted that Richard from its predicament between Allen and Selzer. Next, I pushed the Allen toward the Selzer, and finally, laid the Richard out flat at the beginning. There! That was better—Richard Allen Selzer. But wait! Something was still wrong. It was the Allen. I removed one of its l's, and changed the e to an a to make Richard Alan Selzer. Not perfect, but a name I could live with and did so until decades later when I jettisoned the Alan and became who I am. Each time I changed my name it seemed to give me a new identity as well as a fresh start, rather like a nun who, upon taking the veil, takes a new name to go with it. The truth? I'd rather be called Dick O'Troy than anything else.

I'm as far from being a Great Writer as you can get. To be a Great Writer it's at least as important as genius to lead a colorful life, one that will provide material for a vivid biography when the time comes. (As for genius, I long ago gave that up, and just do the best I can.) Reading the letters of Lord Byron and the life of Hemingway has made me acutely aware of my defects in this regard. I refer to the constant percolation of the lives of Great Writers—plots, counterplots, grievances real and imagined, enemies, scandals, matters of pride and humiliation without which no one can rightly call himself a Great Writer. But I have swum no Hellespont, discovered no new element, hunted no big game. Aside from a few acts of faithlessness on the part of publishers, which I refuse to elevate to the satanic, mine has been a glacial, moribund, and nerveless sojourn in the world of letters. Now that is not good. Where are the duels to be fought? The cruel mistresses? The rivalries, the cheating, the plagiarism? The imitators, the hatred? How can one be expected to write paragraphs seething with passion and vitality when one is forever lying in a meadow of bluets and buttercups in a state of imbecilic contentment? While the rest of the literary world has whipped itself into a sultry chafe, I am the very incarnation of Ferdinand the Bull. Try as I may to work up an outrage, I remain stupidly grateful that I have any readers at all. You're not going to get anywhere that way. Besides, the only "great" writing I've done has been in the hospital charts of my patients. Only there were the words a matter of life and death, and devoid of the vanity of the author or the pomp of language.

∞

I have the urge here to reflect upon my habit of writing. A passion for language was first enkindled when I listened to my mother reading the nursery rhyme "Old King Cole." "He called for his pipe/And he called for his bowl/And he called for his fiddlers three." His fiddlers three? Not his three fiddlers? How come? It was right then that I discovered what could be made by the mere inversion of word order— poetry. St. Paul on the road to Damascus had no more stunning a conversion. I was never to be the same again.

When I was four, Father promised me a silver dollar if I learned to read. Six months later, I read aloud "Jonah and the Whale" from a Bible story book. For years I kept that silver dollar in a cubbyhole of my rolltop desk, until, at sixteen and dying of love, I spent it on a harmonica with which I hoped to win a kiss from Emily Jane. Again and again I played for her the only two songs I knew—"Santa Lucia" and "Flow Gently Sweet Afton." But Emily Jane was not to be blandished.

"Don't you know any others?" she asked. And that was that.

"Just as well," consoled Mother. "A kiss given upon demand gives no delight." But I didn't believe that for a minute. Not then and not now.

From early on, I was encouraged to memorize poems. By age seven, I had in my repertory all of Robert Louis Stevenson's *A Child's Garden of Verses* and, of course, the lyrics to any number of Mother's English music hall and French art songs.

"Stocking up for later," approved Father. "At seven, the brain is at its most retentive." For once, Mother agreed with him.

"Wax and marble," she said. "Wax to receive, marble to keep."

My earliest readings after "Jonah" were those anonymous books of fairy tales, each with a different-colored cover—*The Green Book of Fairy Tales, The Violet, The Red,* and so forth. Then came Edgar Allan Poe, Robert Burns, Sir Walter Scott, and the immortal Raphael Sabatini. These are the true aborigines of my mind. It is sixty years later, and the vessel has kept the scent it first received. It was these four who touched the "darling chord of my heart." While I am not often with Sabatini these days, I return now and then to Stevenson, Scott, and to Poe, who is currently in diminished reputation as decreed by the Arbiters of Taste. It was while reading "The Telltale Heart," "The Pit and the Pendulum," and "The Fall of the House of Usher" that I felt the first of a lifetime of delicious frissons. To make the flesh creep is an ancient and honorable literary endeavor. Years later, when I began to write, I would make use of horror and the grotesque as instruments of illumination, as well as to produce a physiological effect. (Surgeons love horror, don't you know, and instruments.) In doing so, a writer is like a lover who bends every effort to ensure that his beloved is satisfied. Are there decent limits to the use of horror? Not

since the Duke of Cornwall in *King Lear* put out Gloucester's eyes
and cried: "Out, vile jelly! Where is thy lustre now?"

∞

I suppose I've always been a storyteller. All during the years of surgical training, our family of four (the divine Gretchen had not yet been
born) lived in a hospital-owned tenement across the street from the
emergency room. Whenever I could, I'd dash home to visit my cruel
gift upon Jon and Larry, who were five and seven years old when it
began. Throughout supper and their bath, I took pains to build up
suspense for what they knew was coming, a hint dropped, an innu-
endo planted, that sort of thing. Once I had them in the bed they
shared, I turned off the lights, lit a candle, and turned that bedroom
into the boudoir of Scheherezade.

"Once upon a time," I began. Oh, not in the reedy tenor that has
been a lifelong regret, but in a rich, meaty baritone that, once having
left my lips, sank to the floor, causing the furniture to vibrate with virile passion. "Once upon a time, there were two little boys about your
age, I'd say, who lived on the edge of a dark, dark forest." In the bed,
four pupils dilated as one. "One day, they had disobeyed their mother
and gone into the forest to gather nuts and berries. But the two
naughty boys lost track of time, and before you know it, they felt so
tired that they sat down to rest under a big oak tree. Within minutes
they were fast asleep. When they woke up it was nighttime, and pitch
black. Only the bats and owls were awake, hunting for food. All at
once, the boys knew that they were lost. Try as they might to find the
path home, they couldn't. Suddenly, they heard a strange noise nearby,
then another even closer, and another. What could it be? From somewhere in the tree under which they crouched came a long, long moan
followed by a cackle of mad laughter." (I was particularly good at
mad laughter.) "This was followed by the sound of something dripping from the branches of the oak tree. Just then, the moon slid from
behind a cloud and they could see what it was dripping from the
tree. It was blood! What, in God's name, *what* had died up there?" By
this time, my audience was rigid with fear, their skinny arms and legs
wrapped around each other. Their screams of terror echo even now
in my brain.

"Stop! Stop!" they cried. "No more!"

"All right," I agreed. "We'll stop there," and made as if to flick on the light switch. But before ever I could, there came that other cry (as I knew there would): "No! Don't stop! More! More!" Just so did my sons snatch from their father's lips a fearful joy.

∾

Of all the doctor/writers of history, my two favorites are Anton Chekhov and John Keats. Neither one was temperamentally suited to the practice of medicine. Once, while holding a clinic in a small village in Russia, Chekhov was presented with a mother and child, both of whom were weeping loudly. It seemed the child had a large ripe abscess of the neck that simply begged for incision and drainage. But Chekhov, unnerved by the screams of the child and the sobs of the mother, couldn't bring himself to puncture the abscess. Instead, he sent for the nearest doctor, some thirty *versts* away, to come and do it. Well, all right, you say. A genius shouldn't have to lance boils. And I'd agree.

John Keats, pressed to study medicine by his father, was equally reluctant, although he went as far as assisting at surgery and even delivering a few babies before he left the study. Imagine! The "maiden poet of the sensual," delivering a baby! If only one had been there to cover his eyes or send him away from the premises to spare those hypersensitive nerves. As time went by, Keats grew more and more certain that medicine was not for him. In a letter to his brother, he describes his early retirement. Much like the anatomy laboratory at Albany Medical College where I dissected a cadaver, the one where Keats was similarly occupied was a great stone vault with high ceilings perforated by skylights. Arranged in rows were the slabs upon which lay the stately dead. Standing at one of these tables was our desultory poet, bored to death and beyond. All at once, a sunbeam broke through a skylight and lit upon him where he stood. In it, Keats saw a host of fairies and sprites. Laying down his scalpel, he mounted that sunbeam, ascended to the skylight, then out. He never once looked back.

I cannot think of Keats without sorrow over the circumstances of his death from tuberculosis at the age of twenty-five. It is likely that he contracted the disease by nursing his fatally infected brother. For three years, the cough, fever, and hemorrhage grew worse and worse until in desperation the half-dead young man was sent away to Italy, where, it was hoped, the warm sunshine would turn the tide. His sole companion on the long sea voyage was a young painter, Joseph Severn. Once in Italy, they would support themselves by plying each his art. Keats would sell his poems, Severn, his paintings. Quixotic notion! The voyage was a martyrdom for Keats, who could not leave the cabin or even the bed within it. For the entire trip he was feverish, hemorrhaging and seasick. Severn could do nothing but give him what to drink, bathe his friend, and wring his hands. At last, ensconced in rooms near the Spanish Steps in Rome, the condition of the poet deteriorated. An Italian doctor was summoned who told Severn that there was no hope, that the end would come soon. For weeks, Joseph nursed his friend and sat by the deathbed listening to the pathetic struggle to breathe. Now and then, Keats roused from his stupor to look about, then sank back to battle on. Near the end, Keats had a moment of clarity in which he asked Severn if he had ever seen anyone die before. Severn replied that he had not.

"Then," said Keats, "you'd better leave the room." Minutes later, the poet was dead. It was Severn's last duty to see him buried in the English cemetery at Rome. The gravestone bore the epitaph he had written for himself: HERE LIES ONE WHOSE NAME WAS WRIT IN WATER.

Whenever I feel that my eccentricities are getting too noticeable, I take myself off to England, where they are less apt to stand out among the general oddity. Some years ago, during such an attack, I settled into a bed & breakfast in Hampstead on the edge of a vast heath. There was excellent walking, a lively pub nearby called Jackstraw's Castle, and a supply of ink and paper. I had remained holed up for several weeks when a friend, having learned of my whereabouts, came to roust me out. Dannie Abse, too, is a writing doctor. He suggested that we walk to the Keats house, which, unbeknownst to me, was quite nearby. It proved a moving experience, what with the letters to Fanny Brawne, the death mask made by Severn, and a drawing of the dying Keats that showed the extent of his suffering. There too were the very chairs that Keats used while writing—one to sit in, the other placed at right angles, upon whose back the poet rested one arm.

Just outside, in the doorway, was a plum tree said to be the very one Keats had planted. It was also insisted by the curator, despite all evidence to the contrary, that the tree was still alive, a diagnosis that must be arrived at by annual biopsy, I thought.

In a reverent hush, Dannie and I left the house and walked to the end of the street where the heath began. A short way beyond the pavement was a pond where ducks, swans, and other waterbirds swam. It was here, said Dannie, that Keats took a twig and wrote his name in the water.

"Do you the same," said my friend and handed me a fallen twig. Crouching at the edge of the pond, I wrote "Richard Selzer" in the water, then cast the little twig to sail where it would. Just as I did, the whole community of waterbirds lifted off and flew up to Heaven.

"Now," said Dannie, "you are with Keats." If my heart didn't burst then, it never will.

∾

Who was it wrote about the terrible freedom one has when one's father dies? By age fifteen, my formation as a doctor was well under way. That summer, I rode night ambulance for St. Mary's hospital. No doctor, nurse, or emergency medical technician. Just Tim, the driver, and myself. Tim was a toothless skinny Irishman with a Lucky Strike forever clamped between his gums, and a nose that almost touched his chin. He was in his forties but looked twenty years older. His breath came in wheezes and was punctuated by a wet, productive cough. The driver's window had to be kept open even in winter, to enable spitting. For Tim, driving ambulance was the best of all possible jobs, and I was inclined to agree. It was thrilling to go careering through the streets of Troy at all hours of the night, siren blaring, even if we were only going downtown to buy a pack of Luckies. On more legitimate rides we'd screech up to a stoop where already a silent crowd was standing, the way cows will gather in that corner of a pasture where one of them has stumbled, fallen, and is unable to get up. As though they would summon help by the mere presence of their massive bodies. Riding ambulance was an adventure movie in which Tim and I were the stars.

There came the night when we pulled up to a tenement, were

pointed silently upstairs—four flights. I opened the door to a garret room to see a man standing with a rope around his neck. Not standing, I saw next, the way his shoes swung gently in the breeze from the window. On that dark landing, the needle of my heart pointed due north.

"Have to cut him down," said Tim. "You grab him around the middle so he don't fall on the floor with a thud." I wrapped my arms around the suicide and braced myself for the weight. Tim stood on a chair, sawing away. All at once, the dead man came crashing so that we both fell to the floor, arms and legs entangled, the body of the man covering mine in the most ghastly embrace of my life. This isn't death, I thought. Not my old familiar death, the one I'd seen on house calls, nor the death that had cruelly snagged Father three years before. Here was Death as pursuer, pinning me in His arms. Death as rapist!

Tim took hold of an arm and a leg and dragged the corpse off me, snickering as he did so. Back in the ambulance, we lit up and inhaled deeply. I had already become expert in the management of horror by fumigation, a reliance I wasn't to break for half a century. That snicker! I shall never be rid of that soft dry inhuman sound.

On another run, it was an old woman lying in bed. A sort of whitish quilt covered her midsection. Otherwise, she was naked. White, yes, but not the terrible white of a blank page or the equally threatening white of a bride's linen. No, it was the old white of a tusk, parchment, a drumhead, the moon. As I gazed, it dawned on me that while the woman lay still, the quilt was moving! A moment later, I saw that it was no quilt but a mass of maggots going about their slow business at her genitalia. "Horror," wrote Emily Dickinson. " 'Tis so Appalling, it Exhilarates." I know what she meant, for I was strangely exhilarated by everything I saw that summer. I like to think that part of the feeling of pleasure lay in the fact that I had at last set out upon the odyssey at the end of which stood Father, waiting for me. If the way were strewn with hanged men and maggoty women, well, so be it. I knew that he had encountered the same. We were in it together.

My own children are parents themselves and more than three times the age at which I first witnessed death. About death, they are still virginal. Perhaps I have erred in protecting those maidenly three. It isn't wise to distance yourself from death. Doing so increases its power over you. Familiarity is better, to confront the old adversary rather than the unknown knight. Only with familiarity comes the humor and fatalism to deflate the terror and to incorporate death into life. Now I can only hope that the first corpse my children see is not mine. That would be too cruel.

∞

It is twelve years since I walked away from my beloved workbench in the operating room. It was not done with a cheery wave of the hand. For a long time, there was a sense of dislocation as if I were standing on the bank of a stream, and it was the bank that was flowing while the stream stood still. Surgery was my native land. The writer who cuts himself off from his native land does so at great risk. The subject of so much of my writing had been my work as a doctor. Would I be punished for sending myself into exile? Have nothing left to say? I needn't have worried. There is always the sharp and aching tooth of memory. Then too, my dreams are filled with surgery. Every night I am once again at the operating table striving to control bleeding or to repair what had gone wrong. Still, whenever that former self, the surgeon, insists upon being remembered, I'm astonished, as though a prehistoric creature had somehow managed not to die and was now reclaiming its place in my life.

Most days, I go to the Yale Library, where I read and write. Toward evening I take the Yale shuttle bus home. Not long ago, while waiting for the bus, two blond ladies came up, each as homely as virtue. One tall and fat, the other short and fat.

"Hello, Doctor."

"Whom do we have here?"

"You operated on us both." Were they mad? I wouldn't do a thing like that to anyone!

"I was a gallbladder," said Tall and Fat.

"I was hemorrhoids," said Short and Fat. I said how happy and relieved I was to see they'd made it. Curious how pretty they both became at that moment. Along came the bus and I shuttled off.

It is one of the risks of retiring and staying in the town where you have laid open the bodies of half the population. Shortly after I retired, I was asked to give a benefit reading for the local library. Upon

entering the auditorium I was astonished to find that the audience
consisted of two hundred of my former patients. And it seemed to me
that they had grouped themselves anatomically, with the gallbladders
up front, the hernias in the middle and the hemorrhoids at the rear.
I had a moment of panic in which I imagined that at a given signal,
they would rise to show what I had done to them. At least the two
blond ladies would have known where to sit.

On another day, I got on the shuttle bus and took a seat across the
aisle and one row behind the driver, a man I hadn't seen before. A new
bus driver, I decided.

"Where do you want to get off?" he asked.

"The Divinity School. I live nearby." When he turned to listen, I saw
that his chin, lower lip and the entire front of his neck had been
grafted with skin, doubtless to release the contracture of a burn scar.
He appeared to be in his late thirties. From where I sat, I could see
how easily he turned his head from side to side, raised, then lowered
his chin. An excellent functional result, I thought. Not perfect cos-
metically—a ridge here and there, a spot of pallor—but of this the
man seemed unaware. He made no effort at concealment, wore no
scarf or collar. All at once, it dawned upon me that I was the one who
had performed that skin graft, that this bus driver as a child had been
my patient. A moment later, I remembered a small boy, naked, lying
on an operating table, his chin attached to his chest by a great purple
fan of scar tissue. So dense was this scar that the boy could not extend
his head to see but must wrinkle his forehead and peer from the very
top of his vision. The mouth was pulled open and twisted, the lower
lip entirely lost in the wild mass of flesh. I remembered leaning over
him, holding his hand, his struggle not to cry. Moments later he was
asleep with a breathing tube in one nostril.

Now, so many years later, I had an impulse to go up behind the bus
driver to examine, to feel, to ask him to show me the donor site. Perhaps I would recognize it the way one knows his own handwriting.
Perhaps he would remember my name? But I stayed in my seat.

"Divinity!" he called out. I rose to leave the bus. It is best not to trespass upon a previous incarnation. In Book VI of the *Aeneid,* Aeneas
has met up with his father Anchises in the Elysian Fields. They come
upon a crowd of souls waiting by a river. Anchises explains that they

are awaiting the summons to new bodies and must now drink of the waters of the river Lethe to learn forgetfulness of their past lives. Sometimes, mostly at noon or midnight—those twin hinges of the day when both hands of the clock are upthrust in supplication—I have a fleeting memory, it is no more than an inkling, that my own father had once conducted me just as Anchises had done Aeneas, that he had bade me join those who were destined to come back. For some reason—disobedience, I suppose—I didn't drink of the waters of forgetfulness and so it is that I know full well what I had been in my former life: a surgeon. I used to think that the past was safer than the future. It had already happened and could do no more damage. Now I know it is the past to which we are vulnerable, the past that is far more apt to slay us.

∽

Writing came to me late, like a wisdom tooth. I was forty years old when first I laid down the scalpel and picked up the pen. One ought not to expect to write stories seething with virile passion in a hand still pudgy with baby fat. Whatever the reason, I loved the warmth of it, the awkwardness, rather like a newborn chick. And the feeling that no matter what insane world lowered outside my tiny study, here, at least, I was snug. What emerged on that first page was a retelling of my first-read story, "Jonah and the Whale." Now, since I knew what the lining of the stomach looked like better than those biblical authors, I rendered Jonah's new home with a good deal more authenticity. In the three decades since, I have continued as I began, writing in longhand, with a fountain pen. It has to do, partly, with surgery. In both writing and surgery you hold an implement of somewhat the same size. Wield a scalpel, and blood is shed. Wield a pen, and ink is shed upon a page. It is congenial for me to suture words into sentences with a pen. Too, there's the lovely proximity of the word, the sense of its being made, or done, by your body, the way it issues from the end of your fingers like a secretion. The word processor does not exist that offers so personal a feeling of discharge. To say nothing of the graceful act of penmanship itself: the approximation of thumb and forefinger to form a sling whose base is the first web, the sweet pressure of the encircled pen against the more rigidly fixed middle finger at its distal interphalangeal joint, and the whole apparatus given voice by the hissing of the hypothenar eminence as it crosses the page. Such things are important in the practice of a craft.

∽

A word about my desk. It is made of a large slab of oak with three drawers on either side of a kneehole. It has never been planed smooth and the top is as rutted as an old dirt road. I love it as I have never loved any other furniture. My first desk was a small hideous *bonheur-du-jour* given to Father by a patient in lieu of payment. It was inlaid with mother-of-pearl, and encrusted with bits of reflecting glass. You couldn't possibly write at it. There, I was instructed to sit every morning and practice the Palmer Method of Penmanship until the morning oatmeal was ready. At age seven, my hatred for that desk erupted. Home alone, I took a hammer and fractured it into splinters of wood, glass, and mother-of-pearl. I can still see the fragments glittering in the sunlight. Then I sat back to wait for Mother to come home. She surveyed the carnage and nodded sadly.

"I should have smothered you in your bassinet," she said. "But I was not mother enough."

∽

All of my early writing was done between one and three in the morning. Within a few years, these nocturnal creatures began to appear in *Ellery Queen's Mystery Magazine,* where I should have been pleased to stay forever had not a publisher phoned to ask: Had I enough of these stories to make a book?

"Do I!" I cried, and backed the truck up next to his office. Having selected twenty stories, he called the book *Rituals of Surgery.* It had nothing to do with surgery but he thought that might sell books. He was wrong. Never mind, for when in due course the book appeared, I saw it as an illuminated manuscript with the *R*'s and *S*'s in scarlet and gold. It was at the New Haven Public Library on a Wednesday afternoon some weeks after publication that I received my first book review. It has been my custom to visit that library every Wednesday, and the librarian at the desk was by then an old friend. Just ahead of me at the desk, returning (Be still, my heart!) *Rituals of Surgery,* was one of those vestiges of Yankeehood that are still seen on the streets of New England towns and villages. Picket-thin, she was without an ounce more soft tissue than absolutely necessary to hook ligament to bone, and displayed an iron gray bun impacted at the nape. The librarian thought to garner for me a compliment within earshot.

"What did you think of that book?" she asked. Then, holding it between thumb and forefinger as though it were moist and disgusting, the woman let it fall to the desk.

"I would never," she said, "let that man operate on me." It was two o'clock in the afternoon when I fled home, got into bed and pulled the covers over my head. Nor would I come out until my wife came and fed me oatmeal with a long wooden spoon. I have since developed a thicker hide and prefer to agree with the immortal Tallulah Bankhead: "To hell with criticism; praise is good enough for me."

The opinion of that Yankee lady was prophetic. In the years that followed, the book reviewers, in general, have refrained from delivering a fatal blow to my modesty. Just as well, considering the egotism for which surgeons are famous. (There is a surgeon at Yale who, having left the operating room, is quite sure that his disembodied radiance lingers on.) Nor did I win the approval of my surgical colleagues, who felt it was in somewhat ill taste for a surgeon to write, especially if he were going to reveal the secrets of the priesthood.

"Come, come!" they coaxed me (in the words of Richard Wilbur), " 'Forsake those roses of the mind, and tend the true, the mortal flower.' " That is the way the surgeons at Yale speak. But, like Ulysses who poured melted wax into his ears so that he would not hear the song of the Sirens, I turned a deaf ear and went on scribbling.

I learned to write catch-as-catch-can at the hospital, in fifteen-minute bursts, and so am not oversensitive to disturbances, rather like carrying your imagination in a bandanna tied to a stick and quite unlike Rilke, for one, who had to live in isolated castles with all the furniture arranged just so. Oh, there are certain intolerable conditions—the incessant barking of an abandoned dog. If carried on for more than half an hour, the sound turns me murderous. I'm not nearly so sympathetic to the emotional needs of the lower species as was Sir Walter Scott. Financially hard-pressed, and needing to produce a quota of pages every day, Sir Walter needed his sleep. Once,

kept awake all night by the barking of a dog, he wrote in his diary:
"Poor cur! I doubt not that you have troubles of your own to keep you
barking through the night." But then, I'm not the one to write *Ivan-
hoe*, either. I am equally incapacitated by the Westminster chimes of
a clock that ring out every quarter of an hour. To be reminded four
times an hour of the swift passage of wasted time is more than any
writer should have to tolerate.

Shortly after my retirement from medicine, I was asked to lead a
"creative" writing workshop at Yale Medical School. Every Monday
night we sixteen doctors met for three hours in a conference room and
wrote our hearts out. I learned that a medical education ill prepares
one for the rigors of writing. Here follows the sum total of what we
learned in thirteen weeks: the difference between "prostate" and
"prostrate." It is no easy thing, I told them, to lie prostate on the floor,
even for those of us who have one. We learned that "disembosom" has
nothing to do with breast surgery, but is to be used figuratively as in
"permit me to disembosom myself of a secret." "Disembowel," on the
other hand, has every right to be taken literally. We learned the difference between "prone" and "supine," which I admit is a knotty one.
So distinguished a writing doctor as Robin Cook in one of his immortal novels has an obstetrician instruct a nurse to place a woman
in the prone position, that he might do a pelvic examination on her.
I would suggest that any woman so positioned put her clothes back
on and go get a second opinion. Finally, we learned the importance
of punctuation, how it can change the meaning of a sentence. "Good
Heavens!" he ejaculated is not the same as "Good Heavens! He ejaculated!"

∞

Many of these stories were written at Yale's Sterling Library where, day
after day, "shod with felt," I pursue the arachnoid knack of spinning
out words. The language is as far from the Minimal as you can get. It
is my pleasure to use as much of the English language as I can rather
than as little, in what used to be called full-throated ease. Perhaps it
has to do with those decades of restraining the scalpel. Now, when it's
the pen my fingers ride, I'm apt to give it full rein. An outdated style?
There's no such thing as progress in art. The cave paintings of Lascaux

are as up-to-date as the abstractions of Rothko, only with the patina of twenty thousand years.

I have used both humor and the grotesque as instruments of illumination, and recognize in myself both the aghast, lidless witness to horror and the storyteller bent on captivating the reader. I'm of the persuasion that feels its first responsibility is to charm. It's what I caught along with measles and chicken pox among the Trojan Irish. When the subject is that of the human body, how it's made, how it works, and what goes wrong with it, I have kept faith with the factual. In all other matters, I've committed the gentle treason of poetry and betrayed mere fact in search of truth, the real real that lies just beneath the real. Besides, is there anyone who would prefer that Herodotus had given only the facts? If the tone of some of these stories is what some call "high," so be it. If Eve had eaten a turnip, the whole tone of Genesis would be lower and, I think, somewhat less epic.

Not a single thought of social purpose or morality crossed my mind in the writing of these pieces. They were meant to be told for their own sake. Not being gifted, I don't have to feel subdued by those who have gone before me. I long ago gave up the idea of genius and just do the best I can. Nor do I worry about repetition. I write so little and have only a very few subjects, largely having to do with doctoring. My real subject is language itself, which provides a more direct way to experience than the intellect. It is the soul of the writer exteriorized and made visible. To take up a word, then lay it down again to choose another; to set this one down on the page as if it were a pebble and what is being made a mosaic, this is the greatest pleasure. Words so used are as hashish to the mind. There's a certain impatience in the present-day reader. He's in a hurry, going somewhere, hasn't time for anything but the outline or the gist. My ideal reader has taken the day off and is perfectly content to sink six inches deeper into a chair and cozy up to an armful of language. He's a slow reader, may even move his lips while doing it, tasting. Now and then, he pauses to read the same paragraph twice, then drops into a state of enchantment from which he is aroused only by an urgent call. Nor is he the least bit evangelical, seeking to make converts. He is, rather, a Knight Templar caring only to defend the faith.

There are events of the body, pain is one of them, orgasm another, that defy any effort to render them in prose. They are outside the precincts of communicable language and are spoken only by the one who experiences them. Immediately upon cessation, the language of these events—groans, howled vowels—is forgotten and one is no longer conversant in it.

"Tell me what your pain is like," says the doctor. "Is it sharp or dull? Does it come and go, or is it steady? Does it stay in one place or does it radiate, move around? Is it like a heavy weight?" He is trying to make a diagnosis.

"It's a shovel being dug into my ribs," says the patient. Now the doctor has begun to narrow the possibilities. But this patient and his doctor have ignored the admonition of Susan Sontag not to consider illness in metaphoric terms. And they are right to do so. Metaphor may be the only resort of the sick to express himself. Besides, the turn of a phrase, an apt image, even a bon mot or a joke can lighten the yoke of affliction on the shoulders. Take away metaphor from illness and there is left only the suffering. Disease is most conveniently seen as a hostile invasion of the body, whether by bacteria, viruses, cancer cells, or toxic substances. To repel the invader, the patient must be free to marshal every one of his defenses—his own immunity, heredity, willpower, faith, folklore, his doctor's acuity, the talent of technology, and, yes, metaphor. I have, in telling these stories, applied the lamp of language, especially metaphor, to tetanus, radiation sickness, autism, and so forth in order to illuminate the sufferer and the one who tends him. A number of the stories are in the form of a journal or diary. Such *keeping* comes naturally to a doctor who writes every day in the charts of his patients, noting down the vital signs—temperature, blood pressure, pulse—recording the appearance of a wound, or any change in symptoms, hypothesizing, adding up bits of evidence, making diagnoses, prognosticating, and all the while implying his own sadness or elation. Looking back, I cannot help but think that my best writing was done in the charts of my patients. Only there was it devoid of the vanity of the author and the pomp of language. No question but that it had a higher purpose; the life at risk was not my own.

The story "Avalanche" organized out of the pages of my journal. A phrase here, a paragraph there, were interspersed among the daily entries over the course of eight months, until it seemed there was no more to write. Just so had the story become embedded in the diary and had only to be dissected out with a clever scalpel. Once extirpated, the fragments were sutured together and behold! "Avalanche." That the story takes place in Argentina, on the pampas, would seem to be a handicap, as I have never been to Argentina. But the Argentina of the dreaming mind surely serves as well as a round-trip ticket to Buenos Aires. The imagination is the vehicle by which the writer roams far and wide.

> *"How many miles to Babylon?"*
> *"Three score and ten."*
> *"Can I get there by candlelight?"*
> *"Yes, and back again."*

The writer's candle shines brightest in dream, in dream where lies Babylon uncrumbled and teeming.

The impulse to write "The Mirror: A Tale of Aran" came from Richard Ellmann, whose next-door neighbor I was lucky enough to be for seven years. It seems that James Joyce while living in Paris was told by an Irish visitor the story of an aged couple, the sole occupants of the tiniest of the Aran Islands, whose lives were disrupted by the need to go to the mainland. According to Ellmann, Joyce expressed his intention to use this tale in his writing. He never did.

"Why don't you write it?" suggested Richard Ellmann. To turn aside from such an invitation would have been as stupid as it would have been arrogant. It is as close as I have ever come to rubbing shoulders with greatness.

"Luis" and "Whither Thou Goest" were first met up with as news articles in *The New York Times*. I saw them as fables of our time. An early version of "Pipistrel" was published years ago in *Ellery Queen's Mystery Magazine*. "Brute," written some twenty-five years after the event described, is an act of atonement. It has been woefully misread as racist by some and by others as a "missed opportunity for Grace." Neither could be further from the truth. Never mind, we must show compassion for those who do not understand us. Besides, Grace is an unmerited favor; it has the quality of being unexpected. Nor can it be resisted. The title "Witness" descends from the word testament or testimony, the ancient law that there be two witnesses to establish evidence in court. The organ at the center of this story, the testicle, was so named because it and its fellow are witness to the act of copulation, and therefore fatherhood. "Tillim" describes an event that would be given significance by reading William Blake: "If the doors of perception were cleansed, everything would appear as it is, infinite and holy." Were I to point to any story that might be thought autobiographical, it would be "Impostor," a choice calculated to arouse the blood lust of my fellow surgeons.

Some years ago, the curator of Western Americana at Yale's Beinecke Library invited me to read a cache of letters acquired from the descendants of a young Civil War surgeon stationed aboard a hospital steamboat on the Mississippi River. "Pages From a Wound-Dresser's Diary" is the Whitmanesque result. In "Fetishes" I tried to suggest an otherness that lies beyond consciousness, call it what you will—the god-element, the spirit. Not to be rendered precisely, it is a momentary flash of revelation. Seen once and never again, rather like the appearance of a god among mortals.

I suppose I am a fetishist. Many years ago, someone who loved me, who loves me still, gave me an egg-shaped stone of green malachite from Vermont.

"This will keep you safe," she told me. And so it has. I never leave the house without it. Over the years, it has been rubbed smooth, chipped, and dented and bears a good many scars of wounds I'm sure I should have sustained had it not been for my stone. Some mysteries are not made to be solved; they're meant to be deepened.

"Poe's Light-house" (the hyphen is his and therefore a holy relic) was written after reading a biography of the writer. In his final illness, Poe had fallen into a delirium from which he emerged briefly to begin a story, "The Light-house." Some two hundred words were all he managed before he lapsed into the coma from which he would not return. This story is an act of homage in which I dared to take up the pen that had fallen from the hand of my idol.

"'The Black Swan' Revisited" is another homage, this one to Thomas Mann. It is a rewriting of the novella "The Deceived Woman," a late unsuccessful work of the master. Once, long ago, making rounds at the hospital, I passed an open doorway and saw an aged emaciated woman with trembling fingers trying to pass a pendant earring through her earlobe. It was this brave act of adornment that moved me to treat Mann's theme again.

The wound in "Chatterbox" is not physical but mental. I had been reading the letters of St. Catherine of Siena to her confessor, Fra Raimondo. St. Catherine might have made a fine surgeon what with her sensitive response to blood. Once, she was present at the beheading of a young man whom she had converted. While he knelt on one side of the block, she knelt on the other, whispering to him of Paradise. When the ax fell and the head came free in her arms, Catherine almost swooned from the "fragrance" of his blood. Or so she wrote to Fra Raimondo. Catherine Goodhouse is a rough translation of the saint's surname Benincasa. In "Imagine a Woman" I tried to enter the psyche of a woman. It was a great pleasure to be in touch with the feminine in my nature. Other men who have done so were Patrick White, D. H. Lawrence, and William Trevor.

As a doctor, when giving out bad news, I spoke in pastels. "Tell all the truth," wrote Emily Dickinson, "but tell it slant." And so I did, as much for my own sake as for that of the next-of-kin. I could not have borne it otherwise, day in and day out. In writing, I have not spared the sensibility of the reader, and have written in primary colors. Still, the Hippocratic Oath will cause a doctor/writer some hesitation. I am averse to killing off my characters, and have done so only when there was no other way.

Thus speaketh the bastard son of medicine and literature who signs himself Richard Selzer.

Avalanche

*I*t was midsummer when a woman no longer young (neither was she old) found herself en route by train from Buenos Aires to Santa Rosa, a small town at the edge of the pampas. It seemed that the old woman whose nursemaid she had been for many years had died leaving her a small ranch in the interior of the country, in the province of which Santa Rosa was the capital. She herself had not been outside Buenos Aires in thirty years, ever since she had been brought there as a child of nine. No, she had been born in a mountain village outside the small city of Esquel quite close to the border with Chile. One day she had gone with her grandmother to gather mushrooms on the wooded slopes of the Andes. All at once, from afar, they heard the mountain roar, felt it shudder beneath their feet. They ran back to the village, but it was not there. Where it had been—a great strew of boulders and stones. Only they had survived the landslide. When, a year later, her grandmother died, the girl was sent across Argentina to Buenos Aires, to the Convent of Santa Catarina where she would be educated and raised. Twelve years later she was given a choice by the Mother Superior: Join the order or leave. She had left, and for the next eighteen years earned her livelihood as nursemaid to the elderly invalid whose heir she had become. But even now, more than thirty years later, she carried within her the memory of that mountain village where each step upward or downward carved a new configuration of earth and sky; where the looming crags, the trees watched you approach, showed themselves to you in silence, then fell together behind as if to close a breach. Here below, on the flatlands, walk a thousand steps in any direction and nothing changes; earth and sky remain as they were. And a mere woman is powerless.

Now as the train hurtled across the flat prairie, the woman's longing for the mountains of her childhood returned with full force. She yearned for the great heights where even a small Indian girl could create a new world with each step.

To look at her, you would not say that she was an Indian, in spite of the volume of black hair, eyes that went black with surprise or anger, and the bronze color of her skin. But she was, and kept still the slight accent of Quechua in her speech. Her ears were pierced with tiny gold rings that she never removed. At the convent she had known bigotry. Gypsy, she was called, and *indigena*. Still, Buenos Aires had diluted her Indianness; in her gestures, the way she carried herself, her manner had become urban, Spanish.

Gazing out the window of the train hour after hour, she was offered for the first time a glimpse of her life, of how she had lived all these years in a state of slow, dormant expectation. Expectation of what, she didn't know. Some people who lead such uneventful lives, grow more and more invisible with age; they become like jellyfish that are there and not there. Others, not knowing what to do with themselves, become lumpish; they stand in the middle of alleys and narrow passageways always presenting themselves, needing to be avoided or gotten around somehow. This woman had done neither. Instead she had grown . . . well . . . receptacular. Her skin, even her eyelashes had become extraordinarily sensitive so that, like certain insects whose antennae detect tiny shifts in the current of air, she seemed to possess powers of predictability. She could tell, for instance, the moment a cat came into the room. Long solitude had sharpened her senses. But long before the Convent of Santa Catarina, where she had been thought "hypersensitive" and therefore suspect, even as a child in the mountains, she had had a strange avidity of the senses that she had inherited from her grandmother. It was the suppression of this faculty in her that was the achievement of the nuns. Only after she had left them did she permit herself to feel with the spontaneity of childhood. Once, at Santa Catarina, she had seen a photograph of some penguins in a magazine, and she burst out laughing. Commanded to tell why she had thought the penguins funny, she had said: because they looked like nuns. She had been scolded and punished for disrespect, a disrespect she did not feel; in fact she was eager to love the sisters who had taken her in and protected her. Now, the farther the train went from the city, the stronger grew the sense that if ever something were to happen to her that would change her life, it would be on this journey. It was something she knew in the marrow of her bones.

∽

Three days and two nights later, the woman stepped from the train onto a gravel platform. The uniformed arm of a conductor handed down a valise. Even before she had turned away, the train began moving. Moments later it was beyond sight and hearing. Untempered by clouds, the noonday sun struck her across the face, like a slap. She gasped at the impact and might have toppled. Squinting, she waited for the return of equilibrium. Through almost-closed eyelids she saw a tiny deserted stationhouse. Beyond was a street hemmed in by high stone walls on either side. Here and there the monotony of the walls was punctuated by a narrow arched passageway. She guessed that the inhabitants lived on the other side of the walls, that the alley was a kind of public thoroughfare empty now for the siesta. There was no sign of life. Had the people who lived here all been expelled?

At last, scuttling like a small creature that hopes to avoid the exposure of the open center, she went to stand against the wall. Perhaps there would be shade. Leaning against the wall, she felt only half-committed to the town. After all, it wasn't as though she were sitting on a bench. No, she could always at any moment turn around and leave. But, she thought, there wouldn't be another train for days. Once again she must shut her eyes against the blinding, the cruel sunlight; pure light it was, light in a state of perfection, light that devoured everything—street, walls, whatever town there must be, destroyed it, at any rate made it invisible. All at once, she who could tell the instant a cat came into a room, knew that she was being watched. Her skin crawled with the knowledge. But by whom? There was no one. . . . Squinting again, she saw a dark mass organizing at the center of the dazzle, saw the man emerge—emerge like something that had been born of the sunlight, a dark concentrate of it. And there he stood, on the other side of the street, framed in a stone arch cut in the wall. Had he been there all the while? Or had she willed him into existence? When he took a step, just one, to the level of the street, she held her breath, waiting. Hurry, she thought. Hurry, please! Although she could not have said why. Now he too stood outside the shade of the wall. In the brilliant sunshine, he became transparent. She thought she could see right through him. The more transparent, the more mysterious he became. She would never know this man as she wanted. The way he stood there, sizing her up. What arrogance! He was wearing baggy black *bombachas* and a black shirt opened to the navel. His boots were wrinkled like the pleats of an accordion, and in his waistband, at the small of his back so as to be within easy reach, his knife. A *compadrito,* she thought, with some contempt. Oh, she had seen them swaggering in the streets of the capital. Blusterers who loved only their knives, and therefore only each other. Their knives that they kept hidden from sight like private parts of their bodies, and that they treated with the same pride and concern. Ridiculous!

As for him, gazing at the woman in the yellow dress, the way she fanned herself against the heat, the way she pressed herself against the wall for coolness, made him think of a small lizard that held its head up just so, on the alert. He had the sensation of standing, not on the level ground to which he was used, but on the steep slope of a mountain, while she stood on the slope of another. It was the immense gully of the street that separated them. The only way across was an invisible wire that must be paced. A mountain woman, he thought. They bring the mountains with them wherever they go. A sudden tilt of his mind threw him off balance. He had a moment of dizziness in which he might have staggered. Almost at once, it passed. It was then that he began to walk toward her whose feet had also come unstuck from the ground so that she was moving toward him with a step that was eager and light.

To her it seemed that she was strolling away from a body that had become too confining, too heavy for her. When he had come within ten feet, she saw in his hand a leather riding whip, a *rebanque* with a silver handle. In the center of the empty street, he stopped. Why had he stopped! And she saw, or thought she saw, on his face, in the arrogance of his stance, the age-old contempt of the prairie-born for hill people, she had met up with it all her life in Buenos Aires—the suspicion that the people who came down from the mountains were somehow stunted, bowlegged, beetle-browed from having to climb up and down. But she was mistaken. Closer still, she saw his eyes, brown with flecks in them like the skin of a trout. The deep vertical crease that divided his forehead in two; like the wound of an ax in a tree. Otherwise she would not have dared.

"Excuse me," she plunged. "Is there a hotel in this town?" For a long moment she endured his silence. "Hotel," she said again with her courage leaking away. My god! Why doesn't he speak? A tiny movement of his head indicated that she should follow him. The arm that reached for the suitcase was bandaged above the elbow with a stained red bandanna. A knife wound, she thought in her prejudice. She could tell from the way he avoided her gaze, turning so that the arm was hidden. Besides, he was a fugitive; she could smell it on him. Hadn't she read all about the code of honor to which they adhered, the gauchos? Stupid, cruel. Even the great writers of Argentina glorify it in their poems and stories. "It was only a matter of time before the knives would circle each other again." That sort of nonsense. Nonsense! The thought grew vehement within her so that her blood flared up.

The man nodded for her to go ahead, that he would follow. In the noonday heat he walked behind the woman whose hips moved inside the yellow dress as though someone were swinging a lantern. The deserted street, more an alley than a street, with its blind ochre-washed walls and flat paving stones, ended in the Campo Jerusalen, which, if it were the heart of the town, was a heart that was scarcely beating. The Hotel Argentina stood on one side of the small square. It was a ramshackle wooden structure painted a soft shade of rose. There were three stories each with a wraparound balcony divided by wrought-iron partitions. Otherwise it was devoid of ornamentation. Outside the door to the hotel, he set down the suitcase and stood facing her in silence.

"Look," she said. "I need someone to guide me to a place near Quines. Do you know where that is?" She explained about the *estancia*. "I will pay you well."

"There are no roads to that place, beyond Quines," he announced. When he spoke, it was as though two pieces of leather were being rubbed together. He himself was sand-colored and without the least bead of sweat in spite of the heat. Even his white teeth were something that had fallen and lay bleached. It made her thirsty to look at him.

"No roads," she repeated. How stupid she must sound.

"Can you ride?" he asked.

"A horse?" She *was* being stupid. "I haven't ever."

"I can get two horses. One is a tame horse with a soft lip. You only have to sit there, and let the reins go. The horse knows what to do."

"Yes." She nodded. Her glance fell to the bandanna on his arm.

"Is it serious? Your arm? I mean are you able to do all this for me?" He did not answer. Outside the door to the hotel, he set down the suitcase.

"Come inside," she said. "Let me see. It's all right, I tell you. I have experience in dressing wounds." When he would have turned away, she took his arm and drew him into the building, then minutes later upstairs to the room she had taken. From a pitcher on the table, she poured water into a bowl, then soaked the bandanna until it separated freely from the underlying flesh. He submitted in silence.

"My goodness!" she exclaimed. "It's infected." The wound was a deep laceration across the outer arm slicing into the muscle. The base of the wound was covered with a shaggy gray drainage that smelled. Again and again she washed the wound, pouring water into it, holding open the edges, gently swabbing with one of her handkerchiefs. At last she bound it up with a piece of clean linen. "I'll wash the bandanna and give it back to you tomorrow."

∽

What she could not know was that this man too, only lately, some weeks before, had come to Santa Rosa, come walking, or rather hobbling across the immense plateau, moving at night, hiding by day. There had been a fight—some ancient grudge—perhaps the songs were right after all and it had been the knives themselves settling a score; he had killed the other one. The dead man had seven brothers, each of whom had sworn vengeance. And so he had fled, running in the dark, terrified not so much of his pursuers but of stepping on something that would move, letting himself be led by smell and hearing. And just as he could go no farther, he had happened upon the town of Santa Rosa. Parched, exhausted, weakened by hunger and the rigors of the trek, the stupefied man opened his mouth again and again like a fish and gave himself up to the town that would either take him in or not. One thing was certain: it was the end of flight. Here, he would make his final stand. And with that decision, there was an end to fear, as though his bones, where the fear had been lodged, were now washed clean. For weeks he lived in a shed on the edge of town, getting his strength back, eating, drinking, sleeping a great deal—for so long at a time that sometimes he would wake up to find his body laced with spiderwebs. The pain of his wound subsided to a buzz. And with this return to himself, he had begun to wonder what would come next. He had entered a state of expectation that even then he understood was a dangerous thing to do. This was the man who had emerged from the black mouth of the archway into the parched brilliance of the alley and, gazing across the street from the dark stone stairway at the woman in the yellow dress, had had the sensation that he was not standing on the level ground of the pampas, but on the steep slope of a mountain with nearby a fall of water, and currents of cool air. What was happening to him! Why had he stood still, inhaling deeply, feeling his heart race and a surge of jubilation?

He left her at the hotel then, said he would return the next morning to let her know what he had been able to arrange. From the balcony she watched him go. For a man who had spent half his life on horseback, he had a long thin walk, holding his knees together as though to let them go would risk having them splay outward. She watched until he disappeared into the arch of the shadow. After she had bathed and eaten, she took a walk outside the hotel. At dusk the town of Santa Rosa gave an appearance quite different from the lifeless burning street she had seen at her arrival. No longer deserted, Santa Rosa seemed, still, the reduced form of a town that had once been grander. Stores and houses lined the main street. How is it that she had not noticed them before? Directly across the small square from the Hotel Argentina a brick church held up a red-painted steeple. Every hour a bell clanged from within it. A charmless cement government building squatted on another side of the square. Walking away from the center of town she came upon a regimental barracks around which a cadre of unevenly uniformed soldiers loitered. All the life in Santa Rosa was contained in three cantinas side by side in whose doorways curtains of insects shook and from whose upstairs balconies brightly dressed women leaned and flirted open their fans. She could not take her eyes from the women, with their impossibly high-heeled shoes, their slit skirts that closed and opened with each step, the artificial scarlet flowers in their hair, held there by the teeth of combs; the fans that they flirted open and snapped shut. How beautiful they are, she thought, and fashioned for pleasure. And she marveled as once, long ago, as a small terrified Indian girl, she had marveled at the nuns in their cowls and habits, swinging their black wooden rosaries. These are just women, she thought now, dedicated to a different vocation. The thought made her strangely happy, as though she had solved a mystery that had plagued her all her life.

Hours later she heard a commotion in the street, went to look down from her window. A busload of . . . could it be tourists? . . . had arrived. Who would come here? No, not tourists. A posse of caballeros sporting sombreros with wide brims, and each with a bandanna around his neck and riding boots up to the knees. The dangling of their spurs. Soon, the cantinas were noisy with tango; she heard their drunken *vivas*, their shouts and threats.

All that night she lay awake and listened to people putting themselves to bed above, below, and all around her; to laughter, the squeaking of beds, groans on the other side of walls. From the street, once, there came the sudden blare of a trombone that cut open her ear along the neck. Toward dawn it grew quiet. Very distinctly she heard footsteps go down the hall, up a flight of stairs. A door opened and shut. Then silence. At the first pale light, a rooster crowed. Moments later it was followed by several others, then all together in a kind of discord made more raucous by a few laggards. But the gist of their message was not in question: dawn had broken.

When hours passed and he did not come, the woman entered a time of numb despair. Oh, she would just let things happen, take no step, wait and see. Let another dawn break if it would, let a rooster crow, the churchbell fracture the air, an accordion squeeze out tangos across the square where the men drink beer and coca tea, and the women snap their fans. Yes, that seemed best. Just let her arms hang at her side. But in spite of herself, first one hand, than the other, would fly up, plunge into her hair, then tumble back into her lap. Twice she left the hotel to wander in the narrow streets where the houses with their red doors and gourd vines leaned against one another as though they were sleeping off a drunk. He would not come. And she remembered how he had not departed all at once but had paled out, slowly decolorized back into sunshine. It had been a dream, a miscalculation. What would she do? Then the next morning, she awoke to the sound of hoofbeats in the street, raced to the balcony and there he was! Riding one horse and leading another, both animals with bulging saddlebags. The way her heart bounded! When he had dismounted she saw that he was improbably spruce, clean-shaved except for the black mustache, and with his poncho spotless, no knife in sight. When she saw the guitar hanging from the saddle, she could have laughed for joy. It is *you!* she would have cried out in recognition of the event. But she did not.

He helped her to mount, she who had never ridden. At once, she felt the accord that sprang up between the horse and herself, the way its hoofs lifted and struck calmly, with complete assurance; the novelty of living flesh between the thighs. A wave of gratitude toward this animal swept over her. Whatever it was that was coming toward her had begun to roll.

All day they rode deeper into the pampas, she following on the tame horse, absorbed in the gracefulness of the man, the softness of his movements, the way his legs embraced the horse, the way he reached around his thigh, took a leather bottle from the saddlebag at his hip, unplugged the stopper with his teeth and drank, holding the mouth of the bottle at some distance from his own so that the stream jetted through the air. Just so, he drank and her thirst was slaked. Even so, didn't she know that he was displaying himself to her, performing? A gaucho, she thought, and shivered at the notion. He was not tall, but with a strong yoke of shoulders and a deep chest. Darkish, with a triangular head, prominent cheekbones, a sharp chin— like a knife, she thought. He even looks like a knife. Already she knew him, knew him in her skin, on each of the tiny golden hairs that can be seen only in the brightest sunlight. It was a blind, deaf knowledge; he was the first man she ever knew. She may have known him even before she ever saw him.

On and on they rode. She had never endured such heat. They passed a steer lying on its side; flies swarmed. There were the inevitable cantinas, soldiers. What for? Who would want to conquer or defend this place? But there was always somebody able to pay uniformed men to do his bidding. At the doorway of one of the taverns, he dismounted and went to ask directions.

"It is another day's ride," he told her. "Can you?" She nodded. His voice was an arm around her waist.

∞

The *estancia*, then. An adobe farmhouse, low, white and stricken. Neglect was everywhere. Weeds grew up through holes in the porch. The steps were broken. The red-tiled roof seemed held up by a lattice of vines. Two collapsing sheds and a disreputable barn enclosed a barnyard. A small plot for cultivation was fenced-off from the vast open pampas all around. A well stood in the center of the yard. The man lowered a pail on a rope and brought it up. Tasting, he nodded and gave her the ladle. She drank awkwardly, spilling water down her chin. When he drank again, it was with immense grace, even the way he wiped his mouth with the back of his hand, pushing aside his mustache. Inside, the main room was bare except for a wooden table with two straight chairs. Slatted blinds covered the windows. The floor was of naked planking. The only ornament, a crucifix on the wall. It seemed to her more a painting of a room than a real room. The pieces of furniture were flat, oddly remote from each other. Some animal had left its droppings on the floor. The only other room in the house contained an iron bedstead with a horsehair mattress and pillows. A mirror hung on one wall. A stone kitchen completed the house at the rear. The man walked the entire perimeter of the ranch, examining everything minutely.

"What are you going to do with this place?" His words emerged reluctantly, no more than necessary and even they were pried from his lips.

"Oh, sell it, I guess. That is, if anyone would want it. What do you think? So broken down." Again, the man went to peer into the barn, the sheds; he kicked at the broken steps, then returned to face her. Too close! she thought. You are too close, and made as if to draw back from him. His face was only inches from hers. She could feel his breath on her; his black eyes glaring. Fear sprang; her pulse thudded.

"What . . . ?" she began. "What do you want?" But there was no menace in his voice.

"I want to stay here. Let me work here, fix the place up. I will sleep in the barn."

"It's time to bathe your arm." She ladled water from the pail and drenched the bandanna that covered the wound. After a few minutes she removed the cloth.

"What do you say?" There was something of entreaty in his voice.

"It looks better." She separated the edges of the wound with her fingers, let the water run into the wound. "Why do you want to stay here?"

"This place, it is just like me," he murmured. "All by itself."

"But you're not all by yourself, are you?" And with that she committed her destiny to this man whose past she did not know but who had called to her out of need. Something flashed up in his face, then was damped, but did not go out, only turned down and burning low. As though he had seen what was so clear, that she required him, too. Oh, not for the *estancia* which he knew she would have sold or even abandoned without regret. She required him in order to go on living. "All right," she told him. "Stay here with me. We will live here . . . together." She made a futile gesture toward the hacienda. But as if he had not heard, he untied his blanketroll from the saddle and carried it to one of the sheds. He would sleep there.

One day into the next. The man shored up the steps to the veranda, caulked the holes in the roof with mud and canes, planted corn, beans, potatoes. She had found a few chickens ranging free. Where had they come from? And rounded them into a corner of the shed. There would be eggs. Twice a day she changed his dressing. It was always the same. They would sit side by side at the table, his elbow resting in a basin while she poured water from a pitcher to saturate the bandage until it came away easily. Separating the lips of the wound, she irrigated its depths, swabbing gently until the water ran clear. Then she would bind up his arm with a piece of clean linen. Through it all he gave no sign of pain, but sat gazing at the blank wall, submitting.

"Why don't you yell?" she asked him. "I know it hurts." His embarrassed smile informed her that a gaucho knows how to suffer. "It isn't natural. You don't have to be brave for my sake."

Early one morning he rode off alone to get supplies. The cylinder of dust from the horse's hoofs rose, spread, settled. She went to pump water from the well, annoyed by her awkwardness. What if he didn't come back? Oh God! What if he had been seen? And recognized? Let him come back to me, she prayed. When at dusk she saw again the grayish pillar far down the plain, she knelt and gave thanks.

Later, she would try to remember how it happened, that once, when she had finished bathing the wound, wrapped it in one of her handkerchiefs, they had continued to sit side by side in an unbearable silence; how all at once, he had reached out his hand to touch her. Or had it been she who . . . ? Then, with what might have been a roar had he permitted it to sound aloud in his throat, he drew her to him. Never, never would she forget the way he raised his gaze to the horizon and passed his hands over her body as though he were blind, committing it to memory.

"I love you," his lips fumbled with the words; he started in shock at what had come out of him. Now it no longer mattered to her what he might have been—murderer, thief. She no longer wondered. Or cared. She knew only that this was what she had been waiting for all her life. When he said that he loved her, she believed him as a tree believes the wind that blows through its branches. And she reached out for the dirt-encrusted man with his lacerated arm, this man who was not handsome, very far from it—just a long tubular man with a lamb's brown hair, thick and curly, emerging from the stronghold of his chest, and cracked red knuckles that sat speechless upon his speechless knees. Oh yes, this was the man she wanted.

And he, for his part, ached to take her apart as though she were a complicated thing like a clock, turning over and over in his hands this body that she had brought down to him from her mountains and that she had been storing up in a cool dark place as though it were a fruit that must be kept so or it would spoil. But he could not fathom her. He who had made use of many women, and had never removed his clothes to make love. It was not enough to strip her bare, to lie down naked beside her. Even the tiny golden hairs on her arms, her thighs, that were like the down of a peach to his fingertips, did not tell him what he longed to know about this woman. Only when he had placed himself inside her, only when he felt her stiffen, tremble in his arms, heard the breath drawn through her clenched teeth, and when he spied upon that face from which all expression had fled, only then did he feel himself growing close to the molten core of the woman. Perhaps it was her smell that awakened him from what seemed like centuries of sleep. Faintly mossy, cool, like a mountain stream, something, anyway, alive with fish. The moisture of her—the tears that glittered but did not fall, the tendrils of hair at her temples gleaming with sweat, the tiny bubbles of saliva on her straight, white teeth. Even her voice was humid. The way she welcomed his immersion, as if to bathe, to slake.

All that first day and into the night they listened to the delirium of each other's arms and legs; the pillows about their heads burst into flames; and between their close-pressed bodies, first she, then he, felt the pulse captive in the upraised wings of a butterfly open . . . close . . . open. When the moment came, he threw himself into her like a powerful swimmer who quickly captures a pace, lets it lead him, feeling his courage swell until at last his thick man's fluid gathered and hurled itself into the drifting castaway in his arms. Only then did he know this woman.

So! she thought. It is like this! The heat coming out of him, the heat of the pampas—the precise rhythm of their bodies, beyond her control; that place without language or thought to which he brought her. That place that is not present on any map of the world. And afterward she wondered—had she died in this man's arms? She wasn't sure, but then there he lay, still within her, like a man taking shelter from a storm.

For the first time, she did not miss the mountains of her childhood. With a shock she realized that she had not even thought of them in weeks. Why should she? When here at the *estancia* there was the copper smell of tea, the soft barking of his boots on the beaten earth of the yard, the way he tossed one leg over the horse and swung himself erect; and the hot cloudless days that swooned one into the other, the melon sun cracking open on the edge of the horizon, leaking out into the night.

Now those mountains seemed to her deaf, dumb, and blind; all knitted up with narrow paths, rope bridges, sliced by gorges. What had she to do with them anymore?

Weeks went by, weeks in which they moved together and apart, pouring themselves into each other. They might have been jars that needed filling. To the woman, her passion was no longer an ardor that sprang from within but a command from outside of herself that must be obeyed. Once he had returned from a day's ride for supplies with three silver bangles which he slipped on her left wrist.

"So that I can hear them and come to you right away." Between the two trees in the yard, he had slung a rawhide hammock. Sometimes when he had finished eating, he went to lie there; she would spend whole minutes absorbed in the plate from which he had just eaten while the silence hummed in her ear like a big black fly. Until she could not sit still any longer but must go to him in the hammock and bend over him. She could not keep from touching him. As seamed and rough as were his neck and arms (they had the consistency of horn), the skin of his belly and buttocks was as smooth as water flowing through her fingers. Sometimes, she thought, he tolerated it the way a lioness will endure the biting of her cubs until, provoked, she will bite back but with the soft tooth of love. Once, after they had made love, and his regular deep breathing told her he was asleep, she sat up to watch him. The moon was full and she could see an expression of sadness on his face. In the morning, she asked him.

"No," he told her. "Not sad. That's not it."

"What then?" Reading his silence, she guessed it had to do with being a gaucho, something in his past. Had to do with his being a fugitive. On another night she had awakened toward dawn to find him standing in the doorway of the house.

"What are you doing?"

"I'm trying to make it last longer, the night."

"Come back to bed," she coaxed him. In the darkness, she heard him sighing like a man bereaved.

"You are sad. Are you sad?" Thinking: gaucho, bridegroom. If only he knew what thoughts went through her head.

Twice each day when she changed his dressing, the wound brought them together. The act became a kind of foreplay, triggering their passion with a desire edged all around with pain. If only the wound would heal! No longer was there any pus at the base; no longer was there the smell of rot. There was scarcely any seepage or blood, as though the man's veins had silted up. But she could see no sign of healing.

To her, everything about him was gaucho, including his silence. As the weeks went by he had grown even more silent, so that when he did speak she was as startled as if the table had uttered a word. Try as she might, she could not break through his silence. Whole days would go by when he did not utter a word. What she could not know was that for him it was a way of protecting her. To speak of certain things would be to give them a terrible reality. Better to distance them in a cloud of silence. Besides, he told her when she pressed him, there was no language he knew that was good enough for her. He was sure to say something insulting or rude. Then he would reach for his guitar and sing.

> *When on the range I was living*
> *I had worked as a cowpunch.*
> *I would lasso little calves*
> *And take them to the slaughterhouse.*
>
> *I know how to throw the bolo*
> *And to take care of a horse.*
> *And I can skin a cow*
> *Without cutting through the robe.*

"My God!" she would exclaim. "You gauchos only know to sing about killing." Then the man would soften his guitar and lower his voice.

Ama todo cuanto vive
De Dia dios vida se recibe
y donde hay vida hay amor.
(There's nothing got life that doesn't have love.)

They had been at the *estancia* for three months. Once again, at dawn he had ridden off for supplies. He had waited until the night before to tell her that he must go. Once again her heart bounded at the thought that he might be discovered. Still, she who had taken this man and usurped his life in all its particularities, could not voice her fear, could not bring herself to intrude upon what she knew was the gist of his privacy as a man, a gaucho. Besides, what could he tell her? When he saw on her face the terror she was unable to conceal, he spoke.

"I don't go to Quines. Another place. In that direction," he pointed.

"Far away. You'll be safe?" She couldn't resist. From where he sat on the horse, he looked down, tilted his head to one side, closed one eye as if taking her measurements, nodded slightly and rode away. In her anguish all day she had patrolled the house, the yard. It was dusk when, squinting into the distance, she caught sight of him, the saddlebags bulging from the flanks of the horse. She could not have known at that time that each step the horse took was a martyrdom for him. His tongue felt too big for his mouth; his face tingled as if half asleep. Only the throbbing of his arm kept him from tilting out of the saddle to the ground. All that afternoon, in whatever direction he looked he saw her face. She was the dark flame that bowed toward him with each painful intake of breath. Returning to the *estancia,* to her who was waiting, was all that he wanted. With the hacienda once again in view, desire sprang up among the pain, canceling it. Reaching behind him, he slapped the rump of the horse and raced the last mile toward her. She ran to where he had tethered the horse. He turned to embrace her. All at once, his body crashed into hers so that she staggered to remain standing. He would have fallen had she not gripped him in her now powerful arms.

"What?" she began, then saw that his face was fiery, that the sweat was streaming from his temples; the way he shook! His head lolling. "My God! What?" She was whispering as though no one must hear this terrible secret. She half lifted, half dragged the man inside the house, placed him on the bed, undressed him piece by piece until he was naked. So hot, he might have burst into flames; the billows from his body. Fiercely she tamped down the nausea that rose in her throat, blinked away the greenish lights behind her eyes. Soaking cloths, she bathed him until his skin was cool to her touch. Even in his fever, his body responded to her touch. She was moved to tears by the sight of that. At last the rigor passed and he stopped trembling. He spoke.

"I love you," he told her, "and now . . ."

"No!" she shouted in his face. "No! Be still!" She who had tried for so long to unlock his tongue was afraid. She had come to count on the silence that he threatened now to break, and she pressed him to her, rocking back and forth.

For days he drifted in and out of unconsciousness, each time returning by what seemed an act of will. Then he would follow her movements with his eyes, and he would speak in a hoarse whisper. His voice drifting off, barely audible, then wavering back to her. As though he were leaning from the saddle of his horse, his bones clattering across the incalculable pampas, he confided his fear of the revenge that was inevitable. It was his destiny, he told her, openly at last. And why not? Hadn't she again and again pressed her ear to his lips and bade him speak? If silence were the badge of innocence, then *he,* not she, was the virgin, the one who had kept himself pure until now when the delirium unlocked his jaws at last. Even in his ravings, he heard the demand of her blood and in a hesitant, faltering staccato voice, he offered her the inner core of feeling that was his soul; told her that he lived now at her pleasure, only to please her. He had succeeded in giving her power over him, did she understand that?

"So, I have spoiled a good gaucho," she told him. And at the words, a sweetness came over his face, as it does sometimes when there is great suffering. Affliction, she thought, how it can burnish a body until it glows surprisingly. At last the fever abated. His eyes, sunk deep in their sockets, gave proof of fatigue.

"Go to sleep for a bit," she told him. "You want to sleep." But even as she spoke, she wanted him to stay awake, to share wakefulness with her. Sleep would only distance him farther, put him in a different dimension from hers. Even then, had he smiled and lifted his arms, she would have tumbled into them.

Within days, he was confined to the space between the head and foot of the bed. On and on the fever crackled. He was a log in the grate. So violent was the chill when it came that she had to wonder: Was it the bed that was shaking the man? Again and again she sponged his chest and limbs, turned him from side to side to wash his back. At night she listened to the dementia of insects that crowded around the bed and would surely have had their voracious way with him had she not been there to keep them from it. It was worse at night. In the morning, the fever let up; she opened the blinds; let sunlight spill over the skeleton that had begun to assert itself. With the melting-away of his flesh his bones began to take on a grave importance.

All the while she nursed him—wiping away stains, irrigating, carrying away leavings—her desire for him never left her. Even the treasure of his excrement which she carried away, escorted, as though it were the ashes of a saint. Yes! Even that. No one could know. When she lay her hand upon his belly, his thigh, and felt his rod slowly leaf out and blossom among her fingers, tears filled her eyes at the defiance of his desire. The courage of the man! She could not understand such a silence in the face of so much pain and anguish. My God! Hadn't Christ cried out on the Cross? His bravery seemed useless and absurd to her, like the brass ornaments on a casket. The thought brought her hand up to her mouth.

"But why not?" she begged him. "Be more human, holler a little just to please me." But he smiled and shook his head to let her know that suffering was just a bad habit. Gauchos don't have it. Gauchos, she thought, her heart breaking.

There were times during the long nights of her vigil, drifting in and out of sleep, her own mind clouded with dreams, in the mirage-y room, when she wondered! Was he real, or an emanation of her desires, something that she had dredged up from her unconscious. Then she would press herself against him, to feel. No, he was real after all, he was real.

∽

There had been a sudden fierce storm after which came a long flat silence. Water dripped from the roof. A bird shrieked once, then stopped. She did not budge from the chair at the bedside. The house trembled as the man in the bed trembled. When night had entered, and taken command of the room, she went to light the lamp.

"Don't!" he spoke urgently. "Don't light the lamp. Keep watch. Listen." Oh, she knew what he meant: You cannot be seen in the dark. She strove to do his bidding. Before the dawn, she drew the blinds. Not a ray of light. Not one. They must be faithful to the night. She would do as he wished. Besides, when there is only a shadow left, you do not want to waste it like that. Better to hoard the shadow in the dark, so that it will last. Didn't his body give off its own, its proper light? Nothing existed save for that luminous trembling man in the bed. All the life of the farmhouse had gathered there to that bed which, in the heat of the summer, under the fires of the sun, kept its own night, uninfluenced by the revolution of the earth about it. Now, even at the height of the fever, he did not lose consciousness. Nor did he sleep but was held in a state of unbearable somnolence that was not sleep. In this state, halos and echoes enlarged and prolonged the objects and sounds of the room. He listened to her every padded footstep, each one of her sighs. Once, she had awakened from sleep to find him battling.

"What is it? Calm yourself."

" . . . *Siete* . . ." he managed. *"Los hermanos . . . vendetta . . ."* Then she knew that he was being pursued even into his delirium. His voice, between clenched teeth, took on a pale yellowish cast. Only weeks before, his words had been ivory balls that rolled through her one into the other, setting up echoes, clicking. Now he breathed like someone who had forgotten how.

"The lights *are* off. Nobody can see you. Never mind all that. It is a dream." And she poured a few drops of wine into his mouth. "Sleep," she told him, "and don't talk in your sleep anymore." His smile was the slow shifting of dunes. His eyelids weighted down, struggling to open them, dragging his body out of the fever where it toiled, to greet her, to reassure her. Because of his silence, precisely because of that, she had learned to read him without need of language.

"Why are you ashamed?" she asked him. "It's stupid."

"So much attention to me," his eyes alone replied.

"You gaucho! You crazy man!"

There came the day when she looked up to see him smiling. Smiling! She raced to his side, incredulous. A flute of happiness piped through her body, trilling like the panpipes of her native mountains. She laughed aloud to see his joy.

"Why do you smile?" she demanded in mock reproach. "What's so funny? Do you know what you have put me through?" Her voice went liquid with merriment, turned wanton. She pulled her fingers through the extravagance of hair she had neglected to comb, playing the bangles on her wrist. When he made no answer, she nudged him. "What's so funny?" Then she looked and saw that it was not a smile, but a grin, something in which his eyes did not take part. A grin that would not go away, that had no origin from within him but was independent of his thoughts. She bent close to read the small print of his lips and teeth. His eyes gave back to her a deep well of despair. The sudden realization terrified her. Her skin turned senseless, numb; her arms dropped to her side, her legs were as though sunk in the ground; she was turning to stone. And all at once, something within her cracked, the way a stone is riven by lightning. It is too much, she thought. I cannot. At that moment she knew that she would have to ride to Quines for help even though it could give away the secret of his whereabouts. She would have to risk it. It was the grin that broke her. She could not bear to face that grin by herself. No she could not. She would have to go to Quines for a doctor. She would have to leave him for that time while she rode the tame horse to Quines. Even if she rode there and back it would take more than a day. But could she leave him? It was too long! What if he . . . ? She dared not think of it.

"Listen to me." she bent close. "Listen!" she commanded him. The man's eyes swiveled toward, then past her. She pressed her lips to his ear, summoning his brain. And she told him what she must do, that she would ride the tame horse as he had taught her, that she would be back with him the next evening. At last, she saw his eyes focus on her; she could read understanding in them. "Behave yourself!" she told him.

She had not ridden more than out of earshot when the sobs came that tore in and out of her lips. And she who had not howled, howled; had not wept, wept tears. There with only the tame horse to hear, the horse that listened and flicked an ear, she took her portion of suffering and spent it. The slowness of the horse maddened her; it seemed to be counting its steps. She had all she could do to keep from grasping the reins and pulling. She thought that she was going wild. Stop, stop it, she told herself and forced herself to be still. All day she rode, resisting the temptation of the reins, until at last she saw in the distance a wisp of smoke. An hour later she entered the town of Quines. In the square was the clinic of the district doctor. She stayed only long enough to leave word. All the way home, gripping the horse with her thighs, she fought down her terror of what she might find. When at last she slid to the ground and raced inside the house to find him breathing . . . noisily, it was true, but *breathing* . . . she sank to her knees, not so much in prayer as in relief.

"Cough!" she commanded him. "You must cough." When she saw that he could not or would not raise the secretions that filled his throat, she forced open his rigid jaw with a wooden spoon, then using her finger, she cleaned away the gray membrane of phlegm and was rewarded by hours of quiet breathing. Now she fed him water, wine, milk, and tea through a straw she had made from a reed.

Two days later, the doctor arrived. His examination was brief, at the end of which he nodded to himself solemnly. He had solved another puzzle.

"What?" she asked, and saw how the doctor took a firm grip on his authority and thrust it out in front of him.

"Tetanus," he pronounced. "Lockjaw." And explained how the wound, seemingly minor, had become infected with the bacteria that caused tetanus. The man's nervous system had been poisoned. It was that which caused the muscles of his face to contract and stay contracted.

"But the smile . . ." She would have disputed.

"It has the appearance of a smile," he told her. "But, I assure you, it is the appearance only. It is called *risus sardonicus.*" When she made no sign of comprehension, he translated. *"Sonrisa sardonico."*

"What is there to do?"

"It is a matter of days."

"What are you saying?"

"That he will die within days. At most. The end."

The woman's eyes went off like a pair of pistols. She could have killed this man for the tidings he bore her. Oh yes, oh yes, it is true that she had had little hope, but only when that bit was snatched from her did she know how much hope it had been. When the doctor had left, she sank her fingers into her hair, pressed them to her temples, and turned to the man in bed.

"Don't!" she shouted at him. "If you knew how much I love you, you wouldn't think of dying." And she cursed herself for sending for the doctor. For this, for nothing! She had squandered two days! Two days when she could have felt his heart beating beneath her fingers, when she could have kissed his hands, his eyes. What a price! From that moment, she did nothing but tend him—feed, bathe, protect him from insects. Day by day the dry pampas continued to encroach upon the neglected farmhouse. Dust and stones penetrated the full length of the house. In his quiet suffering, he seemed the opposite of the beggar who shows with impudence each one of his sores, badging himself for pity's sake. Now it was the grin that had taken possession of the sickroom, the grin about which everything else—bed, chair, table, mirror, shutters—revolved, as lifeless plants revolve about the sun. His face having been occupied by that false grin, the woman examined his body until she found the true, the fugitive smile that came and went over his chest, that crept down across his abdomen to his thighs. Only in the cleft brow and the corrugation of his eyebrows was the whole of his agony expressed. And all the while, her desire for him never left her. When she had finished her nursing— bathing, dressing, wiping away stains—she would lie down next to him, cover him with her breast, her arms, and kiss the sunken temples already wet with new sweat.

"I'm going to cut your hair," she said. "Can't have my man looking . . ." She would have gone on with it had he not flung his unblinking gaze at her feet, imploring her to stop.

And she would talk to him, wondering all the while if he could hear her. Was she speaking from too far away? When he had not slept for four days and four nights, she brought a metal pail into the room and poured a pitcher of water into it from a height.

"Listen! It's raining! Do you hear it?" The sound of the rain was a weight upon his eyelids and the man slept. Who can stay awake with the sound of rain on a roof? For a long time she watched him, the way he slept without haste, patiently drawing air into his deep chest, holding it there for a moment, then sending it forth to the almost palpable satisfaction of his body. How she relished his sleep. Furtively she bent over him to draw his exhaled breath into her own lungs. Toward morning a bit of color rose to the surface of his cheeks. From time to time a groan issued from what seemed the deepest cave of his chest; his taut lips twitched about the ghost of language. Of what? Of what, she died to know, could he be dreaming? She longed to awaken him if only to rescue him from whatever was pursuing him across the barren pampas but she did not dare to deprive him of a sleep so hard-won. Later when he woke up she asked him.

"What were you dreaming about? Such a lot of mumbling!" But, of course, he could not say. Each time he returned from his dreams as from death, sworn to secrecy.

∽

It was the twenty-third day of his fever. One of those nights when the sky is a goatskin stretched over a kettle. Outside in the darkness, the crickets sizzled. Until now, the man had failed to achieve the mercy of unconsciousness or, rather, he had rejected it by force of will. For her sake, to be for her. At last he could no longer keep his mind from slipping away. All night she sat and roamed the farthest countries of her mind. Was he in pain? Did he think of her still? Know that she was there? Her fingers reeled across his chest. Could he hear her calling out him? And all the while her gaze returned to that grin, that jaw that she could not unlock with her kiss.

"Smile, then, brave man," she told him. "You have earned the right. Brave man, smile." But now the poison had spread to the muscles of his neck and his back which, like his jaws, had gone rigid so that only the back of his head and his heels touched the mattress. His body arched like a fish trying to leap from the surface of the pool that was the only element in which it could live. His breathing had changed; the way he chased his breath until he caught up with it, but only for a moment before it once again broke free and was running away with quick small steps. Exhausted, the man lay as if deciding whether to mount another chase, then all at once, his ribs started up from the bed, and off he went once more, pumping after his wayward breath. And it seemed to her that a pale and fragile light had gathered at the wound on his arm, a phosphorescence that, even as she watched, spread to envelop the entire body of the stricken gaucho. Passing her hand through the luminous vapor, she touched his rigid cheek. And deep within her ear she heard a faint noise, a drubbing. Louder and louder it grew, to a rumble, then a roar. Abruptly, it stopped. In the hush that followed, she spoke.

"Well then, go," she said quietly to the man who was turning to light before her eyes. She would not keep him from it. And with those words, she freed him from the mesh with which she had bound the gaucho to herself. With an immense effort, he opened his eyes, as if to see her one last time. All at once, his skin darkened. His head made a last small movement as when a horse with flies makes its skin quiver, then lay still, with the grin locked upon his face. She gazed and gazed at the broad forehead behind which one minute there had been something that thought and felt, the next, nothing. The way his ears, slightly protuberant, buckled the thick black hair to his head. She stroked his shoulder, his arm, to see: Was there not still a bit of life in that arched and rigid body? The way a tiny worm of flame will curl and uncurl beneath the cinders long after a fire appears to have gone out? She knew there was not, despite the deep furrow that continued to cleave his forehead like the wound of an ax, and the persistence of that sardonic smile in which only the eyes took no part. When he had taken his last breath, she blew out his eyes as if they were candles. Drawing fresh water from the well, she bathed him for the last time, then lay down beside him, pressing him to her so tightly she could feel his smallest bones move.

In the morning she rose, went down to draw a pitcher of water from the well in the courtyard. Returning to the room, she undressed and bathed. Reaching up both hands, she scraped her black hair into an excruciating tight bun at her nape, secured it there with a pin. Walking back and forth, she passed the bed with its terrible contents. In the mirror her shoulders had drooped, her bosom withdrawn into her chest. All that day, because she did not know what else to do, she continued to sit, numb and silent, watching the man. But not touching him. No, not that. His body had become a forbidden place, a garden from which she had been expelled, all the beloved glades and paths overgrown, wild, inaccessible. Death had placed him off-limits. She thought of the way he had undressed her, piece by piece, unveiled her really, his schoolboy's face marveling. And how he led her each time with patience and concern to the end of herself, helped her to climb rock after rock to the summit from which, lofted, she would surrender to him her mystery. The way, in his helplessness, the poverty of his trembling tongue, he would refer to her as a star, a wild horse, or a rainfilled cloud, a guitar—again and again reaching down into himself to pull up the perfect name for her.

"Why do you call me always by these names?"

"It is the only way I have to catch you before you slip away."

"I'm not mysterious!" She had laughed. "The only part of me that is a mystery is the part that is inside you." "And what shall I call *you*?" She was flirting. When he did not answer, she decided that she would call him a name that no one else would know; she would call him only in silence. Something from the mountains—*volcano* or *waterfall. Avalanche.*

But now a sudden uneasiness came upon her, a chill of the mind. Her thoughts leaped, startled. Had a rooster given out an unscheduled cry? Had one of the horses struck his hoof and broken her reverie? No, it was a premonition that she felt as a mist on her skin. Twice she went to peer between the blinds, then returned to her vigil. But even this uncanny woman could not have known that at that moment seven horses and seven riders were galloping across the pampas. Toward her.

All morning she sat at the dead man's side, waiting. But for what? Then, as if a signal had been given, she went outside into the barnyard. Shielding her eyes, she looked into the distance, and saw the cloud of dust, and she knew. Minutes later, she counted: three, four,

five, six, seven. There came the drumming of many hooves. Then
there they were, each with a cowboy hat slung at the back of the
neck; their ponchos billowing. Calmly she waited in the doorway
until at last they had ridden into the yard, dismounted and stood
about her in a circle, their knives drawn. One stepped forward, the eldest, she decided, with a scowling face and heavy shoulders that sat
upon his neck. His voice was like the riding whip with which he
lashed his right boot for emphasis. *Thwack, thwack, thwack.*

"We know he is here." When she did not answer, the blood stood
dark in his face, his nostrils flared; a damp odor rose from his body.
"Whore! Give him up or you die too." The way they whinnied and
barked.

"Whore!" *Thwack.* "Whore!" *Thwack.* "Die!" *Thwack.* How tranquil
she felt in the face of hatred. She watched the sinuous rise of the
whip; and the way it seemed to draw the arm of the man after it in a
flight both alluring and savage. Like the tango, she thought, even as
it struck her across the cheek. She had steeled herself against the
cringe that was expected of her. The avenger took a step nearer, raised
the whip again. His lips were black as coal beneath a black mustache.
The long sideburns were tufted with gray. He had the fierce clear eye
of a man who has at last captured his prey. So close now that she got
a whiff of his lust, a redolence of onions and blood. With a grimace,
the gaucho brought his fist up, putting behind it all the strength of his
shoulder, grunting as if he were sinking an ax into wood. The woman
took the punch squarely in the mouth. Had she parted her lips to receive it? Blood spurted. She sank to her knees in the doorway, fighting off unconsciousness the way the gaucho had taught her; the
raiders trampled her and entered the house. She struggled to her feet
and followed them to the room where he lay in the horsehair bed,
grinning with the grin that had survived his death. She no longer felt
human, but something damned and writhing. And with its blood on
fire. She hoped they would beat her again, kill her, even. It would require pain, the letting of blood, to stamp out what she had become.

"There he is!" she said. "He has been expecting you." She drank in
their confusion.

"He's dead! What's going on here? And he smiles! Why does he smile?" Exultation flooded her so that she, too, smiled over the victory she had given him. The faces of the gauchos were swollen with fury.

She followed them out into the yard and watched as with a speed and efficiency fueled by rage they poured kerosene onto the walls of the hacienda, reentered the house and splashed the bed, then torched it. The first flame was like a blue flail that rose and fell, threshing the farmhouse beneath it. A wind rose and lashed it along. Now the fire glided across the yard, bent its knees and leaped to the roof of the barn and from there to the sheds, turning them scarlet. A moment later, she saw that the men had mounted. There was the muffled sound of their horses' hooves, their shouts. The last of them turned to make his horse rear at the bonfire, then all galloped off.

From the bench by the well she watched the smoke coiling among the fenceposts, licking the trunks of the trees. Closing her eyes, she listened to the hiss and crackle of the burning house and the neighing of the two horses as they danced out of the barn. Now the flames quickened, bits of the house rose and circulated in the currents of heat. Everything—rocks, tree trunks, even the sky turned black with smoke. The house sagged, collapsed and vanished under the towering flames that came from all sides and that would not go out until there was nothing left. Her eyes burned; she was sweating. It shocked her—the speed with which everything was consumed. Once, twice, when the flames threatened to die away and only the embers trembled, she took a pitchfork and poked until the glare rose up again, tending it, feeling the heat on her arms, her face. At last, the embers went black, the ruin silent. There was nothing left for her to do. Nothing but sit there and wait as she had always sat and waited. Day became night with all its anonymous noises, an animal's furtive step, the rind of a melon being cracked open. Then day once more. Rising, she stepped across the virginal yard, covered with white ash, without foot or hoofprint. In the hard surface, no single scar. Measuring distances with her feet she reconstructed a path to the room until at last she stood by the iron bedstead, empty now and strewn all around with ash and bone. So, this is where it happened, she thought, and thrilled as if she had come into a sacred space, as though in this spot an altar had been dressed and fed. She saw how the fire had absorbed his blood, stripped his breast of flesh and spared only these bones in the ritual of extermination. Her nostrils filled with the smell of scorch and smoke. And something else she couldn't name—spice, pepper, rotting leaves, sweat. The horsehair mattress! Yes, that was it! Sighing, the woman knelt and stretched out her hand. It might have been a crippled beggar who dipped her fingers into the ashes, still hot, and lifted them to the burst plum of her lips until her mouth filled with the delicious taste of burnt flesh.

∽

The train wound its way behind the town of Santa Rosa before leveling out toward the east and Buenos Aires. As it curled past the town, the woman raised the window of the compartment and leaned out, inhaling the hot dry air of the pampas for the last time. Already, the death of the gaucho seemed to her miraculous, leaving behind a residue of light, a glory. What did it mean? Had this been life? Her portion of it? For the second time, she felt herself to have stood where an avalanche had passed, and no way to prove that what lay buried under it had been real. If only she could be given a sign, a suggestion, even, that would keep it all rooted. From that moment on she began to live backward in time, receding day by day from the experience of him. I was, she thought. I used to be; I am not anymore. Already, the events of those weeks had begun to pale out. His outline had grown blurred. Where had his chin ended? Were his wrists as thin as she now made them in her mind? He, too, had been; he was not, like a hallucination that utterly convinces only to be nullified in time.

More and more the memory of it all came to her in her dreams. Where, she wondered, did memory leave off and dream begin? In her dreams the man was still alive; dreams do not accept death. Her grandmother too, and her family buried in the landslide so long before were alive and speaking to her in Quechua. The village of her childhood merged with Santa Rosa and then into Buenos Aires, a place where she was herself both a young girl and a woman of forty. Sometimes, she could conjure the gaucho by staring off into space and setting her thoughts just so. After a while, there he was! An image surrounded by shadows; it was always dusk, and he was standing with only his silhouette in view, then as she watched he would turn to face her. At the same moment the image of his body would fade little by little until only the afterimage of the grin remained, disembodied and suspended before her just as she had first seen it and mistaken it for happiness. After a while, that too disappeared.

∽

Upon her return to Buenos Aires, the woman went straight from the train to the convent where she had been raised as a girl. Not out of any strong religious impulse—what she sought, death, did not require faith; only patience. No, she went to stay at the guest house of Santa Catarina because she did not know what else to do. But she did not die. For one year she suffered from insomnia, and the searing pangs of grief. Add to that a hopeless desire for the gaucho and there was a woman on the very edge, she thought, of madness.

At the end of the year, whether it was the peacefulness of the convent, the passage of time, a certain wish to retrieve the dignity of life, whatever, the woman began to sleep. Her appetite returned. She made plans to leave the convent and found an apartment overlooking the river. In time, her longing for the gaucho became a kind of nostalgia triggered perhaps by some trace of smell, a certain warm breeze upon her skin, the sound of hoofbeats. Unannounced it would appear rising slowly in her mind like a waterbird that lifted from the surface of the river below her balcony; and there, where the bird had floated on the water, only a lingering reflection, of brightness that to her who watched and listened, was the distant echo of love.

Angel, Tuning a Lute

In writing a story, it is best to begin with a tiny seed of truth. Some months before leaving for Tuscany to lead a writing workshop, I happened upon Vasari's *Lives of the Painters*. I cannot think now why, only that I spend most of my days in a library and will now and then reach at random for a book. Luca Signorelli, I learned, was one of the most revered painters of the sixteenth century. He was able to paint nude figures so as to make them appear alive, and was the first to show "the true splendor of arms." In his later years, he eschewed the popular biblical subjects—Madonna and Child, The Annunciation, The Gift of the Magi—and devoted himself to historical scenes. Vasari went on to tell of Signorelli's only son, "of whom he was very fond, of beautiful face and figure, having been killed at Cortona, Luca caused the body to be stripped and, with extraordinary fortitude and without shedding a tear, painted the body so that he might always behold in the work of his hands what Nature had given him and cruel Fate had taken away." Reading on, I learned that Signorelli had also painted a beautiful angel tuning a lute. Then and there, I decided to transform these facts into a story.

The writing workshop was held on a country estate, Castelnuovo Tancredi, a short distance from Monte Oliveto, the great Benedictine monastery whose cloister, I was informed, contained many frescoes painted by Luca Signorelli! A coincidence, I thought. And embraced it as one should all coincidences, for you just never know. In the weeks to follow, I would visit Monte Oliveto many times to see the works of Luca Signorelli. Perhaps I would find there the portrait of his son?

Oh yes, this too. Cennino Cennini was also a fifteenth-century painter. While little of his work remains, he achieved immortality by writing a handbook on the craft of painting and sculpture—how to grind and mix colors, how to draw, how to make good brushes, all of that. *Il Libro del Arte* is a book I have loved for many years. In a gesture of homage, I gave Signorelli's apprentice the name Cennino Cennini, and put the teachings of the real Cennino into the mouth of my Signorelli. I trust this reversal of utterance will not offend anyone. I don't care if it does.

✑

From the village of Buonconvento a road branches off toward the abbey, which is set in an oasis of cypress trees, olive groves, and vineyards, all surrounded by an impoverished and hilly desert. A narrow stream glitters at the edge of the cloister. Monte Oliveto! How many times the words had been said, and would be said right on up to the Apocalypse. The air here, rarefied by silence, has a different specific gravity. The churchbells have an ambiguous, fractured sound. Had this place ever been new? I couldn't imagine it without the patina of a thousand years. No part or object within it has been dated or labeled, but each keeps its mystery. You don't know precisely when anything took place, the sequence of events. That in itself is lovely. There are six monks left on the premises. Their work is the restoration of old books under the guidance of one Fra Placido. After the great flood in Florence, many valuable books were brought to Monte Oliveto. Only six! Hardly enough to constitute a choir, and even these six seem part of the past. This abbey is a majestic ship without passengers and going nowhere. The olive grove is scarlet with poppies. At night, the vineyard is alive with uncountable fireflies—a fragment of the Milky Way fallen to earth. In the cypresses, nightingales.

The frescoes in the cloister depict scenes in the life of St. Benedict. Signorelli's muscular males are made three-dimensional by a startling use of white paint. In one fresco, a general is shown kneeling before the saint while his soldiers look on and display their "splendid" thighs and arms. Another has three white-habited Benedictines bagging a devil they've captured. In still another, a nude is being transformed into a devil while a huge lizard licks the blood flowing from his wounds. Everywhere there are miracles; a workman thrown by Satan from a high wall is being brought back to life by the saint who refuses to be "taken in" by a soldier wearing an attractive costume. All the frescoes have been restored to a fare-thee-well. They have the bright vulgarity of kitsch. Among all the horde of beefy monks, androgynous soldiers, and stylized devils, there is no figure that might have been a rendition of the dead son. The cloister of Monte Oliveto is little more than a religious comic book.

Disappointed, I turned aside. No, I would not, after all, write the story of Luca Signorelli's triumph over death. All at once, there stepped a living monk in white, his hair cropped, gaze directed downward. One of the six! Thin, pale, his face an ascetic mask, haunted. Nothing on the walls could match him for truth or beauty. He made his way down the length of the cloister, then disappeared through a door marked in bold letters: CLAUSTRUM. I hurried to follow and managed, just, to keep the door from snapping shut. Was it disappointment in the works of Signorelli, the apparent futility of my quest, or the beauty of the one who had just passed through that caused me to open that door and trespass? I did, and just in time to see the hem of a white habit turn a far corner. I followed, and passed through a second forbidding door to find myself in a large stone room with a single window, the oculus, high under the beamed ceiling. The Chapter House. I recognized it as if long ago I had filed in with the other monks to stand along the walls waiting for the abbot to be seated and for the hebdomedary reader to take his place at the lectern. I was strangely disoriented, could not say for certain in which direction I faced. Was it north? south? east? west? West, I supposed, although I couldn't have said why, only that the oculus might have been placed there to receive the rays of the setting sun. Opposite was a great blank eastern wall. For a long time I stood as if waiting for something or someone to appear, unwilling to take leave of this room that had existed in my mind and with which I felt such strong familiarity. All at once, the room darkened; a pink mist of sunset streamed through the oculus and splashed the eastern wall with a pulsatile glow. It would have been the eastern wall he used, where the setting sun might redden the boy's flesh, giving it the facsimile of life. There I remained until through the clouds an ivory chip of moon came and went across the oculus.

∽

O let me imagine it. The year is 1532. The wheatfields of Tuscany are dotted with scarlet poppies. At night, the vineyards swarm with fireflies. Nightingales sing in the cypress trees. Luca Signorelli is standing on a scaffold in the cloister of Monte Oliveto where he has been commissioned to paint frescoes depicting events in the life of St. Benedict. He has just completed one showing white-robed monks fending off the devil, a reptilian horror with horns, hooves, and tail. In contrast with the pure Benedictines, each of whom sports a pale golden halo, the devil is chock full of dark vice. Long ago, painting frescoes had become a kind of servitude for Luca. All those depictions of the Holy Family, the Annunciation, the Deposition from the Cross had slowly squeezed from him whatever religious belief he had once had. So many years catering to the wishes of mercurial abbots, each of whom insisted upon turning his church or monastery into the ultimate repository of Art. In the end, it had destroyed Luca's faith, leaving in its place only a troublesome nostalgia. He had come to hate the very monasteries where his masterpieces, some call them, are on display for the uplifting of the gullible. Especially this accursed Monte Oliveto to which he had been sentenced, you might say, to decorate the cloister with scenes from the life of St. Benedict. Ridiculous! That one with the three Benedictines stuffing the devil into a sack. It was hard to keep from laughing. And the hypocrisy! Never enough muscular buttocks for these Holy Fathers.

It is just after daybreak. All night long, silence has been heaped up in the cloister like dust, with not even a dog to stir it. All at once, a small brown bird with a scarlet cap, a *cardenello,* as though shot from the branch of a tree, flies straight at the old painter's chest as if to bore a hole in his heart. The bird does not strike him, but dives headlong into the fresco he has just finished painting, then falls to the floor and lies still. Luca shudders and moans aloud. In the absence of faith, superstition does him very well. It is an omen. Something terrible was about to happen!

All day, the painter struggles to focus his attention on the fresco. In the end, he amuses himself by showing the lewdness of two Benedictines on either side of a young knight in colorful tights whose buttocks occupies the center of the fresco. When darkness falls, he lets himself be helped to climb down from the scaffold by his young apprentice, Cennino. Only three months before, this fifteen-year-old boy, a distant relation whose full name is Cennino D'Andrea Cennini, had been lent to Signorelli by his Florentine colleague Agnolo, in whose studio the boy worked. It was understood that he would return to Agnolo when the Monte Oliveto frescoes had been completed. In that short time, Luca had come to love Cennino, and the boy, his master. Once, when Cennino had had a persistent nosebleed, Luca had climbed down to lay a jasper on the boy's neck.

"Where is the little bird?" Luca asks. Cennino produces the tiny corpse. Luca takes it in his hand, strokes the feathers, lifts a wing to see gold wingbars. Later, he would hear Cennino boast to the monks that his master is so great an artist that he could entice the birds to the grapes he has just painted.

But now Luca trembles and draws his cloak tight about his shoulders. This Monte Oliveto! What right does it have to exist? There ought to be a rule against a man stepping aside from the duty of living in the world. *Stabilitas loci,* indeed! Where a monk enters, there he must stay for the rest of his life, tormenting his flesh, each with his cincture and his little bag of whips. Pah! Listen! Luca Signorelli is teaching his apprentice:

"Let us suppose that you have a youthful head to do. When you have got the mortar of your plaster all smoothed down, take a little glazed dish that is tapered like a goblet, with a heavy foot to keep it from spilling over. Now take a bean of ocher into your little dish, add black—the size of a lentil. Add a third of a bean of white lime and as much *cinabrese* as the tip of a knife will hold. Mix all these, then add water. This color is known as *verdaccio* in Florence. In Siena it is called *bazzeo.* It doesn't matter. Make a fine pointed brush out of flexible thin bristles to fit into the quill of a goose feather, and begin to outline the face. In another dish, take a little *terre-verde,* well thinned out. With the wet bristle, half squeezed between thumb and forefinger, start shading under the chin and on the side where the face is to be darker. Go on by shaping up the underside of the mouth, then the rest of the mouth. Under the nose and under the eyebrow, especially in toward the nose. In this way you pick out the whole of the face wherever flesh color is to be applied. Now take a pointed minever brush and crisp up neatly the nose, eyes, lips, and ears with *verdaccio*. Some begin by laying in the face with flesh color, then shaping it up with *verdaccio* and they call it finished. This is a method of those who know little about painting. Follow the way I teach you. The great Giotto did it this way and so does Agnolo, who will be your master in Florence."

They have been working for some hours when, all at once, in the cloister, there is a turmoil. Luca is distracted. He bids Cennino go to the end of the long cloister to quieten whoever it might be. But from the direction of the noise a scene begins to unfold. Luca is near-sighted and cannot make out what is drawing near, only that it is a cluster of white-robed figures. They seem to be carrying something. Another person. Luca watches them approach through his eyelashes. It is a man! A young man whose golden hair hangs down to brush the floor. To each of his arms and legs, a monk has been assigned so that the youth is slung amidst them. Nearer and nearer they come, now in utter silence. Their steps grow slower and slower as though hesitant to reach the scaffold where the old painter is standing. At last, the small retinue is beneath him. Luca sees the shaved heads of the monks, gleaming, polished. Chins, noses and brows, unsoftened by hair, stand out sharply, cruelly. Only their emotions are veiled. Luca's heart bounds against his ribs. Whatever it was that had come hurtling toward him in the form of a bird, had arrived. In the solemnest voice of Luca's life, one of the monks—it is Padre Abate himself—bids the old man descend. When he remains standing on the scaffold, the abbot calls out again, "Luca Signorelli, come down!" Luca watches the words trickle from the thin bluish lips of the abbot, who never ceases to stare at the painter as if by his gaze alone he would keep him from toppling to the floor. A shadow moves across the abbot's face and flows right down under his white habit. When it envelops his feet, the abbot speaks for the third time.

"Come!" Cennino goes to help his master descend. With each step, Luca's horror mounts, for now he can see strewn in death his only son,

Antonio. The abbot tells how, only hours before, the boy had been sent by his mother to carry water from the fountain. With the heavy jug on his shoulder, he was crossing an empty field on the outskirts of Cortona when a serpent, the poisonous *scorzone,* struck. Within minutes, the boy's throat had closed; he could not draw a breath. There were convulsions, until the blessing of death.

"Oh yes," says the abbot, "the *scorzone* has been killed."

The little silver river at the edge of the cloister, it too has seen the dead youth and flees in terror to hide among the low shrubbery. Luca's hand scampers to his neck, goes absolutely still like a small creature on the alert for danger. His head wobbles, floats away from him; his legs give way and he would fall were it not for Cennino. And, like a child, he entrusts his body, turbulent with sobs, to the apprentice who feels the thud-thud of his master's heart pressed against him, and something else—a stirring, as if something inside the bent and writhen man were trying to break out. A moment later, Luca Signorelli straightens, he seems now to be listening. To what? Perhaps to the commotion of the brook? No, he has recognized two men at the rear of the entourage. They are countrymen of his from Cortona. It was they who had brought the corpse to Monte Oliveto.

"Tell me what you saw." Luca is speaking to the two men who had seen the boy fall as he was struck by the adder. The men are silent. He sees that they cannot bring themselves to say it. "No! I want to know. You must tell me!" When they are still silent, Luca turns to the abbot. "Command them, Padre Abate."

"Speak, then," says the abbot.

"We saw him jump back, the way he grabbed his thigh. He stumbled and fell, then crawled about in a circle on all fours. Within minutes, there was a convulsion. Foam bubbled from his lips. His head snapped back; his jaws worked as if he were chewing. And the foam at his mouth turned red."

"What else?" asks Luca. "I must hear it all."

"It seemed to us he was choking, as though his gullet were closing off. His breathing grew shallow and quick until his soul beheld Hades." All this while, Luca Signorelli stands motionless, composed. Now and then he blinks like an old tortoise that pauses from its drinking, raises its head.

"Which of you killed the snake?" The one nods at the other. "Pay them," says the old man to Cennino. Then turns and, in a voice full of authority, orders the monks to carry the body of his son to the Chapter House. To Cennino he instructs that all of the paints, brushes, the mortar and pestle, the dishes and vats, all the materials of his Art be brought to that same room.

With a composure that is not of this world, Luca follows the body of his son into the Chapter House where it is laid upon the cool stone floor. With his own hands, he strips the youth naked, and arranges his limbs in the repose of death. At last, he places his hands on the face of the dead boy, covering it for a long moment as if he would absorb the essential features into his fingers to be transferred precisely to the wall. There must be no delay. He must hurry. It is hot, hot in Tuscany. There has been no rain in weeks. Even the small green lizards stand immobile and panting, their jaws held open, bellies pumping. Already, a tinge of steely blue has appeared at the edges of the boy's skin. A coolness rises from the flesh. Luca cups the toes in his hand, then turns to begin. It will be the task of Cennino to keep his master awake day and night, to see that the candles and lamps are lit, to mix the paints and clean the brushes. All the while, Luca will continue to instruct his apprentice.

"The best place to paint is on a wall. Really, it is most agreeable. I'll show you how it is done. First of all, mix some lime and some sand. Two parts lime to one part sand. They have to be very clean, sifted. Add water and let it cool a bit so the plaster won't crack as soon as you put it on. There! Now sweep the wall with a bunch of feathers and wet it down. Work over the lime mortar with your trowel and smear it on the wall. *Ecco!* Do it twice and get the plaster flat on the surface. Now take a bit of charcoal and begin to draw. Next, with a small pointed bristle brush dipped in ocher as thin as water, shade, shade, always shading with washes of ink. Now comes the delicate part. Using a little sinoper without tempera, mark out the whole figure. Oh Christ! How long it takes! I am too slow!"

Hour after hour, with Time as his goad, Luca produces the outline of the boy on the wall, then paints. Each time the churchbells ring, he winces as though pierced by a thorn. Another hour passed! Cennino glances up at his master, his own face gone soft with compassion. He brings meat and bread, urges the master to eat, but Luca will eat nothing, only drink a little wine every few hours. When Cennino implores him, Luca admonishes.

"It is quite clear that you know nothing as yet. You must be ready to snatch up your brush the instant it bursts into flame." He sees the shame on the boy's face. "No matter, if you cannot abide here with me, go and eat. Go into the church and say your prayers, why don't you? Then come back to me and we will battle on." What Cennino cannot know is that Luca has put aside hunger and thirst, put them into the same sealed compartment where he has put the need for sleep. His body is in a rare state of hibernation. Only his mind blazes on. When Cennino returns, having eaten and prayed, Luca tells him that one day he too will climb a scaffold to leave the earth and tumble among the stars. Even the sorrowful Cennino cannot help but smile at the ornate way his master speaks.

Now and then, Luca sets down his brush to contemplate the wall. Then he will reach out to caress the stone until it should yield under his touch and take on a softer texture. After a while, he will pick up the brush and begin to achieve in reality what had only been imagined.

For five days and five nights, Luca will never cease to dip and apply his brushes to the wall.

"Hurry! We must finish the head today!" And to himself: *te calma,* be calm.

"To paint a dead man, you do not apply any pink at all. Instead, you take a little light ocher and step up the flesh color toward white, but only halfway. All the outlines—nose, ear, eyebrows—mark them with dark sinoper and a little black, tempered. This is called 'sanguine.' The hair too should not look alive; that would be false. For this, you must use *verdaccio.* Learn, little kinsman, learn."

By noon of the third day, the smell is undeniable. Hourly it grows stronger, the voluptuous reek of decay. Cennino tries to mask it with incense taken from the church but cannot keep from gagging every little while. The once pure air of the Chapter House is hung with ropes of stench into which Luca himself seems to be melting. He hears, or sees, the word *addio,* good-bye, floating. More than once, he reaches out to grasp it but the word folds upon itself and billows away. Only yesterday, he thinks, the boy jumped from his mother's breast!

Now it is the beginning of the fourth day and Luca regrets for the first time his absence of faith. More than anything else, he would like to believe that in this stinking puddle now bombinating with flies there had dwelt an immortal substance that was now set free and on its way to eternal life. But he cannot. Oh, he thinks, let there be that rare moment when a stone wall smells freshly of childhood!

Luca can no longer stand upright without the stick upon which he leans with one hand while plying the brush with the other. Cennino is beside himself.

"Maestro, you must rest."

"Keep me awake, I tell you."

"Everyone needs to sleep."

"Sleeping is not for me." Even so, the old man has begun to sway dangerously; his head falls upon his chest; he drifts in and out of consciousness, rouses himself with a start. Cennino has summoned the gatekeeper Vasco to take turns supporting Luca.

"Am I still here?" Luca asks.

"*Sì, maestro,*" Vasco tells him.

If Luca fears, it is not for himself but only that he may not finish before the boy shall have melted or before he himself shall have died. Already the floor about the body is darkly stained with moisture. Here, in this place where time does not matter, time matters! Cennino grinds the pigments to powder, whisks them into paste in the glazed bowls, and gazes up at his master. As the figure begins to emerge on the wall, Luca's brush strokes grow briefer, shyer, more tentative as though to touch that wall in order to alter it would be sacrilegious. But how stupid! The idea of sacrilege for a man who has no faith.

"How the brush feels in your hand is important, Cennino. It must sit comfortably within the circle of the first web space, resting against the knuckle, while the working end is supported lightly by the first three fingertips. In this position, the brush is utterly weightless, balanced."

All night long Cennino lights new candles and trims the wicks of the oil lamps. In the daylight, the flesh of the dead boy takes on a greenish glow. But at night the flames give it the humidity of life, with tints of rose and pearl. Then, involuntary tears glisten on his eyelashes. The mouth is slightly open as though breath were emerging from it.

"See, Cennino, how the eyebrow rises here in abundance, then goes scantier. And the way the red of the lips fades into the pale pink of the skin. Darkness is the absolute out of which light draws shadow. Make the shadow darkest where it originates, then let it go lighter and lighter with distance." Cennino cannot tear his gaze from the scaffold and its precious contents. There are moments when the maestro's face shines with unapproachable exaltation as if he were not the boy's father but his mother, a mother in the molten daze of childbirth, with the unborn Antonio coming to boil within him. Then Cennino knows to keep silent.

It is the evening of the fourth day. Luca has begun to cough, great wet spasms. In the silence of damp stone that surrounds them, the old man's breathing is the only noise. As though a bird were trapped and fluttering inside his chest. The *cardenello*!

"It all depends upon the obedience of the hand, reining it in and giving rein at one and the same time. Sometimes you must let the brush lead you along. Surrender to it, let your hand ride it. And don't think too much. There's no place for thinking here. It puts out the candles."

For the sweat in his eyes, as for the veil of reek, for the incense that billows night and day as for the smoke of candlewick, Luca cannot see his own hand.

"Light! More light!" he implores again and again in a detached pale voice that has no resemblance to the rumbling baritone that only days before had caused the scaffold to vibrate with authority. Each time, to satisfy his master, Cennino puts a fresh taper into the socket of a candelabrum even though one is already burning there. And each time, Luca sighs with relief as if vision had been restored to a blind man. He himself is a candle, all but consumed. The maestro peers into the murk; he sees shadows, hears voices. Who are all these people in the Chapter House, who watch his every move, even climb the scaffold? It is scandalous!

"Get out! Get out!" he shouts.

"Maestro, please! There is only ourselves in the Chapter House."
But Luca is not listening. "Just see how much you have done," says the
apprentice. "It goes well. The wall is thirsty for your paint."

"Yes . . ." Luca consents, but barely.

"The line of a man's body, the grain of his flesh, are there long before your brush can show them. A brush is a small animal that sniffs
the scent. Yours, only to follow. The lids of his eyes! Look! They are
but half-closed, from just beneath the lids comes still a bit of light!"

To Luca, Antonio and Cennino have become one and the same.

"Now, as I show you my son, you will see him, my son. As I show
you, it is night and he is lonely. The darker it is, the clearer his image
on the wall. He is all image, but seen in the dark, gleaming. But I deceive you, Cennino. Painting is a lie. You will only see him when you
close your eyes. Then, on the eastern wall his image is clear. Open
your eyes, and he is gone. Each time you open your eyes he dies
again. Never mind, stand close behind me, Antonio, closer as darkness is falling. Put your strong young arms around your father, hold
me up. Keep me from falling as the darkness falls. Oh! Where does it
come from, this darkness that will not hold itself back? Darkness lies
like wet earth upon my son. His hair alone! It gleams through, will not
stay hidden. No, there is his voice too which I cannot show you but
which I hear, like the cry of a root when it is pulled from the ground."

It is midnight of the fifth day. Cennino counts the bells as they
ring out from the abbey tower. With a soft gasp, the brush slips from
the fingers of the old painter. He totters, and would fall to the floor if
Cennino were not there to catch him. The apprentice kneels, lifts the
master in his arms, pours a few drops of wine onto the dry lips. A moment later, sleep comes to Luca with the suddenness of a blow to the
head, almost fatal. All night long, Cennino cradles the old man upon
whose face he sees the untranslatable alphabet of sleep. When he
awakens, it is morning. Luca hears the chattering of birds—the song
of the *cardenello*. It seems to him that the Chapter House has floated
out to sea, the way it rocks and tilts, with everything in it—benches,
throne, lectern rolling from side to side. For a long time, Luca lies on
the floor and gives himself up to the pitch and toss that seems to him
like the vertigo of resurrection. He feels himself lightening, being
lifted, rising. Soon he would fly up to the vault of the ceiling and out

the oculus. It is the sound of footsteps, made half of leather, half of stone, that bring him back down. He opens his eyes to see Cennino bending over him, applying cool cloths to his face.

With the help of the boy, he stands, sees that the body of his son has been taken away. There is no sign of what had lain there for five days and nights; only a single pool of sunlight. The floor has been scrubbed clean. The morning air is fresh. In a moment, he will lift his gaze to the eastern wall and give his eyes their due. When, at last, he does, he sees for the first time the angel that had burst from his old body to stand against that wall tuning a lute, harkening, plucking. Not dead! But softly breathing the stone-purified air, his lips curved in a smile without the least agony of death, with only the euphoria of boyish farewell.

∞

It is one year later and I have returned to Monte Oliveto, to this monastery where silence and longing wreak havoc with the hearts and minds of the men who live here. Nor can the cool woods of cypress and pine, the trickle of water in the garden, make it up to them. I stand in the choir where once there had been a great file of monks. Ninety-seven, I am told. Here, each seat is carved to show a scene in the life of St. Benedict, and all are polished as if by the squirming of eight centuries of restless monks. It was Gregorian Chant that had been sung here then, something less music than it is the cool unearthly corpse of music. Oh, give me music to dance to—polka, waltz, flamenco with the chatter of castanets; music that will seize a room and shake it by the rafters. No, this choir is a room that died long ago.

Memory is like a bird that flies where it pleases. For one year, mine has been chained to the rock of the event I have imagined, but which is as real to me as anything that ever happened. In my dreams too it has come back, the moment when Death shot out of a cypress in the guise of a bird, and that moment when, obeying the command of the abbot, Luca Signorelli had climbed down the ladder and bent to see what had been brought to him. There was the logic of the boy's death. Oh no! You couldn't fight that, not without God. And God, he did not have. But he was in the vicinity of piety, and that had to count for something. Had it been I . . . my son . . . I should never cease to flee from one exile to another, and in every foreign room where I should spend the night, I would leave my stupid, insincere life, like a discarded object. But with this fresco, Luca had sealed his fate. He would never leave Monte Oliveto and the son he had fathered for the second time. He had become a monk. So, it is true then. In order for God to prevail, someone has to die.

Next to this painting, all his others would be decoration. Here, only here, was the primal corporeal fact, not its fanciful derivative; the body that he had painted not with *verdaccio,* sinoper, ocher, but with the semen of his old age. Of course, Luca would have used the Chapter House! It is the coolest place, with stone walls and floor, the abbot's throne, rows of benches, and the lectern bearing the same huge tome across which lies a silver stylus. It is the stillest room of my life with, underneath its stone floor, the bones of a millennium of monks. The air here isn't the same as the air in the choir or in the garden. I can't put my finger on it—the way it rises and laps at the roofbeams. Breathe it in too long, and you get dizzy. Footsteps and voices give the impression of having originated far away or long ago and have only just now arrived to be heard.

And the life-absorbing eastern wall where the father would accompany his son to stillness, preserving him, defying death. As if the painting of the boy could live on forever! Even as he made the first brushstroke, Luca must have known how meaningless, how pathetic was his gesture. It is not enough to have the gift of art or imagination. There is something beyond technique and facility. Grace must season the painter's hand.

⍟

It is evening. Once again I have passed through the door marked CLAUSTRUM, walked the length of the corridor, then through the second door. If the rest of Tuscany is one color—tawny—this room is another, bloodless, leached. Not white, so much as having had red in its past; not red, but a history of red. It is the color of expectancy, as if the room were waiting all these centuries for the one occupant who would transfuse it back to life. I must think away the cameras, the electricity, the automobile that brought me to this place until what is left is the soft sound of the brushes, the grinding of the "bean" of pigment in the mortar and pestle, the voices of the master and apprentice engaged in the transfer of the craft. Why do I have the sense of trespassing? I look back over my shoulder to see if anyone is watching. No, I am alone. This evening the light is gray, spectral, uncertain. In such a light, nothing is as it seems. "Turn to the East," it is written, "and to the Angel that comes from thence. Fix thyself upon this Angel of the East, and thine understanding shall be enlightened." The eastern wall is a drumhead, the taut tympanum upon which the painter had beaten out the terrible, unmelodious, the funerary cadence of his loss.

All at once, the oculus turns red with the setting sun. Now the whole room is touched with pink, or rather, *violante,* a color edging close to violet. The way the stones soak it up! And upon the eastern wall appears a pale luminescence, a soft shine, barely discernible, that feeds on my gaze, growing, differentiating until what is there is a beautiful angel holding a lute which he is tuning. And I hear, as from deep within my ear, the muffled pounding of my heart.

It is the next day. Driving away from Monte Oliveto, I wonder. Had it been a glimpse of infinity or only the idea of it, something I conjured just as Leonardo did when he gazed at a blank wall and saw apocalyptic horsemen charging? Oh, I could go back to that Chapter House again and see. . . . But I won't. I fear that blank wall as I have feared nothing else.

Whither Thou Goest

Brain-dead," said the doctor. "There is no chance that he will wake up. Ever. Look here." And he unrolled a scroll of paper onto her lap.

"This is the electroencephalograph. It's nothing but a flat line. No blips." Hannah bowed her head over the chart. The doctor cleared his throat, took one of her hands in both of his, and leaned toward her as though about to tell a secret. Hannah submitted to what under any other circumstance she might have considered presumption, submitted because she thought she ought to. It was expected of her. The formality of the occasion and all.

"Hannah, it is three weeks since your husband was shot in the head. The only thing keeping him alive is the respirator."

Hannah waited for the walls of the solarium to burst.

"I'm asking you to let us put an end to it, unplug the machinery, let him go. There is just no sense in prolonging a misfortune." Hannah felt that she should say something, not just sit there, but for the life of her she couldn't think what. The doctor was speaking again.

"But before we do that, we would like your permission to harvest Sam's organs for transplantation."

"Harvest?" said Hannah. "Like the gathering in of wheat?"

"Yes," said the doctor. "That is what we call it when we take the organs. It is for a good cause. That way your husband will live on. He will not really have died. . . ."

"Dead is dead," said Hannah.

64

"I know, I know," said the doctor. And he looked down at his feet for relief. Hannah noticed that he was wearing oxblood wing-tip shoes of a large size. They were the shoes of power.

A week later she received a letter from the doctor.

Dear Mrs. Owen,
You will be pleased and comforted to know that because of your generosity and thanks to the miracle of modern science, seven people right here in the state of Texas are living and well with all their faculties restored to them. Your husband's liver has gone to a lady in Abilene; the right kidney is functioning in Dallas; the left kidney was placed in a teenaged girl in Galveston; the heart was given to a man just your husband's age in a little town near Arkansas; the lungs are in Fort Worth; and the corneas were used on two people right here in Houston. . . .

Hannah folded the letter and put it back in its envelope and then into the bottom drawer of the desk without reading to the end. There was no need. She already knew what had become of the rest of Sam. She had buried it in the family plot of the Evangelical Baptist Church cemetery.

∽

That was three years ago. And still, she had only to close her eyes to have the whole of the horror spring vividly before her, as though it had been painted on the inside of her eyelids. For Sam's thirty-third birthday they had spent the weekend at the beach. Now they were in the pickup truck on the way back to Houston. Hannah had fallen asleep. It was the sudden stop that woke her up.

"We couldn't be there already," she murmured.

"No," said Sam. "I'm just going to change that lady's tire." Hannah sat up and saw the green Buick pulled off to the side of the road. The right rear tire was flat. An elderly woman sitting behind the wheel looked up and smiled when she saw Sam walking toward her with a car jack in one hand and the tire iron in the other. Hannah got out of the truck and went over to talk. "Bless you," the woman said. Sam

hadn't given that jack more than half a dozen pumps when a man—
he looked Mexican—appeared out of nowhere with a gun in his
hand.

"Sam?" Hannah had said in that low, questioning voice that always
made him turn to see if she was upset. For a long moment Sam stayed
where he was, crouched over the jack. When at last he stood, he had
the tire iron in his hand.

"What do you want, mister?" he said. The Mexican made a gesture
as if to turn a key and nodded at the pickup.

"The keys are in the truck," said Sam. The Mexican made no move.
Perhaps he did not understand? Sam raised his arm to point. The
Mexican fired. It took a long time for the echo of that shot to peter
out. When it had, the truck and the Mexican were gone, and Sam lay
on his back wearing a halo of black blood. He was still holding the tire
iron. Something pink squeezed slowly out of the middle of his forehead.

"Dead is dead," she had told that doctor. But now, three years later,
she wasn't so sure. For Hannah had begun to have doubts. Incidents
occurred, like the time months ago when she had gone to the
butcher's. Just ahead of her at the counter a woman had ordered a
chicken. "I want it in parts," she heard the woman say. Hannah had
watched as the butcher scooped out the entrails, cleaved the carcass
through the middle of the breast, and hacked off its thighs, legs, and
wings. The heart, gizzard, neck, and liver he put in a small plastic bag.

"You can keep the feet," said the woman. And then it was Hannah's
turn.

"What'll it be?" said the butcher. And wiped the clots from his fingers onto his apron.

"What do you call that?" she asked, trying not to look at his bloody
hands. As though they were his privates.

"What do you call what?"

"What you just did, cutting up the chicken. What is the name for
it?" The butcher stared at her blankly.

"It's called 'cleaning a chicken.' Why?"

"Cleaning?"

"Look, miss," said the butcher, "I'm real busy. What'll it be?" But
Hannah had already turned to leave.

It was after that that she stopped going to the cemetery to visit the grave. It wasn't Sam in that cemetery, not by a long shot. It was only parts of Sam, the parts that nobody needed. The rest of him was scattered all over Texas. And, unless she had been misinformed, very much alive. And where did that leave her? God knows it was hard enough to be a widow at the age of thirty-three, and her sympathies were all with those women whose husbands had truly, once and for all, died. But widowhood, bleak as it might be, seemed preferable by a whole lot to the not-here, not-there condition into which she had been thrust by "the miracle of modern science." At least if your husband were all dead you could one day get over it and go on with your life. But this! This state of bafflement. Maybe, she thought, maybe it was a matter of percentage—if more than 50 percent of your husband was dead, you were a widow. Whom could she ask?

Along with doubt came resentment. Oh, not just at the doctors. They simply do what they want to anyway, without really thinking. Doctors, she decided, don't think. They just *do,* and cover it all up with language. *Harvest. Transplantation.* The soft words of husbandry and the soil. Even they cannot bear to speak the real names of their deeds—dismemberment, evisceration. What was worse, she had begun to resent Samuel. Here she was, living in this sort of limbo, while he, Sam, was participating in not one but seven lives, none of which had anything to do with her. It wasn't fair. Even if he hadn't chosen it, it wasn't fair.

∞

Hannah's cousin Ivy Lou was also her best friend. Lately she had taken to bringing her lunch over to eat at Hannah's house. One day when she got there, Hannah was standing at the kitchen window, looking out into the backyard. Over the radio came the pitched monotone of a preacher. The subject was the resurrection of the flesh.

"And it says right here in First Corinthians, chapter fifteen: 'For the trumpet shall sound, and the dead shall be raised incorruptible.'

"And here it is again in Romans, chapter eight, verse eleven: 'If the Spirit of him who raised Jesus from the dead dwells in you, he who raised Christ Jesus from the dead will give life to your mortal bodies. . . .' "

"Turn that damn fool off," said Hannah.

"For goodness' sake!" said Ivy Lou. "What's got into you?" Four years ago Ivy Lou had been born again.

"It's a big lie," said Hannah. "It's the way the preachers swindle you."

"I'm sure I don't know what you are talking about," said Ivy Lou.

"There is no such thing as the resurrection of the flesh," said Hannah. "Just tell me at what stage of life we are supposed to be on the day of resurrection, so-called? Do we look as we did when we were babies? At age forty? Or as we are when we die, old and wasted? And tell me this: What about Samuel Owen on your resurrection day? Here he is scattered all over Texas, breathing in Fort Worth, urinating in Dallas *and* Galveston, digesting or whatever it is the liver does in Abilene. They going to put him back together again when the day comes, or is it to the recipients belong the spoils? Tell me that."

"Well," said Ivy Lou. "I don't have the least idea about any of that, but I do know that you are committing the sin of blasphemy. Hannah, I'm real worried about you. Don't you believe in God anymore?" Hannah looked out the window and was silent for a long moment.

"About God," she said at last, "I have only the merest inkling. That's all anyone can have."

✍

Hannah could not have said exactly when the idea first occurred to her. Later, she thought it might have been on the day of the tornado. From the kitchen window her eye had been caught by a frenzy of leaves in the live oak. All that August morning it had been sultry and still, until all at once it turned dark as twilight. Then lightning came to tear open the clouds. And the air, as if desperate to announce great tidings, broke its silence and turned to wind. But such a wind! At the height of the storm Hannah opened the back door and stood to receive the force of the rain on her face, her hair. It stung like pebbles. The violence lasted but a few minutes, after which it settled into a steady drizzle. Then, as abruptly as it had come, the storm passed and the sun came out, leaving Hannah with the feeling that something more than the humidity had been relieved. Something, a pressure that had been building inside her, had boiled its way to the surface, then broke.

That very night she awoke suddenly and sat bolt upright in bed, and she clapped her hand over her mouth as if to hold back what threatened to burst forth from it. A scream? Laughter? She didn't know what. But what she did know, beyond any doubt, as though it had been a revelation, was what it was she must do.

She had been dreaming, and in her dream, she saw two men lying on narrow tables next to each other. One of them was Samuel; the other she could not see clearly. His features were blurred, out of focus. Both of the men were stripped to the waist, and their chests were open in the middle, the halves of their rib cages raised like cellar doors. A surgeon was there, dressed in a blue scrub suit, mask, and cap. As she watched, the surgeon reached his hands into Samuel's chest and lifted forth his heart, held it up like some luminous prize. At that moment, Hannah could see into the chests of both men, see that they were both empty. Then the surgeon turned away from Samuel and lowered the incandescent, glowing heart into the chest of the other man, who promptly sat up, put on his shirt, and walked away.

What was instantly made clear to her—it was so simple—was that she must go to find that man who was carrying Samuel's heart. If she could find him, and listen once more to the heart, she would be healed. She would be able to go on with her life.

In the morning, the idea seemed quite mad. She wondered whether she was losing her mind. And she began to interrogate herself. Why would she do such a thing? What good would it do? To say nothing of the intrusion on the life of a perfect stranger. What made her think he would agree to let her do it? How could she explain it to him when she could not even explain it to herself? What would she say? Would it be like a pilgrim visiting a shrine? No, it had nothing to do with worship. Although, it might be a bit like going to the Delphic oracle for advice. But that wasn't it either. Did she just want to make sure that Sam's heart had found a good home? For God's sake, it wasn't a dog that she had given away. Nor was she the least bit curious about the man himself, other than to know how to find him. "No," Hannah said aloud, addressing the nameless, faceless man of her dream. "Thou shalt be unto my hand as a banister upon a dark staircase, to lead me up to the bright landing above. Once having climbed, I shall most willingly let thee go." The more she thought about it, the more she felt like a woman whose husband had been declared missing in action in a war. What would she have done if that were the case? Why, she would bend every effort to find him—living or dead—even travel to Vietnam or Laos, wherever, and she wouldn't leave until she knew, one way or the other.

Perhaps it *was* a phantom she was chasing, a phantom that would dissolve when she drew near. But she would have to take that chance. Hannah remembered the time, a year after they were married, when she and Samuel were lying in bed and she had said: "Let's tell each other a secret. You first." And Sam had told her about when he was twelve years old and his father had died suddenly of a heart attack. For a long time afterward he would think that he saw his father on the streets of the city. It was always from the back, so he couldn't be sure. But the man was wearing the same gray fedora and holding the cigarette the same way. The more Sam looked, the more certain he became that it was his father whom he saw walking downtown, that he had not really died, but had gone away or been taken away for some reason, and now here he was. And Samuel would quicken his pace, then break into a run to catch up, calling out "Daddy! Daddy!" in his excitement. And each time, when the man turned around to see, it wasn't, no it wasn't, and there was that fresh wave of desolation. One day, a policeman came to the door and told his mother that Sam had been following men on the street and that one of them had reported him, said he might be a pickpocket, or worse.

"Is it true?" asked his mother. When he didn't answer, she asked him why. But he couldn't or wouldn't say why because no one would believe him or understand, and they would think he was crazy.

"Well, don't you dare do it ever again," said his mother in front of the policeman. But he couldn't stop, because the next day he thought he saw his father again and he followed him. After a year it stopped happening and Sam felt a mixture of relief and disappointment. Relief, because at last he had laid to rest his father's ghost; disappointment, because the wild possibility no longer existed. Sam had never told anyone about this before, he said. It was the first time he had ever mentioned it. When he had finished, Hannah hugged him and kissed him and cried and cried for the young boy who couldn't let go of his father.

"You're so pretty," Sam had said after a while to make her stop.

But Sam had been a young boy, and she was a grown woman. No matter—even if it turned out that she, too, was chasing a phantom.

Hannah went to the cupboard where three years before she had placed the doctor's letter, the one telling her about the seven transplantations. She read it again, this time to the end, and made a list. The kidneys, liver, and lungs, she decided, were inaccessible—hidden away in the deepest recesses of the bodies of those who had received them. How could she get to them? And the corneas just didn't seem right. She didn't think she could relate to a cornea. That left the heart. A heart can be listened to. A heart can be felt. And besides, there had been her dream. She would seek to follow the heart. But then there was that man, that other, who had lain on the table next to Samuel and whose face she had not been able to see. What if he refused her, mistook her intentions? No, she would explain it to him, write it all in a letter, and then he would agree. He would have to. In the letter she would tell what happened that night on the highway, how Sam had raised his arm to point to the truck, still holding the tire iron, how the Mexican had fired, and what the doctor had said to her in the hospital.

"That way your husband will not really have died," he had said. And that she had said to him, "Dead is dead," but that now she was not so sure. And how, ever since, she had been living in this gray place, unable to grieve or get on with her life because she no longer knew who or even what she was. All this she would tell him in the letter and he would let her come. He must.

∞

Once she had decided, it was not difficult to get his name and address, a few of the facts of his illness. Hospital records, she learned, were scandalously accessible to whoever might want to see them, whatever the hospitals swore to the contrary. Anyone who really tried could get to see them—lawyers hunting for malpractice suits, legal assistants, reporters, detectives, graduate students gathering statistics, nurses, insurance companies. It was in this last guise that Hannah called the record librarian of the university hospital and made an appointment. She had followed it up with a letter on official stationery of the Aetna Casualty and Life Insurance Company.

She had had to take Ivy Lou into her confidence; Ivy Lou worked as a secretary for Aetna.

Ivy Lou was appalled. "I don't like it one bit. No good will come of it." And at first she had refused. "I just don't see what you could possibly hope to get out of it." And then, when Hannah didn't answer, "Why? Just tell me why."

"I don't know why," said Hannah. How could she say why, when she really didn't know herself? Perhaps it was something like the way a flower can't help but face the sun, or the way a moth goes to the flame.

"Hannah, you're going to get burned," said Ivy Lou as though she had read her mind. "Besides," she went on, "it's not only sick, it's in the grossest ill taste." Ivy Lou set down her teacup and walked to the door, shaking her head.

But then, there was poor Hannah, and in the end Ivy Lou gave in.

"Just don't tell anyone where you got it," she said when she brought the stationery.

The next week at the hospital, the record librarian welcomed her with a smile and showed her to a cubicle where the chart was waiting for her. POPE, HENRY, she read. AGE: 33. NEXT OF KIN: MRS. INEZ POPE. CHILDREN: NONE. ADDRESS: 8 ORCHARD ROAD, AVERY, TEXAS. DIAGNOSIS: CARDIOMYOPATHY, VIRAL. SURGERY: HEART TRANSPLANT. Reading on, she learned of his "intractable heart failure," that his prognosis had been "hopeless"—he had been given an estimated life expectancy of a few months "at most."

And then she came to the part about the operation, which occupied the bulk of the fat chart, and none of which she read. There was no need.

"That didn't take long," said the librarian as Hannah walked by her desk.

"No," said Hannah. "I'm quick."

❧

Avery, Texas. Hannah and Ivy Lou looked for it on a map.

"There it is," said Ivy Lou. "Way up almost into Arkansas."

"How far away is that?"

"Maybe a couple of hundred miles, but, Hannah, I'm telling you— don't. You are making the biggest mistake of your life."

That night, Hannah sat at her kitchen table with a pen and a blank sheet of paper. "Dear Mr. Pope," she wrote, then set down the pen. There was something absurd about that *Mr.,* considering that she had been married for seven years to a significant part of the man. But she would let it stand. The situation called for tact, patience, diplomacy. There would be plenty of time for "Dear Henry," if and when. She picked up the pen and continued.

> My name is Hannah Owen. Could the name mean anything to you? Doubtless not, considering the decorum with which these things are done. I am the wife (some say widow) of Samuel Owen, the man whose heart is even now beating in your chest.
>
> Perhaps you will forgive a woman's curiosity? I am writing to ask how you are since the operation. Your early discharge from the intensive-care unit, and even from the hospital it- self—three weeks! It might be a record of some kind and would seem to show that you had an uneventful recovery. It would follow that you have continued to improve and that by now, three years later, you have completely regained your health? I surely do hope so. It is my dearest wish that the heart is doing as good a job for you as it did for Sam and for me too. Do let me hear from you, please,
>
> > Yours truly,
> > Hannah Owen

There, she thought. That should do it. Nothing whatever to arouse suspicion or to make anyone wonder. Only the shock of who she was. After that, just an expression of well-meaning concern. When she dropped the letter in the slot at the post office and heard the soft siffle as it went down the chute, she sighed. It had begun.

∞

It was two weeks before she saw the envelope in her mailbox written in neat handwriting in black ink. It was postmarked Avery, Texas. How it shook in her hand.

Dear Mrs. Owen,
It was very kind of you to write asking after my husband's health. He is not much of a letter writer and has asked me to tell you that he is stronger and healthier than he has been in years. He says he is the luckiest man on earth. By the way, however did you get hold of our name and address? I had thought such information might be protected, under the circumstances, but—I guess not. Thank you for your interest.
Sincerely,
(Mrs.) Inez Pope

Dear Mr. Pope,
I don't know any other way to say it than to just take a deep breath and come right out with it. What I am going to ask will seem at first quite insane. But I assure you I am no maniac. I want to come and listen to your heart for the space of one hour at a time when it is convenient for you. While I know that at first this request will seem strange to you, I pray that you will say yes. You have no idea how important it is to me.
Yours truly,
Hannah Owen

Dear Mrs. Owen,
My husband and I have tried to understand your position. But we feel that it would not be at all wise for you to come here. Not that we aren't grateful and all of that, but you have to admit it is a little on the bizarre side. So this is good-bye.
Sincerely,
(Mrs.) Henry Pope

P.S. We have consulted with our doctor, who says it is a terrible idea and perhaps you should get some professional attention to get over it. No offense meant.

Dear Mr. Pope,
Your wife does not wish to let me come. I can understand her hesitation. The awkwardness and all. And perhaps it is only human nature, a touch of suspicion. Perhaps I have ulterior motives? I assure you, Mr. Pope, that I do not. As for my interest in you personally, it is limited to you as the carrier of something I used to possess and which I for one reason or another would like to see again. Or rather, hear again. For that is all I want to do—to listen to your heart for the space of one hour. The way a person would like to go back to visit the house where he had grown up. You are in a sense that house. Your doctor doesn't think it is a good idea? Mr. Pope, the doctors don't think. They are unaccustomed to it. Doctors just do whatever they want to, without thinking. If they had thought, perhaps they might have foreseen the predicament into which the "miracle of modern science" has placed me. No, speak to me not of doctors. They haven't the least idea about the human heart except to move it from place to place.
Yours truly,
Hannah Owen

Dear Mrs. Owen,
I am very sorry. But the answer is still no. And that is final. Ever since I got your first letter, I've been feeling awful. Like ungrateful or something. But I know in my heart it wouldn't be a good thing for you either.
Sincerely yours,
Henry Pope

Dear Mr. Pope,
The circumstances of my husband's death were violent and shocking. In case you do not know, he was shot in the head by a bandit on the highway where he had stopped to help an old lady with a flat tire. I was there. After three weeks on the

respirator, they came and told me it was no use, and could they disconnect the respirator? But just before they did that, could they take parts of his body (*harvest* is the word) to transplant to other people? I said yes, and so they took his liver, lungs, heart, corneas, and kidneys. There are seven of you out there. You, Mr. Pope, got the heart, or more exactly, *my* heart, as under the law, I had become the owner of my husband's entire body at the time that he became "brain-dead." Don't worry—I don't want it back. But I do ask you to let me come to Avery for one hour to listen to your heart. It is such a small thing, really, to ask in return for the donation of a human heart. Just to listen. For one hour. That is all, really all. The reasons are private, and anyway, even if I wanted to tell you why, I don't know if I could put it into words. If you see fit to let me come, I will never bother you again, and you will have repaid me in full. Do please let me know when I can come.

Yours truly,
Hannah Owen

P.S. Of course your wife can be in the room all the time. Although, frankly, I would prefer otherwise. Mrs. Pope, what I want to do is no more than what dozens of nurses have done—listen to your husband's heart. Only the reason is different. Couldn't you look at it as just another medical checkup?

Dear Mrs. Owen,
You said there were seven of us recipients. Why me? Or do you plan a statewide reunion with all your husband's organs? And the answer is NO! Please do not keep writing, as it is annoying to say the least, and it is making my wife nervous.

Sincerely,
Henry Pope

Dear Mr. Pope,
You ask "Why me?" And you are right to ask. It is because you have the heart. The others—the liver, lungs, kidneys—are

hidden away. I can't get to them. As for the corneas, well, I just can't relate to corneas somehow. But the heart! A heart can be felt. It can be listened to. You can hear a heart. A heart is reachable. That's why *you.*

> Yours truly,
> Hannah Owen

When there had been no reply for two weeks, Hannah wrote again.

Dear Mr. Pope,
Please.

> Yours truly,
> Hannah Owen

Dear Mrs. Owen,
No, goddammit, and if you don't stop this business and get the hell out of my life, I'm going to notify the police.

> Sincerely yours,
> Henry Pope

Dear Mr. Pope,
And so your answer is still No. Oh, can you imagine how sad I am? Now I am the one who is disheartened. Never mind. I will try to accept it, as I have no alternative. You said I can't come and so I won't. I shall not be bothering you and your wife again. You can relax. I can't resist saying one more time, although it doesn't matter anymore, that I was the owner of the heart. It was mine to give. I think I did mention to you that the body of the deceased is the property of the next of kin. It wasn't Samuel who was the donor at all. It was me. But that is all water over the dam. Now may I ask you for a much smaller favor? I would like to have a photograph of you for my scrapbook. Nothing, for goodness' sake, posed or formal. Just a casual snapshot would be fine. Chalk it up to foolish sentiment. Thank you and good-bye.

> Yours truly,
> Hannah Owen

For three weeks Hannah prowled the house, smoking the cigarettes of disappointment, settling into her despair. Ivy Lou was frankly worried. But she knew better than to suggest a psychiatrist, or a minister, for that matter.

"Hannah," she said. "You have got to pull yourself together and get over it. It was a lousy idea in the first place. What's going to be the end of it?"

"I really don't know," said Hannah and waited for Ivy Lou to go away.

And then there it was, lying at the bottom of her mailbox like a dish of cream waiting to be lapped up. No need to look at the postmark—she could tell that handwriting anywhere. Stifling her excitement, she waited till she was back in her kitchen, sitting at the table, before she opened it. The sole content was a snapshot. No letter.

Hannah studied the photograph. It was three by four inches, black-and-white. The next size up from passport. It showed, at some distance, a thin, dark-haired man slouched against the trunk of a tree, his right knee flexed at right angles, with the sole of his foot braced against the tree. A live oak, she guessed, judging by the girth. His hands bulged the pockets of a zip-up jacket. He wore a baseball cap and was looking off to the left, the head turned almost in profile. The face, what she could see of it, was unremarkable, the eyes, shaded by the peak of the cap, giving away nothing. Only the dark seam of a mouth expressed suffering. Even with the help of a magnifying glass, she could read no more on that face. It was possessed of no mystery. Compared to the large color photograph of Samuel that she kept on the mantel in the parlor, with its generous smile that held nothing back, the snapshot in her hand was of a sick man who had known pain and expected more of it. He looked twenty years older than Samuel, although she knew they were the same age. This was taken before the operation, she decided.

But that he had sent it! Actually looked for and found the photograph, then put it in an envelope and *mailed* it. That heart is *working,* she thought. Hannah smiled and fixed herself a tuna-salad sandwich and a glass of milk.

She waited exactly two weeks—it wasn't easy—before she answered.

Dear Mr. Pope,

Thank you so much for the photo. I have put it in my scrap-book. My friend Ivy Lou, who is sort of an actuary, has cal-culated that your face occupies 2.1 percent of the picture and what with the peaked cap, you are a bit hard to make out. But, still. I like your backyard, is it? Are those azaleas on the right of the live oak you are leaning against? I have a live oak in my backyard too.

Sincerely yours,
Hannah Owen

Six weeks later, another letter arrived.

Dear Mrs. Owen,

My wife Inez will be in Little Rock visiting her parents on the weekend of October 20th. If you still want to come, I don't see why not, so long as you just stay for one hour. I will ex-pect you at the house at ten o'clock Saturday morning. You know where it is, I'm sure.

Yours truly,
Henry Pope

"I wouldn't drive, if I were you," said Ivy Lou. "Not wound as tight as you are. Why, you're as nervous as a bride. See if there's a bus." It was the first piece of Ivy Lou's advice Hannah thought she should take. She didn't trust herself to drive. Besides, she wanted the time to think, to prepare herself. Like a bride, she agreed, but she quickly shooed that notion out of her mind. There was an early-morning bus that got to Avery at nine-thirty, and the next day, before dawn, Han-nah was on it. But once on the bus, she couldn't think, only reached up now and then to touch her right ear, which, when the bus stopped in Avery, would become a mollusk that would attach itself to the rock of Henry Pope's chest and cling through whatever crash of the sea.

∽

Number eight was one of a dozen identical single-family ranch houses that made up the dead end that was Orchard Road, only this one was ennobled by the big live oak at the back, which fringed and softened the flat roof. At precisely ten o'clock Hannah unlatched the front gate and walked up to the door. Before she could ring the bell, the door opened halfway.

"Come in," he said, keeping himself out of sight until the door was closed behind her. The house was in darkness, every shade and blind drawn and shut. It had the same furtive, tense look she saw on the face of the man standing before her.

"No need to call attention," he said. "It would be hard to explain if anyone saw you come in." He was, she saw, a healthy man who looked even younger than she knew him to be. He had put on at least twenty pounds since that picture had been taken. His hair was light brown, almost blond, and curly. He was wearing jeans and a white T-shirt.

He's nervous as a cat, thought Hannah, and that makes two of us.

Hannah followed him into a small room, a den furnished with a sofa, an upholstered easy chair, and a television set. One wall was lined with bookshelves. She guessed that he had spent his convalescence in this room.

"It's your show," he said. "How do you want me?" When she didn't answer, he reached up with both arms and pulled the T-shirt over his head.

"I suppose you want this off," he said. Then Hannah saw on his chest the pale violet stripe that marked the passage of her husband's heart into this man. She felt her pulse racing. She might faint.

"Well, it's your show," he said again. "How do you want to do this? Come on, let's just get it over with. One hour, you said."

"Best, I think, for you to lie down flat," she said. "I'll sit on the edge and lean over." She had gone over it so many times in her mind.

He lay down and slid a small pillow beneath his head, then shifted as far as he could to give her room to sit. When she did, he rose abruptly to his elbows.

"Where is your stethoscope?"

"I don't have a stethoscope."

"How are you going to listen to my heart without a stethoscope?"

"They didn't always have them," she said. "I'm going to listen with my ear." She gave her right ear two short taps. "I have very acute hearing," she added, because he looked dubious, as though he might call the whole thing off. But he didn't, just lay back down and stared straight up at the ceiling with his arms at his sides, as though he were still a patient at the hospital awaiting some painful procedure.

Then Hannah bent her head, turning toward the left, and lowered first to her elbows, then all the way, lowering her ear toward his left, his secret-sharing, nipple. When she touched his skin, she could feel him wince.

Oh, it was Samuel's heart, all right. She knew the minute she heard it. She could have picked it out of a thousand. It wasn't true that you couldn't tell one heart from another by the sound of it. This one was Sam's. Hadn't she listened to it just this way often enough? When they were lying in bed? Hadn't she listened with her head on his chest, just this way, and heard it slow down after they had made love? It was like a little secret that she knew about his body and it had always made her smile to think of the effect she had on him.

Hannah settled and gave herself up to the labor of listening. Closing her eyes, she drew herself down, down into that one sense of hearing, shedding sight and touch and all her other senses, peeling away everything that was not pure hearing until the entire rest of her body was an adjunct to her right ear and she was oblivious to whatever else might be in the world. She listened and received the deep regular beat, the emphatic *lub-dup, lub-dup* to which with all her own heart she surrendered. Almost at once, she felt a sense of comfort that she had not known in three years. She could have stayed there forever, bathed in the sound and touch of that heart. Thus she lay, until her ear and the chest of the man had fused into a single bridge of flesh across which marched, one after the other, in cadence, the parade of that mighty heart. Her own pulse quieted to match it beat for beat. And now it was no longer sound that entered and occupied her, but blood that flowed from one to the other, her own blood driven by the heart that lay just beneath the breast, whose slow rise and fall she rode as though it were a small boat at anchor in a tranquil sea, and she a huddled creature waiting to be born.

At last Hannah opened her eyes and raised her head. Never, never had she felt such a sense of consolation and happiness. Had it been a dream? Had she fallen asleep? It was a moment before she felt his arm about her shoulders. How long, she wondered, had she lain encircled and unaware? She looked up to see that he was smiling down at her. Angels must smile like that, she thought.

"You were trembling," he explained. "It was like holding a bird."

Gently, Hannah disengaged herself and stood, but listening still, cocking her ear for scraps of sound, echoes. And it seemed to her in the darkened room that light emanated from the naked torso of the man and that the chest upon which she had laid her head was a field of golden wheat in which, for this time, it had been given to her to go gleaning.

Henry Pope followed her to the door.

"Will you want to come again, Hannah?" he asked. How soft and low his voice as he uttered her name.

"No," said Hannah. "There will be no need." And she stepped out into the golden kingdom of October with the certainty that she had at last been retrieved from the shadows and set down once more upon the bright lip of her life. All the way home on the bus a residue of splendor sang in her ears.

Imelda

I heard the other day that Hugh Franciscus had died. I knew him once. He was the Chief of Plastic Surgery when I was a medical student at Albany Medical College. Dr. Franciscus was the archetype of the professor of surgery—tall, vigorous, muscular, as precise in his technique as he was impeccable in his dress. Each day a clean lab coat, monkishly starched, that sort of thing. I doubt that he ever read books. One book only, that of the human body, took the place of all others. He never raised his eyes from it. He read it like a printed page as though he knew that in the calligraphy there just beneath the skin were all the secrets of the world. Long before it became visible to anyone else, he could detect the first sign of granulation at the base of a wound, the first blue line of new epithelium at the periphery that would tell him that a wound would heal, or the barest hint of necrosis that presaged failure. This gave him the appearance of a prophet. "This skin graft will take," he would say, and you must believe beyond all cyanosis, exudation, and inflammation that it would.

He had enemies, of course, who said he was arrogant, that he exalted activity for its own sake. Perhaps. But perhaps it was no more than the honesty of one who knows his own worth. Just look at a scalpel, after all. What a feeling of sovereignty, megalomania even, when you know that it is you and you alone who will make certain use of it. It was said, too, that he was a ladies' man. I don't know about that. It was all rumor. Besides, I think he had other things in mind than mere living. Hugh Franciscus was a zealous hunter. Every fall during the season he drove upstate to hunt deer. There was a glass-front case in his office where he showed his guns. How could he shoot a deer? we asked. But he knew better. To us medical students he was someone heroic, someone made up of several gods, beheld at a distance, and always from a lesser height. If he had grown accustomed to his miracles, we had not. He had no close friends on the staff. There was something a little sad in that. As though once long ago he had been flayed by friendship and now the slightest breeze would hurt. Confidences resulted in dishonor. Perhaps the person in whom one confided would scorn him, betray. Even though he spent his days among those less fortunate, weaker than he—the sick, after all—Franciscus seemed aware of an air of personal harshness in his environment to which he reacted by keeping his own counsel, by a certain remoteness. It was what gave him the appearance of being haughty. With the patients he was forthright. All the facts laid out, every question anticipated and answered with specific information. He delivered good news and bad with the same dispassion.

I was a third-year student, just turned onto the wards for the first time, and clerking on Surgery. Everything—the operating room, the morgue, the emergency room, the patients, professors, even the nurses—was terrifying. One picked one's way among the mines and booby traps of the hospital, hoping only to avoid the hemorrhage and perforation of disgrace. The opportunity for humiliation was everywhere.

It all began on ward rounds. Dr. Franciscus was demonstrating a cross-leg flap graft he had constructed to cover a large fleshy defect in the leg of a merchant seaman who had injured himself in a fall. The man was from Spain and spoke no English. There had been a comminuted fracture of the femur, much soft-tissue damage, necrosis. After weeks of debridement and dressings, the wound had been made ready for grafting. Now the patient was in his fifth postoperative day. What we saw was a thick web of pale blue flesh arising from the man's left thigh, and which had been sutured to the open wound on the right thigh. When the surgeon pressed the pedicle with his finger, it blanched; when he let up, there was a slow return of the violaceous color.

"The circulation is good," Franciscus announced. "It will get better." In several weeks, we were told, he would divide the tube of flesh at its site of origin, and tailor it to fit the defect to which, by then, it would have grown more solidly. All at once, the webbed man in the bed reached out, and gripping Franciscus by the arm, began to speak rapidly, pointing to his groin and hip. Franciscus stepped back at once to disengage his arm from the patient's grasp.

"Anyone here know Spanish? I didn't get a word of that."

"The cast is digging into him up above," I said. "The edges of the plaster are rough. When he moves, they hurt."

Without acknowledging my assistance, Dr. Franciscus took a plaster shears from the dressing cart and with several large snips cut away the rough edges of the cast.

"*Gracias, gracias.*" The man in the bed smiled. But Franciscus had already moved on to the next bed. He seemed to me a man of immense strength and ability, yet without affection for the patients. He did not want to be touched by them. It was less kindness that he showed them than a reassurance that he would never give up, that he would bend every effort. If anyone could, he would solve the problems of their flesh.

Ward Rounds had disbanded and I was halfway down the corridor when I heard Dr. Franciscus's voice behind me.

"You speak Spanish." It seemed a command.

"I lived in Spain for two years," I told him.

"I'm taking a surgical team to Honduras next week to operate on the natives down there. I do it every year for three weeks, somewhere. This year, Honduras. I can arrange the time away from your duties here if you'd like to come along. You will act as interpreter. I'll show you how to use the clinical camera. What you'd see would make it worthwhile."

So it was that, a week later, the envy of my classmates, I joined the mobile surgical unit—surgeons, anesthetists, nurses, and equipment—aboard a Military Air Transport plane to spend three weeks performing plastic surgery on people who had been previously selected by an advance team. Honduras. I don't suppose I shall ever see it again. Nor do I especially want to. From the plane it seemed a country made of clay—burnt umber, raw sienna, dry. It had a dead-weight quality, as though the ground had no buoyancy, no air sacs through which a breeze might wander. Our destination was Comayagua, a town in the Central Highlands. The town itself was situated on the edge of one of the flatlands that were linked in a network between the granite mountains. Above, all was brown, with only an occasional Spanish cedar tree; below, patches of luxuriant tropical growth. It was a day's bus ride from the airport. For hours, the town kept appearing and disappearing with the convolutions of the road. At last, there it lay before us, panting and exhausted at the bottom of the mountain.

That was all I was to see of the countryside. From then on, there was only the derelict hospital of Comayagua, with the smell of spoiling bananas and the accumulated odors of everyone who had been sick there for the last hundred years. Of the two, I much preferred the frank smell of the sick. The heat of the place was incendiary. So hot that, as we stepped from the bus, our own words did not carry through the air, but hung limply at our lips and chins. Just in front of the hospital was a thirsty courtyard where mobs of waiting people squatted or lay in the meager shade, and where, on dry days, a fine dust rose through which untethered goats shouldered. Against the walls of this courtyard, gaunt, dejected men stood, their faces, like their country, preternaturally solemn, leaden. Here no one looked up at the sky. Every head was bent beneath a wide-brimmed straw hat. In the days that followed, from the doorway of the dispensary I would watch the brown mountains sliding about, drinking the hospital into their shadow as the afternoon grew later and later, flattening us by their very altitude.

The people were mestizos, of mixed Spanish and Indian blood. They had flat, broad, dumb museum feet. At first they seemed to me indistinguishable the one from the other, without animation. All the vitality, the hidden sexuality, was in their black hair. Soon I was to know them by the fissures with which each face was graven. But, even so, compared to us, they were masked, shut away. My job was to follow Dr. Franciscus around, photograph the patients before and after surgery, interpret and generally act as aide-de-camp. It was exhilarating. Within days I had decided that I was not just useful, but essential. Despite that we spent all day in each other's company, there were no overtures of friendship from Dr. Franciscus. He knew my place, and I knew it, too. In the afternoon he examined the patients scheduled for the next day's surgery. I would call out a name from the doorway to the examining room. In the courtyard someone would rise. I would usher the patient in, and nudge him to the examining table where Franciscus stood, always, I thought, on the verge of irritability. I would read aloud the case history, then wait while he carried out his examination. While I took the "before" photographs, Dr. Franciscus would dictate into a tape recorder:

"Ulcerating basal-cell carcinoma of the right orbit—six by eight centimeters—involving the right eye and extending into the floor of the orbit. Operative plan: wide excision with enucleation of the eye. Later, bone and skin grafting." The next morning we would be in the operating room where the procedure would be carried out.

We were more than two weeks into our tour of duty—a few days to go—when it happened. Earlier in the day I had caught sight of her through the window of the dispensary. A thin, dark Indian girl about fourteen years old. A figurine, orange-brown, terra-cotta, and still attached to the unshaped clay from which she had been carved. An older, sun-weathered woman stood behind and somewhat to the left of the girl. The mother was short and dumpy. She wore a broad-brimmed hat with a high crown, and a shapeless dress like a cassock. The girl had long, loose black hair. There were tiny gold hoops in her ears. The dress she wore could have been her mother's. Far too big, it hung from her thin shoulders at some risk of slipping down her arms. Even with her in it, the dress was empty, something hanging on the back of a door. Her breasts made only the smallest imprint in the cloth, her hips none at all. All the while, she pressed to her mouth a filthy, pink, balled-up rag as though to stanch a flow or buttress against pain. I knew that what she had come to show us, what we were there to see, was hidden beneath that pink cloth. As I watched, the woman handed down to her a gourd from which the girl drank, lapping like a dog. She was the last patient of the day. They had been waiting in the courtyard for hours.

"Imelda Valdez," I called out. Slowly she rose to her feet, the cloth never leaving her mouth, and followed her mother to the examining-room door. I shooed them in.

"You sit up there on the table," I told her. "Mother, you stand over there, please." I read from the chart:

"This is a fourteen-year-old girl with a complete, unilateral, left-sided cleft lip and cleft palate. No other diseases or congenital defects. Laboratory tests, chest X-ray—negative."

"Tell her to take the rag away," said Dr. Franciscus. I did, and the girl shrank back, pressing the cloth all the more firmly.

"Listen, this is silly," said Franciscus. "Tell her I've got to see it. Either she behaves, or send her away."

"Please give me the cloth," I said to the girl as gently as possible. She did not. She could not. Just then, Franciscus reached up and, taking the hand that held the rag, pulled it away with a hard jerk. For an instant the girl's head followed the cloth as it left her face, one arm still upflung against showing. Against all hope, she would hide herself. A moment later, she relaxed and sat still. She seemed to me then like an animal that looks outward at the infinite, at death, without fear, with recognition only.

Set as it was in the center of the girl's face, the defect was utterly hideous—a nude rubbery insect that had fastened there. The upper lip was widely split all the way to the nose. One white tooth perched upon the protruding upper jaw projected through the hole. Some of the bone seemed to have been gnawed away as well. Above the thing, clear almond eyes and long black hair reflected the light. Below, a slender neck where the pulse trilled visibly. Under our gaze the girl's eyes fell to her lap where her hands lay palms upward, half open. She was a beautiful bird with a crushed beak. And tense with the expectation of more shame.

"Open your mouth," said the surgeon. I translated. She did so, and the surgeon tipped back her head to see inside.

"The palate, too. Complete," he said. There was a long silence. At last he spoke.

"What is your name?" The margins of the wound melted until she herself was being sucked into it.

"Imelda." The syllables leaked through the hole with a slosh and a whistle.

"Tomorrow," said the surgeon, "I will fix your lip. *Mañana.*"

It seemed to me that Hugh Franciscus, in spite of his years of experience, in spite of all the dreadful things he had seen, must have been awed by the sight of this girl. I could see it flit across his face for an instant. Perhaps it was her small act of concealment, that he had had to demand that she show him the lip, that he had had to force her to show it to him. Perhaps it was her resistance that intensified the disfigurement. Had she brought her mouth to him willingly, without shame, she would have been for him neither more nor less than any other patient.

He measured the defect with calipers, studied it from different angles, turning her head with a finger at her chin.

"How can it ever be put back together?" I asked.

"Take her picture," he said. And to her, "Look straight ahead." Through the eye of the camera she seemed more pitiful than ever, her humiliation more complete.

"Wait!" The surgeon stopped me. I lowered the camera. A strand of her hair had fallen across her face and found its way to her mouth, becoming stuck there by saliva. He removed the hair and secured it behind her ear.

"Go ahead," he ordered. There was the click of the camera. The girl winced.

"Take three more, just in case."

When the girl and her mother had left, he took paper and pen and with a few lines drew a remarkable likeness of the girl's face.

"Look," he said. "If this dot is A, and this one B, this, C and this, D, the incisions are made A to B, then C to D. CD must equal AB. It is all equilateral triangles." All well and good, but then came X and Y and rotation flaps and the rest.

"Do you see?" he asked.

"It is confusing," I told him.

"It is simply a matter of dropping the upper lip into a normal position, then crossing the gap with two triangular flaps. It is geometry," he said.

"Yes," I said. "Geometry." And relinquished all hope of becoming a plastic surgeon.

∾

In the operating room the next morning the anesthesia had already been administered when we arrived from ward rounds. The tube emerging from the girl's mouth was pressed against her lower lip to be kept out of the field of surgery. Already, a nurse was scrubbing the face which swam in a reddish brown lather. The tiny gold earrings were included in the scrub. Now and then, one of them gave a brave flash. The face was washed for the last time, and dried. Green towels were placed over the face to hide everything but the mouth and nose. The drapes were applied.

"Calipers!" The surgeon measured, locating the peak of the distorted Cupid's bow.

"Marking pen!" He placed the first blue dot at the apex of the bow. The nasal sills were dotted; next, the inferior philtral dimple, the vermilion line. The *A* flap and the *B* flap were outlined. On he worked, peppering the lip and nose, making sense out of chaos, realizing the lip that lay waiting in that deep essential pink, that only he could see. The last dot and line were placed. He was ready.

"Scalpel!" He held the knife above the girl's mouth.

"Okay to go ahead?" he asked the anesthetist.

"Yes."

He lowered the knife.

"No! Wait!" The anesthetist's voice was tense, staccato. "Hold it!"

The surgeon's hand was motionless.

"What's the matter?"

"Something's wrong. I'm not sure. God, she's hot as a pistol. Blood pressure is way up. Pulse one-eighty. Get a rectal temperature." A nurse fumbled beneath the drapes. We waited. The nurse retrieved the thermometer.

"One hundred seven . . . no . . . eight." There was disbelief in her voice.

"Malignant hyperthermia," said the anesthetist. "Ice! Ice! Get lots of ice!" I raced out the door, accosted the first nurse I saw.

"Ice!" I shouted. *"Hielo!* Quickly! *Hielo!"* The woman's expression was blank. I ran to another. *"Hielo! Hielo!* For the love of God, ice!"

"*Hielo?*" She shrugged. "*Nada.*" I ran back to the operating room.

"There isn't any ice," I reported.

Dr. Franciscus had ripped off his rubber gloves and was feeling the skin of the girl's abdomen. Above the mask his eyes were the eyes of a horse in battle.

"The EKG is wild . . ."

"I can't get a pulse . . ."

"What the hell . . ."

The surgeon reached for the girl's groin. No femoral pulse.

"EKG flat. My God! She's dead!"

"She can't be."

"She is."

The surgeon's fingers pressed the groin where there was no pulse to be felt, only his own pulse hammering at the girl's flesh to be let in.

∞

It was noon, four hours later, when we left the operating room. It was a day so hot and humid I felt steamed-open like an envelope. The woman was sitting on a bench in the courtyard in her dress like a cassock. In one hand she held the piece of cloth the girl had used to conceal her mouth. As we watched, she folded it once neatly, and then again, smoothing it, cleaning the cloth which might have been the head of the girl in her lap that she stroked and consoled.

"I'll do the talking here," he said. He would tell her himself, in whatever Spanish he could find. Only if she did not understand was I to speak for him. I watched him brace himself, set his shoulders. How could he tell her? I wondered. What? But I knew he would tell her everything, exactly as it had happened. As much for himself as for her, he needed to explain. But suppose she screamed, fell to the ground, attacked him, even? All that hope of love . . . gone. Even in his discomfort I knew that he was teaching me. The way to do it was professionally. Now he was standing above her. When the woman saw that he did not speak, she lifted her eyes and saw what he held crammed in his mouth to tell her. She knew, and rose to her feet.

"*Señora,*" he began, "I am sorry." All at once he seemed to me shorter than he was, scarcely taller than she. There was a place at the crown of his head where the hair had grown thin. His lips were stones. He could hardly move them. The voice dry, dusty.

"No one could have known. Some bad reaction to the medicine for sleeping. It poisoned her. High fever. She did not wake up." The last, a whisper. The woman studied his lips as though she were deaf. He tried, but could not control a twitching at the corner of his mouth. He raised a thumb and forefinger to press something back into his eyes.

"*Muerte*," the woman announced to herself. Her eyes were human, deadly.

"*Sí, muerte*." At that moment he was like someone cast, still alive, as an effigy for his own tomb. He closed his eyes. Nor did he open them until he felt the touch of the woman's hand on his arm, a touch from which he did not withdraw. Then he looked and saw the grief corroding her face, breaking it down, melting the features so that eyes, nose, mouth ran together in a distortion, like the girl's. For a long time they stood in silence. It seemed to me that minutes passed. At last her face cleared, the features rearranged themselves. She spoke, the words coming slowly to make certain that he understood her. She would go home now. The next day her sons would come for the girl, to take her home for burial. The doctor must not be sad. God has decided. And she was happy now that the harelip had been fixed so that her daughter might go to Heaven without it. Her bare feet retreating were the felted pads of a great bereft animal.

∽

The next morning I did not go to the wards, but stood at the gate leading from the courtyard to the road outside. Two young men in striped ponchos lifted the girl's body wrapped in a straw mat onto the back of a wooden cart. A donkey waited. I had been drawn to this place as one is drawn, inexplicably, to certain scenes of desolation—executions, battlefields. All at once, the woman looked up and saw me. She had taken off her hat. The heavy-hanging coil of her hair made her head seem larger, darker, noble. I pressed some money into her hand.

"For flowers," I said. "A priest." Her cheeks shook as though minutes ago a stone had been dropped into her navel and the ripples were just now reaching her head. I regretted having come to that place.

"*Sí, sí,*" the woman said. Her own face was stitched with flies. "The doctor is one of the angels. He has finished the work of God. My daughter is beautiful."

What could she mean! The lip had not been fixed. The girl had died before he would have done it.

"Only a fine line that God will erase in time," she said.

I reached into the cart and lifted a corner of the mat in which the girl had been rolled. Where the cleft had been there was now a fresh line of tiny sutures. The Cupid's bow was delicately shaped, the vermilion border aligned. The flattened nostril had now the same rounded shape as the other one. I let the mat fall over the face of the dead girl, but not before I had seen the touching place where the finest black hairs sprang from the temple.

"*Adiós, adiós . . .*" And the cart creaked away to the sound of hooves, a tinkling bell.

∽

There are events in a doctor's life that seem to mark the boundary between youth and age, seeing and perceiving. Like certain dreams, they illuminate a whole lifetime of past behavior. After such an event, a doctor is not the same as he was before. It had seemed to me then to have been the act of someone demented, or at least insanely arrogant. An attempt to reorder events. Her death had come to him out of order. It should have come after the lip had been repaired, not before. He could have told the mother that, no, the lip had not been fixed. But he did not. He said nothing. It had been an act of omission, one of those strange lapses to which all of us are subject and which we live to regret. It must have been then, at that moment, that the knowledge of what he would do appeared to him. The words of the mother had not consoled him; they had hunted him down. He had not done it for her. The dire necessity was his. He would not accept that Imelda had died before he could repair her lip. People who do such things break free from society. They follow their own lonely path. They have a secret which they can never reveal. I must never let on that I knew.

∞

How often I have imagined it. Ten o'clock at night. The hospital of Comayagua is all but dark. Here and there lanterns tilt and skitter up and down the corridors. One of these lamps breaks free from the others and descends the stone steps to the underground room that is the morgue of the hospital. This room wears the expression as if it had waited all night for someone to come. No silence so deep as this place with its cargo of newly dead. Only the slow drip of water over stone. The door closes gassily and clicks shut. The lock is turned. There are four tables, each with a body encased in a paper shroud. There is no mistaking her. She is the smallest. The surgeon takes a knife from his pocket and slits open the paper shroud, that part in which the girl's head is enclosed. The wound seems to be living on long after she has died. Waves of heat emanate from it, blurring his vision. All at once, he turns to peer over his shoulder. He sees nothing, only a wooden crucifix on the wall.

He removes a package of instruments from a satchel and arranges them on a tray. Scalpel, scissors, forceps, needle holder. Sutures and gauze sponges are produced. Stealthy, hunched, engaged, he begins. The dots of blue dye are still there upon her mouth. He raises the scalpel, pauses. A second glance into the darkness. From the wall a small lizard watches and accepts. The first cut is made. A sluggish flow of dark blood appears. He wipes it away with a sponge. No new blood comes to take its place. Again and again he cuts, connecting each of the blue dots until the whole of the zigzag slice is made, first on one side of the cleft, then on the other. Now the edges of the cleft are lined with fresh tissue. He sets down the scalpel and takes up scissors and forceps, undermining the little flaps until each triangle is attached only at one side. He rotates each flap into its new position. He must be certain that they can be swung without tension. They can. He is ready to suture. He fits the tiny curved needle into the jaws of the needle holder. Each suture is placed precisely the same number of millimeters from the cut edge, and the same distance apart. He ties each knot down until the edges are apposed. Not too tightly. These are the most meticulous sutures of his life. He cuts each thread close to the knot. It goes well. The vermilion border with its white skin roll is exactly aligned. One more stitch and the Cupid's bow appears as if by magic. The man's face shines with moisture. Now the nostril is incised around the margin, released, and sutured into a round shape to match its mate. He wipes the blood from the face of the girl with gauze that he has dipped in water. Crumbs of light are scattered on the girl's face. The shroud is folded once more about her. The instruments are handed into the satchel. In a moment the morgue is dark and a lone lantern ascends the stairs and is extinguished.

∞

Six weeks later I was in the darkened amphitheater of the Medical School. Tiers of seats rose in a semicircle above the small stage where Hugh Franciscus stood presenting the case material he had encountered in Honduras. It was the highlight of the year. The hall was filled. The night before, he had arranged the slides in the order in which they were to be shown. I was at the controls of the slide projector.

"Next slide!" he would order from time to time in that military voice which had called forth blind obedience from generations of medical students, interns, residents, and patients.

"This is a fifty-seven-year-old man with a severe burn contracture of the neck. You will notice the rigid webbing that has fused the chin to the presternal tissues. No motion of the head on the torso is possible. . . . Next slide!"

Click, went the projector.

"Here he is after the excision of the scar tissue and with the head in full extension for the first time. The defect was then covered. . . . Next slide!"

Click.

". . . with full-thickness drums of skin taken from the abdomen with the Padgett dermatome. Next slide!"

Click.

And suddenly there she was, extracted from the shadows, suspended above and beyond all of us like a resurrection. There was the oval face, the long black hair unbraided, the tiny gold hoops in her ears. And that luminous gnawed mouth. The whole of her life seemed to have been summed up in this photograph. A long silence followed that was the surgeon's alone to break. Almost at once, like the anesthetist in the operating room in Comayagua, I knew that something was wrong. It was not that the man would not speak as that he could not. The audience of doctors, nurses, and students seemed to have been infected by the black, limitless silence. My own pulse doubled. It was hard to breathe. Why did he not call out for the next slide? Why did he not save himself? Why had he not removed this slide from the ones to be shown? All at once I knew that he had used his camera on her again. I could see the long black shadows of her hair flowing into the darker shadows of the morgue. The sudden blinding flash. . . . The next slide would be the one taken in the morgue. He would be exposed.

In the dim light reflected from the slide, I saw him gazing up at her, seeing not the colored photograph, I thought, but the negative of it where the ghost of the girl was. For me, the amphitheater had become Honduras. I saw again that courtyard littered with patients. I could see the dust in the beam of light from the projector. It was then that I knew that she was his measure of perfection and pain—the one lost, the other gained. He, too, had heard the click of the camera, had seen her wince and felt his mercy enlarge. At last he spoke.

"Imelda." It was the one word he had heard her say. At the sound of his voice I removed the next slide from the projector. *Click* . . . and she was gone. *Click* again, and in her place the man with the orbital cancer. For a long moment Franciscus looked up in my direction, on his face an expression that I have given up trying to interpret. Gratitude? Sorrow? It made me think of the gaze of the girl when at last she understood that she must hand over to him the evidence of her body.

"This is a sixty-two-year-old man with a basal-cell carcinoma of the temple eroding into the bony orbit . . ." he began, as though nothing had happened.

At the end of the hour, even before the lights went on, there was loud applause. I hurried to find him among the departing crowd. I could not. Some weeks went by before I caught sight of him. He seemed vaguely convalescent, as though a fever had taken its toll before burning out.

Hugh Franciscus continued to teach for fifteen years, although he operated a good deal less, then gave it up entirely. It was as though he had grown tired of blood, of always having to be involved with blood, of having to draw it, spill it, wipe it away, stanch it. He was a quieter, softer man, I heard, the ferocity diminished. There were no more expeditions to Honduras or anywhere else.

I, too, have not been entirely free of her. Now and then, in the years that have passed, I see that donkey-cart cortege, or his face bent over hers in the morgue. I would like to have told him what I now know, that his unrealistic act was one of goodness, one of those small, persevering acts done, perhaps, to ward off madness. Like lighting a lamp, boiling water for tea, washing a shirt. But, of course, it's too late now.

Fetishes

There is Audrey. And there is Leonard. Audrey had waited until she was thirty-two to marry. Not by choice; no one had asked her. But all the time she had never given up hope, so that when Leonard Blakeslee had come along, she had at once reached out her hands for him as though he were an exotic foreign dish whose very strangeness captured her appetite completely. "You'll love me?" she asked him, and never once in all these years had he given her reason to doubt it. The fact that no children had come along was briefly regretted by both of them, then accepted. Somehow, it suited them.

Leonard is an anthropologist. Every so often he goes off to New Guinea on an expedition among the Asmat. It is the only time they are separated. When he is away Audrey feels only half intact, bisected. And Leonard too, as he wrote in a letter (she has saved them all), is "never done with wanting you at my side, where you ought always to be, my darling." She loved that "ought always to be." It was courtly. When he is not going on in that vein, his letters are anthropological, having to do with the language of the tribe for which he is compiling a dictionary, the artifacts he is collecting, the myths and mores of the people, all of which Audrey reads with affection and even genuine interest. Leonard and his artifacts, she would say to her sister, Violet, with an indulgent smile. Not that Audrey is beautiful. No one but Leonard could accuse her of that. But what she had she had and that was the true love of her husband.

Another thing Audrey has right now is a ten-centimeter cyst on her right ovary which the doctors can't say for certain is benign, and so it will have to come out. Thank heavens Leonard isn't off on one of his expeditions, she thought.

Fifteen years ago, she had been forty-two then, every one of her upper teeth had been extracted while Leonard was in New Guinea. Pyorrhea, the dentist had said. Said it severely. "You've let it go. They are all rotten and ready to fall out on their own."

Audrey was flabbergasted. "I have to think," she had said. "My husband isn't here. He's in New Guinea." She remembered the man's contemptuous little smile. On the way home, she said to Vi, "But . . . Leonard . . ."

"Leonard is not a dentist," said Violet.

And so a few days later Audrey had gone through with it. She hadn't been out of that dentist's office ten minutes when she knew that she had made a dreadful mistake. Vi drove her home afterward. Lying down on the backseat of the car, her mouth numb, her cheeks stuffed with pledgets of cotton, she wondered what Leonard would think, how he would feel. And she recalled something she had heard him say to one of his students, she couldn't remember why: "No one," Leonard had said to the student, "can take your dignity away from you; you might throw it away yourself, but no one can take it away from you." Then and there Audrey decided that Leonard didn't have to know.

"You all right?" Vi asked from behind the wheel, and turned round to see at every red light.

Right from the start, Audrey had refused to take the denture out of her mouth, no matter the pain. There were dark blisters on her gums; she lisped. But she was determined. Leonard would be coming home in two months. Audrey persevered so that with weeks to spare, she had gotten used to the "prosthesis," as they called it, incorporated it. It had become second nature.

Oh, she had had to steel herself against the first times it had to come out, be cleaned, then reinserted. But she had surprised herself. She was calm, curious even, as she turned it over in her hand, examining. Like a pink horseshoe, she decided, and how wise she was to have avoided the vulgarity of pure white. Ivory was more natural.

Ivory has endured; ivory has kept faith. In time her palate had molded itself to fit, her gums were snug and secure in the hollow trough. Never, never would she remove her teeth anywhere but in a locked bathroom. She would keep them in at night. It was a myth that you had to take your dentures out at night. Before long, she had no qualms, didn't mind at all. The denture had become for her a kind of emblem of personal dignity, like one of those Asmat artifacts with magic properties, but this having to do with the one thing that mattered most to Audrey: Leonard. "It isn't really cheating," she told Violet.

"You're lucky," said Vi. "You're one of those people who don't show their teeth when they smile."

When at last Leonard burst into the room, gathered her in his arms and kissed her, she smiled as much from triumph as with happiness. "You never cease to charm me," he had said, and she knew then that she had done it. Leonard would never know.

But now it was fifteen years later. "Total abdominal hysterectomy," the surgeon announced. "A clean sweep." As though she were a kitchen floor! "What does that include?" she asked him. "The uterus, both ovaries, both tubes," he told her. "Why my uterus?" She insisted upon the personal pronoun. "Why my left ovary? My tubes?" He then explained, rather too patiently, she thought, that she didn't need her reproductive organs anymore, that the risk of getting cancer in one of those organs was "not inconsiderable." Human beings do not talk like that, she thought. That is not human speech. "And," the surgeon went on, "as long as we are going to be in there anyway . . ." In there! Audrey could not keep her hand from passing lightly across her abdomen. Then he spoke about the small additional risk of the larger operation, said it was "negligible." But Audrey already knew what it was to go through life missing something. She wished fervently that she had been able to keep her cyst a secret, like her teeth. You would think it would be easier since the ovaries were inside and safely hidden. Imagine having to carry them in a bag between your legs, like testicles. And as for the risk of getting cancer . . . is that a reason to have your organs taken out? All of life is a risk. Living in California is a risk; there might be an earthquake. First, her teeth, and now her . . . her womanhood, yes, it was nothing short of that. All at once the operation seemed part of a plot to take her body apart. And she remembered the clink of coins years ago, as that dentist stirred the change in his pocket, stirred it on and on, enjoying the sound of it before he took up the syringe and injected her with novocaine.

On the wall in back of the surgeon's desk was a colored diagram of the female organs. Altogether, it resembled a sweet-faced cow's head rising to the gentle curve of the horns.

"No," she said, closing down. "No, that cannot be. Only my ovary, the one with the cyst. Nothing else, unless there is cancer." She would sign permission only for that. In the end, she had capitulated. "You're doing the right thing, I assure you, Mrs. Blakeslee," said the surgeon as she signed the permission sheet.

At the hospital, Leonard and Audrey followed the nurse into the room. "Get undressed and into this." The nurse held up a knee-length shirt open at the back. She did and over it put on the pale green brocade bed jacket Leonard had given her the night before. It had been arranged that Leonard was to wait in the solarium outside the operating rooms. The surgeon would talk to him there, let him know what he had found. Afterward, he would wait for Audrey to be wheeled down from the recovery room a few hours later.

"Visiting hours are over," commanded the page operator. "Will all visitors please leave now."

"Good luck," said Leonard with a smile that was much too bright for him. He's frightened, she thought, and felt tears filming her eyes. After Leonard had left, Audrey lay on the bed, thinking of him—the silky feel of the black hairs on his forearms, his smell of permanence, the sound of his singing. Leonard sang bass. It was her favorite. At sixty-one, his voice was as rich as ever. Sometimes, listening in church to that submarine vibrato, she would have moments of unecclesiastical commotion. Once, when she confessed it, Leonard reproached her with a waggle of his finger. Ah, but his was a magic throat.

∽

"I'm Dr. Dowling." The man had knocked and come in at the same time. It is what happens in hospitals, she thought. She was glad to be wearing the green bed jacket. So long as she had it on, there was protection.

"The anesthesiologist," he explained. "I'll be putting you to sleep tomorrow. Any questions?"

Audrey shook her head. He had an important sort of face, florid, with jowls made even more congressional by the white political hair that escaped from beneath his green surgical cap. He was wearing a scrub suit of the same color and, over that, a white laboratory coat. The strings of a mask dangled.

"Open your mouth wide as you can." He peered in.

"I see you have an upper plate. Out it comes in the morning before you leave this room. The nurse will mind it for you."

Mute shadows of words trembled at her lips.

"But I never take it out, only to clean . . ."

"Well, you cannot go to the operating room with it in. I cannot put you to sleep with a foreign body in your mouth."

Foreign body! Audrey felt the blood leave her head. Gongs could not have sounded louder in her ears. Then a final cold ticking.

"For how long . . . ?"

"Until you are fully awake. Certainly till evening."

"But you don't understand . . ." she began. Her voice trailed off. The doctor waited, turned his head, looked at her from the corner of an eye.

"Yes?"

"It is . . . My husband does not know that I have a denture. He has been unaware of it for fifteen years. I would not want him to see me without it. Please," she said very quietly. "It is important to me." She waited for the walls to burst.

"Pride," said the man. "No room for it here. Like modesty. Suppose we had to get at your trachea, your windpipe, in a hurry, and then we had to waste time fishing those teeth out. Suppose they came loose in the middle of the operation. There are a hundred 'supposes.' " He started to go.

"It isn't pride," she managed.

"What, then?"

"It's dignity." Perhaps it had been pride at the very beginning, but it had grown. And something else: Audrey understood that the connubial apparatus of a man is more delicate than a woman's. She saw no need to put it to the test.

"Come now. Mrs. Blakeslee, is it?" He consulted the name on the chart to make sure. Audrey struggled to fend off his voice. "You are making too much of it."

All right, then, she would calculate, be a cat.

"Don't you . . ." she began. "Don't you have a little something hidden away that you wouldn't want anyone to know about?" She smiled, laying it on in almost visible slabs. The doctor was taken off guard.

"No, actually not." But he had hesitated for the fraction of a second, and so she knew.

"How boring," she said, smiling, giving it to him right in his face. "And, of course, I don't for a minute believe you." This doctor could not know it, but Audrey was fighting for her life. But now she saw that he had retreated a vast safe distance behind his lips.

"In any case, you may not keep them in. And that's that." He stood abruptly and walked to the door.

"Have a good night," he called over his shoulder.

After he had left, Audrey felt her heart go small in her chest. Again there was the clink of coins being stirred in a pocket. With a sudden resolve, she decided that there was no longer any need for tact. The situation didn't call for tact. It called for defiance. I'll sign myself out of the hospital, she thought. Against medical advice, as they say. That cyst on her ovary, it might well be benign. They don't know. Leaving it in would be just one more risk. A risk infinitely smaller than having Leonard see her without her denture. Her mouth caved in, wrinkled like a drawstring pouch. She tried to imagine herself saying to Leonard afterward: "All right, then. You have seen what you have seen. Now accept it. Or not." But she could not. That way lay death. Hers or that of something far more delicate and valuable. No, she thought. No. Never again would she cultivate a belief in inevitability.

Audrey reached for the telephone, dialed.

"Leonard, don't come to the hospital at all tomorrow."

"But why?" He was startled. "Of course I'm coming to see you."

"That's just the point, Leonard, please . . ." She heard her voice flapping about her, out of control. "Please." She was imploring him. "Don't come. Promise me."

"I'm sorry, Audrey. I'm just not going to agree to that. So forget it." His tone was severe, as with a child.

"I don't want you to see me like that."

"Like what?" He smiled with his voice. "I have seen it all before, you know." Oh, but you haven't, she thought. You shouldn't.

"What is it, Audrey? You sound distraught. Shall I come right over? I'll make them let me in."

"I just wanted to spare you," she said harshly. "There are times when people need to be alone."

"No," said Leonard. "I'll be there."

Violet managed the gift shop in the lobby of the hospital. She was two years older than Audrey—a big woman, divorced once, widowed once. Violet did not use makeup. I have nothing to hide, she said. Still, she dyed her hair. For business reasons. When you have to meet the public, gray hair automatically dismisses you. Fifteen years before, they had been closer, when Violet had brought her home from the dentist's office and Audrey had sworn her to a lifetime of silence. But somewhere between then and now Vi had become the kind of woman who sat herself down with ceremony in a deep chair to receive the secrets of others. She would be coming up to the room after she closed the gift shop. Audrey would ask her for a ride home. She would deal with Leonard later.

"I'll do no such thing," said Violet. "Do you mean to lie there and tell me that Leonard still doesn't know about your false teeth?" Vi made a point of never saying "denture." "False teeth" had a balder sound and they had drifted too far apart for softness. The venules on Vi's cheeks dilated with indignant blood. Audrey reached for the light switch, flicked it off. It was something to do.

"May I turn off the light?" she asked then. In the dark she could see the glossy mound of her sister's hair.

"Listen, Audrey, this has become a sick obsession with you." Her vehemence was reiterated by flashes of gold at neck and earlobes.

"There are madder things," said Audrey. And she lamented the weakness that made her let down her guard before this stranger who was her sister.

"Besides, it's a lie. People shouldn't lie, no matter what."

"Oh, lies," said Audrey. "That's where you're wrong. People don't lie enough. When people tell the whole truth, that's when things fall apart. Most relationships are like some plants, I think. They need to be kept partly in the shade or they wither." A nurse came in and turned on the light. In the sudden glare Violet leaped up at her.

"Now, Audrey, don't be stupid," she said, standing to leave. "Behave yourself." Violet's teeth would never fall out, Audrey thought. They chew words, worry them; the way they buckle up her mouth.

Almost at once there was a hesitant knock at the door. Oh, God. Now who?

"My name is Dr. Bhimjee. I am the intern on this ward." An Indian or Pakistani, she thought. And lame. He limped toward the bed using his head and one arm in the act of locomotion.

"Mrs. Blakeslee, I see that our names both end with two *e*'s." His face was dark, she suspected, more from fatigue than from racial coloring. More than anything else he resembled an ungainly parcel, something bulgy and ill-wrapped. His hair was almost too thick, too black, but relieved by a single swatch of white near the crown. He is not young, Audrey decided. What has he endured and with how much patience? All at once, a fence came down. Who, after all, is to say where, in whom, one places trust?

"I have false teeth," she said, firing the words into his hair. She was shocked at the ease with which the forbidden words had come. The intern gazed down at her.

"Many people do," he said. The slate-colored skin set off the perfection of his own very white teeth. He is beautiful, she thought. And she threw herself further upon his mercy.

"I have had them for fifteen years. My husband has never seen me without them. He doesn't know that I have them. The anesthetist was here. He says I must leave them here in the room tomorrow. My husband will be waiting for me to come back from the recovery room. He will see me. I can't do that. Please, please." The last words rose like echoes. For a long moment they looked at each other, during which something, a covenant perhaps, Audrey did not know, was exchanged. Audrey lashed her gaze to his long gracile fingers. Then, all at once, deep called unto deep. A rush of profound affection came over her. It was nothing like her feeling for Leonard, but for all she knew, it might have been love.

"Do not worry." The *r*'s rolled very slightly. "In the morning, put them in the nightstand. There is a container. I will take them with me to the operation. I am assigned to your case, so I will be there too. Before you leave the recovery room, I will put them back into your mouth. Do not worry."

∽

Later, when she awoke in the recovery room, the pain of her incision was the second thing that Audrey felt. The first was the denture which she explored with her tongue. Only then came the pain which, so help her, she did not mind. In spite of it, she curled up like a cat in a basket. Once, when she opened her eyes, she saw, or thought she saw, a dark face above her, a white swatch in a tumble of black hair, like a plume of smoke clinging to the chimney of a snug cottage.

"Don't worry," he was saying softly. "Your teeth are in. Take a deep breath. Again." He listened with his stethoscope. "You will be awake soon." He checked her pulse, and was gone. For a long time his voice lingered, lapsing, returning, drifting into darkness. And then there was Leonard, holding her hand, leaning over the bed to kiss her. "The doctor says it was benign." Audrey smiled up at him within the limits of morphine.

During the days that followed, Audrey found herself thinking about Dr. Bhimjee as much as she did about Leonard. There was a peacefulness about him. Not resignation so much as acceptance. No, definitely not resignation. Resignation suggests defeat. Acceptance, rather. Where had he found it? Wrested it, she supposed, barehanded from a tangle of thorns. He had no need to deceive. It had not been given to him to deceive. She saw him differently now from the way she had that first desperate night. What she had thought was fatigue became the sum total of all the suffering he had experienced. It had worn his face down to the bone. The sockets of his eyes were dark cabins of it. Audrey would have liked to take the bony parcel in her arms, to breathe in his dreams.

And soon it was the hour of Audrey's discharge from the hospital. The intern had come to say good-bye.

"My wife tells me that you have been very kind to her," said Leonard. Audrey could not take her gaze from the two men.

"Not at all."

"I want you to know that I will always remember your"—she saw that Leonard was struggling—"your courtesy."

"Please, it was nothing."

"Nevertheless," said Leonard. "Nevertheless," he repeated, "I want you to have this." He held out a small reddish stone.

"What is that?"

"Just a stone that has been dyed red by the Asmat people of New Guinea. See? It has a monkey carved on one side, a parrot on the other. A shaman gave it to me. He's a sort of doctor too. It wards off melancholy, brings good luck. Please, take it." The doctor hesitated.

"I want you to have it," said Leonard. There was in his voice something vivid, mighty. Maybe it was the sun probing between the slats of the venetian blinds, but from her wheelchair it seemed to Audrey that, at the exact moment when the red stone left the white hand of one and entered the dark hand of the other, something flared up that looked for all the world like fire.

Tube Feeding

A man enters a bedroom. He is carrying a lacquered tray upon which stands a glass pitcher of eggnog. There is also a napkin in a napkin ring, a white enamel funnel, and an emesis basin. In the bed a woman lies.

It is eight o'clock in the morning. Precisely as he turns the knob of the door, she hears the church bells. At the sound, a coziness comes over her. There is nothing more certain than that he will appear, when he is most needed, when everything is ready. She has been awake for two hours, considering the treason of her body. But now that is over. She feels privileged to have known ahead of time of his coming, as though it were an event that had been foretold to her. She smiles up at him.

"Lovely," he says, and smiles. He carries the tray to the nightstand near the bed and sets it down. He bends then to kiss her head which is almost bald from the chemotherapy.

"What's lovely?" she asks him.

His smile broadens.

"The morning. Breakfast. You."

"Just lovely," he says again as she knows he will.

He opens the drawer of the nightstand and, after a moment of hesitation, selects a silk scarf. He holds it up.

"This one?" he asks.

She nods. He folds the scarf into a triangle, places it across her forehead and ties two ends of it at the back of her head. He tucks the folds in at the sides with a small flourish. He has become adept at this. Even now, after so many weeks, he marvels at the smallness of her head. It is so tiny and finely veined, no more than a pale knob, really, or a lamp of milk glass etched by the suture lines of the skull.

Before the chemotherapy, she had had dark brown hair which she sometimes braided into pigtails. It had given her a girlish look that amused him until he read somewhere that people who were dying of a lingering illness often took on a childlike appearance. Thereafter he wondered whether a long dying was really a slow retracing of life until the instants of death and conception were the same.

Hours before, she had opened her eyes to see him stepping into the room to give her the dose of pain medication. The moonlight streamed where he stood, an arc of blackness carving the moon of his face in half, hiding the lower part from her view. She wondered what he was thinking then. She thought it might possibly be like what she felt as a child when she picked the crumbs out of her grandfather's beard as he slept.

That was several hours ago. There would still be time before the pain returned. He could always tell when the pain was beginning to come back. Almost before she could. Her eyes took on a glitter that was a presentiment of the pain. All along he had considered the pain to be a mistake on the part of her body. Something had gone awry, been derailed, and so she had the pain. It was the kind of mistake that was an honest piece of ignorance by a person he loved. Between the long prairies of pain, there were narrow strips of relief when the dream of health was still given to her. In these intervals she would lie as on hillocks of cool grass, having caught at last, among her fingertips, the butterfly for which she had such nostalgia.

The man sits, one buttock on the bed, his legs arranged for balance. "Ready?" he asks.

She nods. He never seems to notice the great red beard of tumor that, having begun in her salivary gland, had grown until it fills, now, the space between her face and her chest. There, where once her neck had been, she is swollen to bursting. Like a mating grouse, she thinks, or one of those blowfish. It is as though there is a route which his mind obeys, carefully, so that he sees only her brow where the skin is still pale and smooth, nothing below her eyes. She was someone who had always counted appearance for so much. Her own looks had stood her in such good stead. After all, she would say to him, I caught *you*, didn't I? And then came the cancer which, if it had only remained internal, hidden, would have kept for her the outline of her self. But this tumor had burst forth, exuberant, studding her face, mounding upon her neck, twisting and pulling her features until she was nothing but a grimace trapped in a prow of flesh.

"I look like Popeye," she said once.

He had not smiled.

The man rises, then kneels playfully beside the bed. To the woman, he seems taller in this position than he had while standing. As though, in the act of folding, he had grown. Kneeling *is* the proper posture for prayer, she thinks.

Now the man stands again. He folds down the sheet to the level of the woman's hips. Her abdomen is scaphoid, like an old boat which had been pulled up onto the land long ago, its mast and appointments pirated. Still, in the bend of each rib, there was retained the hint of wind and bright water. From the left upper quadrant of her abdomen, from what looks like a stab wound, there hangs a thick tube of brown rubber. The end of the tube, some eighteen inches from the skin, is closed off by a metal clamp, a pinchcock. The number 34 is stamped in black on the tube, announcing its caliber. The man takes the stiff tube in his left hand, letting it ride across his fingers. He removes the white gauze pad that has been folded over the open end and secured there by a rubber band. Always at this point, she feels that the act is exploratory, as though they are children left alone in a house, and have discovered for the first time how to do something mysterious and adult, each needing the assurance of the other.

The man releases the pinchcock. A few drops of mucoid fluid drip into the emesis basin. Sometimes there is a little blood. He is relieved when there is none. He wipes the end of the tube with the napkin and inserts the nozzle of the calibrated funnel into the gastrostomy tube, setting it firmly lest it slip out during the feeding. They look at each other and smile. She knows what is coming. He holds the empty funnel upright in his hand as though it were a goblet of wine, raising it so that it dances between their faces.

"Bon appetit!" he toasts her.

There is a sound like the bleat of a goat, as gas escapes from her stomach through the tube. He is always touched by the melancholy little noise. The man tests the temperature of the eggnog with the tip of a finger, which he then licks clean.

"Just right," he says.

Now he pours from the pitcher until the topmost mark of the funnel is reached. He gives the funnel to her to hold, the way a parent will indulge a child, letting her participate. Together they watch the level in the funnel slowly fall. The woman gives a deep sigh as she feels the filling of her stomach.

"Is that good?" he asks her.

"Yes," she nods and smiles, then looks away from him, preoccupied with the feeling.

For him it is not unlike a surgical operation that has become fixed and unchanging in the hands of the man who performs it over and again. Each time there are the same instruments; the steps are followed logically; the expectation of success is high. Once it happened that the mouth of the woman suddenly filled with the eggnog. He had administered the feeding too quickly. Overdistention of the stomach had brought on reverse peristalsis, and a column of the white liquid was catapulted up toward the blocked throat with such force that the barricade of tumor was forced, and the mouth achieved. It was sudden, but he was prepared for it. With one hand, he held the curved emesis basin at her chin. With the other, he lowered the tubing to siphon the eggnog back into the funnel. In a minute the spasm was over, and the feeding was resumed. All the while that this was taking place, the man did not cease to murmur to her.

"There, there," he had said, and wiped the woman's chin with the linen napkin. Then he had waited while she struggled to control her coughing.

She had always taken pleasure in his manner toward her—a kind of gallantry that he assumed for occasions—nights when they would go to the theater, or evenings when she knew that later he would make love to her. Now, of course, she understood that his gallantry was a device. She listened to him say "lovely" and "there, there," and she tried to forget for a while what she knew too well, that at the bottom of each of these tube feedings was the sediment of despair.

It is halfway through the feeding. All at once the man is startled by the sight of something white in the bed. For a moment, he does not know what it is. In that moment of uncertainty, a line has been crossed. Then he knows that it is the eggnog running from the hole in her body, the hole from which the tube has slipped! This time, too, he understands what has happened. Just behind the inner tip of the tube, there is a little thin-walled balloon that holds just five cc of water, enough to distend it to a size greater than that of the hole in her stomach, so that the tube will not slip out. The little balloon has broken; the tube has slipped out. Now the man gazes at the empty hole in his wife's abdomen. Despair seizes him, mounts into desperation. He knows that he must replace the old tube with a new one.

"You must do it immediately," the surgeon had warned, "or very soon, the hole will begin to shrink and heal in. Then you will not be able to insert it."

The man rises from where he has been sitting on the bed. He walks to the dresser, where the extra tube is kept. There is a hollowness in him; he hears echoes. He senses that a limit has been reached. But he clenches himself.

"It's all right," he says aloud. "Here's a new one. Don't you fret about it."

But he is sweating and his fingers tremble as he dips the end of the new tube into the pitcher of eggnog to lubricate it. Once again, he is sitting on the bed. He slides the nose of the tube into the hole. It does not go. It will not fit. So soon! Again he tries to advance the tube. It is no use. He cannot. He twists and turns it, pushing harder. The woman winces. He is hurting her! He looks up to see the knobbed purple growth bearding her face. The lopsided head she raises in her distress seems to him a strange tropical fruit, a mutant gourd that has misgrown from having been acted upon by radiation and chemicals. And so it had. It is as though he is seeing it for the first time. Once, long ago, he had gripped her neck in rage. Oh God! Did the cancer come from that? Then he remembers how he used to lap the declivities of that neck.

He pushes the tube harder. What will he do if he cannot get it in? She will starve. All at once there is a terrifying "give," and the tube slides in. He inflates the little balloon with the water he has drawn up into a syringe, injecting it into the tiny tract alongside the main channel of the thing. He pulls back on the tube until he feels it abutting against the wall of her stomach. It is done.

"There," he says.

The man rises from the bed and leaves the room. He hurries down the hall to the bathroom where he reels above the toilet and vomits with as much stealth as he can manage. In the bed, the woman hears his retching. The day before, he had brought her white peonies from the garden. He had thrust his face into the immaculate flowers and inhaled deeply. Then he had arranged them in a vase on the dresser. She gazes at them now. One of the peonies sleeps unopened, resting against the blazing wakefulness of its kin. It will not bloom, she thinks. It is a waste. For a while she had thought it might open, but not anymore. As she watches, a small breeze from the opening door sends the blind bud waving from side to side. No, she thinks. It will live asleep. To awaken would be to die.

The man returns to her bedside. He takes up the funnel to reinsert it in the tube, to resume the feeding. She reaches out and stays his hand.

"It is enough," she says. "No more."

The man flushes the tube through with a small amount of water to prevent clogging, then replaces the gauze square and the clamp.

He pulls the sheet up over her abdomen, then picks up the lacquered tray that holds the pitcher, the napkin ring, the emesis basin, and the white enamel funnel. At the door he turns and smiles.

"You take a nice little nap, now," he says.

Her eyes are already closed.

In the kitchen, the man washes the pitcher and the funnel, and, climbing on a chair, he puts them away on the top shelf of the cupboard. At the rear, where he won't be apt to see them again for a long time.

Pipistrel

pipis•trelle, pip•is•trel (pip´í strel´, pip´í strel´) *n.* [Fr. *pipistrelle* < It.
pipistrello, altered < OIt. *vispistrello* < L. *vespertilio,* bat < *vesper,*
evening: see VESPER] any of a genus *(Pipistrellus)* of small bats that
characteristically fly early in the evening: found in N. America and in
most of the Eastern Hemisphere

*L*ying awake in her bed, Ada heard the boy sigh and permitted a
glance inside herself. Had it really happened? She searched the shadows for scraps of memory. Were it not for the evidence in the next
room, the boy's thin arms and legs strewn in the carelessness of sleep,
she might have doubted that eighteen years ago a young man named
Philip Schuster had come down to Schuylerville from the high pas-
tures beyond Sleeping Giant mountain, his sandy hair combed back
into two soft waves above a trustworthy smile, his boots polished to
the brightest black, and carrying into the house that smell of cud, manure, and milk that ever since had the power to reawaken instantly
the whole of the buried past. From that first Saturday night, he had
made her feel *selected.* For his part, he told her later, he had been beside himself with desire for her. For me! she thought, amazed. And his
was a desire entirely aboveground, a dumb, animal desire that he
brought down from the hills every Saturday and held up for her to
see. Now and then, amid that smile she saw a minute, serious glance
upon her, as if only she had the power to rescue him. Until—was it

only six weeks later?—he had fixed her with a gaze full of longing and told her he wanted to look after her from then on. Standing so close, she could feel the heat that radiated from the man's body, and swaying toward him, she let herself be lit by the conflagration. "You mean get married?" she asked. She had to be sure. She had flashed with excitement at the nakedness of it, his offer that she say yes or no to him while he waited in his misery and hope. Then she took in both of hers the hand he held out to her, turned it over to study the calluses on the cushions of his palm and the long lifeline that went almost up to his wrist. "Yes, I want to," she said into the glow that was his face, and heard his groan of jubilation as he drew her to him and pressed her head against his chest, where she inhaled the sweet clovery breath that emanated from it. Three months to the day after they had met, Ada and Philip Schuster left the First Presbyterian Church as man and wife and went to live on the farm beyond the mountain. And three months after that, he left for Korea, and that was that. Or almost that. For by the end of the year she was a mother and a widow. Philip, she named the boy, so as not to lose track. Long lifeline, indeed.

Ada rose and went to stand by his bed. Search as she would in the boy for his father—a curve of the lip, the lift of an eyebrow, the slow swelling of his features, like the rising of dough, that used to tell her soon he would make love to her—she could not find the least sign of him. What she saw instead was an ill-wrapped bundle of sticks that would not grow beyond four feet tall, with a pointed face as white as chalk and red watery eyes that, even in sleep, seemed to try to avoid the light. And, hovering over that face, the strange vacancy she was to spend the rest of her life trying to fathom. All at once, her son opened his eyes to see her standing over him. Ada smiled and stroked his head, not much bigger than a boxer's fist, the way one strokes a cat.

"Go back to sleep, Pippo," she said. A moment later, having given no sign that he had seen her, the boy turned on his side and closed his eyes. Ada felt her heart expand with love.

When he was four and started at his rocking back and forth (he would keep it up for hours), and he wasn't paying attention or talking except for "Mama" and "Pippo"—which was how he said Philip—she dressed him up in his good chinos and white shirt and took the bus to Albany, to the children's clinic.

"Autistic," said the doctor.

"What's that? Feeble-minded?"

"No. His brain is as good as yours or mine, only the circuits are all broken."

"Can it be fixed?"

"You have to accept it. You'd best put him somewhere nice with others like him and people to look after him."

"What caused it?"

"Nobody knows. It just happens."

"Come on, Pippo," she said then. "Let's go home."

"If it gets to be too much, let us know," said the nurse. "There's a place right here in Albany."

"No thanks," said Ada. And she meant it. That was thirteen years ago. In all those years he hadn't said any but those two words—*Mama* and *Pippo*. Other than that, little barks and chittering noises were what he made, and whimpers whenever he hurt himself. When he was happy, which was most of the time, he smiled and sort of sang, a long quavery singsong, up and down and on and on. To Ada he was the purest, sweetest thing God ever made. You're like an apple, she thought, looking at him, that's been picked too soon, but on purpose, to avoid the possibility of worms.

Oh, he could be stubborn, all right. There were things she couldn't get him to do. Wear his glasses, for one. No matter how she coaxed, or showed him how he could see better if he would, he wouldn't, but clawed them off as though they were burning hot. "All right," she said at last. "You don't have to. You will see what you will see."

At the children's clinic they had told her what she already knew, that he could draw better than anyone else his age. After she'd sold the farm, they'd moved to a small house a mile and a half outside of town, and over the years, new people had moved in and houses had been added to the outskirts, until one day Ada woke up to find herself living on the edge of town with neighbors and their children. And all through the years he had continued to draw, everything—trees, birds, roads, houses, the sky, the earth. Animals were his favorites—cows, sheep, goats, horses, and those pigs with each bristle slanted just so and the black crinkles about their eyes. Everything but people. He never once drew a human being. It was as if the whole world of his imagination did not contain one. He doesn't see us, Ada thought, for the vacancy around him. She couldn't keep him in paper, paint, and pencils. Once a month she'd send for supplies by mail order. A carton would arrive, and by the end of the month it would be used up. And every evening after supper, they'd sit together on the porch or by the stove and he'd show her his pictures. Sometimes he'd make five or six all of the same thing, a particular part of the path to the pond, a willow tree with a nesting bird, a mule cart, did it over and over until somehow he was satisfied.

"You're a perfectionist," she told him. When he gave her that sweet, dumb, blank look, she explained.

"It means you're persnickety. You've got to get it right." He must have drawn that willow tree a hundred times. Every chance she got, Ada brought him to the pond, where it leaned into the water. Sometimes he wouldn't draw, only sat by the edge of the water, gazing into it, and no matter how excited he had been, rocking or worse, banging his head on the wall, it turned him tranquil and dreamy.

"You know what I think?" she said. "I think you're a genius. Are you a genius? Come on and tell me."

After a while, he began to mix the colors himself, until he got what he wanted. He liked soft colors the best—browns, grays, yellows, ochers, and reds. Ada thought it was because they were easier on his eyes. He couldn't stand brightness in his pictures any more than he could in real life, when he would go about with his face scrunched up and his eyes squeezed almost shut to keep out the light, or walk in the yard with his hands over his eyes. You'd think he'd bump into things, but he never did. At the last moment, something would tell him there was a rock or a tree in his path and he'd turn aside just in time. Like a bat, thought Ada. He's like a bat that hears echoes of things and so doesn't collide with them.

All along, she had never stopped talking to him, saying whatever came to mind as though he were a normal person who would hear what she was saying and answer back. Oh, he could hear, all right, more and better than she could—far-off thunder, a train whistle, a flock of geese a mile high. It was as though his hearing made up for what he couldn't see. She'd watch him lift his head and cock his ear.

"What is it, Pippo? Is it thunder?" If he gave a little smile, that meant yes and she knew to take the clothes down off the line and throw the tarp over the woodpile. And sure enough, a couple of hours later, there'd be a storm. Mostly, though, he wouldn't answer, just sit on the floor with his narrow back to her, his shoulder blades outlined under his shirt like the winglets of some flightless bird. But it was not for her to say what got through and what didn't.

Pippo had another gift. Perfect aim. She had found this out when he was twelve. It was the way he picked up a pebble and threw. It was always *at* something, and he would hit it nine times out of ten.

"Let's go out and play," she said to him one day. "I'll set you up." She put a tin can on top of a fence post and watched him pick out the stone he wanted, just the right size and shape. How he walked up and down, back and forth, drawing a bead on that can, settling on the range. And not till he was good and ready would he throw. At last, *ping!* It was amazing, considering that she couldn't hit the side of the toolshed with a shovel. It wasn't play. She could see that. It was business. A year later she was tossing the can up in the air. He'd be off in a corner, quivering as he waited for her to release it, then back would go that skinny white arm and *ping!*

"You!" she laughed, and pulled him to her. "With your weak eyes. It's a grace," she told him. "A donation."

One Sunday in church, the preacher was telling about David and Goliath, how David chose five smooth stones out of the brook and went forth to meet Goliath. How he put his hand in his shepherd's bag and took from thence a stone, and "slang it and smote the Philistine so that he fell upon his face to the earth." All at once, Ada sat straight up in the pew and almost said it out loud: slingshot! As soon as she got home, she looked in the Sunday-school reader for the picture of David, then went rummaging. From a piece of old rawhide, she cut strips for the handles, then stitched them to a swatch of canvas for the pouch. The whole thing didn't take her more than an hour. When she held it up for him to see, and he didn't, she took him outside and swung it round and round over her head. Because he still looked puzzled, she put a pebble in the pouch and showed him again, watched his head circle to follow the path of her arm. When she let go of one of the cords and the pebble shot out, understanding flamed up in his eyes.

"There now," she said. "It's your turn."

It didn't take him more than an hour to figure out how to use it. In six months that boy could hit the tin can in midair no matter where she threw it, or how she tried to trick him by pretending to toss it one way and throwing it back over her shoulder at the last minute. How could he tell? She guessed that he figured it out from the way her arm moved and from the sound the can made as it flew into the air, a sound only he could hear. Then she decided that it was instinct and had nothing to do with air currents or acceleration or curvature. One day she took him for a picnic up on Sleeping Giant, and when she saw him knock a crow out of the air, she knew he could take care of himself if the time came. Ever afterward, she thought it was God telling her what to do that Sunday in church.

He loved her to pet him. Ada never knew when the notion would strike him; he'd come running up to her and throw his arms around her legs, imprisoning her until she dropped everything and took him, big as he was, on her lap, and he'd all but purr. Oh, he did want to be loved, and never once did she turn him down. She knew what it was to want loving and find there was none to be had. Later, she thanked God for every single time she had held that boy in her arms and kissed him.

But as time went on, what was enough for her would not appease the world. There came the day when she heard a commotion out in the yard and looked out to see two big boys laughing and roaring outside the fence. One of them—she thought it was Lloyd Baskin's son—picked up a stone and threw it at Pippo, and then the other boy did the same. She saw Pippo get up from where he was squatting and scamper around the yard, flapping his arms and chittering at the fun, because neither of the stones had hit him. She knew that at that distance he could have hit them every time. But all at once, there was another stone, which hit him in the center of the forehead, and he fell down, bleeding. By the time she got to him, the big boys had run off. She knelt and turned him over into her lap, and saw his thin white face streaming blood.

"It's all right," she said. "All right." But he didn't so much as grasp her hand when she took his. Just lay there bleeding and blinking his little red eyes. Ada did what she knew, scooped him up—he weighed no more than seventy pounds—and carried him into the house and washed his wound and pressed it until it stopped bleeding, and she kissed and kissed him over and over. At that moment, if she could, she would have stuffed him back into her womb to keep him safe. Hours went by as she rocked him in her arms, her tears falling on his cheeks, and Mary, Mother of God, couldn't have felt worse with crucified Jesus on her lap. And Ada saw that over his countenance a veil had dropped. She could feel him falling away from her in a wail, but no sound came. The bright time is over, she said to herself. But it wasn't the wound in his forehead that told her, so much as the bloodless white wound that was his face. He had tasted of the fruit of the world, reached out for it with his heart full of joy, and found it bitter as the apples of Sodom. He wouldn't try again. Next morning, looking down at the purple dent in his forehead with the clotted blood around it, she told him:

"Don't you worry. I'll go outside with you from now on."

It was only weeks later that there was more trouble. It was a rainy day, but she had let him out anyway in his black raincoat.

"I'll be right out in a minute," she said. "You'll be all right."

And then: "Pippo, you're batty," she heard one of them call out; it was the same two boys and now two girls.

"Be a bat, Pippo," said another. All at once, from beyond the fence came a howl of pain. Pippo was standing in the middle of the yard, swinging the slingshot. He let fly another stone, and she heard another yelp behind the fence. She was out the door in a flash, just in time to see a third stone go sailing, the boys and girls running off, roaring, one holding his arm. Ada threw herself on Pippo, grabbing his arm so hard he whimpered.

"Here you, Pippo," she said, and shook him hard. "Don't, I said. Don't you ever do that again." She had never spoken to him like that, so harshly. "Because if you do, I'll take it away from you and you'll never see it again." When he raised his head to look at her, something wild and yellow blazed up in his eyes, then died down. It's fury, she thought. He's mad enough to bite me. The one time that he acted like a man, defending himself, she had stopped him. She held out her arm to his teeth.

"Bite me," she said. "Go ahead and bite me. I know you want to." And I want you to, she thought. Just for a moment, his lips drew back and quivered. But he didn't bite her, just sort of gave, went limp and still. Ada put her arm around him and drew him into the house.

It wasn't an hour later that Lloyd Baskin and two other men were at her door.

"He's dangerous, Ada. Wild. You've got to put him away." The hate in their eyes, the desire for revenge. It frightened her and she could not conceal her fear.

"The idea! Letting that crazy little geek have a slingshot when you know he's got the Devil's own eye. Get him out of here."

"I'll never do that," she said. "Never."

"Whatever happens, then, will be your fault." Please, she wanted to say, please leave us alone. She would have dropped to her knees and kissed the hem of Lloyd Baskin's garment, if she had to. Inside, she knew the boy was listening, still wearing his black raincoat.

It wasn't the same after that. For one thing, he stopped coming to her for her caresses. When she captured him on her lap, he would let her, but that was all. The need had become all hers. And there were no more smiles, only that look of erasure.

"You've got to forget about it," she told him. "Some boys are like that out there, some aren't." And once, she found herself wondering whether she ought to have listened to that doctor and put him away with others of his kind. But only once and never again. And all the while, Ada knew that something was coming, something terrible that she would have to face. She felt it ticking in her ear.

∽

It was eight o'clock on the morning of the first day of June. Pippo was still asleep. She opened the refrigerator to take out the milk, and found there wasn't any. Ada wondered whether she had time to get to the market and back before he woke up. She opened the door to his room. Yes, he was sleeping. Deeply, from his slow, even breathing. She closed the door and left the house. The walk there and back wouldn't take more than twenty minutes if she hurried. Already, it was hot. Her head drummed with sunshine. Coming back, she saw that the front door was open, and she knew. She raced through the house, calling out for him, looking in the closets and out in the yard. But all the while, she knew that he was gone.

Still carrying the bottle of milk, she ran down the path to the pond, crying his name, searching the sky for clues. That afternoon, they organized search parties, fanned out in all directions. He couldn't have gotten far, they told her. Not that half-pint. But Ada knew otherwise. With what was calling out to him or driving him away, he could have gone to China. At nightfall, when there had been no sign of him, they quit for the day. Don't you worry, Ada, they said. He'll come back with his tail between his legs as soon as he's hungry. Tail? she thought. And she might have laughed, if her heart weren't breaking. All night, she prowled the house. Had he left her a sign? But she found nothing, only that he had taken the tackle box with his paints, brushes, charcoal sticks. And his slingshot.

For a week they searched the woods, dragged the pond. A police helicopter rattled back and forth over the house. The sheriff came.

"Give it up, Ada. We're quitting. There's no place we haven't looked. He can't still be alive, not with everything hungry that's prowling out there, and him with no more strength than a newborn chicken, and the little bit of sense he had. Something has taken him by now—a bear, dogs, crows. He's gone. Give it up." But she couldn't give it up. As the weeks went by she could not keep her hands off the thought of him. Time and again she took him who was not there onto her lap, old as he was, and hugged him and sang into his ear until he laughed and scratched it for the tickling.

One day she met Lloyd Baskin on the street.

"It don't look good," he said. She thought he didn't mind letting her know. Well, maybe, but Ada wasn't convinced. And all that day and night she debated with Lloyd Baskin in her mind. When you were like Pippo, you didn't need to get any stronger or bigger or older to survive. You only had to know what was your range, and stay inside it. Besides, whatever instincts for survival he was going to get, he already had. He was born with them. Unless you were talking about human beings, survival wasn't at all a matter of intelligence or wit or even very much experience. It had to do with animal cunning, which is another way of saying intuition, something that seemed to her situated in the nerves and muscles, not the brain. As for being big and strong, that might be more of a handicap than anything. A sparrow didn't want to be big and strong, or a mouse. It wanted to be small and quick, and that's what Pippo was.

"We'll see," she said to Lloyd Baskin. Besides, Pippo had his sling-shot and could hit a crow taking off from a corn patch three out of four times. Maybe there's not much behind it, but he's got an eye up front, where it counts, she thought. Ada had heard about wild boys who were found in the forest after years of living like animals on roots, nuts, and small creatures. Hadn't they managed to survive? He's got all the sense he needs to get himself home. He just doesn't want to come home yet.

But now it was October, four months since he'd gone. For four months she had waited and watched; from behind the curtains, from the farthest edges of the pond, from the woods on the outskirts of the village. She had worn herself out watching. She had walked the streets calling his name out loud and in her heart, hunted in the grass for his footsteps, sniffed the trunks of trees, burned herself at the stove, forgotten to eat, and she who did not stumble, stumbled. And every night she lay herself down like ashes after the fire. She couldn't take it anymore. It was eating her up alive. Hope was worse than finality. Hell was better than limbo. Ada decided to clean out his room.

After the first week, she hadn't gone in there, just couldn't. But now it was time. Without looking to right or left, she marched straight to the closet. The sight of his clothes made her dizzy but she gripped herself hard and started taking down the hangers, carrying things to the bed. Back and forth three times, before she saw, tacked up on the wall behind the clothes rack, a painting she hadn't seen before. He always showed her his paintings, but she hadn't seen this one. Tacked up on the wall, but hidden behind the clothes. She had to wonder.

Ada took the picture down and brought it into the light. He'd used a page from his sketchbook. The picture showed Sleeping Giant in charcoal and watercolors. There was the old man of the mountain, lying on his back, half sunken into or half emerging from the earth. Arms at his sides, that blank Indian face shut in on itself, only here smudged with the shadow of a passing cloud, hands and feet hairy with shrubbery, the bare torso strewn with tawny boulders. Just as she had known it all her life, and Pippo too, from the many times they had gone there. And the whole of the mountain not muted, but yellow and hot with bright sunshine, everything casting a shadow. Her eyes swept across the length of the paper and back, from top to bottom, when, as if a finger had pointed, her gaze was caught and held at the black thumbnail, no more than an eighth of an inch across, near the bottom of the painting. And even that half hidden in tall weeds. Anyone could have missed it. Black, she thought. A black thumbnail? Perhaps it was a jot of charcoal he had meant to fill in, only forgot. No, it was black paint, a dab of it. Besides, he never forgot in his painting. Without reason in much else, he had a reason for every speck and line he drew. And Ada peered and peered until the black thumbnail softened and gave way so that she was looking through it, into a place behind that you could enter, a hole. "The cave," she said out loud.

Ada took off her apron, put a flashlight in her pocket, and left the house. A moment later, she returned, put three plums in her pocket, and left again. Already the sun was three quarters down the sky. It would be dark by the time she got there. It took an hour and a half to reach the foot of Sleeping Giant, then another thirty minutes up the steep path choked with briers. All the way, she berated herself for not finding it before, the message that maybe he had left for her and meant her to find, not to bring him home, but only that she should know. At the giant's hand, she stepped off the path into the underbrush. Not twenty paces in, she stopped, turned in a half circle, and there it was, partially obscured by small gray bushes that leaned across the entrance. The cave! The monstrous cave. She would stand it. She would have to. She stared at the mouth of the cave for a long while, inhaling the sour air that came from it, and she shivered with a premonition that went deep, deeper than sorrow. *No hope,* it seemed to say. *There is no hope.*

Ada stepped into the mouth of the cave, counted her steps to ten, then stopped, waiting for her eyes to accommodate to the darkness. Another ten paces, one blind foot fumbling after the other, her arms outstretched, parting the darkness like a swimmer parting water. Here the passageway was so narrow that she could reach out and touch the sweating walls; there, it broadened and she was left unmoored. The darkness swirled with violent shapes. All at once, fear, which she had not yet felt, slammed into her with an impact that made her stagger. Not of the darkness or whatever else was in it, but of something that dropped to her neck, then skittered off. She prayed for the strength she would need if she found him lying sprawled and lifeless. Or if she stumbled onto him with her foot. Spare me that, she cried to herself. At least not that. With trembling hands, she flicked on the flashlight she had not dared to use because of what she might see, and followed the beam to the wall of the cave. She reached out, palming the slime. She sprayed the light to the high vault, then down at the floor, where she saw, almost at her feet, something pale and gleaming. Bending closer, she drilled it with the light. Her heart hammered against her ribs. A skull! She could make out the jaw, a row of teeth. No, it was too small, and the teeth were those of an animal, a raccoon, perhaps. She touched it with her shoe, tapped it. Nearby there were other bones. A rib, the long bone of a leg, a scattering of dark fur, some feathers. But she could not bring herself to go deeper. Ada backed toward the mouth of the cave, guarding herself with the cone of light until she stood in the entrance. Then she remembered the plums, stepped back inside, and set them down just inside the opening.

When she left the cave, it was raining. On the way down the path she was watched carefully by a doe and her fawn. How they turned their narrow heads and pointed their ears as she passed! All the way home, in her mind, she saw him running into that cave for the first time, his black hair sticking out at his temples, accompanied only by his own terror, which she hoped had not gone inside with him, but had stayed out in the world from which he had run. So long as he stayed in that cave, he was safe. He had found the one place where he could live. From the bones and feathers, she guessed that he had already used his slingshot. Now he had all the darkness he could wish for, and no bright sun to burn his eyes. When she thought about it, the cave wasn't completely dark. The walls glowed with their own light, like phosphorus. After a while, you could see a bit, even without the flashlight. It was as dark as that when her front porch put its long arm around her and drew her inside the house.

The next day, Ada slept until noon. She decided to wait until late afternoon; there was less chance of being seen. At three o'clock, she filled a pint bottle with soup, buttered two slices of bread, and put it all in a paper bag. She unpacked a box of paint tubes that had come after he had gone, stuffed half a dozen in her pockets, tested the flashlight to make sure it was working, and set out for Sleeping Giant. It was five-thirty when she got there. Sunset, she saw, was preparing in the west. Without hesitation, she entered the cave, turned on the light, and edged slowly along the wall. The first thing she noticed was that the plums weren't where she had placed them. So that's it, she thought, and set down the bag of bread and soup.

"Pippo!" she called softly and heard her voice being swallowed by the cave. "Pippo!" She pressed her hand against the wall as if to invoke him from the stone. At twenty steps, the cave took a sharp turn. At thirty, she had to stoop low to get beneath a projection of rock. At fifty, she paused and listened to a tiny sound that grew suddenly, then died an instant later. Something slunk against her legs. When she looked down, there was nothing. When she looked up again, she saw on the wall the painted outline of a small hand. Ada advanced slowly. Another ten steps, another hand. And another. Here the cave narrowed to a cone, so that she had to go sideways and bend double. A dead end, she thought. He's not here. He's gone. Tears of disappointment ran down her face. She would leave—there was no more she could do.

But, look! Here was yet another hand, this one lower on the wall, at the level of her knees. Not pointing, but all the same, she thought, directing her gaze downward. Ada bent to see an opening in the rock, at ground level. It was no more than a foot and a half across, maybe two. The air coming from it was fetid and damp. She knelt down and lowered her head to peer in, but only the long beam of her flashlight was visible in the blackness. It was too small for her to crawl through. Ada flicked off the light and stood there in the dark. A greenish pallor seemed to float toward her from the stone walls.

The next day, Ada began her fast. I'm too fat, she thought. I can't get through, but soon I will, she insisted to some imagined adversary. Don't you worry, I will. It would be bread and water from then on. And it almost was. So help her, she didn't want a mouthful of anything else. It would have gagged her. Every afternoon she set out carrying a basket with the day's food, the flashlight, some painting supplies, a jackknife. Now and then, she'd stoop to pick up a stone that was the right size for the slingshot. Without flinching now, she entered the great cave, where by day all the world's darkness seemed to crowd it-self, massive and dense, until, with dusk, it seeped out to cover the earth once more. Once inside, her feet grew subtle as an animal's, committing the cave to memory. Now, without the flashlight, she could tell just when the cave took that sharp turn, where she had to bend down to keep from hitting her head. Now and then, she called out his name: "Pippo! Pippo!" But she knew he wouldn't answer or make a sign—except that whatever she put down in the entrance was gone the next morning. Something was working, something frag-ile that she knew she mustn't scare away.

Already her fear of the darkness was no longer absolute. She half liked it; half not. There was something sensual about it that was miss-ing in broad daylight. She could almost feel her pupils dilating to take it in, willing herself to become a piece of the darkness. In a cer-tain way, she could see why he hid from the sun. At the end of three weeks, Ada's clothes swam off her shoulders. She was two notches slimmer at the waist. Another week, and she would be ready to try. It would be tight, but she would have to see.

∽

Ada had arrived at the cave at dusk, her usual time, and had made her way inward some forty paces, about halfway to the tunnel, when something told her that the air was full of silent wings, beating. All around her head she heard a whisper, whisper, tiny squeaks. Panting like a dog, she pressed her back against the wall of the cave. Some-thing flickered at her throat. By the time she had raised her hand to brush it off, it had gone, leaving an unclean sensation on her skin. Something else struck her softly on the chest, then on the fingers. In the pale green glow, the roof rolled like something brought to a boil. Now and then a wave swept across it, shaking free fragments of itself to swing like censers. A steady rain of droppings pelted her. The smell of ammonia choked. All at once, the whole ceiling began to billow like a tent come loose from its peggings. In a moment it would collapse. Ada could not hold in her terror, but wailed, and raised her arms against whatever was coming down upon her, forced shut her lips lest she find her mouth filled with something furry, stiff hairs on her tongue. And she forced herself to remain still, to just stand beneath that heaving roof, letting the swarm pass over and around her, buffeting, glancing off. Once, she felt a fluttering inside her chest. It was as though a bat had slipped between her ribs. If she could only stay there and bear it, and not give in to what was coiled tight inside her and ready to lay her screaming on the ground. If she could get through this, she would never be afraid again.

At last it was over. The cave had disgorged its colony for the night's feeding. Ada inhaled deeply and pulled the sudden quiet of the cave into her lungs, stilling herself with it after what had boiled all about her, what had, on its surge to the outside, swept along with it all of her resolve. Hollow and exhausted, she staggered from the cave. No, she thought, I cannot. Not today. She would try tomorrow.

❧

The next day, at noon, Ada was still lying in bed, husbanding her strength for what was to come. Now and then, she slept. Hours later she was aroused by a commotion outside. There was the shouting of men, the sound of running feet, a truck started up urgently. Then more shouting as the truck pulled away.

"Where?"

"One of the caves at Sleeping Giant."

"What was it doing?"

"Squatting in front, skinning something."

"A white man. Big, the kids said, with wild staring eyes, all dressed in black rags. Soon as he saw the kids, he ran into the cave."

"We'll follow you."

Ada ran to the window in time to see the last of the truck. There were three men in it and the barrel of a shotgun rested on its window ledge. That would be Lloyd Baskin. She struggled not to faint, while gold lights came and went behind her eyelids and the pictures on the walls shook as if to fall off. She dressed and ran out of the house. If she took the path by the pond, they wouldn't see her.

Ada ran until she couldn't anymore, then walked, then ran again. At the base of the mountain, she saw where they had left the truck. But they hadn't known the way from there, not the way she did, so that when she came up, it was in time to see the back of a man disappearing into the mouth of the cave. Ada trembled. A moment later, she had slipped through the hole. In the invisibility it bestowed on her, she grew calm. Not more than ten paces ahead, she saw the beams of their searchlights jerking from side to side. When all at once they halted, she knew that it was at the debris of bones. She crept closer to hear. She knew that he could hear them too, that somewhere in the cave he was staring into the darkness and listening.

"Stay close."

"Where are you, Buddy?"

"You never know what it's got to throw at us."

"Watch out! Goddammit." In the torchlight, the faces of the men were the color of butcher's meat. How could they not know she was there? Her heart was as loud to her as a bass drum, and she tried to still it with her hand. Then, a voice from which all the bravery had gone:

"Maybe we should quit for now, Lloyd. Come back in the morning, now we know where he's hiding. It'll be dark outside in a while."

"You think so?"

They're afraid, she thought. She saw them huddling together. Why, she could see right through them, as though they were glass, see their fear. And then she feared them all the more. For she remembered something that happened years ago when she and Philip were living on the farm, before Pippo. Philip had gone up to the pasture and she was alone, in the barnyard, when two huge sows began fighting. They had been scared by the boar in the neighboring pen, which had, somehow, tossed a stone over the railing. She had never seen anything like it. The great tusks thrusting into each other, the hidden teeth burrowing and clamping. The screams, the blood, until they both lay mangled and dead. Ada remembered, and trembled.

She grew crafty. She, who had challenged the darkness again and again, would call upon it now to befriend her. Lifting her eyes and her arms to it, she prayed for twilight and its creatures to stream forth and darken the sky, for the exodus of the bats, which was like an echo of the setting sun. Come, Night! she all but hollered. They'll never stand it, she thought. Not the way she'd had to and would again, gladly. Her mind was a deep well of scorn as she stood there, her arms raised like a witch summoning up spirits and calling out to the vast horde to come down upon them.

But the men had not turned back; they were picking their way forward. Already they had come to the place where the cave angled to the right. A little farther and they would be at the tunnel into which, day and night, for weeks, she had dispatched her soul. Up ahead, she heard voices overlapping, echoing, but full now of the hisses and coughs of trepidation.

"Phew! It stinks here. Batshit."

"Watch your step! What's this? It stops here. Far as she goes."

"Unless we've missed a turnoff. What now?"

"Back, I guess. There's no place else to go. Whatever it was, or wasn't, has gone." Ada held her breath. They hadn't seen it. But just then:

"Here you go! An opening. Look."

"Where?"

"Down near the ground. Looks like a tunnel of some kind, narrow, though, about a foot and a half around, maybe four feet long."

"What do you see? Anything?"

"Nothin'. Empty space."

"Hey you! Come out of there or we'll block it up."

"Yeah, Lloyd. We better block it up." They were torn between the desire to turn and run and the desire to see him, to encircle and goad.

"Let's smoke him out. Throw the canister in." Ada saw the shadow of an upraised arm.

"Stop!" It was her own voice, imperious, as she had never heard it. The beams of light jumped like fish, then swung toward the sound of her voice. She let them come, let them seek her out, travel over her body to her face and stop there, blinding her. She stared straight into them.

"What the hell! Who?"

"Ada! What the hell!"

"I can get through," she said quietly.

"No you don't. Keep out of this, Ada. Now you're here, we can't send you back. But stay the hell out of the way. If you think it's your boy . . ." She headed straight into the converged beams of light, took them full on her breast. Then reached for one of the flashlights. It came free from the hand that held it—willingly, she thought.

"Let her do it, Lloyd. If she can get in, she can damn well get out." Ada was already on her knees in front of the opening, then flat, her thin arms stretched in front. She let go of the flashlight and began scrabbling in the muddy floor. It was tight. For the first foot, there was hope; she clawed and toed her way for several inches, flicked the flashlight ahead with the backs of her fingers. At that point the passage narrowed. The back of her head hit against rock. Pebbly mud slid between her lips. Her shoulders wedged, scraped; more pushing with her toes. Another inch of progress. All at once, her strength left her, and she lay exhausted. Her chest, heaving, strained against the floor. She was clamped in a vise, had swollen to fill it. How could she have thought herself able to do it? Behind her, the voices of the men.

"You makin' it, Ada?" She forced down panic. Expelling all the air from her lungs, she sank her fingers into the stone floor, pushed with her feet. Her shoulders were throbbing with pain, something warm running down from her head. Then, bursting through the narrows, her shoulders spilling out into space. Kicking, pushing with her freed arms, until she was in. She had done it. A place so cool and damp and still, a tomb. No current of air. She stood shakily, reached up to touch her throbbing shoulder, felt the blood on her hand. Now she groped for the flashlight, flicked it on, and turned the beam in a slow, tentative circle. The floor was covered with silt. In the absolute humidity she was breathless. Within minutes she was dripping with the cold condensation. The walls of the chamber were a soft sandy color. At one place, water ran slowly down, screening it darkly. Spectral little beasts—white beetles, crayfish, and pink salamanders—scurried out of range of the light. A recess in the wall coned down into a kind of passageway. She followed it, stooping low, stepping through shallow pools into which small insects plopped.

"Pippo!" she said softly. "Pippo, it's me. Don't be afraid. Please, Pippo, if you are here, let me know." There was no sound other than her own voice. "Pippo!" she called louder, and heard the name come echoing back to her. She must not let the men hear. All at once, her mind filled with the knowledge of his presence. He was here. She knew it. Her heart leaped and volleyed; she was panting. Ada let the light rove the walls, moving it upward little by little. All at once, it jumped in her hand. At one corner of the circle of light, something large and black hovered high, near the ceiling. Perhaps she thought rather than saw it? Holding the light with both hands to steady it, she brought whatever it might be into view.

He was hanging from what must be a narrow ridge, clinging with his fingers. His arms and legs, like sticks, emerged from a tatter of black rags. In the darkness of the cave, his skin was milk-white. The sinews stood out like rods with the effort of clinging. A tangle of black hair framed a face behind which the skull threatened to pop through.

"Pippo," she whispered. "Come down here to me. I won't hurt you. Oh, how I've missed you and worried. Come down." She came closer until she could see the droplets of moisture caught in the cloud of his hair. They glistened as he turned his head to stare down behind him. The little muscles around his nose and mouth twitched. His eyes, no longer red and watery, but dry and white, seemed to reach for her like suckers. The sight of him calmed her. The violent fluttering of her heart slowed. She stepped closer until she was just below him, then raised her hand. The dead-white eyes never left her.

"Take my hand," she said. "Touch me." Even on tiptoe she could not reach him. He made not the smallest movement, but clung motionless to whatever small crevice or jutting he had grasped. It was as though he were speaking to her for the first time. Let me be—he said it to her with his eyes, white as picked lilies. Let me stay—he begged her with his scrabbling fingers. If you take me out, I will die.

From far above, she heard the men calling, their words echoing.

"Ada! Get back here. You come back here right now-ow-ow."

"I'm coming . . . there's nobody here." She turned back to the boy. "Tomorrow," she whispered. "Tomorrow."

Then loudly, over her shoulder, she called out, "I'm coming."

The squeeze through the canal seemed to her not half so hard as before, as though the cave itself were not anxious to retain her. Once through, she stood up. From the other side of the tunnel came a low moan as of air entering an unseen cleft.

"It's empty," she told the men. "There's no one there."

"It's about time, damn you, Ada. We had half a mind to leave you here to rot. Jesus! You're covered with blood."

"Those kids must have made it up."

"Let's get out of here. Those kids are in for one hell of a licking." Ada submitted passively, followed them as they hurried each other along. They couldn't wait to get out. A queer sensation flooded her. It was, she thought, something like the happiness of the outlaw for whom eternal flight was preferable to life as a law-abiding citizen.

"Tomorrow," she whispered to herself. "Tomorrow."

They were no more than fifty steps from the entrance when Ada felt it coming. Felt the entire cave turn over in its sleep, the air thrilling with wings. She willed her body to shut down, to still itself until she was no more than another palpitation in the dark disquiet. And she stood, arms akimbo, in the teeth of the onslaught, fearless and grateful, receiving the fluttering horde, drawing them upon her arms like sleeves, while, ahead, she saw the men flailing about, stamping, yelling in their terror, staggering into one another. Through minutes of it she stood, relishing the plague she had brought down upon their heads to which only she was immune. And she marveled at the power of love that drives even the fear of death out of the heart. "Jesus!" they screamed. And "Jesus!" When it had passed, she saw them gather themselves up, whipped, and leave the cave once and for all. They would not return.

Ada waited until she heard the truck start up and drive off before she, too, stepped from the cave. It was almost midnight when she opened the door of her house, her shoulders throbbing where the stone of the passageway had bitten in, her fingertips stinging raw from the scrabbling to which she had set them. That night she did not go to bed, but sat in the chair rocking, rocking, and thinking of his white forehead boring through the tunnel and of that chamber all about and above her with everything that was alive and quivering in its high reaches. At precisely five o'clock the next afternoon, she rose and washed herself with water from the china pitcher, thrusting her head into the bowl of cold water again and again until she felt clean and hard and sharp. When she left the house, she was carrying only the kerosene lamp and a box of matches. During the whole of that day she had made only one decision—to take a kerosene lantern. A flashlight, she decided, would not do for a chamber what it would a passageway.

∾

The small black eye of the channel gazed gravely up at her. She knelt, then lay down on the slimy floor, her arms stretched forward. She had thrust the lamp on ahead as far as she could. Raking with her fingers, she pulled herself forward, using her hips and knees until once again she lay in the clutch of stone. Then, bending her ankles, she pushed with her toes. It was slow; minutes went by seemingly without a bit of progress. The channel bit into her head, her arms. She felt a hard pressure on her chest. For one moment, she felt a wave of nausea, but she fought it down, and alternated her thrusts with deep exhalations. When she felt the sudden little give, and felt the rock cut deeply into her flesh, she heard herself moan.

Now her head was free and gasping into space. A push, a clawing at nothing, a tiny twist. One shoulder through. Then the other, then gathering her chest, trunk, abdomen, and legs behind her like the segments of a worm, she flung what was left of her torn body through into freedom. She stood, groped for the lamp, touched a match to the wick, and held it aloft. She stepped toward the wall where she had seen him suspended the day before. Back and forth, up and down, she swung the lantern. He was not there. Only, high on the wall, near the recess leading to the next corridor, the imprint of his hand. She went toward the niche, and stooped to enter the next chamber.

Ada found herself in a high-domed room with inward sloping walls. She stepped to the center of the room and raised the lantern; she gasped. Riding across the walls was a frieze of many cattle, their curved horns intersecting, tails describing patterns. Here a bull jumped, while another lowered its horns. There, a donkey waggled its ears. Horses reared. Trees arched near the ceiling, with bats in full flight or hanging like leaves. And the colors—ocher, brown, reddish brown, yellow, gray—his colors. Each figure etched into the wall with something sharp, a rock, she guessed, then outlined in charcoal and painted. She saw how he had used the curves and hollows of the walls to give the animals movement, to make them gallop or pant. The flickering of the lantern gave flight to the bats. Ada had the feeling that she was standing on a great plain where herds were galloping and swirling about her. She seemed to hear their lowing, the shrieking of birds, the thudding of prehistoric hooves, and though she could neither name nor place them, memories were being stirred somewhere deep within her.

It is the creation of the world I am beholding, she thought. But a world not meant to be seen. Why? It was just the urge to make it, she thought. Gazing about her, Ada felt that she could at last see into the heart of the boy, which had always been hidden from her. Here it was, illuminated. She walked the circumference of the chamber, her lamp held high, searching the walls for him. But he was not there. She would go home, then. She had to think. No one could tell her what to do. Ada had turned to leave the chamber when her foot touched something soft, and she stumbled, almost fell. She lowered the lamp to see his foot, thin and white, the delicate toes. He lay where he had fallen, his moth-white face bent backward, too far back, and twisted on his neck. The blinding white stripe of his teeth, his wrinkled nose, the eyes, pale and staring.

In the midst of that glory of herds, that flight of birds, all of his exquisite seed sown there in the darkness, Ada rejoiced in the full-grown manhood that at last he had won. She looked down again at the thin twisted neck, the narrow bloody paws with their tiny talons, the cracked head pasted to the floor of the cave with black blood. Then, all about his head and body, she saw pulsating a halo of pale beetles, crayfish, salamanders, scurrying at his face, his fingers, and her grief welled up anew. Weeping, she set down the lamp, knelt, and wiped her hands again and again across the floor of the cave, gathering the wet silt into her palms, then turned to smear him—cheek, brow, hands, and feet—with the slimy earth. Then Ada lay down beside him, settled herself, and watched the waning lamplight enliven the herds until, at last, the flame died down, blazed up, died down, and went out.

The Masked Marvel's Last Toehold

Morning rounds.

On the fifth floor of the hospital, in the west wing, I know that a man is sitting up in his bed, waiting for me. Elihu Koontz is seventy-five, and he is diabetic. It is two weeks since I amputated his left leg just below the knee. I walk down the corridor, but I do not go straight into his room. Instead, I pause in the doorway. He is not yet aware of my presence, but gazes down at the place in the bed where his leg used to be, and where now there is the collapsed leg of his pajamas. He is totally absorbed, like an athlete appraising the details of his body. What is he thinking? I wonder. Is he dreaming the outline of his toes? Does he see there his foot's incandescent ghost? Could he be angry? Feel that I have taken from him something for which he yearns now with all his heart? Has he forgotten so soon the pain? It was a pain so great as to set him apart from all other men, in a red-hot place where he had no kith or kin. What of those black gorilla toes and the soupy mess that was his heel? I watch him from the doorway. It is a kind of spying, I know.

Save for a white fringe open at the front, Elihu Koontz is bald. The hair has grown too long and is wilted. He wears it as one would wear a day-old laurel wreath. He is naked to the waist, so that I can see his breasts. They are the breasts of Buddha, inverted triangles from which the nipples swing, dark as garnets.

I have seen enough. I step into the room, and he sees that I am there.

"How did the night go, Elihu?"

He looks at me for a long moment. "Shut the door," he says.

I do, and move to the side of the bed. He takes my left hand in both of his, gazes at it, turns it over, then back, fondling, at last holding it up to his cheek. I do not withdraw from this loving. After a while he relinquishes my hand, and looks up at me.

"How is the pain?" I ask.

He does not answer, but continues to look at me in silence. I know at once that he has made a decision.

"Ever hear of the Masked Marvel?" He says this in a low voice, almost a whisper.

"What?"

"The Masked Marvel," he says. "You never heard of him?"

"No."

He clucks his tongue. He is exasperated.

All at once there is a recollection. It is dim, distant, but coming near.

"Do you mean the wrestler?"

Eagerly, he nods, and the breasts bob. How gnomish he looks, oval as the huge helpless egg of some outlandish lizard. He has very long arms, which, now and then, he unfurls to reach for things—a carafe of water, a get-well card. He gazes up at me, urging. He *wants* me to remember.

"Well . . . yes," I say. I am straining backward in time. "I saw him wrestle in Toronto long ago."

"Ha!" He smiles. "You saw *me*." And his index finger, held rigid and upright, bounces in the air.

The man has said something shocking, unacceptable. It must be challenged.

"You?" I am trying to smile.

Again that jab of the finger. "You saw *me*."

"No," I say. But even then, something about Elihu Koontz, those prolonged arms, the shape of his head, the sudden agility with which he leans from his bed to get a large brown envelope from his nightstand, something is forcing me toward a memory. He rummages through his papers, old newspaper clippings, photographs, and I remember. . . .

∾

It is almost forty years ago. I am ten years old. I have been sent to Toronto to spend the summer with relatives. Uncle Max has bought two tickets to the wrestling match. He is taking me that night.

"He isn't allowed," says Aunt Sarah to me. Uncle Max has angina.

"He gets too excited," she says.

"I wish you wouldn't go, Max," she says.

"You mind your own business," he says.

And we go. Out into the warm Canadian evening. I am not only abroad, I am abroad in the *evening!* I have never been taken out in the evening. I am terribly excited. The trolleys, the lights, the horns. It is a bazaar. At the Maple Leaf Gardens, we sit high and near the center. The vast arena is dark except for the brilliance of the ring at the bottom.

It begins.

The wrestlers circle. They grapple. They are all haunch and paunch. I am shocked by their ugliness, but I do not show it. Uncle Max is exhilarated. He leans forward, his eyes unblinking, on his face a look of enormous happiness. One after the other, a pair of wrestlers enter the ring. The two men join, twist, jerk, tug, bend, yank, and throw. Then they leave and are replaced by another pair. At last it is the main event. "The Angel vs. the Masked Marvel."

On the cover of the program notes, there is a picture of the Angel hanging from the limb of a tree, a noose of thick rope around his neck. The Angel hangs just so for an hour every day, it is explained, to strengthen his neck. The Masked Marvel's trademark is a black stocking cap with holes for the eyes and mouth. He is never seen without it, states the program. No one knows who the Masked Marvel really is!

"Good," says Uncle Max. "Now you'll see something." He is fidgeting, waiting for them to appear. They come down separate aisles, climb into the ring from opposite sides. I have never seen anything like them. It is the Angel's neck that first captures the eye. The shaved nape rises in twin columns to puff into the white hood of a sloped and bosselated skull that is too small. As though, strangled by the sinews of that neck, the skull had long since withered and shrunk. The thing about the Angel is the absence of any mystery in his body. It is simply *there*. A monosyllabic announcement. A grunt. One looks and knows everything at once, the fat thighs, the gigantic buttocks, the great spine from which hang knotted ropes and pale aprons of beef. And that prehistoric head. He is all of a single hideous piece, the Angel is. No detachables.

The Masked Marvel seems dwarfish. His fingers dangle kneeward. His short legs are slightly bowed as if under the weight of the cask they are forced to heft about. He has breasts that swing when he moves! I have never seen such breasts on a man before.

There is a sudden ungraceful movement, and they close upon one another. The Angel stoops and hugs the Marvel about the waist, locking his hands behind the Marvel's back. Now he straightens and lifts the Marvel as though he were uprooting a tree. Thus he holds him, then stoops again, thrusts one hand through the Marvel's crotch, and with the other grabs him by the neck. He rears and . . . the Marvel is aloft! For a long moment, the Angel stands as though deciding where to make the toss. Then throws. Was that board or bone that splintered there? Again and again, the Angel hurls himself upon the body of the Masked Marvel.

Now the Angel rises over the fallen Marvel, picks up one foot in both of his hands, and twists the toes downward. It is far beyond the tensile strength of mere ligament, mere cartilage. The Masked Marvel does not hide his agony, but pounds and slaps the floor with his hand, now and then reaching up toward the Angel in an attitude of supplication. I have never seen such suffering. And all the while his black mask rolls from side to side, the mouth pulled to a tight slit through which issues an endless hiss that I can hear from where I sit. All at once, I hear a shouting close by.

"Break it off! Tear off a leg and throw it up here!"

It is Uncle Max. Even in the darkness I can see that he is gray. A band of sweat stands upon his upper lip. He is on his feet now, panting, one fist pressed at his chest, the other raised warlike toward the ring. For the first time I begin to think that something terrible might happen here. Aunt Sarah was right.

"Sit down, Uncle Max," I say. "Take a pill, please."

He reaches for the pillbox, gropes, and swallows without taking his gaze from the wrestlers. I wait for him to sit down.

"That's not fair," I say, "twisting his toes like that."

"It's the toehold," he explains.

"But it's not *fair*," I say again. The whole of the evil is laid open for me to perceive. I am trembling.

And now the Angel does something unspeakable. Holding the foot of the Marvel at full twist with one hand, he bends and grasps the mask where it clings to the back of the Marvel's head. And he pulls. He is going to strip it off! Lay bare an ultimate carnal mystery! Suddenly it is beyond mere physical violence. Now I am on my feet, shouting into the Maple Leaf Gardens.

"Watch out," I scream. "Stop him. Please, somebody, stop him."

Next to me, Uncle Max is chuckling.

Yet the Masked Marvel hears me, I know it. And rallies from his bed of pain. Thrusting with his free heel, he strikes the Angel at the back of the knee. The Angel falls. The Masked Marvel is on top of him, pinning his shoulders to the mat. One! Two! Three! And it is over. Uncle Max is strangely still. I am gasping for breath. All this I remember as I stand at the bedside of Elihu Koontz.

∽

Once again, I am in the operating room. It is two years since I amputated the left leg of Elihu Koontz. Now it is his right leg which is gangrenous. I have already scrubbed. I stand to one side wearing my gown and gloves. And . . . *I am masked.* Upon the table lies Elihu Koontz, pinned in a fierce white light. Spinal anesthesia has been administered. One of his arms is taped to a board placed at a right angle to his body. Into this arm, a needle has been placed. Fluid drips here from a bottle overhead. With his other hand, Elihu Koontz beats feebly at the side of the operating table. His head rolls from side to side. His mouth is pulled into weeping. It seems to me that I have never seen such misery.

An orderly stands at the foot of the table, holding Elihu Koontz's leg aloft by the toes so that the intern can scrub the limb with antiseptic solutions. The intern paints the foot, ankle, leg, and thigh, both front and back, three times. From a corner of the room where I wait, I look down as from an amphitheater. Then I think of Uncle Max yelling, "Tear off a leg. Throw it up here." And I think that forty years later I am making the catch.

"It's not fair," I say aloud. But no one hears me. I step forward to break the Masked Marvel's last toehold.

Mercy

*I*t is October at the Villa Serbelloni, where I have come for a month to write. On the window ledges the cluster flies are dying. The climate is full of uncertainty. Should it cool down? Or warm up? Each day it overshoots the mark, veering from frost to steam. The flies have no uncertainty. They understand that their time has come.

What a lot of energy it takes to die! The frenzy of it. Long after they have collapsed and stayed motionless, the flies are capable of suddenly spinning so rapidly that they cannot be seen. Or seen only as a blurred glitter. They are like dervishes who whirl, then stop, and lay as quiet as before, only now and then waving a leg or two feebly, in a stuporous reenactment of locomotion. Until the very moment of death, the awful buzzing as though to swarm again.

Every morning I scoop up three dozen or so corpses with a dustpan and brush. Into the wastebasket they go, and I sit to begin the day's writing. All at once, from the wastebasket, the frantic knocking of resurrection. Here, death has not yet secured the premises. No matter the numbers slaughtered, no matter that the windows be kept shut all day, each evening the flies gather on the ledges to die, as they have lived, *ensemble*. It must be companionable to die so, matching spin for spin, knock for knock, and buzz for buzz with one's fellows. We humans have no such fraternity, but each of us must buzz and spin and knock alone.

I think of a man in New Haven! He has been my patient for seven years, ever since the day I explored his abdomen in the operating room and found the surprise lurking there—a cancer of the pancreas. He was forty-two years old then. For this man, these have been seven years of famine. For his wife and his mother as well. Until three days ago his suffering was marked by slowly increasing pain, vomiting, and fatigue. Still, it was endurable. With morphine. Three days ago the pain rollicked out of control, and he entered that elect band whose suffering cannot be relieved by any means short of death. In his bed at home he seemed an eighty-pound concentrate of pain from which all other pain must be made by serial dilution. He twisted under the last of it. An ambulance arrived. At the hospital nothing was to be done to prolong his life. Only the administration of large doses of narcotics.

∽

"Please," he begs me. In his open mouth, upon his teeth, a brown paste of saliva. All night long he has thrashed, as though to hollow out a grave in the bed.

"I won't let you suffer," I tell him. In his struggle the sheet is thrust aside. I see the old abandoned incision, the belly stuffed with tumor. His penis, even, is skinny. One foot with five blue toes is exposed. In my cupped hand, they are cold. I think of the twenty bones of that foot laced together with tendon, each ray accompanied by its own nerve and artery. Now, this foot seems a beautiful dead animal that had once been trained to transmit the command of a man's brain to the earth.

"I'll get rid of the pain," I tell his wife.

But there is no way to kill the pain without killing the man who owns it. Morphine to the lethal dose . . . and still he miaows and bays and makes other sounds like a boat breaking up in a heavy sea. I think his pain will live on long after he dies.

"Please," begs his wife, "we cannot go on like this."

"Do it," says the old woman, his mother. "Do it now."

"To give him any more would kill him," I tell her.

"Then do it," she says. The face of the old woman is hoof-beaten with intersecting curves of loose skin. Her hair is donkey brown, donkey gray.

They wait with him while I go to the nurses' station to prepare the syringes. It is a thing that I cannot ask anyone to do for me. When I return to the room, there are three loaded syringes in my hand, a rubber tourniquet, and an alcohol sponge. Alcohol sponge! To prevent infection? The old woman is standing on a small stool and leaning over the side rail of the bed. Her bosom is just above his upturned face, as though she were weaning him with sorrow and gentleness from her still-full breasts. All at once she says severely, the way she must have said it to him years ago:

"Go home, son. Go home now."

I wait just inside the doorway. The only sound is a flapping, a rustling, as in a room to which a small animal, a bat perhaps, has retreated to die. The women turn to leave. There is neither gratitude nor reproach in their gaze. I should be hooded.

At last we are alone. I stand at the bedside.

"Listen," I say, "I can get rid of the pain." The man's eyes regain their focus. His gaze is like a wound that radiates its pain outward so that all upon whom it fell would know the need of relief.

"With these." I hold up the syringes.

"Yes," he gasps. "Yes." And while the rest of his body stirs in answer to the pain, he holds his left, his acquiescent arm, still for the tourniquet. An even dew of sweat covers his body. I wipe the skin with the alcohol sponge, and tap the arm smartly to bring out the veins. There is one that is still patent; the others have long since clotted and broken down. I go to insert the needle, but the tourniquet has come unknotted; the vein has collapsed. Damn! Again I tie the tourniquet. Slowly the vein fills with blood. This time it stays distended.

He reacts not at all to the puncture. In a wild sea what is one tiny wave? I press the barrel and deposit the load, detach the syringe from the needle and replace it with the second syringe. I send this home, and go on to the third. When they are all given, I pull out the needle. A drop of blood blooms on his forearm. I blot it with the alcohol sponge. It is done. In less than a minute, it is done.

"Go home," I say, repeating the words of the old woman. I turn off the light. In the darkness the contents of the bed are theoretical. No! I must watch. I turn the light back on. How reduced he is, a folded parcel, something chipped-away until only its shape and a little breath are left. His impatient bones gleam as though to burst through the papery skin. I am impatient too. I want to get it over with, then step out into the corridor where the women are waiting. His death is like a jewel to them.

My fingers at his pulse. The same rhythm as mine! As though there were one pulse that beat throughout all of nature, and every creature's heart throbbed precisely.

"You can go home now," I say. The familiar emaciated body untenses. The respirations slow down. Eight per minute . . . six . . . It won't be long. The pulse wavers in and out of touch. It won't be long.

"Is that better?" I ask him. His gaze is distant, opaque, preoccupied. Minutes go by. Outside, in the corridor, the murmuring of women's voices.

But this man will not die! The skeleton rouses from its stupor. The snout twitches as if to fend off a fly. What is it that shakes him like a gourd full of beans? The pulse returns, melts away, comes back again, and stays. The respirations are twelve, then fourteen. I have not done it. I did not murder him. I am innocent!

I shall walk out of the room into the corridor. They will look at me, holding their breath, expectant. I lift the sheet to cover him. All at once, there is a sharp sting in my thumb. The same needle with which I meant to kill him has pricked *me*. A drop of blood appears. I press it with the alcohol sponge. My fresh blood deepens the stain of his on the gauze. Never mind. The man in the bed swallows. His Adam's apple bobs slowly. It would be so easy to do it. Three minutes of pressure on the larynx. He is still not conscious, wouldn't feel it, wouldn't know. My thumb and fingertips hover, land on his windpipe. My pulse beating in his neck, his in mine. I look back over my shoulder. No one. Two bare IV poles in a corner, their looped metal eyes witnessing. Do it! Fingers press. Again he swallows. Look back again. How closed the door is. And . . . my hand wilts. I cannot. It is not in me to do it. Not that way. The man's head swivels like an upturned fish. The squadron of ribs battles on.

I back away from the bed, turn and flee toward the doorway. In the mirror, a glimpse of my face. It is the face of someone who has been resuscitated after a long period of cardiac arrest. There is no spot of color in the cheeks, as though this person were in shock at what he had just seen on the yonder side of the grave.

In the corridor the women lean against the wall, against each other. They are like a band of angels dispatched here to take possession of his body. It is the only thing that will satisfy them.

"He didn't die," I say. "He won't . . . or can't." They are silent.

"He isn't ready yet," I say.

"He *is* ready," the old woman says. "*You* ain't."

Poe's Light-house

My name is John Jacob Moran. There would be no reason that the world should take cognizance of me—more than of any other poor young house doctor—had it not been given to me thirty years ago to preside over the death of Edgar Allan Poe. On the third of October in the year 1849 a man by that name was placed under my care at Washington Hospital in Baltimore. The patient presented in critical condition. The cold sweat with which he was drenched, his pallor, the wild tremor of his limbs, the hallucinations in which he conversed with imaginary creatures on the walls, and the odor of alcohol on his breath bespoke the diagnosis of acute alcoholic intoxication with delirium. All this is a matter of record and can be confirmed by reference to the hospital charts written by me thirty years ago. I shall not revisit here the wreckage of the body of Edgar Allan Poe. What is not known is that during the five days of my attendance upon the patient, each one marked by toxic madness and stupor, there were brief episodes of utter clarity in which the poet spoke to me of his enslavement to drink, his dashed hopes, the loss of love, and, in a voice full of bitterness, of having betrayed his art. During one such interval, while I sat at the bedside, he told me that, only days before, he had begun to write a new tale called "The Light-house." At the mention of the title, his face took on a glow of reverie as though he had once again caught up the thread of his story. But in a moment the glow had vanished and was replaced by a look of profound sorrow.

"Now, never to be written," he cried aloud. In an effort to distract the man from his torment and in hopes of lifting his spirits, I asked him to tell me the story. For several minutes he lay silent, eyes closed. He seemed to me to be rummaging through the wild tangle of his thoughts. At last, he gave a deep sigh and began to speak.

" 'The Light-house,' " he said. "By Edgar Allan Poe." Unbeknownst to him, I had motioned to a nurse to bring paper, ink, and pen, for it was my thought to take down the story as he spoke it so that should he by some divine intervention recover, he would be able to complete the manuscript. Should he fail to recover, the world would have this last outpouring of his genius. And so for the space of a quarter of an hour he spoke; and so I wrote. At the end of which, I looked up to see that he had drifted into a peaceful sleep. It was a sleep from which Edgar Allan Poe was not to awaken. Two days later he was dead.

That, as I have said, was thirty years ago. In the three decades that have followed I have attended the last illness of many hundreds of patients, all of whose agonal suffering I have let slip from my memory. It is only to the deathbed of Edgar Allan Poe that I have felt myself summoned time and again as if by the restless whispering of his soul; summoned as well to the fragment of the story that I who have not at all a literary cast of mind now feel compelled by a will other than my own to complete. For where is it written that the ministrations of the doctor must end with his patient's death? What follows is "The Light-house" by Edgar Allan Poe. I offer it in homage to the dead poet. May it lay to rest his ghost. Let the reader divine at what place in the story the master laid down his pen and where I, in all humility, took it into my own hand.

ᨑ

I am one of the damned. Not as others of my race do I wander the earth in futile search of rest. Nor do I twist under the lash of physical torment. No, mine is a sickness of the soul such as to alienate me from my fellow man, to set me apart from all others without hope of love or friendship.

It was as a boy of ten that I first began to exhibit the strange behavior that has persisted over these thirteen years. Until that time, I had led a life of privilege and luxury, as the third son of the Lord of Friesling. I was unacquainted with affliction or grief.

The day was the Sabbath. I had been seated in the ducal chamber among the young courtiers and nobles who composed the household when a sudden uncontrollable urge to shout came over me. To the horror of those assembled, I interrupted the priestly service with a hoarse guttural cry that had no similarity to the voice of a young boy but was more that of an animal snarling. This was followed by another cry, and another. At my father's order, I was led from the premises in disgrace, beaten, and confined to my rooms. It was the first of many such punishments, none of which had the least effect in putting an end to these outrages. Within weeks, I had added to my repertoire peals of hellish laughter and screams of invective that included the most obscene words in the language, words that a boy of so tender an age would not have been thought to know, words that I must evacuate from my mouth or strangle on them. Even now, I shrink to write them down lest the mere ink upon the page be an invocation to the Devil.

Nor did I select my audience but, to the shame and horror of my next of kin and the entire household, gave forth in front of whatever company happened to be present, plucking from my throat the whole orchestra of curses that were my sole means of relief, however transitory. From this beginning, I advanced to the further extravagance of mimicking my elders, repeating again and again, so as seeming to mock them, whatever phrases they spoke. Before long these utterances were accompanied by a violent thrusting of my tongue, spasms of my head and shoulders, all punctuated by the most disgusting barks, grunts, and hisses. The more punishment I received, the more frequent came the seizures until they occurred as often as ten and fifteen times in the course of a day. My parents and brothers, the servants, too, were distraught. The entire atmosphere of the castle turned to one of despair and gloom. What was to be done with me? At last, I was sent, along with an elderly valet, Nils, to live in an isolated hunting lodge on the edge of a great woods in the far corner of my father's estate. Here, under the aegis of a kindly uncle, I was to live out my dishonored life until such time as I had been reformed.

To this lodge each day, a new physician came *en retinue*, each with his own diagnosis and prescription: bloodletting, purgatives, enemas—all the ghastly therapy of subtraction. When these failed, I was plunged alternately into hot and cold baths; stoups, poultices, and plasters of hot oil and turpentine were applied to my entire body. Bees were placed upon my lips so as to swell them shut with stinging. Emetics and all sorts of obnoxious medications were funneled into my mouth. At length a company of soldiers was dispatched to obtain a flagon of salutary water from the fountain of Saint Hildegard, said to be effective against lycanthropy. A single mouthful of the fetid ammoniacal slime produced the most violent retching and abdominal pain. When these medical martyrdoms produced no subsidence of my horrid idiosyncrasies, I was referred to the priests. What was needed was a thorough exorcism, it was decided. On the appointed day, a Goliath of a priest—he could have strangled a wolf with his rosary—advanced upon me, holding aloft a silver crucifix, grinding his teeth, blowing out his cheeks, sweating until it seemed he, not I, harbored the demon. But when a day and a night of holy gymnastics only incited me to yet greater heights of echolalia, the brutish priest struck the Devil a last righteous blow across the face that left me senseless, and departed.

It was decided that I was mad. But, alas, I was not mad. Nor am I now. Possessed? Infested? Perhaps, but utterly sane. And beyond the power of any mere priest or physician to set me free. Subsisting as it does upon the unnatural violation of the laws of man and God, mine is a perversion of such cunning and tenacity as to confound all but the one whose body is its instrument. I grew familiar with the spiteful characteristics which insisted that the outbursts occur only in the presence of another human being. Alone and out of earshot, I remained beautifully silent. Nor, as the old valet told me, did the eruptions occur in sleep. In my isolated dwelling, with only the necessary presence of Nils and the daily visit of my dear uncle, the demon—for that is what I must call it—lay largely dormant, allowing me some dignity. Yet I was far from happy. My perpetual solitude seems to me a living death. I longed for the comrades I knew I could never have. All day I studied and played like a wild thing, to tire myself out.

Upon my eighteenth birthday, the tenth of February, my uncle presented me with a pair of ornate pistols. Toward midnight, faithful Nils departed after seeing to my needs, but not before I had again scourged him with my tongue, though surely not with my heart, for I had come to love the old man. Yet I disclosed nothing to him of the grim purpose that had suddenly revealed itself to me. Alone, I took up one of the pistols. Through the casement, a full moon washed the contents of my room, where, by the bed, I knelt to pray for forgiveness. Youth bids farewell to the moon more easily than to the sun. But prayer would not come, only a last curse that I flung straight in the face of the cruel God who had created such an aberrance as I. No sooner had it been uttered than the door was flung open and my servant pulled me from the room. The house was in flames, and by daybreak, the lodge and with it my beloved uncle had been consumed. The grief that followed was tainted. I mourned, but in my secret heart I could not but feel that my last terrible oath had called down this conflagration. And not even Death would receive me.

When my brothers arrived, I gave myself into their hands. They brought me back to the ancestral house, where once again I was assailed by the numbers and witch words that called forth the demon. Time and again, family and guests were struck to horrified silence when I spat and brayed and barked. At last I was sequestered in an apartment in a far turret of the castle, attended by the old valet who had saved my wretched life. For companions, I had only my dog, Neptune, and the ancient books that lined the shelves of these rooms. One night, unable to sleep, I chose a volume at random and sat down to read. It was a fatal selection. The book was entitled *The Light-houses of Norland,* one of a set of identically bound volumes that comprised a learned treatise on the history and architecture of these structures. From my first glimpse of the etchings and diagrams with which the texts were illustrated, I was drawn to the stark beauty of the lonely towers, to their utter isolation, and to the benevolence of their purpose. For the next months, I studied these volumes night and day. The final volume was a manual of instruction in the daily tasks and responsibilities of the keeper of a certain light-house called Otterhölm. It was a tome of encyclopedic proportions, written in a weighty Old Testament prose that treated the least likely circumstance ad infinitum. Nevertheless, I read it slowly, a page at a time, as if it were the

Book of Ecclesiastes. By summer's end I had committed the entire volume to memory.

I was particularly struck by the last page of the manual, which was entitled "In Extremis." It so instructed that in the event that the integrity of the light-house was violated, either by an inrush of sea through a break in the pediment or in the occasion of a fire, the keeper was duty-bound to ensure as well as possible the preservation of the written log in order that the course of events be made known to the Consistory. The keeper was to immerse the entire manuscript in melted candle wax until it was completely sealed, then cast it into the sea, where it might float to safety. The keeper was then to retreat to the lowermost story of the structure, there to await rescue or an honorable death in the line of duty.

In the course of my studies I learned that the light-house of Otterhölm was situated on a reef in midsea that lay no more than a week's voyage from the coast of my father's lands. By correspondence with DeGrät, the overseer of the realm, I learned further that the beacon of Otterhölm had not been lighted for three years, the keeper having disappeared under certain circumstances and no one found willing to take his place. Since that time, four ships had foundered upon the reef, with much loss of life. All at once my destiny was revealed to me. I would go to Otterhölm as its keeper, there to place my damnation in the service of others. In such worthy solitude I should be rid, if not of the demon, at least of the humiliation that defined my existence on earth.

I made my request at once to DeGrät, and he in turn proposed my appointment to the Consistory. To my surprise, there were difficulties, especially with regard to my refusal of an assistant. The strange fate of my predecessor was mentioned, though I found nothing strange about it. Doubtless the old man, having fallen ill or sustained an injury, and sensing that the end was near, had managed to lash himself to the railing of the upper gallery, where, weeks later, his corpse had been found by the sailors sent to investigate, hideously mangled as if by the feasting of seabirds. The objections of my father had also to be overcome. Would I, he wondered, be able to bear the eternal solitude? Sooner or later it would undermine my sanity, cause me to despair. Nonsense! It was solitude that I sought, solitude that I required. As for companionship, there would be Neptune. In the end, pressure was brought to bear upon several members of the Consistory who were vulnerable; the commission was granted.

∽

It is said that at the moment of departure, turning to gaze upon his homeland for the last time, the exile's eyes blaze at the sight of a beloved cup, a pipe stand, the fiddle of his boyhood—some dear object of remembrance. Not mine. The door I closed, closed upon the artifacts of a life not worth living, not one of which I brought away to dote upon.

Before me, the sea was breathing easily as if in sleep, with scarcely a wrinkle in the open water. "It shall not last," the captain muttered into his beard. Throughout that first night the helmsman kept the cutter's prow in the silver lunaqua. We seemed to be riding in a furrow of the moon. But toward morning, a sudden squall arose, a squall made half of sea, half of sky, such that the sails had to be reefed and the direct course abandoned for a more circuitous route. Five nights and days passed before I had my first glimpse of the light-house. Otterhölm! The very name evoked a museum of polished bones. I seemed to hear their exotic clatter above the uproar of the sea. What a great dark frown of a tower it was, without a sign of hopefulness such as one sees in the upreaching spire of a cathedral. Otterhölm reached for nothing, and at the sight, it was borne home to me how completely I should be thrown back upon myself.

Closer still, the reef came into view, a menacing populace of rocks washed by the sea, now visible, now submerged, as the cutter wallowed and staggered through trough after trough of water and spray. What had seemed from afar smooth rock revealed itself to be fissured and rusticated, and carved into fantastic shapes. Here and there were inscrutable hieroglyphs and the rotten, brine-soaked timbers of old shipwrecks. The light-house had been built upon a flat table of rock on the far end of the reef. From my studies, I knew that to provide a foundation, rocks had been scooped from the sea and heaped into a great pile. Atop this was built a platform of masonry, and all about it a seawall. The only approach to the pediment was by longboat through a narrow passage and into a kind of gully or cove. Here the sea was abnormally convulsed, as the multitude of waves crowded at the opening like sheep at a pasture gate.

With the cutter anchored and its sails furled, the first longboat was lowered into the ill-tempered sea. Supported by two of the crew, I was lifted from the hold of the cutter and swung into the small vessel, and Neptune put down beside me. Here it was all noise, with the booming of the waves and the slaver of the sea mouthing the rock. The oarsmen strove mightily to coordinate our passage through the aperture in the rocks with the inrush of a wave. The slightest miscalculation would have us fractured upon the jagged reef. Overhead, a variety of seabirds—redshanks, oystercatchers, herring gulls—shared my terror. The stones all about were smeared with their guano. We entered safely, and in the gully, the sea was calmer. The longboat was drawn alongside a seawall, from which stone steps ascended to the portal. Once again, I was lifted bodily from the boat to the pediment. I had arrived.

Neptune and the supplies having been unloaded, the captain prepared to return to the cutter. To my shame everlasting, I offered my thanks to these good seamen, not with a clasping of hands but with yet another eruption of curses. I could not doubt their satisfaction at having deposited so vile a creature in the middle of the ocean and left him to his own devices. Turning, I entered the tower that was to become my nest, my den, my cocoon. Asylum! I was like a child who has located that hidden corner of the world where he will live with his imaginary companions. Yet even at that first moment there was something sentient about the light-house, an aloofness that did not entirely welcome my intrusion.

1 January 1796

This day—my first in the light-house—I make this entry in my diary, as agreed upon with DeGrät. As regularly as I can keep the journal, I will. But there is no telling what may happen to a man all alone as I am. I may get sick, or worse. . . . So far well. The longboat had a narrow escape through the aperture in the reef, but why dwell on that, since I am here, all safe? With the seizures abated and my demon again in hibernation, my spirits are beginning to revive already.

The floor of the first story is some twenty feet above sea level, of heavy oak beams. A trapdoor of the same wood leads down into a submarine extension of the shaft that tomorrow I shall explore. Carved into the masonry is a curving stone staircase that leads to the story above, and from thence to each successive story and to the lantern at the top. It is comprised of 180 steps. My first act was to climb to the lantern itself, to step out upon the circular railed gallery that is open to the elements, from which I looked down over the vast expanse of sea that merges with the sky into a single firmament. There, with Neptune at my side, I felt for all the world like Noah on the deck of the Ark, watching the Flood recede. To be in such a light-house is to be aboard a ship that is forever becalmed. No matter the flogging of the wind, it is the very principle of immobility, yet with the sweet illusion of sailing. It is a kingdom measured out in altitude, with a winding staircase for its only road.

The lamp room is a dome made entirely of prisms of glass so as to magnify the light of the beacon. The lantern itself is a great basin of stone with iron fittings. In accordance with the manual of instruction, I filled the basin with oil and fired the wick. Instantly the dome was transformed into a crucible of brightness and heat. The light-house of Otterhölm had returned to life. Once again I stepped out upon the circular gallery and felt the light-house shudder like the deck of a ship trod by its beloved captain.

Immediately below the lantern are the living quarters. These consist of three rooms, the central and largest being a kitchen, on one wall of which is a great hearth. Here there are cupboards, a large table, and two chairs. The masonry walls are fitted out with dark panels of wood, between which are set sconces. A many-tongued candelabrum sits upon the table. The sole ornament is a coat of arms set upon the wall. This consists of the Cross of Saint George with four galleons, one in each quarter, and above, a crowned lion holding a scroll with the motto *trinitas in unitate*. The rooms to each side are simply furnished, each with a bed, chair, and armoire. The two stories beneath are used for storage of oil, wood, and other supplies. At each level, the walls of the light-house are pierced by narrow vertical windows, one of which opens off the kitchen onto an enclosed bay. This will serve as a roost for the carrier pigeons, which, save for the infrequent arrival of the cutter, are to be my sole means of communication with the mainland. It is evening and I am writing at the table in the great kitchen. From far below comes the muffled respiration of the sea. With a fire burning in the grate and the faint redolence of sailcloth and old leather, this room has the intimacy of a ship's cabin.

2 January

Morning. The cutter has a rough passage home, I am sure. But now the sea is again calm. In the distance it lies burnished, like the shield of Achilles. Directly below, the light-house wears a perpetual collar of foam.

5 January

Only four days arrived, and already I am as cozy as an egg in its shell. My duties are surprisingly light. In addition to the tending of the lamp, I am twice daily to make a round of the tower, inspecting it for any disrepair. The solidity of the structure argues against any such dilapidation, as the walls are four feet in thickness and made of blocks of stone, subtly carved so as to dovetail the one into the other. The light-house had been standing for a century already, a triumph of masonry over wind and water.

14 January

How good the sea air may be, only those know who have left the intolerable behind. My affection for Otterhölm grows with each gliding fugitive day of winter. I wake each morning to the soothing artillery of the sea, the knifelike shrieks of the gulls, the thump of Neptune's tail on the floor, and I am at peace. From the gallery, a liturgical light presides over the forces of nature. I have the sense of eternity being filtered through the vast space and I feel as if my spirit is being cleansed as well. Only now and then, in response to some humanlike sound of sea or bird, does the old disquiet stir.

It is time to speak of the Well. I call it that for want of any rational explanation of its presence. Nowhere except in the manual of instruction did I encounter mention of such a submarine extension of a light-house shaft, and there only the repeated instruction—almost a warning—that the trapdoor be kept shut and bolted at all times, save during the weekly inspection of the lower chamber for any cracks that must be caulked. Despite the thickness of the structure's walls, surely this hollowness of its base must make it more vulnerable to the crushing weight of the sea.

It required all of my strength to raise the hatch of the trapdoor. From its depths emanated a cold, sour belch of air. Wooden steps lead down to a ledge that encircles the cavern. A wooden bridge traverses the pool, above which hang strands of mist. Into its depth, by an ingenious tracery of grooves and pipes, is led the rainwater to be used for drinking and bathing. Holding aloft a torch, I descended the steps into what seemed the dark wet gullet of the light-house. In the damp, saturated air the torch burned low, struggling to stay alive. Here the climate is humid and breathing difficult. A pale, greenish gleam arises from the sweating walls, where small plants have taken root in the interstices of the masonry blocks. These are further speckled with patches of lichen. In the subdued light of the torch, strange shadows on the walls break apart, collide, fuse, chase one another in a wild metamorphosis. With each step downward, the darkness thickens, the heaviness of the air presses down upon the intruder. I saw that the walls are not vertical here but form an ever-narrowing cone into which the rainwater collects. And it is silent, for one no longer hears the buffeting of the sea, only feels its immense, silent weight. What could have possessed the builders of this light-house to place at its core this *cisterna magna*, like the lowest circle of Dante's *Inferno*, where Satan weeps "with six eyes"?

In the midst of my exploration, a violent tremor seized me, a dread that was less physical than a terror of the soul. I took the steps as quickly as I dared, lowered the hatch, and ascended to the safety of my room. Even here I shudder at the charge of malignant energy that shot through that compartment beneath the sea.

I have resolved to descend to the Well only to perform the weekly inspection prescribed by the manual. Fortunately, there is a rope by which water may be brought up in a bucket through the hatch.

20 January

One day into the next without event. Here the simplest laws of life impose their ritual, encouraging a discipline the soul welcomes after a lifetime of chaos. The light-house has become for me a microcosm of the earth itself, in which I am to dwell between the Lamp above and the Well below, precisely as between Heaven and Hell. In the simplicity and regularity of my duties, a certain languor has invaded the light-house. If I miss anything from my former life, it is the forest— the crackling of leaves underfoot, the unexpected fall of a dead branch, rain dripping leaf to leaf—but such longings have grown less and less frequent. I should count my contentment complete, save that, now and then, the immensity of my solitude sits like a dark beast upon my chest.

I said I should not visit the Well until I must. But I had not counted on its mysterious attraction. Resolve as I will to avoid it, time and again my thoughts are drawn there until I must return to peer from the ledge at my own hideously distorted reflection. What a deceitful, perfidious liquid that presents itself in the bucket in repose, limpid, with "beaded bubbles winking at the brim." Under no circumstances can I persuade Neptune to accompany me. No sooner do I raise the trapdoor than the poor creature begins to whimper and will not cease until I have emerged and the hatch is again lowered.

1 February

I do not know what it was that caused me to awaken just at dawn with the feeling that something untoward had transpired. I only half remembered a dull grinding noise in my sleep, as of something breaking apart. All day yesterday and far into the night a storm had raged. Looking out, I saw that sea and sky were sealed in a bluish mineral light. I climbed to the dome to find that during the night the lantern had gone out! Caught up in the strange reverie brought on by the storm, I had drifted into sleep without seeing to the fire. I had let my duties lapse. Quickly, I poured oil into the basin of the lamp and relit the fire, then stepped out upon the gallery. Through the spyglass I saw, wedged upon the reef some thousand yards from the light-house, a three-master, her sheets doubly reefed. Her prow was splintered, and the sea poured in and out of the hull. With each salvo of waves, she shuddered, turned as on a pivot, and dipped to lie further on her side like a horse held down for banding. There was no sign of her crew, save, some distance from the wreck, a lone figure lying motionless upon the rocks, his tiny form washed over by the sea. I hastened down the steps and out the doorway, down the rocks to the gully, where the dory was moored. I pulled toward the opening in the rocks, then waited and waited until a receding wave should sweep me through the narrows into the open sea. All about me the pitiless reef bared its teeth. Was it guilt at my dereliction that drove me on? Or the immense burden of my solitude that craved human companionship? How I pulled on the oars, for hours it seemed, until I came to the rocks where shuddered the poor wreck. Through the staved hull I saw the bodies of two men, their faces already studded with crabs. Then out upon the black shoulder of the reef I climbed to kneel by the rock pool all laced with ice where lay the dashed and broken body of the man. I stopped only long enough to determine that life, however faintly, yet stirred in him, then lifted him, limp as the dead, and placed him in the dory. I doubted my strength for the return. But for once, Heaven was looking over my shoulder. At the opening to the gully I waited to receive the carrying wave, surrendered to it, and found myself alongside the pediment. Securing the dory, I carried the man to the room opposite mine, where he now lies—breathing, yes, but little more than that. I stripped off the clothing and saw a great gash in the left breast with a fragment of rib sticking through, and another wound to the thigh. His left arm hangs like a flail. His color is that of the waves, and his respiration the labored gurgling of the moribund. I doubt he will survive.

How I cursed my fatal lassitude that brought about this tragic circumstance. Gazing down at the broken body of the stranger, I felt the sudden unbearable weight of my loneliness. What I wished with all my heart was to know the companionship of a fellow being. In the wild excitement of the moment, I had forgotten that it is only in absolute solitude that I can live without the torment of my affliction. It was my desperate hope to retrieve that man, to retrieve him for myself.

11 February

For ten nights the northern sky has been hung with the curtains of a sickbed. For ten days and nights the sailor has lain insensible, as though his heart could not decide at what moment to cease beating. He has uttered not a sound, except for the clicks, gasps, and sucking noises that accompany his breathing. Again and again, I give thanks for the chest of salves and medicaments thrust upon me by old Nils on my departure. With these herbal decoctions and unguents, I have been able to dress the sailor's wounds, although with scant hope for his life. Yet once, in his delirium, he reached out a hand, which I took between my own and held as if to say to the feverish man, *I am here.* At once he calmed, and a moment later sank into a peaceful sleep.

16 February

This morning I entered the room to see that the sailor's eyes were open, and that when I moved, his gaze followed me. I bent over him to speak.

"You are alive," I told him. It seemed necessary to persuade him of that. And I related briefly the story of the shipwreck and his rescue. He made not the least reply, but gaped blankly as if stunned. I drew a chair to the bed and questioned him as to his name, his past, the points of departure and destination of the wrecked vessel. Still he made no reply. I attributed his silence to the state of shock brought on by his terrible ordeal.

Nor have I yet heard a sound emerge from his lips other than the grunts and hiccups of a man in delirium. The wretchedness of his physical state touches me deeply. The least movement causes him to grimace, his breathing to grow shallow and rapid. Yet still he makes no outcry. It is a rare stoicism.

19 February

It is three days since the sailor has regained his consciousness. He has begun to accept gruel, which I feed him with a wooden spoon. Now and then he lifts his gaze to mine, then lowers his eyes as if to silence what they would tell. Again I questioned him gently about his native land, his name, but he seems to have lost all knowledge of the past and, with seeming lack of understanding, answers neither yea or nay. I offered him pen and paper to write down what he would not speak. By a shake of his head he gave me to understand that he cannot read or write.

1 March

Today I gathered seagull eggs from the nests inside the seawall. I had to smile to see the eagerness with which my patient took the omelet I made from them. His strength improves by the day. The pallor of near-death has been replaced by a whiteness of skin that is startling—as though, by himself, he constitutes a new race. Who could his people be?

I sit at the table writing in the ledger while outside the gulls circulate like smoke. Otterhölm is roofed by a low sky. Seals are crying on the reef with the voices of the drowned. In the next room the mariner sleeps.

12 March

Each day the man grows stronger, eating whatever I place before him. Now and then he looks up at me with the dumb, submissive expression of a beast. I confess to a certain pride in having salvaged this man from the wreck. And yet, with his recovery, something is stirring within me. It is, I know, the demon, who senses the presence of another human being. Day by day the pressure is mounting. Already when I am with him the struggle to contain myself is acute. He must leave by the next cutter. I cannot risk his presence here.

12 April

In Mathias, for that is what I have named him, I recognize a kindred taste for solitude, and a certain nostalgia, as though he exists at some distance from the world. Yet he is no stranger to industry. In what passes for carpentry here he has made traps with which to catch crayfish. And from a plan he has fashioned a fine harpoon. With it, only yesterday he slew a seal that had ventured too close to the seawall. We shall have fresh meat instead of the wormy hardtack to which we are accustomed. At tending the lamp he is utterly dependable. His mariner's soul is visible in the way he gazes at sea and sky, as if to make an offering of himself. He seems to sense long beforehand the coming of a storm, all the mysteries of the tides, the vagaries of the inconstant sea. Twice, when the sea was calm, we rowed to the site of the shipwreck and returned with a load of wood from the hull to supplement our supply. Though he does not speak, there are times when I seem to hear the murmuring of his flesh. Does he place his trust in silence as in the whirlwind? Only one proscription has he placed upon himself: He visits every portion of the reef and every story of the tower, except the Well. That, I see, is to be my precinct.

24 April

By the pantomime we have invented, I have made known to Mathias my intention that he leave the light-house on the next ship. Was it only fancy that I saw upon his face a look of sadness at the news?

2 May

It has happened as I knew it would. I was at my writing table. There, where the floor rises two steps to the embrasure of the kitchen window, Mathias stood gazing out. All at once I felt mounting the terrible urge that will not be defined, felt the hot ball of rage rising in my throat. I bit my lips until the blood ran on my chin. I clamped my very soul shut about the demon. I leaped to my feet, overturning the chair, and covered my face with upflung arms. But in the end, it was no use. The dam burst in my throat, I heard the harsh grating noises, the hideous gargles, curses, all the filth of my speech. On and on I spewed until the rage was spent. In the silence that followed, Mathias gave no sign that he had heard me. When at last he turned and stepped down from the window, I saw only the perfect innocence of his expression. Then it was that I knew the truth. He had not heard. The one human being whom Fate had sent to share my isolation was the only one with whom I could live. Mathias is deaf. His muteness is the silence of the deaf man who has never learned to speak. With that knowledge, a wave of relief, not to say happiness, came over me. And I felt the thwarted demon shrink back into hibernation.

24 June

The cutter has come. Through the glass I watched its approach not with any sense of anticipation, but with mounting dread. Together, from the gallery, Mathias and I watched its perilous approach to the opening of the gully, the letting down of the small boats loaded with provisions. And with each succeeding step in the unloading, my heart grew heavier. I did not want him to go. At the end, I accompanied him to the seawall, from which he was to step into the boat. At the last moment, he turned to me with an imploring look and, I thought, tears in his eyes. I could not be strong. We bade farewell to the men and watched them pole off. The boat rejoined its ship, the anchor was raised, and a blessed length of empty sea appeared between ship and light-house. Together, Mathias and I reentered our tower.

18 August

One day into the other in which Mathias and I carry out our daily round. Side by side, we work in the silence that has been imposed upon us, the silence that is my blessing and, doubtless, his curse. In the absence of speech, I listen to the sounds he makes: the faint strokes of his oars, the scrape of his boot on the floor, something like a hiss when he stoops to retrieve the fresh-caught cod from the dory.

In such quietude, a sneeze or a cough is an oration. And welcome. No more perfect a partner in exile could have been conceived. His small acts of solicitude in the tending of the fire, the preparation of food, the operation of the lantern, he performs without the least show of servitude, but with a kind of dignity. He is at once robust and delicate, a man snugly lodged in his body, and with a pulse that I imagine to be slower than that of other men, as though the fire of his life has been banked. Or is it a pensiveness natural to the deaf, who are said to be gifted with special insight? When we pass each other on the steps, it is as though he is awakening from a dream while I am falling into it. At the moment when we stand together, we become one.

15 September

Word has come from DeGrät by pigeon that the mainland has been swept by a plague. Nor has the noble household been spared. My two brothers have been stricken to death, and I, demonized and isolate, am sole heir. But I should far rather be keeper of this light-house than lord of a realm. Strangely, I am unable to feel the grief natural to a man whose family and homeland have been laid waste, as though the sentiments of patriotism and kinship were of a former life from which I long ago departed into a new incarnation.

19 September

This morning, in accordance with the instructions in the manual, I went to carry out the weekly inspection of the Well. Mathias had left the light-house to gather in crayfish from the traps he had sunk about the reef. No sooner had I raised the hatch of the trapdoor, than I felt once again the presence of evil inherent in that low compartment. The sense of oppression was greater than before, as though whatever presence dwelt therein had swelled, and the very air seemed to have grown viscous, weighting my arms and legs. I made my way along the ledge about the pool, clinging to the whimpers of Neptune above as to a lifeline in a wild sea. Halfway around, the torch blazed up, then died, but not before I had glimpsed a pale, shapeless mass submerged in the dark pool just below where I stood. A moment later, it rolled like a corpse and sank from view with a swarming of eddies. The depth swallowed my strength as if I were a stone cast into it. In the utter blackness I clung to the rail and forced myself to continue toward the opening of the trapdoor. At last I achieved the steps and climbed out to lie panting on the floor. When I had recovered somewhat, I lowered the hatch and, without daring to look back, ascended to my room. There I sat, trembling and unable to steady my pen, the stench of the Well in my nostrils, its damp upon my skin. Suddenly, my dread lifted, and I looked up to see that Mathias had entered the room, bringing with him that special silence which always causes me to hold my breath for fear of shattering it. The very look upon his face restored my composure. Perhaps I had imagined the apparition in the Well? Perhaps it was a hallucination, an odd trick of light and shadow, a configuration brought about by the shimmering of the pool?

12 October

The cutter has arrived but there is too much sea in the gully for the longboat to pass through. And so she must lie to. I have decided not to present myself at the unloading to spare the innocent seamen my unwarranted abuses. Mathias will receive them.

13 October

The sea calmed sufficiently for the previous to be unloaded. Mathias made several trips to the cutter in the longboat. Excellent mariner that he is, familiar with every rocky projection and current of the reef, his guidance proved indispensable. Or so I judged, watching from the gallery. When the longboat had departed for the last time, I descended to find him holding a kitten in his arms. Unaware of my presence, he stroked and kissed the creature, his face suffused with tenderness. So there are to be four of us.

15 October

Toward the newcomer Neptune has shown all the generosity of spirit of which a dog is capable, insisting only upon his sovereignty at the foot of my bed. Mathias keeps the kitten with him. At dawn today, on my way to the lantern, I glanced through the doorway to see the little cat creep from his sleep-tangled arms. I am awed by its domesticating power. By the addition of this one, we are made a family.

30 October

Word by carrier pigeon from DeGrät that we can no longer rely on the cutter for supplies, the mariners having been decimated by the plague. By trimming the lantern during daylight, I have calculated that there is sufficient lamp oil to last another three months. Surely by then we shall be resupplied. As for food and fuel for ourselves, we have no such anxiety. There is the immense fecundity of the sea and its reefs and the ingenuity of Mathias.

When the waters are quiet, he can be seen crouching on the wall over the gully, spear upraised. More often than not, there is fish for our supper. Wood from the shipwreck is ours for the taking, although it still grieves me to think that our warmth depends upon the drowned.

Mathias has no fear of the water. This morning he stood on the seawall, stripped, and leaped into the sea. Moments later, there he was again, glistening like a seal on the rocks. To me, the waves are so many blows in the face. It is a flagellation from which I emerge stinging and red and cold.

We live under the one authority of the lamp, which transforms our every task into a ritual of worship. Pouring oil into the basin of the lantern from an earthenware jug that he tips from his shoulder, Mathias seems to me like some biblical priest preparing the altar, his face in the uprush of flame the gleaming visage of an angel. Feeding the fire, polishing the dome, he and I are companions in a dream, two children creating the night. Later, we sit together at the table, he working a piece of driftwood with his knife, I writing in this journal while the logs in the grate glow and dim, glow and dim, as if in rhythm with the wind that howls about the tower.

Yet there is something about his silence that, argue as I will against it, disturbs me. At moments I doubt the very perfection of it, and wonder whether it is true deafness or some other form of hearing. Perhaps, displaced from his ears, the sense has taken up residence elsewhere in his body. There is a voice, too, I swear it, that rises about him, issuing from his very flesh. It is then that I feel, however faintly, something angry stirring in my soul, something altogether familiar. I must arrest these perverse thoughts.

15 November

Still Mathias's silence torments me. More and more I suspect not true deafness but a refusal to speak that has the quality of a dangerous concealment. This morning, sitting behind him in the dory, I leaned forward and gave a mighty shout. Was it coincidence that made him turn at that instant with a watchful look that vanished almost before I caught it? Why should he deceive me, who rescued him?

20 November

The past weeks have been full of toil. In addition to our routine we have undertaken to clean and polish the light-house as though it were a ship. Mathias has accepted the wearying pace I have imposed upon us without the least sign of resentment, while I, in a frenzy of activity, hope like the monk who doubles his prayers to stifle what threatens to defile me from within.

With suspicion, the light-house itself has become a tower of shadows that each day grows more tenebrous. No longer is Otterhölm my haven of solitude, my refuge. But still it may be my university, where I shall learn the truth.

I have become a secret watcher, a spy. Oh, this distrust that breeds itself anew each day and which alone is capable of calling up the creature who lusts to be heard! For some days I have felt the premonitory aura. Daily the pressure mounts. How is it that I only now perceive a certain subtlety about him?

22 November

Again! We had just finished our evening meal. I had seated myself at the table to begin to write. Mathias was tending the grate. All at once,

I felt the involuntary movements of my mouth, the baring and crunching of my teeth, the bursting-apart of my throat. Then out came the curses, black as ravens, flapping and cawing from my mouth. The ill-said words disgorged, my lips torn as if by the passage of thorns, I watched him turn toward me, saw his face redden as if slapped. He hears! I know it! Or was it a glow from the flames over which he bent? I will conquer these insane suspicions or I will go mad.

24 November

At noon I opened the trapdoor to haul up fresh water from the Well only to find that the rope had broken. It would be necessary to descend to retrieve the bucket. For a long time I held the frayed end of the rope, fingering the groove in the stone where it had ridden. At last I descended to the Well, upon whose scabbed and oozing walls the torch cast veins of light. Once again, from the footbridge, I beheld the creature stalking me from beneath the surface of the black liquid element in which it lives and which is surely not water but something like blood. By a will other than my own, my gaze was held fast to what now appeared as a loose, voluptuous bag, whose undifferentiated contents flowed from one part to another, causing the whole to ripple in languorous sacculations and invaginations, as though the beast were taking sensual pleasure in itself. No chimera of the brain this, but an amphibian reality perceived through the unconscious reflexes of the spinal cord—boneless, bloodless, fleshless, composed of some primordial jelly that existed at the beginning of life. Upon what does it feed if not its own miasma that has the odor of gangrene? Even as I watched, the creature grew turgid, polypoid, like something possessed of a fierce embryonic energy and undergoing metamorphosis, evolving toward a yet more evil incarnation. And I knew beyond any doubt that *here* is manufactured the dark concentrate of evil itself, which emanates to spread across the earth and pass into the bodies of men, there ceaselessly to excite the inmost self in gross circumvention of natural law. At last I tore myself from the hypnotic pool and fled up to my room to lie trembling upon the bed. At length, exhaustion overcame me and I slept.

Hours later, I awoke with the odor of gangrene still strong in my nostrils. With a start I recollected that in my haste and terror, *I had not shut the trapdoor.* At the black mouth of the hatchway, I found poor Neptune, stiff, already cold, his bloody muzzle overhanging the edge.

4 December

I know now that whatever dwells beneath Otterhölm is gathering itself, the way darkness thickens to form night. All day I prowl the light-house, a trespasser fearing discovery. I press my ear to the walls, to the trapdoor even, but this evil makes no sound that I can hear. Only its smell grows stronger, clinging to me like smoke. At night I am awakened by cold fingers of mucus in my throat. As if in conspiracy with the creature, the man Mathias continues his daily round, only now he makes as if to hide as I pass. Is he a man? Or only something pretending to be one? Oh, this expectancy is unbearable. If it will come, let it come now.

20 December

The equinoctial gales have begun. I awoke to a sky of steel-blue tones that darkened by the hour to purple, then black, as the storm gathered. Archipelagoes of clouds advanced upon the light-house. Just before nightfall, broke such a storm as I have not seen in my tenure at Otterhölm. Within minutes the sea was a creature in estrus, bellowing for its mate; above it raged a wind that could strip flesh from bone. So vast an expanse of liquid in motion cannot but awaken an antique terror, yet tinged with the strange pleasure one feels when snugly enclosed in its midst. Now and then the tower shudders as a great boulder wrenched from the depths crashes against the pediment. Up and down the steps Mathias and I climb like sleepwalkers. To comfort the frightened little cat, he has placed it inside his shirt. Amid the thunderclaps, his own face is a blank page, except— But no, I tell myself, it was an apocalyptic streak of lightning that caused him once to flinch, stiffen. Still, more than ever, he eyes me a thousand times with a single look.

The Next Day

In the midst of the tempest, Mathias came to inform me that the lantern had gone out. Together we climbed to the dome, each with a pail of oil. Mathias held the torch. As soon as it was lit, I hurried to fetch another pail of oil, and another. Thus we toiled in the brightness and heat until the cistern was full and the beacon once again in full blaze. To escape the heat of the dome Mathias stepped out upon the gallery. From within, I watched him leaning on the railing as if it were the deck of a foundering ship, his eyes neither opened nor closed, but like those of a marble head; his lips parted as if to *speak!* Through the refracting prismatic dome he was transfigured, with wings of fire rising from his shoulders and all about him a brilliance that rendered him translucent.

What followed took place as if in a dream. I recall only the sudden epilepsy of rage, the lurching of my body from the dome to the gallery, the familiar pressure in my throat; how he turned toward me, his face a mask of innocence, how slowly my hands returned to me, balled into fists. I did not see him fall, if fall he did. Only heard a cry, a single pure call like the sound of the last trumpet that rang out for the time it would take a man to plunge to the reef.

✎

Shrouded in whiteness, the light-house totters. The next blast will send it crashing. Already the glass dome is shattered, the gallery avulsed from the wall. A great jagged fault has appeared at the base of the tower. With each hour, it extends itself upward with a crackling sound as the masonry splits. In all the light-house there is no living thing but I. I, and that which awaits me in the Well. For the last time I sit at the table in the room where Mathias and I have shared so many silences. From the sconces and from the tongues of the candelabrum, I have taken the tapers. My only light is the flames of the hearth, where the wax melts. In accordance with the instructions in the manual, the journal must be dipped and cooled three times until it is completely encased. When that is done, and this book consigned to the waves, I shall descend the steps of Otterhölm for the last time to rejoin the depravity of which I am no more than an outpost, to stare myself back into it, to have its eyes stare out of mine, to fuse with the unrefusable. There is nothing else left for me, nothing at all. Should this record I have kept only to give pain a name survive to wash upon some distant shore, I pray that the finder be not lettered, for I have come to know the terrible contagion of words, their power to destroy.

Tillim

The boy's face is the color of the Torah, as though in the years of bending over the scrolls, his skin had become infiltrated with something, a vapor, that rose from the parchment. But here inscribed with acne. He seems almost another species, a thin messy breed, with a nose too large for the narrow recessed mandible below. Metal bands all but hide his yellow teeth. A blue velvet yarmulke pinned to his dark hair is embroidered in heavy gold thread. From beneath his shirt hang the four fringes of a prayer shawl. They are dirty, glutinous. He plays with them, twisting the threads in his fingers. It is private, automatic.

"How old are you?" I ask him.

"Seventeen."

He looks to be thirteen or fourteen. The strangeness, the unkemptness distance me. I am very tired.

"What is the matter?"

"I have an ingrown toenail," he says. "It is infected."

"Climb up on the table," I say. He does so, not sitting on the edge and bracing his hands to lift himself, but facing the table, putting up first one knee, then the other, kneeling there, hesitating, and finally turning to a sitting position. The roll of paper covering the table tears. It has taken him a full minute to do this.

"Take off your shoe." It is the end of the day. I am growing snappish. He does.

"Your sock, please."

The left big toe is swollen and red. Pus has gathered there where the nail is deeply embedded in the flesh. Part of the nail will have to be cut away.

"Lie down, please." Each time, he complies, but only just. He uses his whole body to delay. I force my voice to gentleness.

"You will feel two needle pricks, one at either side at the base of the toe. Not in the sore part." I show him where.

All at once, he sits up. He is agitated. He cannot control his terror.

"After that," I say, "you will feel nothing. Your toe will be numb."

In a loud voice and with an edge of desperation, he calls out to his father who is in the waiting room.

"Tateh! Tateh!"

A man opens the door of the examining room. He is tall and handsome, with a red beard and blue, German eyes. He is wearing an impeccable new fedora. One finger keeps his place among the pages of a black leather-bound book. The barest tips of spotless white fringes show beneath his jacket.

"Shah! Shah!" He speaks firmly, coldly to the boy. His face is taut with anger. The presence of the man calms, domesticates the boy.

"Lie down, please," I say to the boy. I wipe his toe with alcohol on a sponge, and advance with the syringe. But he draws back his foot, twists free. There is no violence in him. He cannot do it. He just *cannot.*

All right, then, I think. Don't give in. There has already been too much submission. But I am tired.

"Let's get this over with," I say.

"Why don't you call upon your spiritual resources?" I say. It is a mean remark. I am ashamed of having said it. But somehow, it is a suggestion that he can accept. He lies still upon the table, covers his eyes with one arm, and lets come from his lips an unceasing silken whisper of Hebrew. I grasp the toe firmly with one hand, pinching it and bending it down. Not out of callousness. It is to distract him from the prick of the needle. Still, there is pain. The whisper pauses, but only for an instant, then rushes on. The first injection has been given.

"What is it that you are reciting?" I ask him.

The whisper has stopped, but he does not answer.

"*Tillim*," says the father. "Hebrew psalms."

"That is a good thing to do," I say. "Here is the last needle."

Again the whisper, and I am made sorrowful by the sound. He seems far away from me, exalted. I think of the others who went to the sealed chambers murmuring *tillim*. I think of this ancient sibilance mingling with the hiss of gas.

"Now there will be no more pain," I say. Firmly, I massage the base of the toe to hasten the spread of the anesthetic in the tissues. I insert one blade of the scissors beneath the toenail and advance toward the base, cutting until the root of the nail is divided.

"Where do you go to school?"

"I go to the yeshiva. In New York," he says. He is animated.

"I come home for weekends. There is very strict discipline there." He smiles. "With boys," he says, "you need discipline." He looks at his father and smiles faintly. I know from his voice that he needs none. He has never done any rebellious thing. He cannot.

I grasp that third of the toenail that is to be removed, with a heavy clamp. With a sharp tug, I avulse it from the nail bed. It comes away intact.

"Do you have brothers?"

"No. I am the only one. That is why I have trouble getting along with the other boys."

I turn to the father. "Are you a rabbi?"

"No."

"What do you do?"

"I am a businessman." He looks down, smooths the crease of his pants.

"But still I study Talmud," he says. "Every day."

With a scalpel, I cut away the overgrown infected tissue. Then I cauterize it with silver nitrate. I bandage the toe. Only when he is certain that the toe is concealed by the dressing, only then does the boy raise his head to look down. Abruptly, he sits up. His agitation returns, but it is different. It is not fear that goads him, but something no less intense, as though he were pursuing an idea, a knowledge, ferreting it out. It is a truth that he *must* know. He needs it. In order to survive after his body has been put to torture, some piece of it slain.

The questions pour from him. Exactly what did you do? How should I take care of it? Will it be all right from now on? Are you sure it will not come back? Will it hurt when the anesthetic wears off? He asks the same things over and over. It is a kind of talmudic questioning.

"Can I see your scissors?" he asks. I hand them to him. His blood still wets the blades.

"Oh," he says, "my blood!" And he draws in his breath. He wears the handle of the scissors on his thumb and forefinger, and snips at the air. This movement, too, is awkward. His fingers are tangled. He opens the scissors to their widest, and reads aloud.

"Made in Germany." He falls silent. I think that he will ask no more questions. But he does. "Can I see it?" he asks.

"Can you see what?"

"My toenail. The part you cut off."

I pick up the fragment of the toenail with a forceps, and deposit it on a gauze sponge.

"Here," I say, and hold up the sponge for him to see.

Ignoring the gauze, he takes up the nail in his fingers. He holds it close to his face, studying it. So close . . . for a moment I am afraid that he is going to pop it into his mouth. Suddenly, with a swift movement, he throws the toenail on the floor.

"Ach," he says and wipes his hand on his fringe. "Feh!"

He shudders, and smiles faintly.

I should make him pick it up, I think. But I do not.

Later, when they have gone, I bend to pick up the toenail. I hold it in my palm for a little time, then lift it to the light. It is translucent. At the margins, where it is reddened with the boy's blood, there is a glow, as of stained glass. At last, I go to flick the nail into the trash can. But it sticks to my fingers. It will not leave me. In the end, I grasp it with the steel forceps and tap the instrument against the rim of the can. The toenail falls then, and, as the lid drops shut, there is a blazing-up within the receptacle as though something has been ignited.

Sarcophagus

We are six who labor here in the night. No . . . seven! For the man horizontal upon the table strives as well. But we do not acknowledge his struggle. It is our own that preoccupies us.

I am the surgeon.

David is the anesthesiologist. You will see how kind, how soft he is. Each patient is, for him, a preparation respectfully controlled. Blood pressure, pulse, heartbeat, flow of urine, loss of blood, temperature, whatever is measurable, David measures. And he is a titrator, adding a little gas, drug, oxygen, fluid, blood in order to maintain the dynamic equilibrium that is the only state compatible with life. He is in the very center of the battle, yet he is one step removed; he has not known the patient before this time, nor will he deal with the next of kin. But for him, the occasion is no less momentous.

Heriberto Paz is an assistant resident in surgery. He is deft, tiny, mercurial. I have known him for three years. One day he will be the best surgeon in Mexico.

Evelyn, the scrub nurse, is a young Irish woman. For seven years we have worked together. Shortly after her immigration, she led her young husband into my office to show me a lump on his neck. One year ago he died of Hodgkin's disease. For the last two years of his life, he was paralyzed from the waist down. Evelyn has one child, a boy named Liam.

Brenda is a black woman of forty-five. She is the circulating nurse, who will conduct the affairs of this room, serving our table, adjusting the lights, counting the sponges, ministering to us from the unsterile world.

Roy is a medical student who is beginning his surgical clerkship. He has been assigned to me for the next six weeks. This is his first day, his first operation.

David is inducing anesthesia. In cases where the stomach is not empty through fasting, the tube is passed into the windpipe while the patient is awake. Such an "awake" intubation is called crashing. It is done to avoid vomiting and the aspiration of stomach contents into the lungs while the muscles that control coughing are paralyzed.

We stand around the table. To receive a tube in the windpipe while fully awake is a terrifying thing.

"Open your mouth wide," David says to the man. The man's mouth opens slowly to its fullest, as though to shriek. But instead, he yawns. We smile down at him behind our masks.

"Okay. Open again. Real wide."

David sprays the throat of the man with a local anesthetic. He does this three times. Then, into the man's mouth, David inserts a metal tongue depressor which bears a light at the tip. It is called a laryngo-scope. It is to light up the throat, reveal the glottic chink through which the tube must be shoved. All this while, the man holds his mouth agape, submitting to the hard pressure of the laryngoscope. But suddenly, he cannot submit. The man on the table gags, struggles to free himself, to spit out the instrument. In his frenzy his lip is pinched by the metal blade.

There is little blood.

"Suction," says David.

Secretions at the back of the throat obscure the view. David suctions them away with a plastic catheter.

"Open," commands David. More gagging. Another pass with the scope. Another thrust with the tube. Violent coughing informs us that the tube is in the right place. It has entered the windpipe. Quickly the balloon is inflated to snug it against the wall of the trachea. A bolus of Pentothal is injected into a vein in the man's arm. It takes fifteen seconds for the drug to travel from his arm to his heart, then on to his brain. I count them. In fifteen seconds, the coughing stops, the man's body relaxes. He is asleep.

∽

"All set?" I ask David.

"Go ahead," he nods.

A long incision. You do not know how much room you will need. This part of the operation is swift, tidy. Fat . . . muscle . . . fascia . . . the peritoneum is snapped open and a giant shining eggplant presents itself. It is the stomach, black from the blood it contains and that threatens to burst it. We must open that stomach, evacuate its contents, explore.

Silk sutures are placed in the wall of the stomach as guidelines between which the incision will be made. They are like the pitons of a mountaineer. I cut again. No sooner is the cavity of the stomach achieved, than a columnar geyser of blood stands from the small opening I have made. Quickly, I slice open the whole front of the stomach. We scoop out handfuls of clot, great black gelatinous masses that shimmy from the drapes to rest against our own bellies as though, having been evicted from one body, they must find another in which to dwell. Now and then we step back to let them slidder to the floor. They are under our feet. We slip in them. "Jesus," I say. "He is bleeding all over North America." Now my hand is inside the stomach, feeling, pressing. There! A tumor spreads across the back wall of this stomach. A great hard craterous plain, the dreaded linitis plastica (leather bottle) that is not content with seizing one area, but infiltrates between the layers until the entire organ is stiff with cancer. It is that, of course, which is bleeding. I stuff wads of gauze against the tumor. I press my fist against the mass of cloth. The blood slows. I press harder. The bleeding stops.

A quick glance at Roy. His gown and gloves, even his mask, are sprinkled with blood. Now is he dipped; and I, his baptist.

David has opened a second line into the man's veins. He is pumping blood into both tubings.

"Where do we stand?" I ask him.

"Still behind. Three units." He checks the blood pressure.

"Low, but coming up," he says.

"Shall I wait till you catch up?"

"No. Go ahead. I'll keep pumping."

I try to remove my fist from the stomach, but as soon as I do, there is a fresh river of blood.

"More light," I say. "I need more light."

Brenda stands on a platform behind me. She adjusts the lamps.

"More light," I say, like a man going blind.

"That's it," she says. "There is no more light."

"We'll go around from the outside," I say. Heriberto nods agreement. "Free up the greater curvature first, then the lesser, lift the stomach up and get some control from behind."

I must work with one hand. The other continues as the compressor. It is the tiredest hand of my life. One hand, then, inside the stomach, while the other creeps behind. Between them . . . a ridge of tumor. The left hand fumbles, gropes toward its mate. They swim together. I lift the stomach forward to find that *nothing* separates my hands from each other. The wall of the stomach has been eaten through by the tumor. One finger enters a large tubular structure. It is the aorta. The incision in the stomach has released the tamponade of blood and brought us to this rocky place.

"Curved aortic clamp."

A blind grab with the clamp, high up at the diaphragm. The bleeding slackens, dwindles. I release the pressure warily. A moment later there is a great bang of blood. The clamp has bitten through the cancerous aorta.

"Zero silk on a big Mayo needle."

I throw the heavy sutures, one after the other, into the pool of blood, hoping to snag with my needle some bit of tissue to close over the rent in the aorta, to hold back the blood. There is no tissue. Each time, the needle pulls through the crumble of tumor. I stop. I repack the stomach. Now there is a buttress of packing both outside and inside the stomach. The bleeding is controlled. We wait. Slowly, something is gathering here, organizing. What had been vague and shapeless before is now declaring itself. All at once, I know what it is. There is nothing to do.

For what tool shall I ask? With what device fight off this bleeding? A knife? There is nothing here to cut. Clamps? Where place the jaws of a hemostat? A scissors? Forceps? Nothing. The instrument does not exist that knows such deep red jugglery. Not all my clever picks, my rasp . . . A miner's lamp, I think, to cast a brave glow.

∞

David has been pumping blood steadily.

"He is stable at the moment," he says. "Where do we go from here?"

"No place. He's going to die. The minute I take away my pressure, he'll bleed to death."

I try to think of possibilities, alternatives. I cannot; there are none. Minutes pass. We listen to the cardiac monitor, the gassy piston of the anesthesia machine.

"More light!" I say. "Fix the light."

The light seems dim, aquarial, a dilute beam slanting through a green sea. At such a fathom the fingers are clumsy. There is pressure. It is cold.

"Dave," I say, "stop the transfusion." I hear my voice coming as from a great distance. "Stop it," I say again.

David and I look at each other, standing among the drenched rags, the smeared equipment.

"I can't," he says.

"Then I will," I say, and with my free hand I reach across the boundary that separates the sterile field from the outside world, and I close the clamp on the intravenous tubing. It is the act of an outlaw, someone who does not know right from wrong. But I know. I know that this is right to do.

"The oxygen," I say. "Turn it off."

"You want it turned off, you do it," he says.

"Hold this," I say to Heriberto, and I give over the packing to him. I step back from the table, and go to the gas tanks.

"This one?" I have to ask him.

"Yes," David nods.

I turn it off. We stand there, waiting, listening to the beeping of the electrocardiograph. It remains even, regular, relentless. Minutes go by, and the sound continues. The man will not die. At last, the intervals on the screen grow longer, the shape of the curve changes, the rhythm grows wild, furious. The line droops, flattens. The man is dead.

It is silent in the room. Now we are no longer a team, each with his circumscribed duties to perform. It is Evelyn who speaks first.

"It is a blessing," she says. I think of her husband's endless dying.

"No," says Brenda. "Better for the family if they have a few days . . . to get used to the idea of it."

"But, look at all the pain he's been spared."

"Still, for the ones that are left, it's better to have a little time."

I listen to the two women murmuring, debating without rancor, speaking in hushed tones of the newly dead as women have done for thousands of years.

"May I have the name of the operation?" It is Brenda, picking up her duties. She is ready with pen and paper.

"Exploratory laparotomy. Attempt to suture malignant aorto-gastric fistula."

"Is he pronounced?"

"What time is it?"

"Eleven-twenty."

"Shall I put that down?"

"Yes."

"Sew him up," I say to Heriberto. "I'll talk to the family."

To Roy I say, "You come with me."

Roy's face is speckled with blood. He seems to me a child with the measles. What, in God's name, is he doing here?

From the doorway, I hear the voices of the others, resuming.

"Stitch," says Heriberto.

✧

Roy and I go to change our bloody scrub suits. We put on long white coats. In the elevator, we do not speak. For the duration of the ride to the floor where the family is waiting, I am reasonable. I understand that in its cellular wisdom, the body of this man had sought out the murderous function of my scalpel, and stretched itself upon the table to receive the final stabbing. For this little time, I know that it is not a murder committed but a mercy bestowed. Tonight's knife is no assassin, but the kind scythe of time.

We enter the solarium. The family rises in unison. There are so many! How ruthless the eyes of the next of kin.

"I am terribly sorry . . ." I begin. Their faces tighten, take guard. "There was nothing we could do."

I tell them of the lesion, tell of how it began somewhere at the back of the stomach; how, long ago, no one knows why, a cell lost the rhythm of the body, fell out of step, sprang, furious, into rebellion. I tell of how the cell divided and begat two of its kind, which begat four more and so on, until there was a whole race of lunatic cells, which is called cancer.

I tell of how the cancer spread until it had replaced the whole back of the stomach, invading, chewing until it had broken into the main artery of the body. Then it was, I tell them, that the great artery poured its blood into the stomach. I tell of how I could not stop the bleeding, how my clamps bit through the crumbling tissue, how my stitches would not hold, how there was nothing to be done. All of this I tell.

A woman speaks. She has not heard my words, only caught the tone of my voice.

"Do you mean he is dead?"

Should I say "passed away" instead of "died"? No. I cannot.

"Yes," I tell her, "he is dead."

Her question and my answer unleash their anguish. Roy and I stand among the welter of bodies that tangle, grapple, rock, split apart to form new couplings. Their keening is exuberant, wild. It is more than I can stand. All at once, a young man slams his fist into the wall with great force.

"Son of a bitch!" he cries.

"Stop that!" I tell him sharply. Then, more softly, "Please try to control yourself."

The other men crowd about him, patting, puffing, grunting. They are all fat, with huge underslung bellies. Like their father's. A young woman in a nun's habit hugs each of the women in turn.

"Shit!" says one of the men.

The nun hears, turns away her face. Later, I see the man apologizing to her.

The women, too, are fat. One of them has a great pile of yellowish hair that has been sprayed and rendered motionless. All at once, she begins to whine. A single note, coming louder and louder. I ask a nurse to bring tranquilizer pills. She does, and I hand them out, one to each, as though they were the wafers of communion. They urge the pills upon each other.

"Go on, Theresa, take it. Make her take one."

Roy and I are busy with cups of water. Gradually it grows quiet. One of the men speaks.

"What's the next step?"

"Do you have an undertaker in mind?"

They look at each other, shrug. Someone mentions a name. The rest nod.

"Give the undertaker a call. Let him know. He'll take care of everything."

I turn to leave.

"Just a minute," one of the men calls. "Thanks, Doc. You did what you could."

∽

Once again in the operating room. Blood is everywhere. There is a wild smell, as though a fox had come and gone. The others, clotted about the table, work on. They are silent, ravaged.

"How did the family take it?"

"They were good, good."

Heriberto has finished reefing up the abdomen. The drapes are peeled back. The man on the table seems more than just dead. He seems to have gone beyond that, into a state where expression is possible—reproach and scorn. I study him. His baldness had advanced beyond the halfway mark. The remaining strands of hair had been gallantly dyed. They are, even now, neatly combed and crenellated. A stripe of black mustache rides his upper lip. Once, he had been spruce!

We all help lift the man from the table to the stretcher.

"On three," says David. "One . . . two . . . three."

And we heft him over, using the sheet as a sling. My hand brushes his shoulder. It is cool. I shudder as though he were infested with lice. He has become something that I do not want to touch.

More questions from the women.

"Is a priest coming?"

"Does the family want to view him?"

"Yes. No. Don't bother me with these things."

"Come on," I say to Roy. We go to the locker room and sit together on a bench. We light cigarettes.

"Well?" I ask him.

"When you were scooping out the clots, I thought I was going to swoon."

I pause over the word. It is too quaint, too genteel for this time. I feel, at that moment, a great affection for him.

"But you fought it."

"Yes. I forced it back down. But, almost. . . ."

"Good," I say. Who knows what I mean by it? I want him to know that I count it for something.

"And you?" he asks me. The students are not shy these days.

"It was terrible, his refusal to die."

I want him to say that it was right to call it quits, that I did the best I could. But he says nothing. We take off our scrub suits and go to the shower. There are two stalls opposite each other. They are curtained. But we do not draw the curtains. We need to see each other's healthy bodies. I watch Roy turn his face directly upward into the blinding fall of water. His mouth is open to receive it. As though it were milk flowing from the breasts of God. For me, too, this water is like a well in a wilderness.

In the locker room, we dress in silence.

"Well, good night."

Awkwardly our words come out in unison.

"In the morning . . ."

"Yes, yes, later."

"Good night."

I watch him leave through the elevator door.

✎

For the third time I go to that operating room. The others have long since finished and left. It is empty, dark. I turn on the great lamps above the table that stands in the center of the room. The pediments of the table and the floor have been scrubbed clean. There is no sign of the struggle. I close my eyes and see again the great pale body of the man, like a white bullock, bled. The line of stitches on his abdomen is a hieroglyph. Already, the events of this night are hidden from me by these strange untranslatable markings.

Pages from a Wound Dresser's Diary

I am a dresser of wounds.

My name is William. My beard is grayer than it is black, but I am childless.

I make my rounds on the decks of the steamboat *January.*

I dress the farmers who make up the regiments of Tennessee, Ohio, and Kentucky. I plant my acreage of gauze, then stand back to wait for the dark red fruit to appear.

The *January* runs from Pittsburgh Landing to St. Louis, taking on casualties and carrying them north to the great hospitals. Sometimes we stop for stragglers who have made it to the banks of the river, lone soldiers who wave their arms and call out to us. Their urgency is spectral. To them we are no fat asthmatic auntie, but a musicked barque drawn by dolphins.

We are a hospital boat. We are also a pest house and morgue. We freight typhoid and tuberculosis and measles as well. At night we stop to bury the dead along the banks. There are two coffin makers aboard. They are very busy. At night, I lie in my berth and feel the river slapping against me. It is more Styx than Mississippi. I am more Charon than William.

The things I have seen on this river.

I have seen two drowned men hustling each other along the current, jostling, glancing off, rearing up over rocks and shoals, as exuberant as boys racing downhill.

I have seen rats swimming among planks of ice.

I have seen a horse and rider lying half submerged at the bank so that only the head of the man and the hind parts of the horse are visible, a centaur that had lost its way, its beautiful nostrils gone knobbly with rot.

I have seen the sleeping bellies of soldiers, soft as the bread women bake.

I have seen that path of moonlight on water for which there is no word.

❦

Say that a man is missing a finger. So forever after he is known as "Fingers." It is a peasant wisdom that invents a man from what he does not have. There is a fine accuracy to such nicknames; I call this river "Bridges," for it has hardly any. Chug away an entire day, two even, and you do not see a bridge.

But when there is one, there is that long anticipation from the instant it is sighted far ahead, the exultation when at last the sun is carved from view and . . . hush! You are *in,* a quick narrow place that is cool and green and dark. How reluctantly you emerge from such an arcade into heat and light, all the usual affairs of August.

This Mississippi unspanned is no place to be.

❦

Two Rebel boys among the day's haul. Their eyes are covered with bloodstained cloths tied around their heads. Side by side, they sit on a bench, waiting. I untie the bandages. I saturate the dressings with water, and only when they are heavy with the water do I dare tease away the cloth from the underlying tissues lest I pull away valuable flesh. Once. Twice. Three times and four I lay bare . . . no eye, but an empty socket at the base of which puddles a yellowish ichor. One burst globe droops from its stalk upon the cheek below. A snip of the scissors, and it, too, is gone. The boy is startled by the sound.

"What was that?" he asks.

"Nothing," I say, "a bit of dead flesh. Something you didn't need anymore."

But vision is too cunning a thing to be killed by the putting out of eyes. It were an arrogance of anatomists to believe it so. No, vision is a nomad. He'll tent where he can—in the knees, the hands, the groove at the back of the neck. He will peer from behind the bars of rib cages, watching, and seeing no less than were he in his proper sockets.

∽

Dawn. In the pilothouse. We have been at river for an hour. A dozen crows have stayed the night in a great cottonwood tree that looks like clackety Death with his graspers out and waving. The crows hunch one to a branch, sawing at the air and working each other into a rage. As though beckoned, the community lifts. One after another dislocates his wings and flaps off, twelve black rags shaking away to God-knows-what ghastly food. For crows, this is the land of plenty. A blind peck at the earth will yield some morsel of new flesh.

It has begun to rain. A passionless fall that is unlikely to spend itself imprudently and so will persevere all day. A dead man is sighted on the bank. The crows have seen him too. Already the vanguard is grounded and stepping close. I rush with two others in the small boat to do the burial. One man rows, and we others shout and wave our shovels at the crows. We race them for the prize. The birds pull at their work until we are within arm's reach. Only then do they hop sideways a bit, sizzling to get back. The soldier's face is gouged, one wrist ripped, tendons unstrung.

But rain has filled his open mouth and runs across his chin. Who would imagine that from this fixed scream such a limpid brook could run? His papers state that he is Secesh from Mississippi. We dig in the mud and lay him in. It is far too wet for a grave. In three days he will seep into the river and the fish will have him.

I don't know why we think that's better than crows.

∽

Our cargo is typhoid, and worse by far than the most terrible battle wounds. These men bed in their excrement, too weak to raise themselves from where they lie. Most are doomed by the time they are carried aboard. There are so many, I cannot tend them all. I pour a few drops of midnight whiskey upon their black tongues and listen to their breathing. Some are pricked by a sudden delirium to spend their last caches of strength in wild careering about the deck. One man rises abruptly from his pallet and, as though chased, runs to the railing, calling out in tongues. Before he can be restrained, he has thrown himself over the side.

A man lies down to die. He sweeps a man-sized space of the deck, wraps himself in a blanket, turns half a circle and, doglike, settles to the boards. The wounded lie about among the dead, indistinguishable from them save for the occasional hand reaching upward to retrieve a beloved something that floats just away and away. So shyly, so gently do men die, that I found myself having just injected one man, a calico printer from Georgia, only to discover that he was long since cold and lifeless. An hour before, I had heard him swapping accounts of the battle with his fellows.

Even the *January* is ailing. It is hard to write, the old nanny quakes so.

∽

A bend in the river is a risk. What will be around it? New horror? Or more of the same horror? At three o'clock, standing at the railing of the upper deck, I see a lone woman on the west bank. I could not be more overcome by the sight were she some species of ape. She stares at the steamboat. As we draw abreast of her, she raises one hand and waves. It is the most tentative, the wariest of gestures. In the same manner, I wave in return. We are neither of us soldiers. Merely, we hope not to be shot.

∽

This morning I amputated the leg of an Illinois farmer, a man of forty-five years. We have run out of chloroform, and it must all be done without. I had hardened my heart for screams, but the man made no single sound. Now and again, I looked up to see was he conscious. He was. Once he opened his mouth as if to cry out, but . . . he merely yawned. There are such men who bear a legging bravely, as though bravery were the best in human character. But I think this kind of courage redemptive only in a wicked man, for in him it stands forth like a beacon in a wild gray sea. I would sooner trust a man who owns more honest tissues, who would not hesitate to shriek and bawl. Even Jesus wept. Not to unleash the throat in such circumstance is to misunderstand the natural purpose of outcry which is twofold: To comfort the uncomfortable with the sound of your own voice. What could be better proof that you are still alive? And to summon aid from all within earshot.

Still, as the leg of the Illinois farmer fell free and was lifted away by the orderly, the fellow raised his head to gaze after it. Once, in the woods, I came upon a snake in the midst of his shedding. And a neat, deliberate job it was the serpent did. Yet even as he slithered off, the creature turned to gaze one last time at the sad transparent crumple on the ground.

∾

Midnight. I sit at a small table on the covered deck. All about me in close neat rows lies the sick freight. A thick fog obscures all but my pen and notebook. The light of my lamp is turned back upon itself by the mist it cannot penetrate. The darkness is absolute. To the left of me a man coughs, then spits. Nearby, a rattling breath, caught on a bolus of phlegm, hesitates. For a long minute it ceases. I hold my own breath. At last I hear it again, and we breathe. Here and there the involuntary flux of dysentery sputters. Forlorn cracklings, the untranslatable fragments of a lost language. I may one day forget the words and deeds of this time, but I shall never rinse from memory the sound of a man turning into watery stool, his own mass diminishing as the puddle of his excrement widens and spreads until . . . the transubstantiation is complete.

"Oh, Jesus," someone cries.

And flowing beneath these sounds the low ceaseless murmuring of three hundred men drifting in and out of private dreams. I cannot tell where their whispering leaves off and the whispering of the river begins.

Strange shapes gather in the exhalations of dying soldiers! These are jets of vaporized pain shot from the wounds themselves. No mouth could make such air. Above the cots, currents hang, opaque with memories of battle. Now and then, budged by some impalpable breeze, they commingle, then part, then roll together in a thunder soundless and profound. I gaze, and kindle into dreams. I see Shiloh. I hear the hornetry of working muskets in the peach orchard, shouts, and the brave bugle blowing hullabaloo.

All at once, there is a scream—a blend of bell and cannon. It rings with majesty. I look across the field to the peach orchard, and see . . . Pegasus galloping through the trees. He is riderless, and his famous wings are beating at the dazzled air. Again he neighs! The spaces are not large enough for him, and his wing tips bruise against the stubborn branches. No orchard could contain him. Now he rears and sets his feathered parts in motion. They are impossibly high, arched, grabbing air to their undersurfaces, gathering it into gusts, churning it into a wind to rise upon. But he does not go aloft. He cannot. Again he rears, and now I see the bayoneted belly, that dark slit through which presents, like half-delivered twins, a double loop of pinkest bowel.

Fifty, no, a hundred yards he races, sidestepping, straining, his great boxy teeth biting at the peach blossoms, then stops, and, as though at his prayers, kneels into the horse pond at the edge of the orchard. The wings of Pegasus are broken. They flap with the sound of dry straw. It is a creaking. At last they come up, like the sleeves of a kimono drawn across the velvety nostrils. Bubbling, the great horse lies on his side, showing the whole fall of his intestines. He is everywhere soiled with blood.

Overhead and all around, the flowering peaches.

∽

Headache. All day the boilers hammering and the crepitation of muskets. We shall be deep imbrued by nightfall. The men say there is no ground uncovered by a fallen body. One strides them like a carpet, they say. Yesterday I counted twenty-seven bullet wounds in a single corpse.

I feel myself being taken over by the river. Soon I shall be more catfish on the prowl than man. I tell this to Mr. Forbes, the pilot. He laughs. Mr. Forbes is a huge man with a red beard that makes him appear both calm and wild. I judge him to weigh no less than 250 pounds. He knows every crook and turn in the river, just when it will turn peevish and throw up a snag, or a sawyer.

"If I thought," he says, "this war was to put a stop to slavery, I should not lift a finger to check the rebellion. The children of Ham are to be slaves for all time."

Just then a deck hand calls out a sounding.

"How is the river today?" I ask him.

"Low," Mr. Forbes says, and smiles. "Don't worry," he continues. "When it runs dry I can tap a keg of beer and run four miles on the suds."

∽

Old lady *January* is sick and undergoing surgery at the Cairo dock. Rupture of the boiler, I am told. But the way she coughed all the way to Cairo, I think pneumonia has set in too. Now she lies nuzzling the levee, sniffling rope, and waiting for the doctor.

At the St. Charles Hotel, we are in hearing distance of the guns. The hotel has been commandeered for bivouac, and everywhere there are soldiers recounting and bragging and deploring the generals. Now and then, a man will display his souvenirs, a sword or regimental flag. The streets are sodden and throng with men walking, just walking, all aimless in their motion. A cavalry officer gallops by, sending up gobbets of mud from the hooves. Everywhere there are wagons, munitions. In the main square, I see a stand of a thousand rifles.

I drink a whiskey at the saloon of the St. Charles, and go down to the levee to watch the repairs. I cannot keep my distance from that boat and that river. The short while I am ashore, I am on alien land. The customs are exotic, the language unintelligible. In the berth next to the *January*, the *Paris C. Brown* is being loaded with bales of cotton. Fifteen blacks, barefoot and stripped to the waist, work the cargo from one another in a line.

Ole roustabout ain' got no home.
Makes his livin' by his shoulder bone!

Oh I whoop my woman and I black her eye
But I won't cut her th'oat kaze I skeered she might die.

Up sack! You gone.
Up sack! You gone.
N'Yawlins niggers ain' got no sense.
Up sack! You gone.

Coonjine songs. They would tempt back all my dead.

∞

A fourteen-year-old fifer has been taken aboard. His brow has been torn away by a minié ball, and his right thigh is fractured. He has pale yellow hair and blue eyes. I carry him from the litter to a cot, and his head falls against my chest. Suddenly I feel myself to be a comet hurtling through the sky.

The boy shudders. I follow his gaze to my hands where the finger-nails are edged with old dried blood. Who can blame a boy for shud-dering at the claws of an old bear?

Now and then, one of the other men will start to sing. Soon he is joined by another, then another, until a great tuneless chorus rises.

I listen, and this whole world of men becomes for me a pantry that is rattled by the river until, one by one, the cup handles slip their hooks, and each china plate falls its little fall, and shatters.

∞

If it were not for the chloroform, I could not do it, amputate the arms and legs. I have not the stomach nor the heart for this hacking. Last night I probed the neck of a boy to retrieve a minié ball that had got lodged next to his great artery, the lantern held by a man barely able to stand. Each time I got near to dislodging the pill, the boy screamed out, "Jesus, help me," and each time I felt like Pontius Pi-late.

Two of the new amputees have got the rigors. It is horrible to watch them struggle to unlock their jaws for speaking. Their eyes are thrown upward in staring, their necks and spines so arched and rigid that only the back of the head and the remaining heel are in contact with the bed. Finally, awake to the very end, they strangle in convulsions.

Here, Death, you beauty, you outdo yourself.

∾

Another dawn. I stand on the upper deck. A strange elation has seized me, so that I am unable to sleep, except fitfully. The *January* rocks at her pier to the rhythm of faroff Minnesota springs. It is a soothing, amniotic pulse. On the opposite shore, a great hairy cypress surmounts the stream, dangling tendrils in the water.

∾

Scouts have warned of the approach of two Rebel rams, and we waddle up the Yazoo River for a distance of ten miles to hide. The rams are steamboats that have been fitted out with steel beaks at the prow. They are for goring.

The Yazoo is nimble and narrow. We huff against her current in our haste to get hidden. A few miles upstream, we see a great solemn rising in the middle of the river. It is the tilted hulk of a half-sunken steamboat, an old corpse, I know, from the shroudage of creepers that drape the upper deck and wind into the pilothouse. These riverlands of the South are everywhere red with such ulcerous ruins, all their chugging done, then banged out in a great flame as the boilers burst and exploded. Still, this corpse has kept something of itself, some boathood, calling to mind better days, with tapered banners notched at one end, and harmonicas playing in the saloon, and bales of cotton piled on the deck. A silence falls as we pass. On a tiny island that is no more than a yard of sand, a great blue heron stands, one leg folded upon its breast. Boatmen and water birds have the same dreams.

Still we lie sequestered among the vines of the Yazoo. Elisha, the fifer boy, lies upon the deck as though carved into the wood. I spend much of my time sitting by him, listening to his childish tales of the battle. How bravely he must have marched beside the drummer, tootling his fife. Were I a Tennessee soldier, I would have followed that sound into death. And so his elder brother did.

At noon today, he begs me to carry him to the edge of the deck so that he can look down into the water. I do, and lay him face down at the railing, lifting and holding him so that he peers straight down along the side of the vessel. He is delighted to see his reflection in the still water.

"Take off my bandage," he says. "I want to see my wound."

"No," I say. "Why would you see your wound?"

"Because I want to see what I have suffered for my country."

I unwrap the gauze from his forehead and hold him once again over the side of the boat. Looking down into the Yazoo, we can see the avulsion of his brow. It cannot be stitched, so much tissue having been torn away. Elisha studies it. And as I gaze with him down into the river, I see in the water behind his head the yellow noonday sun. There is the great red star-shape on his forehead, and, behind it, the sun. For a moment, I cannot say for certain. Is it the wound that hangs in the sky and the sun that blazes between the eyes of the boy?

∞

The men have caught an alligator and keep it below the deck in a box that the coffin makers have made for it. It is the river god, they say, and as long as we've got him on board, the *January* is safe from the Rebel rammers. Sometimes in the evening, when they feed it a rat, I hear the jaws snap shut. The sound carries to the deck where the sick men lie, and it makes them smile to think of the fun of it.

How bored the men are. When they hear the sounds of battle, they grow eager and hot-eyed. Like a horse kept too long in its stall will chew the wood of the barn for want of something to do. Those that are able crawl out upon the uncovered deck to feel the sun. Elisha lies among them. The men offer him bits of candy, little presents, a whittled stick. They ask him to play his fife for them. But he has not breath enough. What shall I do?

∞

The Union ram, *Queen of the West,* has been ordered to the mouth of the Yazoo to clear the way for us. We saunter off behind her. An hour later, what excitement! The Rebel stegosaurus, *General Leighton,* is waiting. The *Queen of the West*'s beak took the *Leighton* squarely on the guards twenty feet back of her stern, cut through her like a ripsaw, clove her timbers apart, pierced her entrails. The dark waters rushed madly into the hull, and she settled rapidly. But the wounded *Leighton* gripped the beak of the *Queen* and held fast to pull her conqueror down with her. The *Queen* backed off, and the two vessels ground and wallowed past each other like churning giants, the sinking *Leighton* taking on water like a thirsty sailor. Full speed! Within minutes, we can no longer see the men of the *Leighton* floundering in the river. We won!

Once again, we are heading downstream toward Pittsburgh Landing to pick up a load of wounded. Elisha's fever rages. The wound has begun to stink. One of the coffin makers has been carving for him a pair of crutches out of a Rebel flagstaff. I am impatient for them, asking the man again and again, "Aren't they finished?"

∽

There are three hundred sick and wounded on the middle deck. Overnight we have become a barge smeared with shit from typhoid and dysentery. From below, there is the ceaseless hammering of the coffin makers. Each day, dozens of these men die, and each night we bury them along the banks, the graves hurried scoopings in the earth. On the next trip we will be reminded of our haste when we see poking from the earth some portion of an uncoffined body, an arm groping, a leg dancing up into the sunshine. If waking from the dead is as painful as this dying, I'll have none of the Resurrection, thank you.

∽

It is three years that I have ferried the dead over these dark waters. A terrible sameness discolors my days. It is as though the river has turned upon itself, taken its tail into its mouth to make a circle around which I am doomed to chunter. How I long for something . . . a waterfall! Yes, a cataract. Oh let me imagine it! At first a drubbing, barely audible; then a quickening of the stream. The noise rises, a thunder greater than the hum of these miles of cliffs along the bank. I look ahead and see that the river has ended, all at once, in blank open space. The *January* captured and pulled along. We tilt; we hang; we plummet. Ah, there is an end to it! In a cloud of wrack and lovely foam!

∽

The boy will let only me dress his wound. Sweet tyranny! He cannot read nor write. I write down a letter to his mother.

> Dear, kind Maw,
> I have been brave, but I have sinned greatly. I hope that the sinning will not win over the brave part when the time comes soon to be chosen for Heaven. I thank you for your prayers. I am sure they will help me.
> Your boy Lishe.

He has been with me for four weeks. I have kept him with me. He begged me to keep him with me. I have forgotten how it was he came on board. But it must have been like Moses out of the bulrushes. Sometimes I take the notion that the slattern *January* and I are man and wife. And it is upon this old squaw that the boy Elisha was begot. When he is able, he plays "Yankee Doodle" on his fife for the men on the deck, and they lose their last bit of fluid in tears.

∽

One of the wounded is a Rebel lieutenant from Alabama. There is a sucking wound in the left side of his chest. With each inspiration, air is expelled through this ragged opening despite that I have plugged it with oiled lint. His fever rages. He is dying, certain. I sit with him during his final hour, and, all the while, he talks of the reasons for the war, why it is necessary.

At the last, he tears a brass button from his gray coat and places it in my hand. There is that telltale "give," the taut arms gone limpsy, the onrush of silence that fills the space abandoned by labored breathing, moans; and I, visiting such new silences every hour.

∽

Prisoners released from a Rebel jail. So thin that the origin and insertion of each muscle is visible. The bony eminences all but burst through the skin. Only one man is hugely fat. He is but slightly wounded—a bullet in the buttock. I shall have to dig for it, I suppose. His corpulence is an insult to the others and to me that must go after the pellet. I watch the fat man manage the boarding plank. He grunts and puffs like a cow in a barn. They say some are eating human flesh.

∽

What is this that gathers in me as I watch the boy struggling to die like a man and cannot? A kind of madness that urges me to kill him, to save him from death. A caged animal will kill its young. Is it to save it from the long death of captivity that the bear takes up her cub in her jaws, shakes it, and dashes it against the bars?

∽

It is a day of amputating, dressing, and pronouncing death. In the midst of it, I am told by an orderly that Elisha has died. Near the end, the boy called out for me. William! William! although he never called me anything but Doctor. It was the delirium, the orderly said, but I was not there to see that. For me, now, these many "Williams" are the urgent whispers of love. How quickly in war love springs full-grown—at least as fast as death. And how gently the one falls into the other. He is to be buried with the others this night. The gravediggers promise to mark the spot.

In the evening I watch from the deck as the coffins are unloaded and carted up the bank. One of the crutches I have given to be placed upright alongside the grave. The other I throw into the river. Now I accompany the coffin up the bank. I stand over it as the grave is dug. I gaze down at the coffin, then bend to stroke it, to feel, not boy, but board.

Later, from the deck of the *January,* the hillock is starred with the large fireflies that cloud in these parts, making it appear to me, far below, that the entire bank lies already in the sky. I stand at the railing until that burglar, night, has finished stealing from me the gravesite of that boy. I turn back toward the deck where the wounded lie. The odor of a rose would suffocate me, the color of sky madden. I hate every lovely thing. Let me hear screams and weeping. I begin to dress a wound, a soupy crater in the flank of a man too old by far to have fought in any war. "A vulture would turn me down," he says. He shakes with fever; I could light a match to his skin.

I probe the putrid depths of the great sore. The man shudders to feel me there. My finger meets the hard blunt tip of a minié ball. I fish it out and hold it up for the man to see. Very faintly, he smiles. All at once a strange feeling comes over me. It is happiness. I cannot resist it. And I know that if love came once, it may come again. If love should not come, still I know why I am alive.

The Mirror: A Tale of Aran

*B*itter and fell is winter in the islands of Aran. All night the cold sharpens itself on the rasp of the wind, and by dawn is gone so hard there is nothing more it can do, nowhere else it can but into burning. So that the line between heat and cold is muddled, and one feels a fierce silver bead in the chest. Underneath the breastbone cringes the heart. There is an island called Inishmar that is the smallest of those that are inhabited. Inishmar has not the consolation of trees. The only soil has been scraped from here and there, shovel by hard shovel, and packed into holes and sheltered gulleys. Such islands are like insects that long ago were shaken off in annoyance by the great masses of land and ever since lie shiny and helpless at some decent remove from the back of the earth.

Once upon a time, not so long ago as to be forgotten, nor so recently as to be part of this time, an old man and an old woman lived on the island. It seemed they had always been there, and except for once, neither had left it. When the old man was a boy of seven years, there had been a winter harsher than ever before. Not for a minute did the murderous sea lighten or cease to slide back and forth across all but the very highest part of the rock, where the cottage stood. They had run out of food, and he had begun to cough. His mother blamed it on the fairies who had vexed her all her life and would not let up, she said, until they had pestered her to death. In the autumn, she had dug her potatoes and found that one had been scooped out and filled with blood. And now there was this wild winter. They had run out of food altogether, and the boy had gotten a bad chest. It was the fairies all right, she said.

Ye've got to go, the boy heard her say to his father, and take the boy to Ireland. A moment later, without waiting for his answer, she said, Well, go then, and that was all. He remembered being lifted into the curragh, and the hellish rowing of the man. How his father gripped the oars so that man and wood seemed to have fused. And he remembered the terrible groans that came from his father's mouth, that were gathered from somewhere in his back and flung to the wind. They frightened him, these loud, passionate sounds. All the more because he could not marry them to the man who often spent an entire day without speech. He could not remember his father's face, only the whiteness of it, and the way his beard blew over one shoulder. When they reached Ireland, his father had pulled the boat up on the beach, and died. Just toppled back into the boat. Heartburst, he had heard the men say. The next day they had taken him back. There were two curraghs this time. In one was his father and three men. He was in the other with three more. He had never been away from Inishmar since then.

The men of Ireland had carried the body of his father to the hut, and showed it to his mother. They asked her where it was to be buried, for there seemed to them no plot of ground large enough on this rock. She led them to a place nearby, which was a basin in the stone, molded by the curling of the seas that washed over the top and back again. Sand and earth and bits of shell and seaweed had been gathered here and packed in this place which was for them a garden. Here, she said, put him here.

And the men had measured out the size of the grave with sticks, leaving just an inch to spare, for they knew the cost of the ground to this woman and her child. And there they dug, scooping out the meager soil with great care. The boy had never seen so much earth laid bare, and to him it was like the sight of jewels. And then their shovels struck something hard. Ah, said one of the men, it is too shallow here. But they dug farther to lay bare the rock, and saw that it was no rock but something white and smooth. And when his mother saw it, she knelt by the side of the grave and reached in and drew out the skull of her own mother, for it was just here, in this place, that they had laid her long ago. And the boy watched her where she had howled then, this woman who had not yet wept, but whose grief had been set in motion by the touch of her mother's skull. In the end, the men laid them in together, covered them up and tamped it down. Then they went into their curraghs and they rowed away.

Now it was sixty years later and a fierce winter again. The old man and the old woman had never felt so bad a time. There was food enough for but a few more days. Soon they would be too weak to keep the fire going. When it went out, they would die. Days went by, and they did not speak to each other, for each feared that any words would let loose the dread they had been holding in. At last, she saw him go to the box where the few coins were. He tied them into a piece of cloth and put it inside his shirt. Then, he walked to the door, silent until his hand was lifting the very latch itself, holding out still against the words, fearing the magical effect they would surely have, and the old woman felt helpless with her unshuttered ears.

"I'll have to be going now," he said.

His voice startled her. She had not heard him speak in three days, and it sounded alien to her, like the noise of an animal that had somehow come to a place which was not its native habitat. Perhaps it had ridden there on an iceberg, or been blown to it on the wind, and now that she heard its cry, the sound made her shiver with fright, the way she did when she heard the fairies bark and giggle in the corners.

"Well, go then," she said after a long time. And they both understood that the time of horror was upon them.

The old woman stood in the doorway and watched him climb down to the wet rocks. They were alternately silvery with the foam of the waves, and black with the wetness left behind. She watched him heft the curragh to his back. His head was hidden by it, so that all she could see of him were his sticklike legs and that boat shell that he wore like a beetle. Now he was standing in the sea holding the curragh in front of him, waiting for an opening in the waves so that he could race between them and slam the curragh down for just time enough to jump in and keep it from swamping. She had seen him do it many times before, but now it seemed to her impossible to do, and that in a while he would back out of the sea, set down the curragh, and climb back up to her so that they could just let it go, give it up. At the last minute, she decided that was what she had wanted all along, and she almost started to run down to the rocks to call out to him to come back, to stop. But she did not, could not. Not after all the silence. And a shyness came over the old woman, and she stayed in the doorway watching him as though he were a strange man that she had watched every day and wanted to speak to but could not.

Then she saw him take a running step and fall forward into the boat with his hands gripping the gunwales on either side, balancing the curragh somehow while it scooped wildly. In a minute he had the oars unshipped, was sitting there, pulling. And with each pull, getting smaller until he was just a speck in her eye, a speck which she wiped away with one finger, after which she turned and went back into the cottage and closed the door. The old woman bent to stir the turf in the fire, then sat down to wait.

It was bad luck to let a fire go out. Someone always died, or the roof fell in, or the fairies came and poisoned the potatoes with their urine. Most of her life, the old woman had picked at the fire, separating bits of turf, then heaping them together, turning them over this way and that. For her, keeping fire on this island all surrounded and washed with water was a victory of some kind, and, like all triumphs, had taken upon itself certain magic properties. Only once, the fire had gone out. In the middle of the night, she had awakened with a terrible choking in her chest. She could not catch her breath, and sat up to find that the fire had gone out. Then she had heard a dog wailing, and the next day she had dug her potatoes and found that one had been filled with blood. The fairies would never lose a chance like that.

All that day the old man rowed, bending, straightening, then doubling again in the rhythm pounded out for him by the thumping of the sea against the bottom of the curragh. The sounds that came from his throat with each pull were the grunts of a body laboring to be delivered of something impacted deep inside. His lips and eyes burned; his beard, which in the beginning rose and fell with his body, now lay still, pulled to one shoulder, and frozen there, fused to the ice of his shoulder.

It was toward dusk. Already the first stars were dividing up the sky.

In an hour there would be no more sight, only hearing. On and on he rowed, an ancient machine that would soon run down when its momentum was spent. Dimly, he saw a gull stooping to the waves. All at once, the man felt a strange uncertainty of his flesh, as though it were pausing for a moment, confused, wondering which way to fall, then deciding at last that toward the oars would be best. He tumbled upon them, swiveling back and forth with the energy with which he had infused them. Now that he was through, they had enough to go on without him, and they did—or so it seemed to the old man, cradled and waiting to die.

When the shout came, the shout that was not a bird, nor a false construction of wind and wave, but a sound from the mouth of a fellow human being, he did not move. Who can trust the hailing from the shadowy banks of such a river? It was better to lie rocking, with the eyes closed.

More shouting. The old man smiled, floated. When the hands gripped his shoulders, tipped him backward, he was ready to be taken, offered his breast. He would not resist. And they seized him! And lifted him, and carried him to where there was no motion but a solid hard place that he recognized as . . . the Earth. The old man was sorrowful then, as though something—a prize—for which he had labored with all his might had been denied him at the last minute. All that rowing, that cold, that sea. He opened his eyes and saw the sky infected with gray, felt the cold spray, touched stones at his fingertips. He had rowed all the way to Ireland! The way his father had done. And with that thought came a landslide of coughs and retching, the gasps that made him feel a fish disenfranchised from the sea.

When he awoke, he knew that he had eaten. He was warm and dry. They told him that it was two days since he had come. Later, he rose and walked to the sea. It was calm as death. He thought, now it is time to go back. The old woman was waiting for him. The men of Ireland put the grain and potatoes into the curragh and lifted it into the water, held it while he climbed in and took hold of the oars. They pushed him off. He was in the sea again.

But now something burned against the skin of his chest, beneath his sweaters and coat. He felt it and smiled and did not mind the pain in his joints as he pulled the oars. For he had narrowed all his senses down to that one spot on the left side of his chest over the ribs, near the heart. It was what the old man had stolen—he who had never stolen before. From whom should he steal? The old woman?

In Ireland one night, he had awakened on the mat they had laid for him by the fire. The others lay sleeping nearby. He had gotten up to go outside to relieve himself. When he returned, he saw upon a shelf a piece of glass encased in a thin wooden frame with a handle attached. He had picked it up, brought it to the fire, and looked at it, then *in* it, and had seen there a face—a terrible old face—like a wild man's, whose sunken eyes were blue as fairy-flax, with a tempest of white hair, and lips caked with something dark that had gathered in the corners of the mouth and dried there. Terrible as it was, something held him to it, perhaps the answering stare of him who was trapped there within the glass. And soon a recollection gathered, faint and dim, from his childhood, something he did not know the name of. He saw the awakening, the wild surmise grow in the face of the man in the glass as well. At last the old man brought the mirror closer to his face, straining, reaching out for whatever it was that was coming near to him after so many years, and then, with the glass touching his lips, he heard his own voice whisper, "Da . . . Da."

And the sound of the word was like the hissing of fire, for he saw the lips of the other one form the very word he had whispered. Then he knew that trapped within that glass was the father who had rowed all the way to Ireland so long ago, and whom he had thought to have died, whom he had seen buried, but who was somehow living and imprisoned in the bit of glass! He knew also that he would have that bit of glass, would steal it, must. There would be this rescue. He had been saved for it. And he, who had never stolen, became sly. He slipped the glass beneath his shirt, and lay back upon the mat, feeling the part of him it touched shiver and burn, as hot and bright as the sun.

Now in the curragh, the old man felt strangely aroused. It was an agitation. Sudden sweat broke from his papery skin. A fine trembling took his chest. But they were more the symptoms of an acute illness than the effects of the charge that he, all at once, understood had been laid upon him. By whom? He did not know, only that he had come through his ordeal and had made a discovery, had found the surprise at the very center of his life, and that it had changed him. He would never be the same as he was.

For the old man, the rowing home was an escape, a getting-away, and, as such, was done with that remarkable ease with which superhuman feats are accomplished by men who are goaded by fire, or placed in combat with ferocious beasts. A new juice flows; there is a numbness wherein pain is not felt, nor fear realized. In just such a state of blind vigor, the old man rowed across the sea. It was an act of rescue. And, all the while, he felt the mirror against his chest as though it were a mouth applied there, through which energy surged from some mysterious source into his body, flooding it, galvanizing his stiff joints, his stringy muscles, moistening and lubricating him until he was once again a working machine.

Somewhere in that time of bending and straightening, he thought, I'll not show it to her. "No," he said aloud, "no, it is mine." And although the words were ripped from his lips by the wind so that the old man did not hear the sound of his voice, they were as irrevocable as the thought that produced them.

At last the old man pulled the curragh out of the water and secured it upon the high rocks of Inishmar. Inside the hut, the old woman was bending at the fire, stirring it. She looked up to see him, and gladness came over her. "So you are back," she said, and continued to stir the fire. She knew without asking what he had endured, all the rigor of it. He carried the sacks from the curragh to the hut, and she stored them, marking her efforts with little grunts and whispers.

That night, as the old woman lay asleep, he rose from his pallet, and stepped to the far side of the chimney. There he gouged with his knife into the hardened mud that was the caulking between the stones until he had loosened a large one, level with his head. Slowly then, he drew it out, and, in the little space behind, he placed the mirror. He put back the stone, and returned to his bed. Each day when the old woman left the hut to gather seaweed from the rocks for drying, he would go to the fireplace, slide out the stone, and hold up the mirror to the light. "Da," he said over and over, and he would see his father's face take on that soft gaze of love for which he had yearned all of his life. When he saw the old woman approaching the door, he would quickly replace the mirror and the stone and walk away.

Weeks passed, and one day as he was looking into the mirror, he saw that she had come back, and was standing in the doorway. "What have you?" she said. "It is nothing," he said. "A bit of stone." And he hid it in his hand. But the old woman had seen. And she stalked him, until one night, as she pretended to lie asleep, she saw him rise from his bed and go to the fireplace, saw him take out the *thing* which now she must see. She watched him hold it over the open fire and gaze at it, and saw how his face grew tender and soft, and all at once she knew that it was the picture of a young, beautiful girl that he had met in Ireland, and with whom he had fallen in love. And for the first time she sensed the horror of her life on the island, Inishmar, that had become for her the image of her mind. She saw herself as bald, barren, a boulder against which the sea crashed, and whose buffeting she had not felt until that moment.

Now! She watched him, waiting for his sleep, anticipating it with more excitement than she thought still danced in her nerves. At last, she saw the letting-go, that small collapse that told her that the old man slept. In the hazy light of the turf fire, his face seemed made of plaster upon which crept, now here, now there, a gray mold. And she thought of a corpse she had seen years ago rolling in the sea, crashing again and again upon the rocks. She remembered how oblivious it was to the banging, how its solemn expression never changed. For a brief moment, she was swept by a kind of sorrow for the old man, and she remembered how once he had been as cool and fresh as a seagull. She lay back upon her pallet then. But when she could no longer see his face, she thought of what he had done, how he was cheating her of something. And her rage blazed, for she fed it with an image of soft golden hair and smooth breasts and cheeks.

She stood then, looking down at him. At that moment, there was more life in her than she could sustain. She was afraid that she might fall down and die of it then and there. But that she could not do, not until she had seen the picture. At the side of the fireplace, she felt blindly, ran her flapping fingers over the stones until she found the loose one. Then scrabbling, rocking, pulling and scraping, she edged it out. How heavy it was! It fell back against her chest, where she clutched it tightly. The old woman lowered the stone to the hearth with utmost daintiness. She reached into the space. Yes! It was there, that thing that was only his, and not hers, and that she had to see even though she knew it would kill her to see it. Once she had it in her hand, she grew calm, as though its hardness were given over somehow to her flesh. She stopped her trembling. She could no longer feel the pressure of her heartbeat against her jaw.

Suddenly, the old man groaned in his sleep, and raised his thin arms as though to ward off a bad dream. She waited for him to go still again, then knelt upon the hearth and leaned as far as she could into the firelight. The old woman held up the mirror . . . and recoiled. This was no beautiful young girl, but an ugly old hag! With a drooping nose over thin gray lips and a bundle of dead hair. A thousand wrinkles carved up this horror. It was the ugliest face she had ever seen. A witch, she thought, a horrible witch, and shuddering with disgust, she watched the face in the mirror draw back its lips in a grimace. All at once, her whole body felt as though it were being squeezed into a place that was too small for it, and raising her arm high above her head, the old woman threw the mirror against the hearthstones with all her might.

The noise of the shattering woke the old man, and he spoke into the darkness, without turning to see, "What is it?"

"Nothing," said the old woman. "Nothing at all. It's the fairies have been and gone."

Alexis St. Martin

At that very place where the waters of three Great Lakes, Huron, Michigan, and Superior, come together, there humps the turtlish island called Michilimackinac. Here, in the year 1822, a shotgun was fired that blew open the body of a man and founded the science of gastroenterology. Aesculapius, the god of medicine, must have set all Olympus booming with laughter when he arranged that mayhem in Mackinac, and set in motion this unlikely Passion.

The dramatis personae are two: Alexis St. Martin, an illiterate nineteen-year-old fur trapper, one of an army of such, recruited by the American Fur Company, John Jacob Astor's corporate device with which he proposed to debeaver the forests of the Northwest and enmuskrat the women of Europe. The other was William Beaumont, age twenty-five, born of landed gentry in Lebanon, Connecticut, now an army doctor stationed at Fort Mackinac.

If St. Martin was a natural man, at home only in the trackless woods of Canada, or gliding across that country's numberless lakes on silent, home-hewn bateaux, Beaumont was the true heir of colonial solidity, a self-made man whose evenings were spent reading Shakespeare and copying into his journal Benjamin Franklin's essay *On the Achievement of Moral Perfection.*

History is more often a chronology of accidents that befall individual men than the grand sweep of forces, or the relief of inexorable planetary pressures. So it was that on the morning of June 6, 1822, the trading post on the island of Mackinac was crowded with trappers shouting to each other in the patois of French Canada. The stench of untreated hides, piled to the roof beams, would have nauseated a wolf. Still, it did not stifle the atmosphere of exhilaration. For these "voyageurs" were waiting to be paid for their winter's harvest of fur. Later, there would be whiskey, singing, squaws, and the fighting that they loved more than any of these others. All at once, there was the stunning explosion of a shotgun inadvertently fired from a distance of three feet. One of the young men, Alexis St. Martin, dropped to the floor, blood pouring from a fist-sized hole in his left side. William Beaumont, the lone physician on the island, was summoned. He arrived minutes later and neatly extracted part of the shot from the wound, as well as pieces of clothing that had been driven inward. He then departed, with no hope for the patient's survival.

When Beaumont returned several hours later, he was astonished to find St. Martin still alive. Further debridement and dressing of the wound were carried out, and the patient was then removed to the small army hospital under Beaumont's care.

Beaumont's journal described the blast as

> carrying away the integuments more than the size of a man's hand: blowing off the 6th rib, fracturing the 5th, Rupturing the lower portion of the left lung, and lacerating the Stomach by a spicula of the rib that was blown through its coat.

The surrounding flesh and clothing were burned to a crisp.

Further, he described

> a portion of the lung as large as a turkey's egg protruding through the wound, lacerated and burnt, and below this another protrusion resembling a portion of the Stomach with a puncture large enough to receive my forefinger, and through which a portion of his food which he had taken for breakfast had come out and lodged among his apparel.

Each day, many times each day, Dr. Beaumont treated the wound, cutting away the devitalized bone and lung, and applying poultices "to excite local reaction." On the fifth day,

> a partial sloughing took place and the febrile symptoms abated. The protruded portion of the lungs and stomach sloughed and left the puncture of the stomach plain to be seen, and large enough to admit my forefinger its whole length directly into the cavity of the stomach.

On the tenth day,

> a more extensive sloughing took place. The febrile symptoms all subsided, and the whole surface of the wound put on a healthy granulating appearance . . . nature kindly performing what human foresight viewed as hopeless and professional skill might calculate upon with dubious odds. A lucky circumstance to which his miraculous survival can be attributed was the protruded portion of the stomach, instead of falling back into the cavity of the abdomen, adhered to the body wall, and by this means afforded a free passage out.

After about three weeks, Alexis was feeling quite well, and the process of scarring had begun. Despite all of the doctor's efforts, he reports that the stomach showed not the least disposition to close, gradually resembling in its appearance "a natural anus." Each time he removed the dressing, the contents of the stomach would run out.

From this point, Beaumont began to see Alexis, not on appointed rounds, but throughout the day. He observed the boy making the best of his oddness—perhaps, even, being playful with it. Wrote the doctor:

> He will drink a quart of water or eat a dish of soup, and then, by removing the dressings and compress, can immediately throw it out through the wound. . . . When he lies on the opposite side I can look directly into the cavity of the

stomach, and almost see the process of digestion. I can pour in water with a funnel, or put in food with a spoon, and draw them out again with a syphon. I have frequently suspended flesh, raw and wasted, and other substances into the perforation to ascertain the length of time required to digest each.

The months from September 1822 until the following May were marked by a series of abscesses, ulcerations, and sinus tracts, to each of which William Beaumont gave his daily meticulous attention. At this time, the county refused any further assistance to St. Martin, and Beaumont reported in his journal:

I took him into my own family from mere motives of charity and a disposition to save his life, or at least to make him comfortable, where he has continued improving in health and condition, and is now able to perform any kind of labor from the whittling of a stick to the chopping of logs, and is as healthy, active, and strong as he ever was in his life, or any man in Mackinac, and with the aperture still present and presumed permanent.

In 1825 there began a series of experiments performed upon the person of Alexis St. Martin by William Beaumont, experiments which were to become for the one man a magnificent obsession and for the other a hated martyrdom. Countless were the physical and chemical manipulations carried out and endured; inestimable the value of the observations made.

At what point did William Beaumont first perceive the possibilities inherent in St. Martin's wound? Gordon S. Hubbard, an official in the American Fur Company, was an eyewitness to the event. Years later, recalling the circumstances, he wrote:

"I knew Dr. Beaumont very well. The experiment of introducing food into the stomach through the orifice, purposely kept open and healed with that object, was conceived by the doctor soon after the first examination" in the trading post. "About this time . . . the doctor announced that he was treating his patient with a view to experimenting on his stomach."

Yet the daily entries in the medical chart kept by Beaumont give the lie to Hubbard's recollection. Would the doctor who recorded each debridement, each sloughing of necrotic tissue, each happy mound of new granulation tissue, would he be likely to harbor the secret hope that the wound would *not* heal? That all of his surgical efforts would fail?

Where lies the truth? Perhaps there are no "facts." Perhaps all of history is conjecture, interpretation, and, in the end, faith. Doubtless Beaumont's recognition of the importance of the wound to science was early. Why then, all the more honor to him who left no stone unturned in his meticulous efforts to bring about the healing of it. Since history fails to inform absolutely in this critical matter, one is left to one's own interpretative devices. I prefer to think of Beaumont as tortured by his conflicting desires: to keep the wound from healing, and to ensure that it healed. I like to think that Beaumont struggled with his temptations and overcame them. That in the end he behaved as a good doctor would: His patient's well-being came first. The fact that the wound did fail to heal may be thought of by incurable romantics as a kind of divine retribution for having behaved irreproachably.

And so the experiments were begun.

Imagine, then, Alexis. He reclines on a cot, naked to the waist, ordered to lie on his right side for hours at a time while the inserted material is digesting. Then ordered to lie on his left side that the gastric juice might run the more freely, be the more easily collected. Then asked to carry the vials of this fluid in his armpits so as to achieve for it the body's temperature. All these things he is commanded to do day and night and many times each day. Now see William. Approaching the bed whereon the other lies, he pauses at his table to select a hollow reed for insertion. He peels the stopper of lint from the orifice of the wound, and hastens to catch the fluid in his vials. His face is a study in earnestness. Having made his measurements, he sits at his desk, recording the data, amounts, temperatures, stages of digestion, in his notebooks. All this while, Alexis must lie still, or he must fast, or eat only certain foods. And all to a purpose whose significance Alexis cannot comprehend, and that for him has no importance at all.

How much does a man owe to another man who has saved his life? Does he owe him the remainder of his own?

Nowhere in the countless retelling of this story is one invited into the heart of Alexis St. Martin, young, well muscled, and strong as he has often been described, homesick for his lakes and forests, despondent, not permitted even the automatic pacing that is the prerogative of the caged leopard, but coerced into lying down, even as that leopard, *couchant, regardant.* His keeper, the man who *saved his life,* ties a string around the piece of meat that Alexis *knows* is coming, knows that the other man is going to poke into his body. With what a sign of resignation does he raise his left arm out of the way, the better to proffer his wound, the better to submit again to the intrusion that is for him a kind of rape. How can he know that Beaumont is never more alive than when he is pursuing him? That, even as he, St. Martin, mopes, Beaumont is exhilarated, expectant, buoyed by the hope of discovery?

Implicit in the word *voyageur* is the intention to return home. Without this expectation, the voyageur becomes an exile. For Alexis, the house of Beaumont is a place of exile, a wild island upon which he has been cast by a roughneck fate. And just as he is an innocent prisoner, so is Beaumont a jailer both benevolent and slightly cruel. William Beaumont has given back to Alexis St. Martin not his life, but the mere appearance of it.

But eventually the spirit of Alexis St. Martin began to suffocate. Having been strung and pipetted and measured beyond endurance, he bolted back to the woods and lakes of his homeland. Wrote Beaumont in a letter to the publisher of his experiments:

> I regret very much that it is not in my power to offer more varied and satisfactory results, but, unfortunately for me . . . he has absconded and gone to Canada, at the very time I was commencing a number of more interesting and important experiments upon the process of digestion and power of the gastric liquors, and I very much fear I shall not be able to recover possession of him again. He was unwilling to be experimented upon, though it caused him but little pain or distress.

For William Beaumont, the defection of St. Martin was no less than the thievery of his dreams, the petulant act of a stupid ungrateful boy. He would get him back if it was the last thing he did.

The year was 1825. Such was St. Martin's vaunted frailty that he had easily managed the solo journey back to his native Quebec, a distance of two thousand miles, in an open canoe. For the next two years, William Beaumont wanted only one thing: he wanted the "ungrateful boy" back. In desperation he appealed to the officers of the American Fur Company, asking them to be on the lookout for him, and, whatever the cost, to bring him back. At last, word! From one of these officers who reported that the ungrateful boy was now married to an Indian woman, and living in the country, "poor and miserable beyond description." Two years later, at the urging of a petty constable, Alexis returned to Beaumont accompanied by his Indian wife. During those four previous years, Alexis had worked hard to support his family, as a voyageur for the Hudson Bay Fur Company. All this time he had remained robust and well.

From 1829 to 1831, St. Martin and his wife lived at the home of Beaumont and his wife in a sort of *Upstairs, Downstairs* arrangement. The second set of experiments were carried out. And Alexis acted as servant to the Beaumonts, chopping wood, carrying bundles. During this time, he also fathered more children, working toward his grand total of seventeen.

That these second experiments, too, were impeccable, flawless, and simple, is a matter of fact.

Experiment No. 34
March 14, 1830
At 8 o'clock 15 mins. introduced two ounces of rare roasted beef, suspended by a string, into the stomach, and at the same time put one drachm of the same kind of meat into twelve drachms of gastric juice, contained in a vial, and put it into his [Alexis's] bosom. The piece in his stomach, examined every hour till 12 o'clock . . . exhibited a uniform but very slow process of digestion, confined entirely to the surface of the meat. In four hours about half of it only was dissolved and gone. That in the bosom, at the same time,

digested still slower, owing probably to the circumstances that the fluid in the vial had been taken out when the stomach was in a morbid condition, and had been permitted to get cold, even to the freezing point. This last circumstance, however, was probably of less importance than the other. The meat in the stomach was too much confined by the string, was not permitted to move about freely in the gastric fluids by the natural motions of the stomach, and consequently did not digest so fast as it otherwise would have done. Another circumstance or two may also have contributed to interrupt the progress of digestion, such as anger and impatience, which were manifested by the subject during this experiment.

One can hardly be surprised.

Alexis left again in 1831 and returned in 1832, at which time Beaumont, skittish over the possibility of permanent separation, attempted to bind Alexis to him with a legal contract.

> ". . . And the said Alexis covenants and agrees to submit to, assist and promote by all means in his power such Physiological or Medical experiments as the said William shall direct . . . on the Stomach of him, the said Alexis, either through or by means of the aperture or opening thereto in the side of him, the said Alexis . . . and will obey, suffer, and comply with all reasonable and proper orders. . . ."

in return for which Beaumont agreed to pay St. Martin the fee of $150 "for the service of a year."

For a period of ten years, Alexis intermittently endured and fled. For ten years Beaumont experimented or pursued him. Here, then, are the appearances of what happened. Whether they constitute, in fact, the realities is what makes the study of history no mere memorialization of events or the handing down of sacred prejudice, but a subject open to interpretation by thoughtful men and women.

Why tell once more this oft-recounted story of Beaumont and St. Martin? It is the best-known, most-beloved tale in all of American medicine. Beaumont's experiments, crude but meticulous, have long since entered the living literature. Beaumont himself is most securely elevated and enshrined. Everywhere there are Beaumont rooms, tablets, portraits, memorabilia. Everything but a constellation in the heavens, and over this only Aesculapius has jurisdiction. It is precisely to recast this event in terms truer to the dear and faulty nature of man that I here conjecture anew.

There are risks in such an undertaking. A profession that fails to pay homage to its heroes will surely fall on hard times. Not so long ago heresy was punishable by burning at the stake. Still, let us dare.

And so, two men, one the son of Congregationalist landed gentry in Lebanon, Connecticut: solemn, moral, and dutiful down to his Yankee bones; the other a carefree child of the Canadian backwoods: strong, wise in the way of the forests, his mind uncluttered with literacy or other unnatural contrivances. Whilst Beaumont read Shakespeare, Pope, and Robert Burns to while away his time, and even copied Ben Franklin's essay *On the Achievement of Moral Perfection,* Alexis learned to traverse the woods as silently as an Indian, to trap muskrat and beaver, to fight with his fists, and to drink whiskey. Who is to say that wisdom lies at the end of one path over the other? It were an arrogance to ascribe to either one the role of the model man. They were . . . what they were. That it was Alexis who lay blasted open on the floor of the trading center, the recipient of the skill and professional devotion of William, and not William lost and helpless in the depths of the trackless forests of the Northwest until Alexis should happen by to lead him to safety, that such was the turn of events is the accident of fate.

Two men. Neither one noticeably graced with a sense of humor. The one grimly following his purpose, self-righteous, pious; the other a roisterer grown morose through a lifetime of invalidism and pain. A feisty cockerel doomed to the tireless chaffing of his fellows who called him "the man with the lid on his stomach." What, for God's sake, did they talk about all those hours and days and weeks and years while they lived in service to The Wound? While Alexis reclined on a bed, and William sat next to him, dangling his infernal string, or inserting his little tube? Did they tell each other jokes? Make up stories? Play word games? Did Alexis undertake to teach William the patois of

French Canada? Did William teach Alexis chemistry? Was there any affection between them? Any love? Or were they two self-serving con artists, each out for his own; Beaumont for fame and glory, St. Martin for the money to buy liquor? Was it just Beaumont buying and Alexis selling? A sullen ten-year commerce in gastric juice?

The idea for the experiments once having seized Beaumont, it was never to turn him loose. It was as though the doctor himself had been seized between the jaws of that wound, and that it was, in fact, Alexis St. Martin who kept William Beaumont in thrall. Alexis had long since become the grail after which Beaumont was to yearn for the rest of his life. For Beaumont the Measurer, there was a magical exhilaration in the adventure. Once having stepped through the mangled portieres of St. Martin's body, he was never to look back. Not Orpheus on his way to Hell owned such a feverish expectancy. What was his anguish when again and again he was halted, turned back by the capricious petulance, the coquetry, the recalcitrance of St. Martin?

For every man there is one single enterprise that describes his life, and that makes of all that went before, all that is to follow, mere anticipation or recollection. For some it is the selection of a mate, for others the death of a child, for still others the consummation of a passion, be it for God, woman, fame, or power. For Beaumont it was the experimentation that he conducted upon the person of Alexis St. Martin. Never mind that the event was that which happened to St. Martin, and that Beaumont's role was but to seize upon it and to turn it to his purpose. What kind of man was William Beaumont?

Such a man was able to write to the absconded Alexis, encouraging him to leave his wife and family "for only two years." It could not possibly be a hardship, he wrote. And, yet, though Beaumont had himself experienced the love of a wife, the joys of fatherhood, he did not shrink to ask another man to forgo these companies. At last, he offered him more money. Beaumont demanded of St. Martin that he earn his livelihood by selling his body for the glory of science. As well ask an agnostic to take a little bag of whips out into the desert to mortify his flesh for the glory of God. Is Beaumont aware of the true nature of his role as pimp and libertine? When offered the choice between martyr and whore, it does not astonish that St. Martin opted for the latter, more easily comprehending himself as a commodity than as a sacrifice.

How much does one man owe to another man who has saved his life? Does he owe him indentured servitude for the rest of his life? His undying and daily manifested gratitude?

By 1832, Beaumont was famous, the darling of the medical world, and the pet of the surgeon general. Alexis, now twenty-eight, "dark hair, dark eyes, dark complexion, and five feet five inches tall," was drinking heavily. In many of the ensuing 116 experiments done between 1832 and 1833, Beaumont reported evidence of this: "The diseased appearance of the stomach was probably the effect of intoxication the day before."

On and on they battled, Beaumont to "procure," "secure," and "gain control of" his laboratory animal; St. Martin for his freedom from the demonic doctor who, he must never forget, had *saved his life*. "I am determined to [complete the experiments] if I even have to shut myself up with Alexis in a convent." Again and again, they part only to come together. It is as much a reflection of Alexis's loyalty as it is of Beaumont's personal magnetism.

But here, in 1834, is Beaumont writing to the surgeon general after still another jilting by the elusive St. Martin.

"I know well his disposition and his ugliness, and hope rightly to defeat them." Beaumont resolved to forgo any attempts to retrieve St. Martin, but to wait until such time as

> He will have spent all the money I advanced him to provide for his family for the year ensuing, become miserably poor and wretched, and be willing to recant his villainous obstinacy and ugliness, and then I shall be able to regain possession of him again, I have no doubt.

Add a horrible leer, and some hand rubbing, and presto, Fagin the Viper.

By 1846, Beaumont, having been separated from St. Martin for a decade, is undeterred in his efforts to get him back. He learns that Alexis has given up drinking, that he is in good health, and that several of his children have died. Letters were exchanged, those of Alexis being dictations to which he affixed his sign.

This from Alexis, "You who are a married man and a father, can easily conceive how very difficult it is for me to tear myself forcibly away from here without a reason for doing so."

And this from William:

> You know the embarrassment and interruption that have occurred heretofore to the prosecution of my experiments upon you on account of having your family with you. . . . I can conceive no difficulty, unreasonableness, or cruelty in leaving your family comfortably situated and provided for with their friends for the short space of a year or two, while you came to fulfill your obligations to me faithfully and honestly.

And again from Alexis: "I am happy where I am. I can earn sufficient to support them here. Money is of no object to me alone. My only wish is to see my family satisfied." Now, who can blame Alexis St. Martin for adding to this statement of sweet reasonableness: "Several medical men of Montreal have asked me to hire to them for that purpose, but I did not decide. . . ."

As late as 1852, Beaumont the Wily is appealing to the better nature of his guinea pig.

> Mon ami:
> . . . Alexis, you know what I have done for you many years since; what I have been trying and am still anxious and wishing to do with and for you; what efforts, anxieties, anticipations and disappointments I have suffered from your nonfulfillment of my expectations. Don't disappoint me more, nor forfeit the bounties and blessings reserved for you.

Beaumont was furious. Elsewhere he comments:

> This's just for a snatch of Monsieur's ways, thus goes he on in *tricks* and *lies*, and thinking to get well paid for it.

He never saw Alexis again.

William Beaumont died in April 1853. He had fallen and struck his head the month before. The cause of death was sepsis emanating from a carbuncle of the neck. Even with Beaumont safely in Heaven, Alexis St. Martin was pursued by his doctor's ghost in the form of Sir William Osler, who endeavored to obtain permission for an autopsy to be performed, the famous stomach to be retrieved for the Army Medical Museum in Washington. In this he was foiled by the peasant cunning that had oft and again proved the exasperation of Dr. Beaumont. Outraged by the suggestion of the autopsy and determined to prevent its occurrence, the family of the little voyageur "kept the body at home much longer than usual and during a hot spell of weather, so as to allow decomposition to set in and baffle the doctors." By the time of the funeral, the body was in such an advanced stage of decomposition that it could not be admitted to the church, but had to be left outside.

Two men. As bloodless as a stick, Beaumont subjugates his passions. He will do good for mankind, and wend not his way to the fleshpots. It is one of the sublime ironies that, with all of his good intentions, it was precisely toward the rarest fleshpot in the world that William Beaumont turned. Once having arrived, the dazzled doctor's hunger could not be assuaged by a lifetime of probing and stringing and instilling. St. Martin becomes the noble savage, the bearer of the Miraculous Wound, which sets him apart from all other men. But St. Martin does not remain the virginal creation of Beaumont's Puritan dream. Alexis's own concupiscence is at last aroused. Soon he becomes what he must, the virgin turned whore, selling himself bit by bit, drop by drop to his assiduous purchaser, asking higher and higher prices for his services, turning petulant and surly when denied, a wily peasant now rather than a fresh-eyed savage. He would coax from the landed gentry every last bit of payment that was his due. Thus did St. Martin, daily stoked with wads of bacon by the scrupulous, minute, self-taxing Beaumont, fall from innocence.

Was William Beaumont really bloodless in his unending violation of Alexis St. Martin's civil rights? Or did something else, besides his obsession for discovery, goad him to assume the role of hunter, with Alexis St. Martin as his pelted prey? Consider the language of metaphor which Beaumont employs in his descriptions of the wound. Again and again, he compares it to a mouth, or an anus, and finally to a "half-blown rose." To a lover, the beloved and all his parts are beautiful. For one three-year period, Beaumont forsook his family to travel with St. Martin, to Washington, to New York, to consultations with such authorities as Benjamin Silliman. A longed-for journey to Europe with Alexis failed to materialize. During this time another 116 experiments were conducted. From 1832 to 1835, Beaumont lived away from his family, and with Alexis.

If one is to invoke Aesculapius as the prime mover of these events, and Artemis, goddess of the hunt, as his henchwoman, in that it was she who contrived the endless flight and pursuit of the two, is it not possible that Aphrodite, she of the seafoam, was equally conspirator, inflicting unrelieved passion upon the luckless Beaumont. Was William Beaumont gay?

What! Hear Beaumont pleading with Alexis to stay—just a little longer—stay, for I need you? See the distraught doctor clinging to the defiant St. Martin who wrenches free, leaving a torn shirt in the heart-broken Beaumont's grasp, as his beautiful wound-bearer plunges from the hated house into the woods for which he hungers, the lakes for which he thirsts? No. That would be to make of this story a romance, a legend, to give it a grand significance that it does not deserve.

That Beaumont was a passionate man is illustrated by an incident involving a matter of honor, the original insult of which has been lost. A certain Lieutenant Richards announced that Beaumont was no gentleman. Beaumont retorted that Richards was a liar, a base villain, and a poltroon. If vituperation alone be the measure, why Beaumont is clearly the victor. Beaumont further showed his mettle, if not his common sense, by challenging Richards to a duel in order to settle the affair. Richards refused to receive the letter of challenge, reiterating haughtily that he would not accept unto his hand the communication of a man who was so patently not a gentleman. Whereupon Beaumont circulated a public announcement that Richards was indeed those three things which he said he was in the beginning . . . a liar, a base villain, and a poltroon. Oh well. But it does leave the reader of biography with a piquant mystery—why was Beaumont, in the eyes of Richards, no gentleman? Was their altercation over a woman? Unlikely, given Beaumont's singleness of purpose. Was it over money? Unlikelier still. Was it a difference of opinion over Beaumont's treatment of a case? Perhaps. The age-old boredom of military life has been known to reduce even the most elegant men to indignant capons, the one demanding satisfaction and the other not deigning to condescend. Or, shame on me, had Beaumont touched the dark underside of life and Richards been witness to it?

A man of passion, then, himself, how is it that Beaumont was blind to the passion of Alexis St. Martin? They could not have been friends. Friends, by definition, consider the emotional needs of one another. Remember the tone, sulky and severe, in which Beaumont insisted that Alexis leave his family for two years.

It is no wonder that, in the end, St. Martin, no longer naive, squeezes cash from his user, penny upon penny, and then one penny more. By just such dunning does he announce his very existence. It is necessary to him. He *must* believe that he is getting back a little of his own.

As if to show in the end that he knew something that Beaumont did not, St. Martin survived his doctor by twenty-eight years. What cheek!

Raccoon

*D*on't come in! Stay out!"

Just so does the woman answer my knocking. But I am already inside the room. On hospital rounds, a knock is only a gesture.

"Are you all right?" I ask her through the bathroom door. There is no answer.

"I'll be back in a few minutes. Please get back in bed. I want to examine you." I turn to leave. Then I see advancing from beneath the closed door the blot of dark shine. I step closer. I crouch, peering. I slide open the door which separates us. In a hospital the doors cannot be locked.

The woman is naked. She sits on the toilet, bent forward, her pale white feet floating on the jammy floor. Nearby, a razor blade dropped from one painted hand. The other hand cannot be seen; it is sunk to the wrist within the incision in her abdomen. Bits of black silk, still knotted, bestrew the floor about her feet. They are like the corpses of slain insects. The elbow which points out from her body moves in answer to those hidden fingers which are working . . . working.

For a moment she does not seem to notice that I am there. Her face is turned upward, its gaze fixed on some galaxy beyond me. It is vacant, ecstatic. Something has fled from it. What does she knead? For what is she reaching? A precious coin that she will, *must* deliver herself of? A baby? And so she dilates the opening with her fist, and so gropes for the limbs of her fetus?

For a moment I cannot move or speak. I have been struck and minted at that spot. But then she sees me. And her face leaps back across vast distances. Now she is a woman surprised at her most secret act.

"You should not have come in," she says. Her voice is gaunt, quiet. "I was almost finished. You should have waited."

Her hand remains immersed in her body. She does not withdraw it. But now the elbow is still.

"What are you doing!" I say. "What have you done! Stand up here and come back to bed!"

"I almost had it," she says.

"What? What did you 'almost have'? You have opened up your incision. It is only five days since your operation. That was a terrible thing to do. Stand up now," I say firmly. "Come with me."

Then, more gently: "It's all right. Don't worry. We'll fix it. You didn't realize . . ."

I take her by the arm, lifting, and as I do, the plunged hand is extracted with a small wet sound. It is a fist, shiny, beaded with yellow globules of fat.

But a fist is a mystery. I must see what it holds. I pry open the fingers, all bridges with clots. It is raw and scalded . . . and empty. She whimpers, but not in pain. It is longing that she expresses. She sighs, and stands. A sash of intestine hangs from her belly. I reach one hand to cup it, to keep it from prolapsing further. The loop shudders in my palm.

The woman lies on the bed. I call out for assistance. In a moment a nurse arrives.

"Oh!" says the nurse quietly, and sucks back her saliva.

"Get me gauze packing, Betadine solution, instruments, and gloves."

Gently, I replace the coil of intestine inside the abdominal cavity. I clamp and suture the few points that are still bleeding. I pack the wound with yards of gauze, and drench it with the Betadine.

"That would really be painful, wouldn't it?" the woman asks me. "If that were my real body, I mean. It would hurt. But I don't feel anything at all."

All at once I know what it was, what she was reaching for, deep inside. It was her pain! The hot nugget of her pain that, still hissing, she would cast away. I almost had it, she said. You should have waited, she said.

Like a raccoon, I think. A raccoon whose leg is caught in a trap. A raccoon will gnaw through his thigh, cracking the bone between his jaws, licking away the blood and the fur. So has she torn open her incision to rummage in the furnace of her body for the white ingot inside. I close my eyes and see the raccoon rise. He hobbles from the trap. He will not die *there*. Now he turns his beautiful head to glance back at his dead paw. His molten eyes are full of longing.

But this woman feels no pain at my probing, my packing. Perhaps she is wrong. Perhaps she did find what she was looking for, and threw it away. Perhaps I did wait long enough.

"When you are calm," I say, "we'll go back to the operating room, and I will stitch you up again."

"I *am* calm," she says. "You are the one who isn't calm."

Four Appointments with the Discus Thrower

ONE

I spy on my patients. Ought not a doctor to observe his patients by any means and from any stance, that he might the more fully assemble the evidence? So I stand in the doorways of hospital rooms and gaze. Oh, it is not all that furtive an act. Those in bed need only look up in order to discover me. But they never do.

From the doorway of room 542, the man in the bed seems deeply tanned. Blue eyes and close-cropped white hair give him the appearance of vigor and good health. But I know that his skin in not brown from the sun. It is rusted, rather, in the last stage of containing the vile repose within. And the blue eyes are frosted, looking inward like the windows of a snowbound cottage. This man is blind. This man is also legless—the right leg missing from midthigh down, the left from just below the knee. It gives him the look of an ornamental tree, roots and branches pruned to the purpose that the thing should suggest a great tree but be the dwarfed facsimile thereof.

Propped on pillows, he cups his right thigh in both hands. Now and then, he shakes his head as though acknowledging the intensity of his suffering. In all of this, he makes no sound. Is he mute as well as blind?

If he is in pain, why do I not see it in his face? Why is the mouth not opened for shrieking? The eyes not spun skyward? Where are tears? He appears to be waiting for something, something that a

227

blind man cannot watch for, but for which he is no less alert. He is listening.

The room in which he dwells is empty of all possessions—the get-well cards, the small private caches of food, the day-old flowers, the slippers—all the usual kickshaws of the sickroom. There is only a bed, a chair, a nightstand, and a tray on wheels that can be swung across his lap for meals. It is a wild island upon which he has been cast. It is room 542.

TWO

"What time is it?" he asks.

"Three o'clock."

"Morning or afternoon?"

"Afternoon."

He is silent. There is nothing else he wants to know. Only that another block of time has passed.

"How are you?" I say.

"Who is it?" he asks.

"It's the doctor. How do you feel?"

He does not answer right away.

"Feel?" he says.

"I hope you feel better," I say.

I press the button at the side of the bed.

"Down you go," I say.

"Yes, down," he says.

He falls back upon the bed awkwardly. His stumps, unweighted by legs and feet, rise in the air, presenting themselves. I unwrap the bandages from the stumps, and begin to cut away the black scabs and the dead glazed fat with scissors and forceps. A shard of white bone comes loose. I pick it away. I wash the wounds with disinfectant and redress the stumps. All this while, he does not speak. What is he thinking behind those lids that do not blink? Is he remembering the burry prickle of love? A time when he was whole? Does he dream of feet? Of when his body was not a rotting log?

He lies solid and inert. In spite of everything, he remains beautiful, as though he were a sailor standing athwart a slanting deck.

"Anything more I can do for you?" I ask.

For a long moment he is silent.

"Yes," he says at last and without the least irony, "you can bring me a pair of shoes."

In the corridor, the head nurse is waiting for me.

"We have to do something about him," she says. "Every morning he orders scrambled eggs for breakfast, and instead of eating them, he picks up the plate and throws it against the wall."

"Throws his plate?"

"Nasty. That's what he is. No wonder his family doesn't come to visit. They probably can't stand him any more than we can."

She is waiting for me to do something.

"Well?"

"We'll see," I say.

THREE

The next morning, I am waiting in the corridor when the kitchen delivers his breakfast. I watch the aide place the tray on the stand and swing it across his lap. She presses the button to raise the head of the bed. Then she leaves.

In this time, which he has somehow identified as morning, the man reaches to find the rim of the tray, then on to find the dome of the covered dish. He lifts off the cover and places it on the stand. He fingers across the plate until he probes the eggs. He lifts the plate in both of his hands, sets it on the palm of his right hand, centers it, balances it. He hefts it up and down slightly, getting the feel of it. Abruptly, he draws back his right arm as far as he can.

There is the crack of the plate breaking against the wall at the foot of his bed and the small wet sound of the scrambled eggs dropping to the floor. Just so does this man break his fast.

And then he laughs. It is a sound you have never heard. It is something new under the sun.

Out in the corridor the eyes of the head nurse narrow.

"Laughed, did he?"

She writes something down on her clipboard.

A second aide arrives, brings a second breakfast tray, puts it on the nightstand out of his reach. She looks over at me, shaking her head and making her mouth go. I see that we are to be accomplices.

"I've got to feed you," she says to the man.

"Oh, no you don't," the man says.

"Oh, yes I do," the aide says, "after what you just did. Nurse says so."

"Get me my shoes," the man says.

"Here's oatmeal," the aide says. "Open." And she touches the spoon to his lower lip.

"I ordered scrambled eggs," says the man.

"That's right," the aide says.

I step forward.

"Is there anything I can do?" I say.

"Who are you?" the man asks.

FOUR

In the evening, I go once more to that ward to make my rounds. The head nurse reports to me that room 542 is deceased. She has discovered this quite by accident, she says. No, there had been no sound. Nothing. It's a blessing, she says.

I go into his room, a spy looking for secrets. He is still there in his bed. His face is relaxed, grave, dignified, as the faces of the newly dead are. After a while, I turn to leave. My gaze sweeps the wall at the foot of the bed, and I see the place where it has been repeatedly washed, where the wall looks very clean and very white in contrast to the rest, which is dirty and gray.

Luis

. . . And there fell a great star from heaven, burning as it were a lamp, and it fell upon the third part of the rivers, and upon the fountains of waters; And the name of the star is called Wormwood: and the third part of the waters became wormwood; and many men died of the waters, because they were made bitter.

Apocalypse 8:10–11

*E*very morning at precisely eight o'clock—you could set your watch by him—Arnaldo Cherubini, professor of medicine at the National University, steps into the black limousine with the bulletproof windows and is driven down the mountain to the medical center, where he is distinguished chairman of the Department of Radiation Therapy. The road is steep and serpentine that leads down from the walled and patrolled enclaves where live the great and wealthy families of the city, protected from the threat of the unknown. Pedro, the chauffeur, has learned every inch of this road through the soles of his feet, so often has he driven it. Unfortunately, now part of the way lies along the northern boundary of the municipal dump. Naturally, Pedro keeps the blue-tinted windows of the car closed until this area is well past, because of the smell.

It has not always been a dump. Once, it was the municipal park, El Jardim Público, the chief ornament of the city, a vast green acreage laced with paths and shaded by large trees, among which lay topiary gardens, beds of flowers, and, at the center, a white bandstand, all gifts of the foundation established with the fortune built by the professor's grandfather, the mining tycoon Martin Cherubini. But with the bloating of the city and a daily ocean of garbage to be disposed of, it had been decided that a dump was more to the point. For weeks, there had been pious expressions of regret by the government, outrage in the newspapers, but in the end, the citizenry had bowed its head. What else was there to do? And so, with steam shovels and bulldozers, the beautiful belly of the city was gouged open until there was an excavation to a depth of fifteen feet. All but a handful of the ornamental trees were cut down. Even the ancient sundial, which Cherubini's men had commandeered in Bolivia and brought home in triumph, tumbled before the earth movers. For some days, it lay half sunken, with time frozen on its face, then disappeared beneath the surface. By the time the mistake was discovered, no one knew where it was. Even before the digging was finished, the first trucks arrived with their loads of *rejectimenta*—old tires, shattered glass, plastic containers, and, from a city grown rich and profligate, sprung sofas, rancid carpets, automobiles, refrigerators, and a jumble of dismantled machinery.

In time, the city recoiled from this ulceration at its center, sending suburbs, sinuous and leafy, up into the canyons. The distance one lived from the dump became the measure of one's good fortune. Should a tactless visitor mention the site, a citizen will shrug, give an ironic smile, and say: "Aha! So you have seen our beautiful park."

Any map of the dump would be useless, for each day it is molded anew by the giant earth movers. Yesterday's path has vanished, leaving no trace; what was then a towering mound will have been flattened. Even the margins shift and stretch from day to day, as the dump bites another mouthful from the flank of the city. A listing of the flora and fauna would be more reliable. Only a single species of tree exists here. Stunted and tumorous, it grows root-heavy below its bare, ruined superstructure. Nourished by decay, and less vulnerable than leaves to the poisonous fumes, these roots arch from the ground with a monstrous vitality. Sometimes, when the underground fires burn close, these trees claw at the ground and flail their branches in a kind of histrionic woe. Giant weeds spring up overnight, huge whorish flowers that bloom briefly and die, their generative parts waxy and smelling of vomit.

As for creatures, there are rats, of course, flies, mosquitoes, and pale butterflies. A pack of wild dogs roam here, and solitary cats, each one bearing its unique pattern of scars and fresh wounds. Vultures, gulls, and crows throng the air; here and there the surface undulates with carpets of maggots. And hunkering amid the strands of brownish smoke are the human scavengers, each with a burnt-out cigarette in the corner of his mouth.

A ceaseless gray ash from the fires drifts through the air. Now and then a bit of hot ash falls on the bare back of a digger, causing him to cry out. What with these glowing flakes, the fireflies that abound, and the stars in the sky, it is no wonder that the night scavengers (scavenging is forbidden during the day when the trucks are unloading) are afflicted with a strange confusion. At dawn, when they emerge, they have the dazzled look of men who have undergone a long bombardment. All during the day, the garbage trucks grind in slow lines. An endless evacuation of the waste of the city, an endless replenishment of the smoldering landscape. A muddy path leads away from the dump. At all times it bears the imprint of bare feet, wagon wheels, and the hooves of donkeys. This is the way taken by the scavengers to and from the *favela,* a vast strew of ramshackle huts veined by alleys that are little more than open sewers, every doorway emitting the same stench of excrement, urine, and rotting vegetation. This *favela,* no less than the dump, is deplored by those citizens who look down upon it from the roof gardens of their mountain fortresses. To them it is a scabby rash that creeps up the hillsides. From the same vantage, the dump at night, with its points of light that are the kerosene lanterns of the scavengers, resembles a remote, sleeping village. Should Professor Cherubini point his telescope in that direction, it might seem to him that the scavengers are acting with some colonial purpose, but it is not so. Each of them works alone. Even when they crowd onto a freshly dumped heap, they maintain the aloofness of snakes in a nest who crawl over, under, and around each other without the least sign of recognition. Being a man of cultivation and science, the professor is apt to ponder the phenomenon. More than begging, stealing, or prostitution, it seems to him, scavenging is the rudimentary act of civilized life, as the scavenger requires no presence but his own, and he acts without sense of past or future, with neither superstition, faith, or mercy. To be a scavenger, Dr. Cherubini has decided, is to have reached bottom.

∽

On any given night, Luis Figueira can be found at the dump. From a distance, there is nothing to distinguish him from the hundreds of other boys who swarm out of the *favela* to beg, steal, or sell their bodies to the gringo tourists. Closer up, you would see that he is of mixed blood—Indian and Portuguese. It is the Indian that predominates, in the small triangular head, aquiline nose, and pointed chin. A butterfly of dark freckles crosses his face, as though in the mixing of his blood, the pigment had been unevenly scattered. He is of small stature, with slightly bowed legs. If you guess his age at seventeen, you would be a year or two shy of the truth. Like the others, he wears tattered blue jeans, a T-shirt of no recognizable color, and a bandanna tied about his neck. Even his name would not precisely identify him, for doubtless there are ten thousand Luis Figueiras in Brazil, many, it would be safe to say, of mixed Indian and Portuguese blood with amber-colored skin and a crop of black hair.

Seven years ago, Luis left the village of Araguaia, a cluster of houses with its back to the rain forest and facing a great river. The whole village was elevated on wooden stilts, lest the river overflow its banks. For years the transport of rubber and bananas supported the town, but Luis's father was a potter. The boy's earliest memories are of his father's large brown feet working the treadle, his thumbs hollowing out a spinning ball of clay. Now and then, he would pause to ladle water from a bucket to soften the mass or slice away a strip of excess with his knife, all the while humming the half dozen songs with which he accompanied himself and which, he told Luis, made the bowls and jars lighter, gave them rhythm. Sometimes he would reach out a muddy arm and pull Luis onto his lap, show him how to guide the shapeless mass into a bowl with his fist. Each time, it seemed to Luis, his father had performed a miracle. When the pots had been glazed and baked, his mother would take them to the dock to sell to the missionaries and tourists passing through. One day, it was understood, Luis would become a potter too.

But when Luis was twelve, his father stopped humming. The buzz of the wheel was punctuated by a cough. The phlegm on the ground was red.

One day, his mother returned from the dock breathless with excitement. From her basket she drew a crucifix for which she had traded six of the bowls. It had been carved by an Indian from the gnarled wood of a jungle vine. The tortuous grain of the vine was incorporated in the torso of Christ. It was brown and yellow and smooth from handling. The face of Christ was thin and triangular like the faces of the Indians. His hair was long and dark. His head drooped upon a narrow chest in which each rib was visible; about his waist, an elaborate loincloth. As the girth of the vine had not been great, a portion of the crossbar was missing, and the arms ended in jagged stumps. Luis had never seen anything so sad or so beautiful. His mother hung it on the wall. Often, it was the last thing he saw before falling asleep.

The rubber trade dwindled, and with it the river traffic that had sustained the village. For the first time, Araguaia knew hunger. One by one, Luis's brothers and sisters left for the cities to find work, until only he was left at home.

"I will send for you in time," each of them had promised. But he never heard a word.

For six months, his father lay on a woven mat beneath the crucifix, coughing and strangling, and filling the house with the smell of rotting flesh. The other villagers hurried by, holding cloth over their noses and mouths, but still the stench seeped into their skin. Senhor Figueira died before he had passed on his craft to his son, but not before he had bequeathed to him his illness. When Luis's cough persisted, his mother took him down the river to another village from which a path led into the jungle. In a thatched hut, an old Indian woman drew him toward the chair where she sat as on a throne. She pressed her ear to his chest, her hair rancid under his chin. When she had heard enough she left the room, returning with a small slate-colored pouch from which she took a bowl of hard black gum. This she heated over a flame until it was soft, then kneaded and rolled it until it was a flattened disk, which she pasted over his left nipple.

"He will cough for half as long a time as he has lived," said the old woman. "Then he will cough no more."

One day, Luis's mother lay down on the mat where his father had died and did not rise again. It took her two weeks of hard struggle to die. "Mamá! Mamá!" Luis called out to her, but she did not answer. Only when he coughed would she, out of some vestige of maternal anxiety, turn her head to him. When she died, Luis took the crucifix from the wall and placed it in her hand. Afterward, a handful of old men and women came to help bury her.

"What about that?" An old woman pointed to the crucifix.

"Let it go with her," said Luis. A week later, he stood on the deck of a small launch, gazing at his receding village. In return for his passage to the city he was to load and unload the cargo of beans.

∽

Arnaldo Cherubini looks every bit the distinguished professor. Doña Horténsia sees to that. his silver hair is punctually trimmed, as are his beard and mustache, although in recent years, much to his wife's dismay, he has permitted himself a bit of shagginess around the mouth. But then, his eminence allows for it. Doña Horténsia is proud of her husband's appearance. His suits are of the finest fabrics, and perfectly cut. His shoes, handmade abroad, are all but weightless and of such a softness as to suggest that the leather had been chewed for days by Italian workmen. All this he wears with a natural grace, as though it were an elegant hide inside which his body, whatever its imperfections, might move with ease.

Thirty years ago, when the time had come to choose which field of medicine he would pursue, Arnaldo Cherubini had at once decided on radiology. It had been a brilliant, albeit natural, selection. For from childhood he was possessed of an innate fastidiousness that caused him to step back, to recoil even, from the unlovely facts of the flesh— the way it snorted, spat, sweated, defecated, putrefied. The X-ray beams stripped the body of its distasteful functions as of all its superfluities, and so redeemed it in his eyes. To be a radiologist, he decided, was congenial to his instrument, and he had never once regretted his choice.

There is no doubt in the mind of Doña Horténsia that her husband is a genius.

"Everything in Arnaldo," she is fond of saying, "is in balance. He sees things that the rest of us cannot see. But then . . ." and here she shakes her head and gives a musical laugh, "he has always been refined. I think he was born refined. I cannot imagine what could take away his dignity."

If Arnaldo Cherubini has one shortcoming, it is his devotion to tobacco. "The fumes of learning," he calls it. To the sorrow of his colleagues and the dismay of his students, he persists in this vile habit, shrugging off their dire prophecies.

"All this nagging," he retorts. "It cannot possibly be good for anyone. It is worse than a little tobacco." A little! Were you to be admitted to his office at the university, or chance to be invited to his rooftop garden, you would see him enveloped in an aromatic cloud. "Like Zeus on Mount Olympus," as Doña Horténsia puts it. "Sometimes, Arnaldo," she said to him once, flicking her little ivory fan to clear the air, "sometimes, I think you make all this smoke so that I cannot find you. You like to hide in it."

Truth to tell, Doña Horténsia is worried about her husband, but it has nothing to do with his smoking. He so rarely smiles these days.

∞

For the first two years Luis lived on the streets of the *favela*, one of a horde of homeless, half-starved children, each one longing for the village left behind. Even the meanest, most malarial hometown became a paradise in their memories. For an Indian boy alone in the city, the choices are few. Initially, Luis had gone begging. Even with his small size and the cough that he learned to use to advantage, there were seldom enough coins at the end of the day to buy something to eat. After some months, he joined one of the street gangs who, in groups of three or four, slit open the purses of the gringos or jostled the men while picking their pockets. But in stealing, a cough was not an asset.

More than once he had spoiled a robbery. Twice he had been caught and beaten by police. Afterward, the other boys had turned on him angrily.

One evening, when he had had nothing to eat for days, and clawed at his belly as though the hunger were a thing he could rip out, he had gone down to the beachfront lined with tourist hotels. He had learned from the others how it was done; you stand in a place where you are sure to be seen, but in the shadows, not in the open. When a gringo looks, you look back. When he nods, you nod in return. Always do it outdoors, on the beach, in the bushes. Never go to his room. Trembling against a palm tree, Luis waited. It was only his body, after all. A man appeared, walked by, looked. Luis looked back. The man nodded; Luis nodded. Minutes later, when the man reappeared, Luis steeled himself. But in the end, he had cried out in pain and the man, in disgust, had slapped him hard. Luis would not go there again. He would rather starve. That left only the dump.

From the beginning, Luis was strangely drawn to the dump. Somehow it reminded him of the jungle that pressed against Araguaia, fecund and dangerous. But in the forest the dense canopy of treetops holds your thoughts down below. The dump is a jungle with its lid torn away.

Should you descend into the dump at night, you would find Luis among the other scavengers, squatting by his lantern, his bare feet sunk to the ankles, his hands thrust beneath the surface, working, working. If the stench is nauseating, Luis does not acknowledge it. He has long since become inured to it, as he has to the rats and the flies with which he competes. Only when the baying dogs draw near do his armpits itch, for he has never lost his fear of them. To Luis, they are the devils of the dump. Now and then, to his relief, the guards, stationed there to prevent scavenging during the day when the trucks are unloading, will shoot the whole pack out of boredom. Then you can see their half dozen carcasses mantled by the wings of vultures. Within days, other dogs have found their way to the place; a new pack forms.

Luis sits on his heels more comfortably than he once sat in a chair. Early on, he discovered that he had the feet for it—flat, squelchy, Indian feet with which to ride the swiveling dump. The trick is to ride the inner boil as if it were the deck of a ship. More than once he has pulled himself up by ropes of air. From nightfall to daybreak hunger narrows his focus. Hour after hour he sifts with his fingers or digs with the short hoe that, along with his lantern and a small makeshift wagon, are the tools of his trade. His fingers grow raw from the moisture. Now and then, he holds up to the lantern a dripping possibility, then lets it fall. Only a week before, driven by hunger, he had tried to steal into the dump before dark and had been chased by the guards. His ribs are still sore from their blows. On the night that you see him, he has found only a few spoiled oranges. But then—what luck!—a paper plate to which a paste of beans has stuck. He eats it, plate and all. Still, it is surprising what one can find here that might be traded or even sold.

When one of the ever-burning fires engulfs a rubber tire, the already putrid air turns thick as jelly and settles in his chest so that he must give in to the cough that shakes him as though he were a bundle of sticks. Now and then a fight breaks out. Two of the scavengers leap toward each other, cursing, snarling. Fists are raised, knives drawn. Over and over they roll, thumping, slashing, until rage is spent. Or is it rage? Perhaps they are like cats under the pull of estrus who must mate no matter what. Luis knows that one day he, too, will have to fight. The scavenger who turns from such a challenge is as good as lost. From his thieving days Luis has kept the knife he used to slash women's purse straps. He wears it in a straw sheath at his belt.

For a long time, Luis was plagued by homesickness. Again and again, in his mind, he ran through all the old familiar losses: the death of his parents, the departure of his brothers and sisters. He could not stop thinking of the villagers, who were so used to one another that when they spoke in their careless quick dialect, no stranger could understand them; how their sentences had no beginning or end but were a continuation of what had been said yesterday and what would be said tomorrow.

In time, the garrulous old ghosts were still. He no longer heard their sweet jabbering. The dump had become his village, and hunger brooks no rivals. Besides, he had become a stargazer. Among whatever crowd of burrowers in the earth, there is always the one who will lift up his eyes. Such a one is Luis. Many nights in Araguaia his father had pointed to the night sky and shown him there the jaguar, the scorpion, the giant tortoise. Now, night after night, he sends his fingers blindly into the earth and his gaze to the teeming sky. For Luis, it is charged with meaning, a great page of hieroglyphs that he never tires of reading. There, directly overhead, is the bent hook like the one on which his father hung the ladle for wetting down the clay. And there, nearby, the ladle itself. Farther away he sees the flock of parakeets forever about to fly over the rim of the sky. But then the sky changes, and the flock of parakeets turn into a woman who pursues her one-legged husband. Another time, in the same place, he sees a tapir making love to a woman. It is almost as though each night he creates the sky with his eyes.

Nights of discovery. Hour by hour his right arm goes on by itself with a mechanical intelligence of its own. Now and then, he switches the hoe to his left hand, then back again. Always just beneath the surface there is something unformed and invisible waiting to be found: bird bones, chunks of animals, rotting fruit—everything gnawed and ripped. Once, he had followed a descent of gulls to a large plastic bag. In a moment it had been beaked open, spilling fetuses. Two things he has found that he keeps—a fragment of a bowl exactly like the ones his father made, and a flute. The flute is carved of wood, part of what had once been a set of panpipes. When he unplugged the four note holes, he blew into it and was startled at the sweetness of the notes— hollow and reverberant, as though they came from far away. He does not dare part with it. For all his years of street life, Luis still endows certain objects with hidden power. One day, shortly after he turned eighteen, he was playing the flute when he felt something dislodge deep within his chest, as though a stone had been rolled away. All at once his mouth filled with a sour fluid, which, leaning forward on his elbows, he let flow to the ground. On and on it flowed and all the while Luis felt the tightness in his chest lifting as though a wire band had been unwound from about his body. When at last he had spat the last of it, he inhaled deeply, easily, he for whom no single breath in six years had been free.

Each morning Luis pulls his wagon from stall to stall in the marketplace of the *favela*, offering what he has found—an umbrella with two broken struts, a straw hat with a torn brim, a plastic vase still holding a few artificial flowers. One day he caught sight of a woman begging in a corner of the marketplace. In one arm she held a baby at her breast. Another child slept across her lap, and a third sat on the ground playing with pebbles. It was a moment before he saw that the woman was his sister Clara.

That night, Clara told him how she had left Araguaia by boat, then walked for many days until she was picked up by a truck driver. It was the truck driver's cousin Ramón whom she had married. Well, not really married. She told him how two years before, Ramón had left for Amazonia to find work. She had not heard any word in that time.

Luis and Clara sized each other up. There was a great open sore on Clara's ankle; she had lost many teeth. An old woman of twenty-four.

Since then Luis has been sleeping on a mat on the floor of her hut. What with Clara's begging and his scavenging, the children have something to eat.

∽

After many hours, Luis has found six tin cans, a plastic bottle such as is used to carry kerosene, a small wooden crate. Nothing to eat. In the sky he has found the heart-shaped vulture, its head drawn down into its neck. It is summer and the great tortoise has crawled into the southern sky. The hot, dry time has begun. Toward morning, a wind takes the fire so that flags of flame fly from the trees, lizards of it slithering on the heaps. Among the drifting smoke move the dark, indistinguishable shapes of the scavengers. Their spittle sizzles where it falls. A rat jumps up and bites its own scorched leg. Even on a night like this, the flowers cannot be kept from erupting in violent blooms of purple, orange, red.

All at once, Luis hears a hoarse sawing cry that is not that of an animal. There is too much despair in it. A wake of silence follows. Perhaps he has imagined it? But then comes the low growling of dogs. A hundred, two hundred yards Luis creeps, until he hears the sound of flesh ripping, the cracking of bones. Closer still he draws, then sees by the light of his upheld lantern a circle of bloody snouts tugging sideways against each other. It was an old woman, he sees, with gray hair and gold hoops in her ears. Her nose and lips are gone but the eyes, open and staring, give back to him his own horrified stare; the dogs had not waited. It is daybreak when they finish. A vulture flaps down to take up the feast. When Luis swipes at it with his hoe, the bird hops to one side. One of the earrings lies alongside what had been her head, embedded still in a bit of flesh. He cuts it free with his knife. For a long time, despite the daylight, Luis stays to comb the remains but he cannot find the other earring. For a week, he, Clara, and the children eat well.

∞

One night, Luis digs in a mound of new garbage. On the other side work two older men and a younger, whom Luis has seen in the *favela*. His name is Manuel. When Luis hears him calling out "Monkey!" and "Son of a whore!" he knows. A plume of burning embers lands at his feet, then Manuel emerges, his eyes glittering under pitch-black brows. Luis's heart gives a sickening lurch before he makes it go still as a stone in his chest. Only the hoe in his hand continues to rise and fall, like a watch that goes on ticking in the pocket of a dead man. Into the terrible stillness a bottle is hurled that explodes into a galaxy about him. The sharp wetness on his thigh is his own blood. His knife leaps from belt to hand, the hilt sticky in his fist as he rises to greet his challenger. Even in his fear, he marvels at the young man's head, which is like a knob of excellent wood carved and polished. All at once, Manuel throws back his head and gives a hoarse shout. Abruptly the two close upon each other. Each grabs the wrist of a knife-holding hand. With the other, they punch, pull hair. The blows are dull and painful. Now they are down. Over and over they roll, their hard legs entwined, kicking, kneeing, butting with their heads so as to break a rib, trying to stay out of reach of teeth. At the last, it is Luis who is astride. With all his might, he manages the wrist of the other toward a smoldering ember. He sees Manuel's face dissolve in a grimace of pain, hears him whimper. When Luis sees the knife fall to the ground, he leaps up and out of reach. There is pain in the eyes of the other but no fight left. It is over. Trembling, Luis sheathes his knife and walks away. He will not have to fight again. Weeks later, he will pass Manuel in an alley of the *favela*. They will look at each other shyly, with the tiniest snake of a smile, as though they have shared some shameful secret.

∞

In the twenty years of his tenure at the National University Hospital, Arnaldo Cherubini has conducted his country into the era of modern radiation therapy. His department has become the standard against which all other hospitals must be measured. And thanks to Cherubini tin and emeralds, the entire university has flourished. Students and scientists have gathered to study at the feet of the professor and his colleagues. No request for new equipment is denied, and no sooner does a piece of machinery become outmoded, however slightly, than it is discarded and replaced by a newer model. For the professor himself there is nothing but affection and even reverence. Nor has such prestige robbed him of a measure of modesty. He likes to think of himself as just another doctor. Should he so express himself amid the orchestration of lights, crystal, ice, and jewelry at one of his wife's fetes, Doña Horténsia will smile warmly at her guests and say, "Professor Cherubini has both the kingly and the common touch."

From his days as a medical student in Baltimore, where, amid a sea of poverty, he and his fellows learned their trade on the bodies of charity patients, he has retained the quaint idea that suffering is as much the child of poverty as is evil. Still, he forgives his friends and neighbors their small insensitivities in favor of the pleasure of their company.

At night the professor has taken to observing through his telescope the scavengers at the dump, their lanterns distant as the stars. By the time he steps into the darkened limousine each morning, they have departed for the day.

One morning, he sees through the tinted window a young man just inside the boundary of the dump, pulling a wagon piled high with tin cans. Impulsively, he presses the button to lower his window. As the limousine passes him, the young man—a boy, really—glances up, and the eyes of the two meet for an instant before they are torn apart by the foot of the chauffeur on the accelerator. Arnaldo Cherubini wonders whether the tin in those cans was taken from one of the Cherubini mines.

∾

After years of silence, Ramón has come back from Amazonia. Or most of him. One leg is missing. One day he simply appears in the doorway of the hut and swings himself through on his crutches. When he sees the infant lying in the arms of the oldest child, he sucks in his breath, lets one crutch fall to the floor, raises his hand, and brings it down across Clara's face. Luis, awakened by the noise, leaps up, kicks away the remaining crutch, and watches his brother-in-law fall.

"I shall work," he says. "And you shall eat."

After a long silence, the man on the floor nods. "Rum," he says.

∾

Once again the giant tortoise has crept into the southern sky. A terrible drought has descended upon the city. For weeks Luis has pulled an empty wagon back to the *favela*. At the dump the fires rage out of control. He has burned the soles of his feet. All through the night, hoeing, hoeing, as if to uncover a new way of life, he watches the wings of birds parting the smoke. Here and there he sees the folded body of one of them on the ground like a sealed envelope.

Already the children of the *favela* have begun to starve. After two days of vomiting blood, Vittorio, Clara's second child, has died. For the first time, Luis has doubts that his scavenging will sustain them. He himself is weak from lack of food. Still he goes nightly to the dump, which roars and throbs like the hot oily hull of a riverboat. More and more, the scavengers resemble the scrawny contorted trees. Only the sky is the same.

One night the sky is alive with shooting stars. Luis watches them dart and vanish like the fish in the river of Araguaia when a net has been thrown—a flash, then afterward a moment of radiance. All at once, he sees that one of the stars does not blink out, but bursts free in a great curving arc. Brighter and brighter it grows, and nearer, as though it has plunged through the sky. Now it is so close that Luis can see the wake of its blazing tail. The sky is charged with meaning, alive with messages that concern him. With each breath he takes, the whole canopy of heaven billows about him. He is plunging too, from one world to another. Perhaps he will faint.

When Luis opens his eyes, he sees at his feet a glowing disk, all about it a pale cloud of light. Kneeling, he takes it up into his hands, and the hairs of light stream between his fingers. The dump sucks at his feet, moving him where it will. Above it, he towers like a soul rising. He looks up at the community of stars from which this one has fallen. To him! To Luis the scavenger! And he falls to his knees and gives thanks to whatever had lifted aside the veil of heaven and cast it down.

When at last the spell is broken, it is as though Luis has awakened from a deep dream of peace. In the sky, the moon, the stars are paling. The star in his hand is also fading. Luis unties the bandanna from around his neck and wraps the star in it. Looking about to see if he has been watched, he goes to one of the trees, kneels to scoop the muck from beneath its arching roots, places the star deep among them, then covers it up again. He will tell no one what has taken place, what he has found. This, if nothing else, will belong to him alone. Hope fills his heart. In the afternoon, it begins to rain. The drought has broken.

The next evening, Luis runs all the way to the dump. At the tree, he drops to his knees, slides his hand among the grappling roots. It is there! Drawing it forth, he is amazed anew at the strange brilliance that turns his amber skin to deep violet. To the left and right of him, the dump is blue in the lesser moonlight. Holding the star to himself, does he imagine that his chest grows warm from its touch?

A month goes by. Time and again, Luis leaves off his digging to unearth the star hidden at the base of the tree. How it pulsates with the rhythm of his own heartbeat. When his eyes have had their fill, he replaces it and returns to his labor. The star will see to his needs, he is sure.

✑

One day, as Luis makes one last visit to the hiding place, he sees a guard watching him through field glasses. The guard calls out to another guard, to whom he hands the glasses. From the distance he sees their heads move in conversation. His hiding place has been discovered. He wraps the star in the bandanna and places it in the wagon beneath the bottles and tin cans. Slowly, so as not to rouse suspicion, he leaves, pulling the wagon behind him. The guards do not follow. When night comes, he will find another place to hide the star. But now he must bring it home with him. He will leave it in the wagon, beneath his pile of gleanings. He will not sleep.

At noon, he must leave the hut to relieve himself. When he steps back through the doorway, he sees what the little girl holds. Ramón sees too, and on his face is a look of cunning. Luis lunges for the star, but Ramón has snatched it away with one hand. In the other a knife glistens.

"You must give it back," says Luis, but he knows he has lost the star. A wave of dizziness comes over him, the same vertigo of dislocation he had experienced years before when, from the deck of the riverboat, he had watched his village recede from view.

Within minutes, the news has spread through the *favela*. Soon a crowd has gathered in the open doorway, where Ramón holds up the star for them to see. How bravely it glows in the light of day.

"Block out the light from the door. You will see how brightly it shines." Ramón's face is tight with avarice.

"It is a miracle!"

"A piece! A tiny piece! To save us." And soon there is a line of women at the door. Each hands money to Clara, each holds open a pouch into which Ramón shaves a fragment of the star. The women murmur and cross themselves. In the street, embarrassed and ex-cited, the men stand in groups, smoking and drinking beer. The *favela* is swept by rapture, brims with the seeds of hope.

Hour by hour, Luis watches the star shrink beneath Ramón's knife. Paler and paler it grows, smaller and smaller, until only a handful of dust remains, which Clara scatters about the hut.

"To bring us good fortune," she exclaims, laughing with joy. Ramón closes the door. In the windowless room, the scattered dust gives off a sad glow.

∞

At precisely three o'clock on Friday afternoon, Professor Cherubini, in a starched and immaculate coat, enters the auditorium for radiology grand rounds. The students, interns, and residents fall silent. *El Catedrático*, they call him behind his back. A cathedral of a man. Lumbering, as if under the weight of his honors, he makes his way to a chair at the center of the first row, facing a bank of viewing boxes. An intern rises to give a brief résumé of the history, physical findings, and laboratory data of the first case. The lights are turned off. A row of skulls looks down at the conferees from the panel of viewing boxes. Beneath, a second row of skulls gazes to the left like figures in an Egyptian frieze. The patient, it has been explained, has a tumor of the pituitary gland. Dr. Cherubini rises to stand closer to the X-rays, peering, milking an earlobe for thoughts. At last, he motions for the students to draw near. There is a brief subdued hubbub until twenty are grouped about him, each head cocked to catch whatever scraps of wisdom will fall from his lips. The scene has reminded more than one visitor of a painting by Rembrandt. Pointing with a thin gold pencil, the professor shows the erosion of the sella turcica where the expanding tumor has compressed it. Dr. Cherubini resumes his chair. The others do likewise. The CAT scan is then shown, followed by the arteriogram. Here, the professor comments upon the "blush" of abnormal blood vessels, the displacement of the arteries. Last to be shown are the pictures obtained by the use of the Cherubini Foundation's latest gift, a nuclear magnetic resonator. Now the intern tells the number and dosage of radiation treatments and the portals through which they have been delivered. A third panel of viewing boxes is flicked on. These show the post-treatment X-rays. There is no evidence whatsoever of a space-occupying mass. The sella turcica has begun to fill in with new bone. The blood vessels have returned to a normal pattern. The intern relates that the patient no longer suffers double vision, headache, or mental confusion. Her condition appears normal. When the intern has finished his report a self-congratulatory murmur fills the room.

∽

It is dusk. Already the moon has risen. Luis is pulling the wagon along the road, scanning for fresh tire tracks that will show him a fresh mound in which to forage. In the month since he has lost the star, he has come to see the dump as the tourists do, as do those who live high on the mountainside. It seems to him the malevolent working intestine of the city, and himself no better than a maggot feeding on decay. Each time he looks up at the stars, his grief flares anew for what he was given, for what he has lost.

All at once he is aware of someone standing directly in front of him. Automatically he raises his hands. Then he sees that it is a girl, her gaze turned upward. She might be his own age or younger. Her face seems to have gathered all the moon's light to itself. A shyness comes over Luis. He is on the point of walking on when she speaks.

"How big it is, how close."

"You mustn't stare at it so."

She turns to face him. Has he seen her before? In some alley of the *favela*, squatting over a heap of mangos at the market? He cannot remember, but somewhere is the memory of this milk-and-gray girl.

"Why shouldn't I?"

"The moon can drive you crazy when it's full. Better to look at the stars. You'd be surprised at what you can see." She is either a whore or a witch, he thinks.

"Show me, then. Show me something you see in the stars."

"I don't have time for that. I have to go to work."

"Oh." There is a disappointment in her voice. "Then you must go." So. She is not a whore. A whore wouldn't tell you to go.

Suddenly she gives a low moan and sways. Luis steps forward and catches her about the waist. How frail she is, he notices.

"Are you sick?"

"The smell." She frees herself from his arm.

"Oh, that. I don't notice anymore. Are you all right?"

"It's nothing. I get dizzy from many things."

"Are you hungry?"

"No." But he sees that she is.

"I get dizzy when I look up at the sky," she says.

"That's because you don't know how to do it." He does not want her to leave. "All right, I suppose I can show you. But only one." He turns the wagon into the dump and begins to walk briskly. When she does not follow, he calls back over his shoulder.

"Well, aren't you coming? Or did you change your mind?"

"I can't see," she says. He returns to her.

"Give me your hand." He leads her into the dump. "What's your name?"

"Joaña."

"Listen, Joaña, I have two potatoes. I will roast them in the fire. One is for you. Meanwhile, we can look at the stars."

A hundred yards into the dump, he stops.

"Here is a good place." She watches in silence while he lights a small fire and sets the potatoes. When he is done, he goes to stand next to her.

"Look there," he points upward. "That is the great hook just like the one in my father's house where he used to hang the ladle."

"You mustn't point at the stars," she interrupts, pressing his hand down. "You'll get a wart on your finger."

"Where did you hear such nonsense? And there, look, is the vulture with its head drawn down into its neck. Why are you squinting? Keep your eyes open."

"I am myopic. I can't see faraway things. It helps to squint." Strands of her hair brush his cheek. "Why is everything in the sky tilted?"

"It is the way you are looking. You have to learn how."

"Show me one more."

He shows her the flock of parakeets. "Five, six, seven, eight. They're going to fly over the rim of the sky."

When she has eaten with gusto and delicacy, she says, "I must go now, but I don't know the way." Once again into his callused palm he takes her smooth tiny hand that life has not coarsened. Together they retrace their steps.

"Why do you come to this horrible place?" she shivers.

"It isn't horrible."

"The smell, everything rotting. The rats."

Luis cannot help laughing. "The rats? They are only trying to stay alive too. I have learned from them how to do it."

"May I come again sometime?"

He looks down at her hands. "The dump is not for you."

"How do you know what is for me?" Her face is young but knowing. She, too, has made her own way, he thinks.

"Do what you want," he says gruffly. "I don't own the dump." Without another word, the girl turns and runs down the path. Luis returns to the wagon. Immediately he begins to sift the garbage with his hands. But on this night, his eyes are full not of the stars but of her luminous image.

The next night she is there, at the same place in the path. She has brought a piece of calico of the same printed pattern as her dress. He watches her fold the square of cloth neatly, again and again, pressing it with her hand until it is a narrow band. Then, standing on tiptoe, she places it about his forehead, tying it at the back. Her bare arms lie along his temples while he stares down at her like an animal that does not know whether it is to be beaten or caressed.

On the third night, he waits for her on the path, swinging his lantern, until with a rush of despair he thinks she is not coming. But then there she is, and he forces himself not to run toward her.

Beneath three trees in a narrow valley among the mounds he has spread a mat for her. She waits, watching his back, the methodical rise and fall of the hoe in his upraised hand, the way a small animal waits to be discovered. Up and down goes the hoe, up and down. At last, he turns toward her. When she lowers her head, a strand of her hair falls forward over her eyes. It is the sign he has been waiting for. He lifts the strand and tucks it behind her ear. Then they are lying together on the mat, listening to the delirium of each other's arms and legs while all about the living earth beats in rhythm with their hearts and they feel between their close-pressed bodies the wings of a moth open and close.

Later, lying behind her, he watches the slow rise and fall of her shoulder as she sleeps. She seems to him full of secrets. In the acute restlessness of his joy, he does not know what to do with himself. He squats to dig with a kind of frenzy, rises to pace back and forth, then, beside himself, he takes out the flute. She is awake, listening. Turning, she sees that his face has taken on an expression like sleep, or as though the sky were passing through him.

∽

Before daybreak, Joaña leaves to fetch another load of mangos from the country. At the marketplace she will pick her way among the vendors—butchers selling tripe, oxtails, the bloody heads of sheep; women selling hanks of cloth, pots and pans, religious trinkets, cheap rum—until she comes to the open yard thronged with peddlers of fruit and vegetables. She will spread a woven mat on the ground, then wash and set out her mangos. Here she will remain—one day, two, three—until she has sold them or they have spoiled.

Sifting through ashes, Luis feels a buzzing in his fingertips and a strange, not unpleasant heat spreading over his hands as though they have come too near the fire. He holds them to the lantern. Has he been stung? Burned? He scrubs them in the air, then dismisses it from his mind.

But the next night the buzzing is stronger and with it, a feeling of fullness in his fingers as though there were too much blood in them. By daylight he sees that the skin of his hands is pink, shiny, and taut. He cannot close his fists. Twice, the hoe has slipped from his grasp. By the next day, the pain has declared itself. Luis is conscious of the blood streaming through his body, pounding for exit against his swollen fingertips. On the palm of his right hand, a great blister has risen. Pressing it with a finger, he sees fluid moving under his skin. Beneath his touch, the blister breaks; a warm fluid runs across his palm. Luis takes hold of the torn skin and peels it from his hand. What comes off is a glove with two fingers. Alone, he gives in to a conflagration of childlike weeping that burns itself out in sleep, where he is once again in Araguaia, the river flowing cool through him.

Joaña has returned. She stares at the moist raw flesh to which already the first flies have been drawn. Together they study the sores that have opened up at the tips of his fingers.

⁓

With his ruined hands, Luis is no match for the rats, dogs, and crows. He envies them their teeth, beaks, and claws. For the first time, he is afraid of the dump.

"Never mind," says Joaña. "You will tell me where to dig."

Luis looks down at her small delicate hands and his heart fills with sorrow. "Only until you are all better," she says. "I will not leave you." Now it is she who pulls the wagon and lifts the hoe while Luis sits on his heels, rocks back and forth to the throbbing. By day, they take turns sleeping in the streets of the *favela*.

Within days his hands have begun to smell. The death face of his father returns to him.

"It is no good," he tells her.

"What are you saying? Don't be foolish," she says. But she, too, has smelled the odor of decay, and the words limp unconvincingly from her mouth. At last she cries, and when Luis can bear her sorrow no longer, he tells her of the night of the shooting stars, and how he had not kept his vow to protect what had been given to him.

"Now you see," he tells her, lifting his hands. "I have been punished."

At length she says, "Then I shall be your hands. But first, tomorrow, we must go to the clinic at the hospital, to show the doctors. Perhaps there is a medicine, something to do."

∽

In a cubicle of the clinic Luis is sitting on a stretcher. His hands are wrapped in filthy rags tied at the wrists. Joaña stands nearby. Between them there is the formality that such situations confer even upon lovers. A nurse peels away the cloths, dousing them with water when they will not come unstuck. Her lips and nostrils are compressed in judgment of the stench of dead tissue. What is laid bare is only black leather, yellow bone, pus. Two doctors come and go, then stop just outside of the cubicle.

"What could have produced those lesions?

"Wet gangrene."

"Is it circulatory?"

"No. The pulses are strong and full. Besides, he's only nineteen."

"Burns, then."

"From what? And both hands?"

"These stupid Indians and their kerosene."

"Perhaps something he picked up at the dump?"

"He won't be rummaging there anymore." The doctors reenter the cubicle. Joaña eats them with her eyes.

"We don't know what caused it. Was there anything you might

have picked up that could have burned you?" Joaña flashes a glance at Luis. When there is no answer, the doctor speaks again.

"You must go now for X-rays. After that, you can go home." He motions for the nurse to dress the wound. "But you must come back tomorrow."

When Luis and Joaña have left, the doctors linger in the cubicle.

"They never tell the truth, those *favelados*. It is like practicing veterinary medicine."

∽

The next day, Luis and Joaña return to the clinic. Outside the doorway, the two doctors are muttering to each other.

"How could this have happened?"

"It must have been tossed out with the old machine, the one Cherubini replaced a couple of months ago. No one thought to remove the cesium. It ended up at the dump, where he found it. God knows how long he's been playing with it. It's just the sort of thing to make a scandal."

"How do you know for sure?"

"When he went for X-rays, the Geiger counter went wild."

"Does Cherubini know?"

"He's on the way over now."

"Here? To the clinic?" The doctors step into the cubicle.

"Well, well, Luis. How do you—" He is stopped by the girl.

"There is something," she says. "Something that he touched." She hesitates.

"What is it? Come on, come on! The professor will be here in a few minutes. Speak!"

"A star," says Joana.

"A star?"

"Yes, a star." Luis flings the word at them with one trembling stump. "I saw it fall from the sky right where I stood. I hid it under a tree and each night I took it out to see how it glowed until . . ."

"Until what?"

"Until one day I had to bring it home because the guards had seen. It was taken away from me and broken into pieces to sell to the others."

"What did it look like, your star?"

"Like a star."

"What shape was it?"

"It had the shape of a star."

The doctors leave. Through the open doorway, Joaña and Luis hear them speaking. "Professor," they hear, and "star."

"God knows how many others . . ."

"By now, it is all through the *favela* . . ."

Arnaldo Cherubini enters the cubicle. He wears his immaculate starched white laboratory coat. His mouth seems to have sunk into the nest of gray hair gathered about it. He wears dark-tinted, horn-rimmed glasses. There is about him an air of disguise, as though he were an actor playing the role of a doctor. At the sight of Luis, he starts. Does he remember that brief glance exchanged months before through the window of his car? Or perhaps it is something else that tells him that he has met the one patient who will change his life.

For a long time he stands in silence, looking down at Luis, the knuckles of one fist pressed hard into his beard. Luis feels the man's gaze upon him like a weight pressing him down. Behind the beard and the dark glasses lies something still and rapt. Luis cannot know that with his simple offering of wounds, his appearance is just as marvelous to the doctor as the shooting star had been to him.

At last, Cherubini clears his throat and, with a gesture of immense weariness, reaches up to take off the glasses. A deep crease rises from the bridge of his nose to the middle of his brow as though a nail had been driven into his forehead. He steps closer to the stretcher. The smell rising from the hands brings tears to his eyes.

"Is there much pain?" he asks. Luis looks down at his hands as if imploring them to answer for him. "But surely you can tell me if you have pain," Cherubini urges.

Luis shakes his head wistfully. "Not now. In the beginning, yes. Now they are just . . . dead."

"Look, Luis." The doctor's voice is heavy with regret. "We know what happened to your hands. There has been a terrible accident." And he recounts how one day an old broken machine had been taken out of the hospital to make room for a new one. How inside the old machine was a piece of metal that gives off dangerous rays that kill human flesh. "We use these rays to cure people of tumors. Somehow, when the machine was loaded on the dump truck, the hot metal had been left inside. When the machine was dumped, the metal fell out. That is what you found. It is true that at night the metal glows so that you can see its light. Like a star," he says gently, "but not a star. It is what has burned you."

Cherubini coughs into his fist and motions for the nurse to bandage the boy's hands. "The only thing to do now is to cut here . . . and here." He draws a finger across each of Luis's arms above the elbow. "Where the flesh is healthy and has a chance to heal." At the touch, the stump of the boy's right hand jerks upward in a sudden reflex. The doctor recoils as if threatened with a blow. "They are already dead, Luis. You have said so yourself. The hospital will pay for everything and you will have enough money to live on from now on. I promise you that!"

But the boy has turned to stone. It is the girl who speaks, but only to Luis.

"Come, we will go home now."

Cherubini turns to face her. "I cannot let you do this," he whispers. "As for the star, it was a false enchantment. A dream. I want to make it up to you for . . . it is our . . . it is my fault that this happened. You must let me . . . please?" He feels the corner of his lip twitching. He is certain that it can be seen despite the beard and mustache. He presses his fingers there to still it, but cannot.

Already the pair are making their way across the dusty courtyard thronged with patients. Should one of them happen to look up, he would see in the doorway of the clinic a doctor in a white laboratory coat holding out his hand like someone who is trying to see if it is raining. "Please!" he is calling out. "Please!" He holds on to the word as though it would keep him afloat.

Outside the gates of the hospital, Joaña helps Luis into the wagon. She places a straw hat on his head and takes up the handle.

"What does it mean—'false enchantment'?" Luis asks her.

"It is a lie," she replies. "There is no such thing. About enchantment, you cannot choose."

"I have seen what I have seen," says Luis.

"Don't talk," she says. "Rest."

It is evening when they reach the dump. "Come on," she says. "You will tell me where to dig. You always know the best place." She helps him out of the wagon to sit with his back against a tree. A small wind plays among the twisted branches, and Luis, too, trembles. In and out of the pocket of moonlight in which they are huddled, a huge ghost-colored moth is floating. From somewhere comes an angry gabbling and the thump of vultures buffeting each other with their wings.

"What are you thinking?" she asks him.

"Thinking?"

"Tell me."

"I was thinking . . . it is not wise to become too attached to your hands. One day they may be taken away from you."

When she sees that he has fallen asleep she takes up the hoe and begins to turn the earth, singing softly to herself. Hours later, he awakens with a start.

"How long have I been asleep?"

"Long enough."

They speak no longer of the past or the future, as though they have agreed that there is only the present. Again and again, Luis tries to remember what had been the last act, the last gesture of his hands. It seems as important to remember this as it would be to remember the last words of the dying.

⊷

It is midsummer. The tempo of the dump quickens. The ground heaves with the larvae of insects. Luis's left arm ends in an ulcerated black knob at the wrist; the right is an open shaft from which a dry yellow bone protrudes. Swallowing has become painful. When he stands, colored lights flash behind his eyes. His ears are full of whispers. More and more his dreams are of Araguaia. The river shivers, the nets are shaken out. *"Pull, Luis! Pull!"* cry his brothers. From a doorway, his father's voice rises with a song, then stops. Already his memories are scampering off like rats. Overhead, vultures turn like the hands of a clock.

"It won't be long," he tells Joaña.

"You must drink," she says. From the market she has brought a pint of rum. She cradles his head, lifts it to his lips.

He is fully awake now, lucid. "Listen, Joaña. When the time comes, you must take the hoe, dig a deep hole, and put me there."

She covers her mouth and looks away. With effort, Luis hitches himself closer to her.

"You must promise. Do you promise?"

"How will I know when it is time?" Her voice is barely audible, tired. "I have never seen anyone die before."

"When you can't see your reflection in my eyes anymore. That will be the last thing." He reaches out to stroke her face, then remembers. It is hard to break the habit of hands; they go on reaching for things.

∾

Once again it is time for the radiology grand rounds. From the majesty with which Arnaldo Cherubini enters and takes his seat in the front row, you could not know that he has spent the night prowling his rooftop garden, now and then pausing to peer through the telescope at the dump with its many points of light that are as remote from him as the stars. But in the middle of the presentation of the first case, he rises and, without a word, leaves the room.

Under the pretext of persistent headache, Cherubini has asked his chief technician to take an X-ray of his head. He is not to mention this to anyone. Now the professor sits alone in his locked office before a bank of viewing boxes that illuminate the image of his own skull. He does not see the cranial suture lines, the zygomatic arches, the styloid processes, any of the other anatomical features. What he sees, gazing deep into the orbital sockets, is the nakedness of it. It is as though he is looking at the death that lies hidden beneath his skin, only waiting to be released. "You have lived too long among X-rays," he says aloud to the skull.

It is three days since he watched Joaña and Luis leave the clinic. For three days he has waited for them to return. During this time, men in lead-lined suits and gloves have fanned out through the *favela,* holding up Geiger counters that tick loud and soft, loud and soft, in accordance with a will of which the people have no inkling. Only when they see their houses nailed shut and plastered with skull and cross-bones do they suspect. No one knows how many have been rounded up. Trucks equipped with megaphones have cruised the alleys, calling out, "Diarrhea, vomiting, bleeding from the mouth, loss of hair, sores, loose teeth . . ." But who doesn't have one or two of these? Probably it is just another trick by the government to take from them the little that they have. Let them go to hell.

For three days Arnaldo Cherubini has waited. He can wait no longer. He flicks off the viewing box and presses the button on his desk to notify Pedro that he is ready to leave. It will take the chauffeur five minutes to bring the car to the door of the hospital.

At half past four, Pedro pulls the limousine to the side of the road and opens the rear door.

"Wait here for me. It will be some time. Do not look for me. I will come when I am ready." The chauffeur cannot hide his puzzlement. The doctor silences him with a wave of his hand.

"Do as you are told," he says, though not unkindly. Then he turns toward the dump. In a moment he has disappeared down the embankment. Pedro sighs and lights the first of many cigarettes.

Slowly, for the muck drags at his feet, Arnaldo Cherubini makes his way among the heaps. From time to time the stench causes him to retch and cover his mouth. He makes no effort to brush away the flies clouding about him. Now and then, he pauses to turn a bit of refuse with the toe of his shoe, bends to examine it, then moves on.

He remembers the park that had been the pride of the city. Now, in those colorless mounds and puddles, the whole of the hideous topography, he sees only a menacing X-ray of the grottoes, lawns, hedges, and avenues that were once the beautiful Jardim Público. It seems to him now the very delta of hell. Soon, the thin, delicate soles of his shoes are slick with garbage. Twice he stumbles. Awkward and huffing, one hand braced against a stunted tree, he pulls the laces of his shoes, pries them off, then his socks. He feels the dump beneath his toes. With a sudden raucous mewing, a flight of gulls lifts, circles once, then descends to a new site. A rat scampers. At some distance, a fire is smoldering. When a breeze takes the smoke and blows it toward him, he must take quick shallow breaths. Time itself has slowed, become viscous. Wherever he looks he sees the same fever-dark eyes in an amber-colored face, and that girl—like a battered bag that one would throw away.

Day into night, and now the dump is fully awake. At first only the crusts are lit, then minute by minute the great heaps brighten until moonlight seeps deeper into the craters of the earth. Through the soles of his feet, Cherubini feels how it rises and falls as if in respiration.

From the top of a mound, El Catedrático looks down and sees the hundred lanterns, sees dimly the shapes of men squatting, their hands threshing, scattering. For a moment he stands between the stars and the lanterns, which confuse, waver, melt, and flow one into the other so that he loses all sense of up and down. What time is it? he wonders. He takes the watch from his vest pocket and sees that it has stopped. He descends. The air is silky with bats. Underfoot, the dump sighs and streams.

Dawn is coming, the first faint acidity of it. X-ray time, full of shadows dark and light that illuminate without pity the whole of human misery. Within minutes, the tip of the mountain is bright with sun. The professor stirs and shivers. All at once, a wave of horror comes over him. Blindly he staggers toward the road, where the limousine is waiting. Dimly, he hears the soft growl of the motor, feels himself being borne away.

∽

In another part of the dump sits Joaña. Luis's body, silvered by the moon, lies across her lap, head upon her arm. But for the fine grain of her lips, the tiny bubbles between her white teeth, the way her fingers climb the rungs of his ribs, pausing to knead the meager flesh as though to create something, the two might be a carving in gleaming wood. A jaguar of dappled light stalks the shadows. Through the fleshless chest, she watches the heart beating itself out. Each time the eyes float out of reach, she coaxes them back with her own unwavering gaze. At last she feels a slight movement of the head. Luis opens his mouth as if to speak, or yawn.

"What?" she whispers, then sees the light receding slowly from his eyes. It seems to her that their last vision is not of her but of something over her shoulder in the sky. Turning to follow his gaze, she sees just below the handle of the bent hook a cluster of four stars, faint but brightening as she looks. She squints to sharpen the focus. There are three stars in a triangle, with a fourth held somewhat apart. Like a hoe in the upraised hand of a small figure, crouching.

Imagine a Woman

*I*magine a woman, youngish, not quite thirty. Her brown hair falls toward her arm as she sits at a small table, writing in a notebook. It is night and the single lamp behind her chair gives a meager light. Now and again, she rises to pace the small room. Then you can see that she is thin, but with the large belly of pregnancy, perhaps six months. When she feels the child move, she winces and presses her hand to her abdomen as though to still it. Once outside the circle of lamplight, she is no more than a concentrate of darkness. Only when she returns to sit can you see that she is pale, with delicate features—not beautiful, but there is a grace in the way she turns her head or moves her hand across the page. Imagine the quick tiny hiss as it slides along the paper an inch at a time, from left to right, then the longer hiss from right to left as she begins a new line.

My dear Hugh,

I confess to an ignoble pleasure as I imagine you holding this package in your hands, turning it over, reading the return address. Who in the world is S. Gallant? you wonder, before taking a scissors to the twine that Madame Durand, in accordance with my precise instructions, will have tied around the wrapping paper. Veyrier, France? But by then you will have recognized the handwriting and torn your way through to the contents. You and I have been here before—do you remember? Ten years ago, when we were driving from Geneva to Avignon, we stopped in Annecy to see the Convent of La Visitation. Afterward, going south along the lake, we passed through Veyrier. I remembered the sign. I even glimpsed this *pension,* the Hotel les Acacias, by the side of the road, midway between the mountain and the lake below, as we drove by. It is just an old farmhouse, really, with a steeply slanted roof and wide overhanging eaves and, in front, a terrace set with tables.

It is one year since I left. This journal, the first words you will have had from me since then, will also be the last. If as I implored you, you have made no attempt to find me, I thank you for that. If you have made such attempts, you see that they were in vain. It is laughably easy to disappear. I will not tell you the details of my zigzag journey, only that a number of borders were violated and more than one palm crossed with silver. . . . Oh, dear! All at once my pen has turned stiff and arthritic. How to begin?

Under the circumstances, divorce was absurd. Squander the little time left to me in recriminations and remorse? Staying with you was equally absurd. You see, Hugh, while I do not hate you, neither do I love you. I think now that I never did. They say that in illness one is laid open to revelation. The truth is—don't take offense—I ceased to think about you at all. It is the egotism of the sick, a shortcoming for which I forgive myself with the suspicion that it was never me whom you loved; it was marriage, the idea of it. That having been said, there was this, too: I did not want to die prematurely of a virus; I wanted to have *lived,* for no matter how short a time. I could never do that had I stayed.

∞

It was best that I knew first. Had it been you, I wonder whether you could have withstood the anguish of telling me.

"There is something I must tell you," the obstetrician said. Oh, the voice, the face of a man who can bear such tidings. Even before he had finished, a tiny needle of ice had punctured my heart.

"And the child?" I wanted to know.

"There is every likelihood of that too."

I went home with my secret and waited like an assassin until your back was turned before I thrust the words between your shoulder blades. I watched you stiffen, turn, your gaze lashed to mine.

"How do you think it happened?" you said.

"I don't know. And you?"

"No," you said, so quietly. But it was a lie, for there had been Manuel. How easily I write his name, as if he were someone I knew or had seen. I used to try to give him a physical appearance. All I know is that he is a Filipino, and that he is twenty-nine, my age. From these threads I have stitched a slender, short, fine-boned man with black hair and dark complexion. His eyes, too, are dark, with a slight tilt. While I was at it, I gave him even, white teeth and a sweet smile, this stranger come from the other side of the world with his fatal gift of beauty.

✌

From my note you have known everything that, up to now, I have wanted you to know: that I had taken enough money and morphine (again, do not ask) to free myself from anxiety and discomfort, and that I did not hate you. You are hardly to blame for the gray rain of virus that is falling over the earth. Nor do I condemn your secret love. Despite all, I continue to marvel at love however one locates it.

I left to reclaim the life I had surrendered to a convention that kept me from the *real* real—the one that exists just beneath the surface of things. It is what I have come here to find. Already it has begun to happen. I have become strangely receptive to the moon, the waterfall, the trees, the bread, the wine, all the components of this magic village. As my immunity to the germs has dwindled, so has my resistance to these "influences." It is the heightened sensitivity of fever, some might say, or the clarifying effect of pain.

Do you think that I am bored? Not at all. Boredom is a symptom of civilization, and I have become a pagan. It is as though a fog has blown away and I live in a clear, crystalline air, where everything has a voice. I am not so naive or sentimental as to believe that there are spirits in the rocks, forests, and mountains, spirits that must be placated. It is something else, a property of the elements itself that is capable of affecting one for better or for worse. Do you imagine tears falling on the page? Don't. If weeping could coax fate, then perhaps I would weep. But I have given up all my lamentations. When there is no one to tell your grief to, it makes sense to stop.

∞

Madame Durand, the concierge, appears to be in her seventies. When she is not trudging up and down the stairs in her felt slippers, Madame sits in a cubbyhole off the front hall knitting or with her cheek resting on a forefinger, eyes half-shut like a sleepy old tabby cat, but not missing a trick. She has the obligatory dyed-blond hair of the postmenopausal Frenchwoman, which, along with the bright yellows, reds, and purples she favors, gives her the look of a clump of mixed tulips. She has a slight limp, the residue of a hip operation.

You can imagine the state of fatigue and discomfort in which I arrived. Madame asked me no questions, nor did she show the least sign of surprise or curiosity that a pregnant women, wild-eyed and panting, should appear unannounced at her hotel at ten o'clock at night. I had the unaccountable feeling that she had been expecting me. I followed her up the two flights of stairs to my little room under the eaves. "*Dormez,*" she said with a great solemnity as she left. And sleep I did, fell into bed like an apple from a tree, and slept until the sun crossed the mountain behind the house and burst into my window. Or was it the baby stirring that woke me?

There are fourteen rooms in the hotel. Mine is at the front, on the third floor in the corner. The stairs are narrow, steep, and dark, but I am not yet so ill that I cannot manage them.

If asked to describe my soul, I would describe this room. Great wooden beams divide the ceiling. The single tall French window has an inner ledge that is wide enough to sit on. Leaning out, with my long hair hanging down, I feel like Rapunzel. At one time, this was a loft where chickens and geese were kept in winter. They roosted in the niche carved in one wall, which is occupied now by a toilet, sink, and mirror. There is a narrow bed with a long cylindrical pillow that I must fold in thirds in order to sleep. It is easier to breathe that way. To write, I sit on this ladder-back chair at a plain table, both of walnut, as is the small armoire. The room was obviously not consulted about the wallpaper, which is a neoclassic pattern that I rather like—

women in drapery carrying amphorae and lolling about columns, all done in faded ivory and silver. Of all the rooms of my life, this is surely the most congenial.

From my window, I look down over the rooftops of the village to the lake. Directly below is the dining terrace, punctuated by the seven old acacia trees from which the hotel takes its name. A new highway has diverted much of the traffic that used to run in front of the inn. Now only bicycles, horse-drawn carts, and the occasional bus pass by. Most of the time it is quiet, save for the waterfall and the *"hola!"* a farmer calls to his horse.

This morning I told Madame that I would be staying for an indefinite period of time. My accommodation goes by the name *demipension,* under which I do not select from the menu but am to be fed whatever is prepared in the kitchen for the help. It is delightfully inexpensive. Anyway, I do not want to think about food; I do not plan to eat much of it.

As for worldly diversions, I might as well be living in a cloister. The only "life" takes place on the terrace, where, in good weather, meals are served. Even when I can eat nothing, I go to sit there. I wouldn't miss it for the world. There are fifteen tables set under the acacias. The trunks are as big and strong as men, and their foliage is dense enough to shelter us from any but a vigorous downpour. All through dinner we are kept company by a family of saucy sparrows. Only a raised boot-heel directly overhead will scatter them, and as soon as the all-clear sounds, they're once again pecking the gravel for tidbits or perched on the back of a chair.

Quiet as it is all day, at dinner the tables on the terrace are filled. Most of the other guests are French and Swiss, many of whom I take to be regulars from the warmth with which Madame and the Portuguese girls greet them. Each table is covered with a starched white cloth. Alongside each plate is a linen envelope embroidered with the number of your room. Mine is number fourteen. The napkin inside it is changed once a week, on Monday. It is expected that each of us, at the end of the meal, will fold the napkin and replace it in the envelope. A beautifully frugal custom. No human being is entitled to a fresh linen napkin every day.

In addition to Madame, there is Philippe, her grandson, a husky *savoyard* of seventeen, with the square head and short-barreled torso of the men of this region. He has lovely big ears that shine when sunlight passes through them, and a yoke of shoulders already powerful. Toward me, he is shy and courteous in equal part. Two pretty, cheerful Portuguese girls, each about twenty, wait on the tables. If there is a restaurant in Heaven, these two will be hired to serve the gods. It is their favorite pastime to tease Philippe, and his calvary to endure it. His suffering takes the form of a tuneless whistling in which he wraps himself. Still, if I were those Portuguese flirts, I would take care. Philippe is almost a man. With every step he deepens his hold on this hotel, which will one day be his. And more than once, I have caught sight of something like phosphorus blazing in his eyes.

Somewhere inside the kitchen, there is a chef—there must be, but no one has ever seen him. Perhaps he is kept on a tether lest he fly off to the Ritz. I can eat only as much as one of the sparrows. More is not urged upon me, thank God. It is a wisdom of the body that anorexia be the proper condition of the fatally ill; one must lighten oneself for the crossing-over.

The village is small, no more than two thousand feet long, bracketing the narrow gravel road. At night it has a hallucinated look. Perhaps it is the moonlight that dapples the trees and cottages and is drawn out into a shining filament across the lake. The two silent cows that are left to spend the night in the yard are flecked with it, and the stripe of road goes dark and bright as it ascends. Everything—houses, trees, animals—appears to have surrendered its solidity and to be permeable, wavering, as if at any moment Veyrier itself will turn molten and begin to flow. The only thing here that is dense and corporeal is me; I am like the pit of a peach about which this soft incandescent village has deposited itself.

∞

I have not seen a watch or clock in weeks. (You wouldn't survive here for a day.) Now it is the hour of the Angelus, when the bells of La Visitation come visiting me from across the lake. *Bong! Bong! Bong!* In the vast choir of French bells, this one is the baritone. I like to think of that convent full of virgins lying beneath such a deep-chested Don Giovanni, obeying his every summons.

✐

A bluish spot has appeared on my arm, the size of a grain of rice. I was told to expect them. Fever, night sweats, shortness of breath. All night I paddled my bed around the room, like a canoe in whitewater. In and out of the alcove swam phosphorescent fish. And the sounds that came from my chest! Like two pieces of dry leather rubbing together, then the click of billiard balls colliding. Toward morning I forced myself to lie still, as though I were already dead and had no need to move, had forgotten how to move. Then sleep came. I awoke to the bells that came across the lake like skipping stones. Aside from the convent bells and the mute presence of a small church opposite the *mairie*, I see no evidence here of "religion." So far as I know, the people do not go to mass; nor have I seen a priest.

✐

This morning I arose and went to take a bath; only to find that the tub had been filled, the soap and towels at hand. When I returned to my room, a fire had been laid in the little stove, and bundles of lavender and thyme had been placed in with the kindling. When I touched it with a match, the room filled with the odor of herbs. Within moments, my breathing had calmed. Who is so good to me?

✐

Dawn: A mule, his ears still drowsy, pulls a cart noisily down to the market. It is piled so high with logs that it scarcely clears the lower branches of the plane trees.

Noon: A blue heat presses down on the village.

Evening: After dinner I walked down to the village, no more than two hundred paces, but about all I could manage.

I feel as though I have lived here before and have returned after a long journey. Nothing—not a shed or a hedge or a cobblestone or a crooked lamp—strikes me with the least surprise. Rather, for every object I feel a faint, fond sense of recognition. And also I feel the telepathic undercurrent that binds each house to the next, and each inhabitant to the others. I long to tap into it, to become porous.

✑

It is April, and the noise of the waterfall drowns out any other sound. Some distance behind the hotel the melting snow plunges down the sheer face of the mountain to form a pool whose runoff surges straight for Les Acacias. Just before we should be swamped, the torrent politely divides into twin channels that course on either side of us and disappear beneath the road on their way to the lake below. We are, as it were, islanded, and after a while, one does not even hear the roar of the water. It is strangely cleansing, and gives me the illusion that I am no longer infected—in the same way, I suppose, that a paraplegic is given back the motion of his limbs when he lies on the deck of a small sailboat. On some damp days I walk as far as the pool at the foot of the waterfall to stand in the mist. You can't go any farther, as beyond that the mountain defends itself with a Maginot Line of briers. As for the lake, Hugh, first imagine the Dead Sea; then conceive of its opposite, and you have this lake of Annecy that lies among the mountains like a boss on Achilles' shield.

✑

A half dozen black doctors from Mali have come to the hotel. Four men and two women, all slender and tall, the men in suits and neckties, the women in vivid robes and hats. They had been attending a conference in Geneva. They are exceedingly polite to one another. The knives and forks leap in their long fingers, and they meet my gaze with the most refined nod of greeting. After dinner, the girls sang for them in Portuguese.

✑

The doctors of Mali have left, and now the *pension* is full of Swiss. My God, they are hideous—misshapen, tuberous, and gray from a lifetime of having eaten too many potatoes, with gigantic buttocks and only the vaguest impression of a face imprinted on a slab of flesh. I watched one man tearing meat from a bone like a dog, gargling beer. At the end, he broke off a piece of bread and cleaned his teeth with

it! How different from the slender, mercurial Africans with their flash-
ing eyes and teeth, their spidery fingers. Nor do they have the innate
courtesy of the Malinese. They stared at me so, I could only hope that
the vestiges of my human form would suffice. Now there's your old
Monica—the asp in a basket of fig leaves. I'd better close for today. So
much of this journal has been written by moonlight. Can you tell?
From the strain of lunacy that runs through it?

⁇

It is Midsummer Eve. In the mountain villages, huge bonfires have
been set. One by one they were lit until the lake was ringed with
points of fire. On the terrace, red and yellow paper lanterns have
been strung in the acacias. Though it is too early for dinner, I am sitting at my table watching the preparations. Madame emerges from the
doorway and, leaning on her cane, makes her way to where I am sitting. She is carrying a glass of white wine.

"For the appetite," she explains, and observes while I take a sip.
There is something volcanic hidden in this wine that sends it shooting through the arteries. It is Monday and the Portuguese girls are
doing the napkins. Since I have eaten almost nothing for a week except what Madame has brought to my room, my napkin is unsoiled.

"No need," I tell the Portuguese girl. "I have not used it. I'll keep it
for another week."

She is distressed. "No, no, Madame Gallant," she says. "You must
have a fresh napkin."

"But why?"

"It is the way of Les Acacias. Each Monday, when you receive your
new napkin, we know and we rejoice that you will remain with us for
another week."

I eat a bit of cheese called Tomme de Savoie. It is strong and hard,
with an aftertaste like the smell of freshly cut wood. Another sip of
wine and I am through.

⁇

At midnight I was awakened by the ringing of bells, singing, drums,
a fiddle, and one fatal flute. There was the sound of many footsteps
on the road. Torchlight moved across the walls. I got out of bed and

went to the window to see the procession pass by. Over the lake hung a lone star like the pendant of some ancient Order of Chivalry. All at once—I blame the flute—tears. I could not hold them back. Toward daybreak, there came through the open window the watery song of a bird, then another, and another. Green finches. The jangling of a bicycle bell, the abrasive sound of ashes being strewn on the road. And, out on the lake, someone trying to start a motorboat. There it is again.

∾

I haven't told you yet about Monsieur. Every now and then he arrives unexpectedly. I can always tell the moment he has come; the metabolism of the place doubles. And for as long as he stays, a week or two, we are in a state of frenzy. Two steps are taken where before one would do; such a calling out of instructions, such a clatter of crockery and cutlery. I had thought him to be Madame's husband, which assumption was greeted with the rolling up of the principal's eyes and the screams of the Portuguese girls. Even Philippe's chin quivered when he heard about it. So I gather Monsieur is what you might call *un ami de la maison*—a friend of the house.

Monsieur, like Madame, is given to iridescence of wardrobe. The reds! The blues! The yellow-greens! All the rich colors preferred in childhood before maturity dulls the retina. He is tiny, mercurial, with a spruce little mustache and a high silver pompadour. His nose is narrow and curved like a beak and he has something less than hands—fingerlings, I suppose. And the daintiest feet in France. Madame calls him *le perruche*, the parakeet. It is Monsieur's role to ensure that everyone on the premises is talking at once. He can no more live in silence than a cat can live under water. And what roulades of language does he deliver, with such flourishes of lip and eyebrow, and such a repertoire of splendid gestures. When there is no one to talk to, he speaks to the wine. On the terrace he circulates from table to table, swirling a glass, inhaling an aroma and *parlez-vous*-ing a mile a minute. So far as food is concerned, he is worse than I am. I have never seen him eat so much as a single grape. No need. Such a perfect nosegay of a human being lives on his own charm.

✀

The light of the lamp hurts my eyes. They are full of hot ashes. I weep for no other reason and so assured Madame, whose expression said she thought otherwise. The next thing you know there was Philippe, bearing an old Roman oil lamp with a pointed lip, into which he had poured wax around a wick. In this bronze, pulsating light, I am perfectly at ease. Just to watch the play of it on my arms makes me feel attended. Such a light is a living presence, like a nurse at bedside.

✀

Thirst and fatigue. For the one, since I cannot swallow lately, I go to stand in the slaking sound of the waterfall. For the fatigue, a half hour in the sun restores me. Water and sun—the life of a plant.

✀

There is a grand villa with a cherry orchard by the lake, called Les Pensières. The caretaker, Monsieur le Gribi, a Moroccan, is a friend of Madame. She has arranged for me to go whenever I can to sit on the low stone wall that borders the lake. There is a break in the wall where stone steps lead down into the water. The third step is awash, the fourth submerged. The sound of the water lapping at the stone has the same cooling effect as the wind chimes you hung from the rafters on the back porch. The village itself is empty. I have taken to going there at noon, when the heat is greatest. I share the wall with the lizards and red ladybugs that live among the ferns and wild geraniums that grow between the stones. A pair of crested grebes—like ducks, only with sensible lobed feet and no tails—sit in the water in front of the wall, their long necks straight. Now one, now the other, lifts its rump and dives, only to surface again a minute later at some distance. Then it shakes the water from its head and lies to until something says: Do it again. To fly they must beat their small wings like bundles of sticks, but at courting they are grace itself, sending passionate messages to each other with their beaks and wings and the sinuous twining of their necks.

Can you imagine my happiness when I sit on my wall, satisfying the immemorial desire of hot feet for a cold lake?

∾

Philippe has given me something I have wanted all my life, only never knew it—a walking stick. One night a storm swept through the village. What a sight! On the terrace, every tree mad as the Bride of Lammermoor. Over went the tables; the chairs blew about. All at once a loud crack, and down went a large dead branch of one of the acacias. Under my window the next morning, I heard someone say, "Thank God the American woman was not sitting under it. She would have been killed."

"No," said Madame. "*Jamais.* An acacia does not kill."

From the branch Philippe has carved for me a walking stick. That is my idea of a benevolent tree. He stood there gravely watching as I took a few steps with it, to make sure it was the right height, then raised his cap and wished me *bonne promenade.* When I thanked him, he looked down at his shoes. If I could, I'd hang his tiny smile around my neck for an amulet. From Madame, too, a gift—a little leather traveling cup that I can tie to my wrist or belt. Every morning I find it next to my bread and chocolate, filled with an ounce or two of the white wine of Seyssel that is refreshing just to look at. Each evening I return it to the table. When, in the heat of the afternoon, I pour a few drops into my mouth, I feel like one of Bacchus's maidens.

∾

For days, a piece of music has been going through my mind. Something I used to play, by Debussy, but not "Claire de Lune." Splendid chords and ambiguities—you would recognize it at once. I heard it yesterday when I tossed a stone into the lake and watched the ripples. When it comes at night I imagine that all of Veyrier is sinking into the lake, the water flowing in and out of every window, door, and chimney and that, come daybreak, it will rise again.

∾

This stick of mine has become a guide, and a rather high-handed one, I must say. Each day it decides where we shall walk—one day to the waterfall, another to Les Pensières, and so forth. Should

I try to resist, he turns stubborn and throws his skinny shadow across my path. More often than not, lately, he refuses to come out of the armoire at all, thereby informing me that we shall not be going abroad today. But this morning he said, *Allons-y!* and took me to the little square opposite the church, where once a week the farmers come down from the mountain villages with their produce— circles of cheese, fat leeks, mushrooms, melons of every color, and baskets of little red berries. FROMAGE, said the stick with a kind of wooden insistence, so I approached a woman in a peasant dress who stood with her back to me. When she turned, I had to catch my breath. It was like looking into a mirror that held my image from a year ago: the same hair and eyes, the same mouth and chin, even the same mole on the left side of the neck. Only now she is pink and plump and I have purple swatches under my eyes and a dark seam for a mouth. I saw the spark of recognition in her face, too. For a long moment we stared, as though I were gazing into my past and she into her future. Then we both shrugged, laughed, and the spell was broken. When I tried to pay her for the cheese, she re- fused.

"No, no. It is something that I give to myself."

∽

There is another lone woman at the hotel, a blonde with dark eye- brows penciled high on her forehead and a silent-upon-a-peak-in- Darien look on her face that brooks no effort at familiarity. She is always dressed to the nines—silk blouse, high heels—and moves about in a cloud of perfume. Her table is nearest to mine on the ter- race. She is accompanied everywhere by a small dog named Bonbon, the size of a toy poodle, only with long, coarse brown hair that goes silver at the tips. Bonbon has a penetrating metallic yip and is dread- fully testy and spoiled. She carries him under her arm to her table and places him on her lap, where he remains throughout the meal. Now and then she offers him a piece of kidney or a bit of chicken from her long red fingernails. *Je déteste le chien.*

The woman occupies the room at the end of the hall on the same floor as mine. Number eleven. What with the roar of the waterfall, I do not hear a sound, not even from Bonbon. This is a perfect house for keeping secrets. I know mine, but what could hers be? She seems to be waiting for something. Or someone. We have not spoken, not even *bonsoir.* Perhaps she senses my antipathy for Bonbon. You know very well my affection for dogs. I have always thought even the most splathery, weather-headed mutt more open to the possibility of redemption than some of our human friends. But here we have Bonbon and I am no longer sure.

∾

Louis-Antoine is the village baker. Always he wears that weary look that is the sober badge of office. In Veyrier, bread is a calling. His entire repertoire consists of long, thin crusty loaves made of yeast, water, flour, and salt, the most delicious I have ever tasted. I have been twice now to visit him at his oven, which is an igloo-shaped, igloo-sized brick structure located in the dead center of Veyrier. Every morning Louis-Antoine fills it with well-seasoned oak logs and fills the whole village with the anticipation of fresh bread. His face, beneath the dark blue beret that sits flat on his head, has a permanently scalded look. His hands, too, look boiled, the nails caked with flour. The end of his beard and even his eyebrows are singed. Once a month in the late afternoon, when the oven has cooled, he crawls into the igloo and scrapes the soot. Seen through the oven door, he is a great crouched loaf himself.

∾

Last night, when the pain came, I rose from bed and went to the open window. I have never been so close to the moon. It makes you dizzy. There I sat, Hugh, with my moon, combing my hair (the one part of me that is thriving—it has grown very long), combing and combing with long, slow strokes, combing out the pain. I read somewhere that the women of Sparta sat in the moonlight combing their hair until their sorrows went away. It works. I fell asleep while combing, and dreamed a long peaceful dream in which I combed on and on. When I awoke, I was spent, as after a night of passion, and the pain was gone. I can just see that skeptical eyebrow of yours lifting. Never mind. Perhaps the only good thing about pain is that it cannot be shared, and so gives its owner a certain latitude of the imagination.

Like my walking stick, this pen of mine goes where it wishes. I have become the servant of my implements.

∞

I have become friendly with Nicole, the market woman who looks like me. The other day she took me with her to the small farm halfway up the mountain where she lives with her husband, Auguste, and their baby.

It was a bumpy ride in the old truck, what with the road little more than a gully of stones. Soon enough we were there, but then I was unable to step down from the high seat. It was quite funny the way Nicole came around, scooped me up all matter-of-fact as though I were an ungainly, ill-wrapped parcel (which believe me, I am), and carried me to the porch.

"You are lighter than a baby goat," she said, and deposited me in a chair.

The farmhouse is a little cottage with a steeply slanted roof and a chimney wearing a feather of smoke. There is a barn, an orchard, a field of melons, and a yard with animals. It was exactly as though one of my childhood picture books had come to life.

Auguste is a calm-eyed man who, without turning from his bee-hives, tossed me two gruff *bonjours* full of promise. *Just you wait!* they seemed to say. Later he gave me a perfect red tomato that precisely fit my palm, and a speckled pheasant's egg borrowed from the nest for my delectation. There is also an old grandmother—in France there usually is—who, having paid her tuition with a lifetime of household chores, now presides over the porch.

The first thing Nicole did was to fetch the baby from its cradle to nurse. Watching the muscular exertion of the baby's pursed lips, his total engagement in the feast, was strangely erotic—like the recurrence of a libidinous dream of my own infancy.

After a while, I felt able to walk into the barnyard. It is a grand thing to be among beasts—cows, goats, geese, chickens. I knew I was welcome when a nanny goat scattered her dry pellets on the beaten earth at my feet. Toward evening, Nicole deposited me at Les Acacias with a small jar of apricot jam she had put up. On my table, it hints at something in a past life that the memory sees but cannot put into words.

✑

A night of clatter and rustle, as though a small creature were looking for a way out of my chest. I awoke from an endless dream in which I was wandering through the tunnels beneath a great hospital, wrapped only in a sheet. A trail of my blood stretched behind me. Overhead ran great pipes from which came a filthy gurgling. So narrow and low were the passageways in some parts that I had to crouch and turn sideways. It was hot. I grew more and more faint, weaker and weaker. At last I came upon a door, pushed it open, and found my-self in a cool, dark space occupied by stone tables. With my last bit of energy I lay down upon one of them. Imagine my relief to wake up and find myself in my beloved room.

All day I lay listening to the lovely grammatical chant of French rain on the roof. Toward dusk it stopped, and the sky cleared. Slowly the thing on the bed became a body again, tried out its joints to see if they still worked. Enough of them did to let it get itself to the window ledge. In time, the moon rose and cast a beam across the lake. I could have walked across it. It is scandalous that such a thing of beauty should have no name in English, nor, according to Madame Durand, in French. To redress the lapse, I have invented a word for *path of moonlight on the water.* It is *lunaqua.* Keep your Hudson River with its heaving current, its gleaming vaporous mornings, its nights of netted stars, and give me the midnight lake at Veyrier with its silver lunaqua. Since I have no other, this word shall be my legacy.

✑

Among the things I am shedding is my skin, though with none of the grace of a snake, just shreds and peels of rind. Parts of me are quite raw. Why do they call it shingles? I cannot bear even the weight of the sheet on my chest. Once again Madame has provided: a loose, flow-ing white cotton gown that covers me wrist to ankle, with a mantle to raise against the sun. Monsieur le Gribi says it is a djellaba. What a strange sight I must offer to the vines and hedges on the path to the lake. I could be an Ishmaelite woman leading out my nomadic, ex-temporaneous life.

∽

Once again, I have visited Louis-Antoine. Bent over his kneading trough, he did not at first see me, and I watched for a few moments his strong fingers pressing, punching, squeezing. Without looking up he reached for the pitcher to add a little more water, then thrust his hands into the pliant dough. At last, I had to break the voluptuous silence with a cough. Louis-Antoine straightened, wiped the clots of dough that webbed his fingers, and drew up a bench for me to sit. One by one, he molded the loaves, laid them out on trays. Like unborn babies they seemed, each with the same unstoppable urge to rise as this belly of mine. When, all at once, the child kicked, and I was reminded that I was not one of Louis-Antoine's loaves, I felt something between disappointment and envy.

∽

Where did I read about a plant that flourishes only in places where there is much seasonal rainfall? (Perhaps it was you who told me?) During long dry periods, it extricates its roots from the parched earth, grows dry and weightless until it is lifted and carried by the wind to another wetland, perhaps hundreds of miles away. There it sets down roots and grows green until another drought comes and it must move on. It is the exact description of the life cycle of my mind, which for several weeks now has been aloft on a hot wind with no moist bed in sight.

∽

I had been unable to write for several weeks because of the swelling in my hands. How stupid hands are when idle. But now you see that I am once again at my notebook. Here's what happened: Early this morning Nicole came in the truck to bring me to the farm for the day. August was at the bees. One is never out of earshot of their coppery buzz. All afternoon Nicole coaxed the ewes to come and be milked. I must have fallen asleep. When I awoke, there was Auguste, still tending his hives. Nicole went to where her husband was working, reached out, and captured a handful of the bees. She came to where I was sitting. Then, as though it were the most natural thing in the world, she grasped one bee between thumb and forefinger and placed it on my right arm near the elbow. At the sting I jumped, out of pain and surprise. But Nicole smiled and shook her head as though to reassure a child. She took another bee from her fist and applied it to my other arm. Another sting. The rest of the bees she released and waved away. Within minutes, my arms, which had been cold and lifeless and stiff, grew pink and warm. I felt currents of electricity flowing into my dead fingers, which became, and still are now, limber. Can you see the improvement in my handwriting? When I asked her about it, she gave me one of those tiny smiles in her repertoire and said simply, *"C'est le lait des abeilles."*

❧

I have not felt the baby stir for three days. It is strangely still, as though gathering its strength for the ordeal of birth. It is the only thing I dread. Tonight, unable to sleep, I looked at the moon so long that when at last I turned away from it, my eyes in the mirror seemed to glow with the same soft light. Below me the roofs of Veyrier pulsated like the fontanelle of a newborn child. And now I feel suffused with an internal languor, as though I were a cup in which tea leaves were slowly settling, all but one. Soon, soon.

❧

I will make this short. What you shall have, Hugh, are one or two of the facts and the truth.

This morning Madame brought me a steaming resinous cup in which herbs floated. "What is that?" I asked, but I knew.

She stood by the bed and watched me sip it to the dregs, then placed an hourglass on the table, turned it over, and left. When the last of the sand had run through, the pains began and Madame returned. She stayed with me the whole time.

All day long, like a deaf woman, I felt, but could not hear, the shrieks tearing through my throat. The child was born dead. When it was over, Madame took it from me.

I didn't have the courage to look, but I named him Louis-Antoine, for the baker and his perfect bread. There are things that, even now, I cannot bring myself to do. I cannot leave behind a nameless child, not even a dead one, in this village where every path, cottage, and beast has a name. I felt no grief, only exhaustion, and the relief at having cheated a voracious fate. All the same, it is hard. Later, Nicole came and combed my hair with great long strokes.

✂

A new spot has appeared on my thigh. That makes three. A week ago I used the last of the morphine, but along with it, I seem to have used up the pain as well. Perhaps it has left me for some meatier bones to gnaw. There has been no bleeding for three weeks. I have the feeling that I have passed one trial and am being made ready for another.

✂

Monsieur le Gribi has taken me by car to Seyssel, a town on the banks of the Rhône. The river there is broad and wild. No wonder Madame Sévigné was frantic at the thought of her daughter crossing it on a raft. We sat by the river. Monsieur le Gribi drank several glasses of pastis. I sipped from my leather bottle.

"You cannot buy such wine in America," Monsieur le Gribi said.

"Why not?"

"Such a wine does not survive a journey. If you try to take it away from Haute-Savoie, it will collapse into vinegar."

"Like me," I said.

We watched the men playing *pétanque,* a game with wooden balls that is midway between billiards and croquet, only played with the hand. The men are of the same tribe—short, squarish, not at all fat, but solid. Topped with berets, their good-looking heads seem to me to have been chipped from the same block of wood by a single-minded clever ax. By the time we returned to the hotel, I had to be carried upstairs. Never mind—such an afternoon was worth the currency.

✂

Today I sat on the wall at Les Pensiéres in the noonday sun and dangled my shadow in the lake like bait. Leaning over, I gazed until the stony mountain behind the hotel slipped its tether and escaped through the water. That which on earth cannot be, in water becomes.

I must have nodded, because next thing I knew, there was a man before me, with water streaming from his shoulders. He had hard green eyes and a beard of precise curls arrayed in rows like a statue's, and only a pair of black bathing trunks to persuade that he was a mere mortal. I could not have been more startled had a centaur pranced out of the orchard. To me he seemed one of those creatures that are the dream of childhood and for which the adult never stops longing. A sweet-water Triton! It is just as well, Hugh, that you are rid of me. I have become insufferably particular. Now that I have seen a Triton, I would never be satisfied with a mere man.

"You frightened me," I said. "Who are you?"

His name was Luc, he replied, and smiled a smile that went straight through me. *"Je suis plongeur."*

"A diver?"

"Yes."

"What is it like down below?"

"It is cool and green," he said.

He looked at me with something like roguery and tenderness, but without the least ambiguity. I had to lower my gaze to the wall, where, all at once, the tiny ferns between the stones took on a vast importance.

"One day, when you are ready, you can come with me," he said swiftly. Then, *"À bientôt."* I watched him dive into the water, his gleaming body now curvetting above, now submerging, until he was nothing but a lustrous residue churned by the waves. All the way back to the hotel, there was a bright sting in my mouth as though I had just bitten into a crisp young radish.

✆

I asked Madame if she knew the diver. A tiny smile flitted.

"I have heard things," she murmured. I asked her to tell me what she had heard, every last detail. Was he married? I wondered. I died to know.

"He does not marry," she replied, and left me.

✆

Fever! The way it pulls the skin taut over one's skeleton, like a drum, then beats on it.

Awake and asleep I dream about the lake, endlessly cleansing itself from a thousand springs, from the infusion of melted snow from the mountains, from the rain. It is new each day. What does not change are the hidden forests and chasms, the kingdom in its depths. Looking into the lake doubles the earth, lending it a celestial magnitude.

∽

Every few days Nicole comes to Les Acacias, each time bringing me some bit of food. Today, a brown and speckled free-range egg and a cup of stewed apricots. Then I, who can eat virtually nothing, devour what she brings. In her hands, goat cheese and bread turn into Belshazzar's feast. I asked Nicole to tell me exactly where he found the egg. Was it in the marshy field? In the pasture? She had found it in a little patch of blackberries farther up the mountainside, where she had gone to extricate a ram that had gotten caught in the thicket. Madame poached the egg, and minutes later, there I was wiping the last of it from the plate with a crust of bread. And with gusto! When I had eaten, Nicole and Madame together disinterred me from the bed and brought me forth for an airing. Where did they learn this profound courtesy for the flesh?

∽

I have now been here long enough to see the lack of religious conviction of the mountain. In the winter he was a Dominican friar with his white cowl. In spring he turned Jewish and wore a skullcap. Now it is autumn, and he has gone Buddhist and shaved his head. In the face of such fickleness, I have clung devoutly to my atheism. There is something to be said for constancy.

∽

Quite often the Triton comes from the lake to sit on the lowermost step of the wall. When he does not, I am desolate.

"It is cruel of you to abandon me," I told him. He laughed with delight.

"Throw a little stone into the water. I will know it, even from the farthest end of the lake." So I did just that today. Within minutes, there he was! Rising from the depths, taut, pulsating, his nostrils dilated, blowing off foam. Now that is what I call telegraphy. Twice he has made a cradle of his arms and carried me into the cold caldron of rebirth that is the lake, and each time, I felt the fever leaving my body. How the water hissed and steamed about me! In his arms, water is not another element, only a heavier, darker air. When I am with him, he is absolutely real. When he has left me, I wonder.

∾

News! The blond woman with the dog has a visitor. A swarthy man in a fez—a Moroccan, I would guess. This evening he mounted the steps from the road and stood there for a moment mastering the geography and population of the terrace with his marvelously glittering eye, then made his way straight to the woman's table. Such a yipping and growling from Bonbon, whose hackles rose in outrage. It is obvious that man and dog know each other, to their mutual regret. The conversation was unintelligible to me—Arabic? Still I could see by the violent way she worked her eyebrows that she was *blazing*. At one point, the man reached into his pocket and handed something to her, a small packet that he palmed expertly and that she received with equal finesse into her sleeve. And that was that. Smugglers, I say. Or spies. When the fez pushed back his chair and stood to rise, she sank her long red nails into the meat on her plate and offered it to Bonbon. The fez grimaced in disgust and went quickly into the hotel.

∾

The man in the fez has come again and gone. All afternoon he and the blond woman stayed in the room at the end of the hall. Once, I imagined voices raised, a muffled commotion. Minutes later, the sound of a car driving away. The noise of the motor had barely faded when it began, a terrible howling from the end of the hall. On and on, without respite, feeding on its impetus, like a fierce wind from the north, subduing even the noise of the waterfall. A naked grief. All night she wailed. At breakfast, the Portuguese girl told me that Bonbon was dead. I didn't like the dog, but, God forgive me, I only wished it away. When the woman appeared, gray and deflated, I would gladly have had it back. It is pitiful to see her sitting alone at her table. Her misery is terrible to behold. Although no one would say, I suspect poison. But what a rage for the terrific I am developing here! It is what happens in small hotels. The mind goes lurid.

∾

If I didn't know better, I'd say that my legs are fifty years older than the rest of me. Still, I cough very little and have even, I think, gained a bit of weight, thanks to the treats brought by Nicole—not the least of which is Auguste's honey, which I have been spooning down. I am on my second jar. Has the beast let me fall for a time from his jaws? If so, I am stupidly grateful. In the morning I emerge, not from sleep so much as from a kind of dazzled rest, and without fatigue.

A Dutch family has arrived. A mother, a father, and four very pale children. I should think fair skin in a child a great nuisance. It shows the dirt more. When I told this to Madame, she split her sides. "*Méchante!*"

∾

There is a basement where the Portuguese girls do the laundry. I love to sit at the top of the stairs, where I can inhale the smell of boiling sheets and starch. In the courtyard out back are lines from which the sheets are hung. All at once, Philippe comes across the yard with a great basket of soiled linen. In a second, the girls are at him.

First Portuguese girl: "*Ah, mon cher, mon amant. Venez à moi*—come here, you great beautiful ox. I have a kiss for you."

Philippe: "*Taisez-vous.*" The slamming of a door, much laughter from the girls.

First Portuguese girl: "Never mind. A bucket of water over the head will cool him off."

Second Portuguese girl: "In a year he will leap out at you from behind the clothesline."

I swear these girls have wine in their veins instead of blood, the hot black wine of Portugal. Later, when they took down the billowing sheets, my own blood stirred at the sight of them draped in linen like souls in ascent.

∽

I have fallen in love with the Triton. I know exactly when it happened.

"I am thirsty," I said. Whereupon he ladled clear cold water into his cupped hands and held them out for me to drink. It was precisely then, when my face, like the snout of some small animal, entered that living cup, that I opened my eyes and saw through the pool of water the calluses, like scales, and the markings in the cushions of his palms, it was then that I fell in love with him. I drank like a parched animal.

∽

For three days I did not see the blond woman. On the fourth it turned abruptly cold. I looked up from my table to see her standing in the doorway, hesitant, dazed, yet with her eyebrows freshly penciled and her face a mask of cosmetics. Beautifully dressed, as usual. On a sudden impulse, I called out to her.

"Please," I said. "Tonight you must join me." For a moment she hesitated. Then, as if obeying a command, she came and sat.

"I am sorry for your loss," I said. The words unleashed her grief and she began to weep—bawl, really, her chin all snot and saliva. Within minutes, her handkerchief, a tiny square of sheer cotton edged with lace, was soaked. I could not help recoiling.

"He, Bonbon, was the only one I could trust," she sobbed. "The others have all betrayed me."

What could I say? "Yes, yes," I said, and "Ah! and "I see," the syllables of condolence, which are all one has to offer the inconsolable. What is this *thing*, I wondered, that could turn this woman's face, a face I had thought incapable of expression, into a dripping cistern? What I felt was, I confess, revulsion. But something else too, something akin to envy.

"Come," I said. "We will go to your room." I led her, still sobbing, through the tables. The stares of the other diners, to which she was oblivious, shamed me. In her room, I helped her to undress and put her into bed. In the darkening room, her grief was less visible.

"I am so ashamed," she said.

"It doesn't matter," I told her. "Madame told me that you will be leaving soon. You can leave your shame here with me."

When she smiled, I felt my heart break. How well I know, how completely I understand that we all have things that no one else must be permitted to see.

∾

The blond woman has returned to her table, the one nearest mine. Her hand is in a small brown-and-silver muff on her lap. There she sits, gazing sadly down at the lake, absently running her red nails through the fur.

∾

This evening the blond woman and I had a talk. I had already left the table and had just passed her seat when I heard her say very quietly, almost a whisper, "Madame."

I turned. She gestured for me to sit. For several moments we sat in silence, inhaling the sweet smell of the acacias. At last she spoke.

"Already it grows cold in the evening," she said. "The snow is piling up on the mountain. Soon it will be winter. I have heard the wolves howling up there."

"There are no wolves," I said. "Perhaps it was the wind." Was she mad? Perhaps, but no madder than I. And more of a woman, who can grieve. (I could not take my eyes from the muff.) Mad or not, she refuses to let go, in the face of all reason, at no matter what cost to her dignity. I am in awe of it. All at once, she reached out and took my hand.

"So cold," she said, studying my palm. I shivered, but not from the cold. "Tomorrow," she said, "I shall go away for good. I want you to have this. I want you to wear it. You must promise to." When I hesitated, she slipped the muff from her hand and placed it around mine.

∾

The blond woman left before dawn. At noon, I heard a car pull up out front and two doors slam. A moment later two men, clean-shaven, in

fedoras and neckties, climbed to the terrace. They paused, surveyed
the empty tables, then strode to the door of the hotel, where Madame
appeared, her hands aflutter. I heard the words *gendarmes* and *sûreté*
and my heart contracted to a hard rubber ball that bounced against
my ribs. I knew at once that they had come for me, that somehow you
had traced me, that now, when it was almost . . . I would be snatched
up and sent back to you like an escaped criminal. Oh God, how I
cursed you. I saw the two men shoulder past Madame into the front
hall. You can imagine my terror. I lay on my bed and heard their
heavy footsteps on the stairs. Then I heard Madame.

"It is a small hotel, mine, *messieurs*. There is no one such as you describe. Yes, yes, two women alone, but I assure you that neither of
them . . . The one has already left. I don't know where."

"And the other?" They were at the door to number eleven. A rattling
of keys, a scuffling of shoes, a door opening, a long pause, the door
closing. The footsteps came closer. They were just outside my door.
Madame's voice took on an edge of granite. She raised it for me to hear.

"Here," she said, "the room of Madame Gallant, an American. I
shall open the door for you to see. There will be a young woman
lying in bed with her eyes closed. She will not open them. She will not
speak to you. I think you will not speak to her, when you have seen."
A soft knock. Me, palpitating in the bed.

"Madame!" she called out to me. "I shall open the door for a moment only. *N'avez pas peur*—do not be afraid. No one will come in."
Oh, my heart! The door opened halfway. I did not turn to see, only
lay as Madame had instructed me, with my eyes closed and my hands
folded on my chest, like a corpse. In a moment, the door closed and
the footsteps receded. Minutes later, I heard the car drive off.
Madame's footsteps returned. When she had come into my room, I
opened my eyes for the first time.

"It was not for you that they came," she said. "They wanted the
other. Number eleven." She smiled faintly. "They are too late."

"But where . . . ?"

"She was not a bad woman. Not at all. She was brave. How she
loved her little dog." Madame's glance took in the muff. "Ah," she
said softly. "So." Then she helped me to sit up. "Come, we shall go to
the kitchen; we shall have a cup of soup."

∞

October. And a full moon in every rain barrel. Now, when nothing is compatible with the raw channel my mouth has become, I can still drink a dipper of this water-of-the-moon. It is a year since I arrived in Veyrier. In the mirror, what I see is a head small with disease, the skull imprinted on the skin. The rest is indistinct, clouded as from a coating of mist. A woman's first real awareness of her body, they say, comes through love or childbirth. Maybe so, but for me it came with the discovery of my sickness, when I began the process of separating from it. And what a fragile thing it is, the body. And how absurd to grow so attached to it. I should like to give it up with grace. Not to thrash about like someone drowning, but rather like . . . after the last reverberation of a bell when, in the pure silence, something in the belfry settles itself and folds its wings.

Hugh, I shall not be writing in this journal any longer. I have no more than a dozen words left in me. Too often now my eyes are full of hot ashes; my wrist is like a handful of dice that have been miscast. Just as well. Writing is rather like driving a car; at a certain age, one ought sensibly to forget how to do it. Reading over these pages, I can only wonder why I wrote them at all. They make no sense, tell no story, not the story I had wanted them to. I have called it a journal, but it is a journal only in that it contains no past or future, just a present. And even that is meager. From the many pages I have left blank, I suspect that the real events of this year have taken place behind my back. And so what you will have, since I promised, are a few hieroglypics scrawled among long empty silences. Make of it what you will.

For weeks I have been awaiting a sign. Just this Monday it was given to me. At breakfast on the terrace I withdrew my napkin from its linen envelope and lo! it was the same one I had used all last week. There were the stains of the wine my trembling fingers had spilled the night before. When I looked up, the face of the Portuguese girl was beautifully neutral. In the doorway stood Madame, one finger pressed against her cheek, a tiny peaceful smile at her mouth. Philippe crossed the terrace carrying a carafe of wine. How he has grown this year, more bone than fat, his broad Savoyard shoulders, his hair ferociously tamed to his scalp, his whole body silent, alert. Yet still upon his face, the sad, comic despair of the teenage male, as though all the distressed maidens of Savoie had been rescued without waiting for him.

I no longer go down to the terrace. For some days now, I have been dizzy. All around me the hotel moves with a lovely fluidity, the way waltzing couples cause the ballroom itself to dip and turn. I am quite pleasantly numb. In my room, I sleep, I sleep, I sleep. Awake, I sleep on. The sun comes through the window and tries to lift my head from the pillow, but I sleep on. Today I dreamed—no, I saw—that Nicole had come to my room. For the first time she has brought no food for me to eat.

"And today?" she asked, her eyes accepting the two small stains of blood on the pillow. Her hay-scented breath was so sweet that she blew out all the hard hours of the night like so many candles.

"Today?" I replied. "Today I want to go down to the lake, to lie on the wall for a while."

I will tell you how she raised me from the bed in her strong arms and helped me to bathe and to put on the clean white loose gown that Madame had laid out. How Philippe came and together they managed me, oiled and arrayed like a bride, toward the lake. How Madame accompanied us to the edge of the terrace, then stood leaning on her cane, gazing after. How Philippe lifted me to the wall, and Nicole set a small pillow under my head. How, at the top of the path, they turned to wave, shielding their eyes from the sun. How above the hotel, the foam of the cataract was bearing a rainbow down the mountain. How I lay in the sun with my eyes closed, no longer able to store up energy like a battery, but now like an animal, listening, waiting. How, after a while, I heard that longed-for splash as the waters parted.

"Is it you?" I asked.

I felt the cool shadow of my Triton. "Open your eyes," he said. When I couldn't he raised my eyelids with the gentlest touch of his fingers. In his eyes, I could see the dim aquarial landscape, undulant, tossing. His face was as close as the moon from my window. He gathered me up. I heard the sweet palaver of the lake and the stone steps. There was the shock of the water on my skin, my gown filled with it, my hair floating.

"Down," I said. "I want to go down."

"Yes," he said. "You are ready. We will go now. Look! Here are the fish to welcome you, and the birds to see you off." The last sound I heard was the soft applause of their wings. The next moment my head filled with green. A rush, a rapture, a delirium of green.

⁓

I have asked Madame to send you this notebook one month from tomorrow. She has promised to do so. Tomorrow I will have crossed over. I would not have traded a century for these four seasons in Veyrier, where a single moment is like a year of mortal life and where I have located the wellsprings of a power beyond annihilation.

One thing more, Hugh. Your first impulse will be to come here. Please don't. There will be nothing of me that is reachable here. Madame, Philippe, Nicole—none of them will have anything to tell you that I have not already written. No mournful pilgrimages. Veyrier does not deserve your sighs, your loitering. Let us be.

"The Black Swan" Revisited

In Homage to Thomas Mann

PREFACE

The impulse to rewrite "The Black Swan" came less from the desire to pay homage to Thomas Mann, although that is surely what I shall always wish to do, than from a scene momentarily witnessed at the hospital where I work. I was on evening rounds and I passed the open door of a room occupied by someone who was not my own patient. Glancing in without breaking stride, I saw a very old and emaciated woman lying propped on pillows. She could have weighed no more than seventy pounds. Every bone threatened to burst through parchment. Her hands were spiders at the end of sticks. No matter, she was totally engaged in working a long gold pendant earring through her earlobe. Her head was inclined toward shaking fingers; a look of fierce concentration pleated her face as she probed for the hole. This I saw, and nothing more. But it constituted a moment of clarity in which her act of adornment took on incalculable significance. Once again, a hospital bed had been transformed into a draperied couch by the person lying in it. In that moment the old woman had taken on for me the persona of Rosalie von Tummler, and I knew that I would begin to tell her story again that very night.

ൟ

In that period of deception between the two great wars, in the city of Düsseldorf-on-the-Rhine, on an almost-fashionable street called Magenstrasse, there lived a widow, Rosalie von Tummler, and her two children. From the beginning, Edward, a pale spidery boy of seventeen, had been slated by his father for a military career. Come October he was to leave for the Academy. The elder, Anna, a spinster of twenty-eight, had been born with a clubfoot which had resisted a series of attempts at surgical correction. From childhood on she had studied art and only lately had developed a small reputation in the city for her paintings. Herr von Tummler, may God rest his soul, had died ten years before in an accident the details of which to this day remained fuzzy in his widow's mind. It had to do, Rosalie understood vaguely, with another woman. But it had never occurred to her to be resentful. That was a man's nature, and Rosalie was prepared to accept nature in all of its numberless aspects. Rosalie attributed her sensitivity to the natural world to having been born in April when every living thing on the planet was beginning what she called its "grand investigation." Often, on her bird-watching or rock-collecting treks, she could almost hear the slow rising of the sap in the trees or the infinitesimally small noise of plant cells dividing and multiplying. When she told this to the children, Edward would circle one of his ears with a finger and Anna would smile.

It was this same acceptance of nature's ways that had enabled Rosalie to go through her change of life some five years before with equanimity. For her, none of the irritability, headaches, hot flashes, and melancholy of other women. Sensibly, Rosalie rejected these symptoms and, in the end, declared herself relieved to have it all over with. No event in nature, she said to Anna, is without its purpose.

As luck would have it, Herr von Tummler had left a moderate inheritance, and so the three were able to live, if not in luxury, in a state very far from deprivation. Within those limits Rosalie had seen to it that the household was decorous and calm, and that the talents of each of her children were developed as far as possible. She herself had taken courses in botany and zoology at the university, even going so far as to dissect a fetal pig. Had she been a man, she told Anna, she would have been a scientist. As it was, she studied and collected things. Frau von Tummler was one of those small women who, in middle age, take on a certain physical solidity. Still, she had what might be called an elderly beauty. For instance, she had not entirely lost her figure, the bosom and hips being accentuated by the narrower waist about which she always wore a belt, or a sash with an elusive pattern. The open-wide smile was still there, and her heavy braids, while dusted with gray, were full. Twisted and secured about her head, they shone in the sunlight. In fact, the more one gazed at Rosalie von Tummler, the nearer one came to the image of a pretty young woman of years ago. Now and then, Anna would be coaxed into accompanying her mother on one of her specimen-gathering walks in the countryside. From the distance, seeing the petite mother's graceful stride, taking one step to every limping one and a half of the taller, thinner, prematurely dessicated Anna, one would have guessed their roles reversed. Anna's clubfoot had made intimates of them, each confiding in the other without embarrassment.

With just the same equanimity as Rosalie had accepted the biological news of her menopause, so had Anna one day set down her easel for a moment, gazed at some distant horizon, then accepted her spinsterhood. Anna's paintings were in the abstract mode. To Rosalie, the naturalist, the canvases held nothing recognizable. She simply did not understand them. Try as she might to conjure a leaf or a bird in flight from a shapeless swirl of the brush, she could not.

"How do you do it?" she asked Anna.

"First, I make a mark with the brush. This leads me to the second stroke. These two, their relationship to each other, induce the third, and so on."

"How do you know when it is done?"

"When there is no more room on the canvas," Anna laughed.

The week prior to Anna's twenty-ninth birthday, Rosalie saw on the back page of the newspaper a small discreet advertisement for private English lessons to be given at the homes of the pupils. The name of the teacher was Ken Keaton. English, thought Rosalie. No, American. The Ken gives it away. Immediately, she decided to present these lessons to Anna for her birthday, and arranged an interview by mail. A young American in his middle twenties arrived. Pleased with his informal manner and his Irish good looks, Rosalie at once pronounced him suitable. It was decided that he would come every Tuesday and Thursday at four o'clock. The lessons would take place in the parlor to which large French doors would give privacy and where teacher and pupil might work uninterrupted by the noise of the household. Anna declared herself delighted with her present, and so it happened that Ken Keaton entered the placid rhythm of the house on Magenstrasse. Twice each week at precisely five minutes to four in the afternoon, Rosalie would answer the knocking at the door and lead the young man to the oval mahogany table in the bay window of the parlor. She would pull the draperies across the window and leave. Moments later there would be the heavy drag of Anna's footstep on the stairs. In this way, weeks went by. Now and then, Rosalie would tiptoe to the closed door, press her ear against it, and when she heard Anna responding to the teacher's question in English, she would shiver with a mother's satisfaction.

It must be said that to a woman of Rosalie's romantic nature the thought that an affection might grow between her daughter and the young man had more than once entered her mind. She had once or twice felt wistful about the possibility. But just as quickly she would dismiss the notion. Not likely, she would think. Not for Anna. But still . . .

"He's a nice young man, isn't he?" she said to Anna.

"Quite nice, yes."

"Really, what do you think of him?"

"Really, Mother, I don't think of him much." Rosalie was not ungrateful for the terminal placement of that "much."

Once, the lesson having gone on for some minutes past the hour, Rosalie knocked on the door, excused herself, and suggested to Ken that he stay for dinner. He accepted at once. The evening had proved pleasant and sociable. It was the first of many dinners Ken Keaton was to take at the von Tummlers'. At times it seemed to Anna that he would purposely prolong the lesson to position himself for an invitation. Each time, when asked, he would accept without hesitation. As often as not, immediately after coffee, Anna would excuse herself and clomp upstairs to her studio, leaving the two others to linger at the table. Rosalie would pour Ken a brandy and herself a glass of port.

Now and then Rosalie was acutely conscious that Anna could hear them laughing from upstairs. At such times, she would feel a twinge of guilt.

One day, Rosalie sat at the small table where the lessons took place. She did not hear him enter the room. Only when he had come to stand in her line of vision, blocking out her view of the sky and the garden outside, did she notice. At first, she tried to peer around him in annoyance, then felt her focus shortening from the world beyond the window to the world this side of it, which at that moment was filled to the exclusion of all else with the body of Ken Keaton.

Rosalie could not have said just when it happened that she fell in love with him, what specific sight or sound had caused desire, long outgrown, to bounce back to its feet. Had it been that hot August day when he arrived in shorts and sleeveless shirt? Then, at the sight of the tufts of light brown hair at his armpits, each strand bearing a droplet of perspiration, she had smelled his sweat and felt herself redden.

"What is that?" she bent over him, studying the bunched violet scar on his thigh. It was star-shaped, the pitted center being of the deepest hue, and paling out along the points, one of which disappeared beneath the cloth of his shorts. Here and there a ridge caught the light and shone tightly.

"I was wounded," said Ken simply. He made no move to cover it. Instead, with an unself-consciousness that Rosalie had come to think of as peculiarly American, he pulled up his shorts to show her more.

"It goes even higher," he said.

"Is it painful still?"

"No. Only now and then when I sweat, it itches as though something, a bug, were crawling on it, something that I cannot scratch."

That night Rosalie could not sleep. In the turmoil of her bed she closed her eyes and saw the scar again and again, the way it wandered up beneath his shorts to end . . . where? All at once, she sat upright, her heart pounding. What is the matter with me? she thought. What is happening to me? And clapped one hand over her mouth because what she wanted to do more than anything was to run her tongue over that scar.

Or had it been the day when, unobserved, she had watched them through the barely opened door to the parlor? Anna and Ken were speaking softly. She could not hear them. So profoundly were they absorbed, so still, that they seemed to Rosalie to be figures woven into a tapestry. Anna's face appeared dark, smudged in half-light; Ken's illuminated by the lamp, was a forbidden spectacle—something like a transfiguration. When, suddenly, he caught sight of her and smiled, she had to lean against the door. In any case, from that moment, Rosalie felt a circle had been drawn about her out of which she could not step. Intemperate! she thought. That was the word for it. You would think that a lifetime of propriety would offer some immunity against a rashness that could end only in humiliation. Again and again she tried to think of her husband, dead these many years. But all she could remember of him was the monocle he wore and which every little while he would disimpact from his eyesocket and wipe. And the gold incisor tooth which in the early days of her marriage had given her that extra feeling of opulence when he kissed her. Who, she asked herself, what, was this Ken Keaton who seemed to live from day to day without much vivacity or wit? He was nothing. Yet there was something like distinction or heroism about him. Remembering his face, Rosalie decided that it was the genius of beauty.

Had she been offered a choice—whether to stay as she had been, in a state of harmony, enjoying nature, her children, her garden—or to fall in love, she would have rejected the abstraction of Ken Keaton. But that was not given her. Love, she discovered, cannot be elected or declined. Like illness, it comes, and that is that. Rosalie felt there was something violent and graceless about her suffering. Surely it would give her away. Now and then, without warning, saliva would gather in her mouth; once it had made her choke. Or sweat would spring to her upper lip and nose. At such times, she would weep for the hopelessness of it. The gnawing pain of it. The beauty.

She could not keep her gaze from him. Once, feeling perhaps the hot point of it between his shoulder blades, he turned so suddenly that she had been caught off guard and had burst into awkward tears that to the young man were inexplicable.

"What is it?" he asked. "Is something the matter?"

"Nothing. It is nothing. A sudden female emotion. It is not

unheard-of at my age. Pay it no mind." He had smiled then, in relief. My God! She must be more careful.

Another time, he had come upon her unexpectedly while she was cutting roses in the garden. Beautiful, he had said. The roses leaped in her hand. A drop of blood bloomed at her fingertip. Oh, she had said. Look! And she had held it up for him to see. At once he turned his face aside.

"Ugh! Blood," he said. "I hate the sight of it."

How lucky other women are, she thought, keeping on with their moderately turning lives while she felt herself wasting from a grotesque desire. In the heightened isolation of love, she would think of these others, the women of her neighborhood, as sheep mindlessly grazing. One day toward the beginning of April, returning from the market, Rosalie was hailed by her friend Lisa who also had been widowed but was now unhappily remarried.

"You seem, Rosalie, to have come through the winter with even greater liveliness than before. There is such a color in your cheeks. Is it rouge? And you have become slender! Look, it's true." And she encircled Rosalie's waist with her arm. "If I did not know you better, I would say that you have taken a lover." The woman laughed. Rosalie was certain that the pounding of her heart and the fluttering of the lace collar of her dress was noticed. She held one hand to the collar, but the woman had not seen.

"It is easier," Lisa went on, "for a woman alone to find happiness. Domesticity, and all that goes with it—boredom, frustrated passion— it ages one so."

"Lisa . . ." said Rosalie. But she could speak no more than the woman's name.

As for sleep, it was a place she could not enter. She would urge herself toward it, but a gate was barred. She was like an animal trying to crawl back into its lair, only to find the burrow blocked by heavy stones. But it was at the dinner table that Rosalie fully engaged her martyrdom. A dozen times during a meal she spied on his face, eating him with her eyes. He filled her so that she could eat nothing else.

"You have eaten nothing," Anna once said. Instead of speaking, Rosalie raised her wineglass to her lips and kept watch for the moist tip of his tongue when he opened his mouth to eat. What had she fed upon, what had nourished her, before this? For the life of her, she could not remember.

As Rosalie stood to refill his glass, pouring the wine as though it were a sacrament, she caught sight of herself in the tarnished mirror on the wall. The face she saw was a face in pain and which gave pain. The line, like a deep fault that, year after year, rose farther from the bridge of her nose to bisect her forehead, there was no smoothing it out. All at once a single violent tremor shook her hand so that the stream of red wine wobbled over the dark wood of the table. She felt the quick glance of the other two.

"Never mind," said Anna, mopping with her napkin. But Rosalie stared at the scattered red puddles that remained. It shocked her to think just how far she had departed from life before the arrival of Ken. When she looked back upon her years of serene widowhood, she felt only that they held a kind of obsolete charm to which she could no longer relate. The whole idea of her former life was what she had relinquished. She would not return to it again. Now she seemed to be outlined by a frame, waiting for something to happen.

‰

Just so did the autumn pass unnoticed by the suffering woman. It was Christmas Eve when Rosalie told Anna. Mother and daughter had been trimming the tree.

"Anna," she said. "Your mother is a foolish old woman."

"What now?" laughed Anna.

"I have fallen in love. With Ken," she said simply.

Anna stood motionless and turned to study her mother's face, reading there what she had never seen before: humiliation and naked pleasure.

"But that is ridiculous. He is younger than I am."

"Yes. That is what is so terrible and unnatural. Nevertheless, it is true. I cannot deceive myself." Suddenly, the older woman sank to her knees, her body shaking with sobs.

"What is it that you feel?" said Anna gently. "Try to say exactly." Rosalie shrugged and shook her head. She could not put the symptoms of love into words any more than a woman, immediately after childbirth, can describe the pain of it. Only, she knew, that it must find release or she would die of it. There were times when her body was un-inhabitable for another instant. There was no room for her in it. Something else was crowding her out.

"Why don't you try writing it down?" said Anna. "Just putting it into words on a page will make it recede. In any case, you might feel better. I read somewhere that there is an ancient magic in writing a sorrow down, then burning the paper upon which it is written. It makes the affliction go away. Perhaps it will work for a hopeless desire as well." When Anna left the room, Rosalie sat at the writing table and did indeed try to write it all down. Yes, she would burn the paper, and when she saw the thing writhe in the flames, she would be rid of it. But all that appeared on the papers were the words *Ken* and *Love*. In the end she could not bring herself to throw the piece of paper into the fire. It would be an unnatural act, she decided.

Even in Anna's absence, she fought with herself. It is not love, she would argue. It is lust. An obsession with his body. After all, she knew nothing about his mind, which was a territory she was little moved to explore. But no, said Rosalie aloud in the privacy of her room. No. It is love. To call it anything else—infatuation, obsession—would be an act of cowardice. And a lie. I love him.

"But it is dangerous," said Anna. "There is the possibility of ridicule. You must admit that there is something a bit . . . well . . . laughable about it."

"I suppose there is. Yes, laughable. But Sarah laughed at the idea of getting a child with Abraham at the age of ninety-nine."

"Can't you just like him for what he represents? Youth, good health, an intact body, potential?" Anna was running out of patience with her mother. "Can't you just adore him spiritually? It would be so much more sensible."

"Does he know?" asked Anna. Rosalie shook her head. But he must know, she thought. On some level, he must be aware. The little half-smiles he gave her. Was he young and callow enough to be flattered? Pleased to have made a conquest? Any conquest? Yes! That was it exactly. But Rosalie did not care. I will have him on any terms, she thought miserably.

That night in her room Rosalie studied herself in the mirror. Why, Lisa was right, she thought. Despite everything, I must say I look well. I have not grown into an old woman. She stepped nearer to the glass, peering for evidence. It was true. Her hair was quite lively in the lamplight; it had certainly grown no grayer. And she had lost just enough weight to rid her of that bit of thickening around the middle. I am slender, she said aloud. As the days went by, Rosalie's preoccupation with her appearance grew. Each night, she would stand before the mirror in her room, examining. It seemed to her that her eyes were once again as bright as a girl's. The skin of her arms and neck was pale, pale as ivory. And smooth. She had always been proud of her complexion. But this! Is this what love does to a woman? she thought. Try as she might to brush aside the notion, she could not entirely rid herself of the idea that she looked younger than she had in years. Certainly, she felt younger. Even her voice had taken on a clear girlishness. One night, in fact, she dreamed that she had been given the body of a young girl.

Six months to the day after Ken's first visit to the house on the Magenstrasse, Rosalie von Tummler lay in her bed and did battle. It was past midnight and through the drawn curtain a shifty moon teased. Black leaves waggled at the windowsill. Another night of it, she thought. Slowly, all but imperceptibly, she felt the first cramp building low in her abdomen. It grew big, the way thunder grows big from the smallest beginning, and rolled as thunder rolls before ebbing away. In a moment, another, and another. It has reached the point of pain, thought Rosalie, and turned on her side, drawing her knees up, pressing them into her belly, squeezing the pain from her body. How much farther was there to go? Even her breasts felt the longing; they were tender, engorged, the nipples registering discomfort beneath the sheets. The curled position gave her relief and presently she fell asleep. It was still dark when she awoke. Rosalie pushed herself upward to sit on the edge of the bed, to stand and leave that bed which had just given her so little rest and so much suffering. As she stood, Rosalie felt a warmth moving on her inner thigh, then something slide down her leg. She put her hand there to feel a moisture. Even before she saw the dark stain on her fingers, she knew that it was blood. It is happening, she marveled. I am menstruating! Once again, a woman, after so many years. It is the miracle of love. Love, she thought, is making me young again to be worthy of him. Of course!

How is it that I had not recognized it before this? The tenderness and sensitivity of my breasts, the cramps. A wave of triumph swept her body.

How differently men and women think about bleeding. For Rosalie it bore the promise of love and youth. Whereas Ken . . . Had he not told her that day in the garden when she pricked herself, had he not told her that he could not stand the sight of blood? It is the men who are frail. They perceive the shedding of so much as a single drop of their blood as a reminder that they will one day sicken and die. In three days, the bleeding had stopped. Rosalie noted the dwindling of the flow, then the cessation, almost with reluctance. When, the next month, she experienced the premonitory signs, she was overjoyed and gave herself up to the anticipation of the flow. She was not disappointed; there was again pain and bleeding. Again! she thought. She could not wait to tell Anna.

"Anna! Anna!" she called. But Anna had gone for a walk. Rosalie waited impatiently for her daughter to return. She died to tell her the news. At last she saw from the upstairs window the younger woman limping up the walk, and she rapped a signal on the pane with her thimble. Even then, she thought that, minus her limp, Anna would be unnoticeable.

"But, Mama, you are imagining it." Anna looked genuinely frightened as though she had heard evidence of her mother's insanity.

"Miracles!" said Anna, unable to keep the contempt out of her tone. "It is so unlike you, Mama. All your life you have preferred facts and virtues. Now, suddenly you depend upon miracles. Which is the more reliable, I ask you?" When her mother made no reply, Anna felt the anger mounting within her.

"How could you have let this happen?"

"That is easy for you to say," said Rosalie. "Love is a hardship which you have been spared."

Anna looked down at her mother, saw the violet swatch that had lately appeared beneath each of her eyes.

"If this be love, I'll have none of it."

Anna knew that her mother would never renounce him. She had never learned the art of renunciation. As I have, she thought. As I have had to.

"Then there is only one thing to do, as I see it," she said. "You must tell him."

"And if he refuses? Makes fun of me?"

"You must prepare yourself for that."

"I should not live long after that," said Rosalie quietly. "I should not want to."

Anna's eyes filled with tears. "But that is a terrible thing to say. Don't I mean anything to you? Doesn't Edward? Mama, if he refuses you, the sky will still be blue, the grass green. There will be still all of your beloved nature. Aren't these reasons for going on? And besides," she added, "there is always the possibility . . ."

"We must choose a time and a place, then."

"Not in this house," said Anna quickly. "There is Edward, after all."

"Where, then?"

"An outing. The four of us. We'll pack a picnic lunch and take the boat up the Rhine to the park. The one with the old castle and the bird pond."

"When?"

"The sooner the better. This Sunday. At least we shall know."

∞

Standing on the deck of the boat, Rosalie stared into the wake and could not tell in which direction the river was flowing. It was as though she were seeing it for the first time, seeing it as it really was. It seemed to her that she was standing in the teeth of a wind although the air was calm save for the small breeze of their passage. For weeks she had wondered how he would respond to her declaration. Now, here, on the boat she permitted herself a moment of confidence. After all, it was spring. The banks were every shade of green. There was the silent tide of sap, the speckled eggs that she knew lay hidden in the bushes. One day soon, boughs would be parted; a tiny new bird would be disgorged from straining shrubbery. No summer, however splendid, could fulfill the prophecy of such a spring. Had not nature given her back her youth to be worthy of his love? Only two days before, she had finished with her monthly flow. Again! And with each flux she felt age flowing away from her. To what blessed state was she returning? How far into youth would the miracle take her? A wave of giddiness overtook her so that she had to cling to the railing of the boat. If she had let herself go at that moment, she could have fainted.

It had been arranged between mother and daughter that Anna and Edward would go off to explore the gardens while Rosalie and Ken would visit the old castle ruin. An hour later, they were to meet at the pond. It would have been settled by then. One way or the other. Rosalie watched her children walking away from her. Go! Go! she thought in a burst of impatience. Then she turned to Ken, slipped her arm through his and drew him toward the ancient pile of stone that had been a castle and that lay half-tumbled down the slope of a long lawn. An empty moat surrounded the ruin. They crossed the bridge and walked around to the far side where an expectant archway led to a flight of descending stone steps, each one spotted with a rash of gray lichen. At the bottom of the stairs was a stone door to what must have been a cellar. Ken tried the door but it was locked and bolted. The steps were moist and slimy, covered with rotting leaves. The smell of mold and earth filled the well. At the bottom, they were quite hidden from view. Rosalie had untied the ends of her veil and they hung limply over her shoulders, like braids of pale girlish hair. All at once she heard herself calling out his name, "Ken! Ken!" in a voice so clear and young it startled her. Minutes later she was clinging to him unable to control the sobbing breaths that chased the confession from her mouth. At last, he lifted her chin and bent to kiss her.

"When?" he asked. "Where?"

Rosalie grew suddenly calm as though a storm had passed. Only the odor of decaying leaves gave her a feeling of queasiness.

"Tomorrow. Three o'clock. The cafe across the square from the library. There are rooms upstairs." Leaning into his embrace, Rosalie felt the stones of the old wall stir gently. She listened and heard the honey-colored sap flowing in the trees nearby, saw the beads of it press themselves between the ridges of bark. It was not his kiss but the whole weight of the eternal afternoon that pressed the breath from her parted lips. She felt that she needed twice as much oxygen as anyone else, and she thanked God for the pressure of Ken's hand at her waist, stilling her, calling her back from a state beyond control.

"A terrible stench," said Ken, "these rotting leaves. Let's go back now." At the top of the steps a sudden shaft of sunlight struck, making her stagger. Ken disengaged his arm from hers and bent to scrape away the damp leaves that had become stuck to the soles of his shoes. Then once again, arm in arm, they walked toward the pond.

From the distance she saw them, up to their wings in the water, motionless. Three pairs of white swans. And a single black.

". . . two, three, four, five, six, seven," she counted. "That's something! And all so lovely." She was wild with excitement. "But the black. He is another matter entirely. See how he shovels the water with that red bill of his. And he is alone. He has no mate. I do like him the best."

Ken fished in his pocket. "The bread," he said. "I almost forgot that we brought it to feed them." At the familiar gesture, the black swan swam toward them. All at once, Rosalie snatched the bread from Ken's hand, still warm from the heat of his body, and stuffed it into her mouth. Furious at having been cheated, the black swan raised its wings as though for flight, then thrust toward her, hissing through its blood-red bill. So close did the great bird come to the bank that the shadow of its lifted wings touched Rosalie's feet. She took a quick step backward and threw the rest of the bread to the angry swan. Then Rosalie laughed, throwing the laughter from her throat like lumps of gristle. It was less a human sound than an issuance more akin to the hissing of the swan. Shocked, Ken turned to stare at her, to see from what galled place it had come forth. But Rosalie took no notice.

Once again aboard the riverboat, Rosalie stood alone upon the deck. The others had retreated from the evening chill to the ward room where tea was being served. Far from refreshing her spirit, Rosalie found the river depressing. Sluggish, this Rhine, she thought. Almost stagnant. Breeding flies as though it were a dead animal. Furthermore, she felt unwell. Febrile. When she looked from side to side, her eyeballs ached. The touch of the breeze on her skin was unbearable. She was panting as though the air found passage through her veil difficult. Her head was like a torch in the wind. She was being consumed. Still, gripping the iron railing, she yawned with suppressed desire. Her womb had turned molten with it.

That night Rosalie fell into a deep sleep from which she was coaxed hours later by the rhythmic pounding of driven rain upon the roof. In her half-awakened state she imagined hooves galloping across the slate. All at once, she became aware of a familiar sensation of warmth and moisture between her thighs. A tickling. A cramp rolled across her belly. But it is too soon, she thought. It is not my time. She threw back the covers, raised her head to see. And saw the great dark glistening clot that covered her abdomen and thighs, the puddling in the sheets.

"Anna!" she screamed. "Anna!" And fainted back upon the pillow.

∞

Anna waited in the hospital solarium for the doctor to complete his examination. At last he appeared.

"Cancer," he said. "The neck of the womb. It is beyond surgery, I'm afraid. We must resort to radium to control the bleeding. She is receiving blood transfusions now." He paused. "It is not good." He spoke more softly. "We are in trouble here."

∞

Rosalie awoke to find the doctor standing at the bedside.

". . . radium therapy," she heard him say.

"Shall I be cured, then?"

"That? . . . No. It is meant to stop the bleeding, to give time." His gaze was solemn, not unkind. He was used to this, she saw. Perhaps as a younger man, he had practiced the expression.

"And the pain?"

"Morphine," he said. Rosalie shook her head.

"I think not," she said at last.

"You will not undergo the radium treatments?" The doctor's voice had a note of incredulity. "But surely you do not wish to bleed to death?"

Her voice was calm and final. "There are symptoms too merciful to be placed in the hands of a doctor."

"Be reasonable, Frau von Tummler. It is unnatural to reject the assistance of medical science. Some would call it suicide."

"Some," said Rosalie, "would be wrong." With distaste she submitted to the pressure of his fingers at her pulse. For a minute he counted in silence.

"But what, then, is the point of my attending you?"

"None, I think." She closed her eyes and waited for him to withdraw.

At the door, he turned, and Rosalie imagined she heard him click his heels faintly.

"Frau von Tummler," he said, acknowledging his dismissal.

∾

In the six weeks since the outing in the park, Rosalie had shed what seemed half of her body. A collapsed pouch, she thought, looking down at what remained in the bed. She felt empty, yet strangely heavy, as though her weight had doubled, rather than halved. Her arm, when she tried to lift it from the sheet, was as tired as if it had been holding up a candle for her to see her way down an interminable corridor.

"No," she thought. "I shall not be so foolish as to escape a benevolent and easy death. The doctor is wrong. It is very far from suicide. That other: the radium, the morphine, that is how the doctors swindle human beings." Still, she knew, there would be Anna to deal with.

To Anna the woman on the bed had the look of a young girl, as though the illness, with its fever and wasting, had returned her to a state of . . . well . . . girlishness. She could think of no other word. She gazed down at the long thick braids hanging at either side of her mother's face, by their very immensity accentuating the tiny fragile chin. Now, thought Anna sadly, you have your wish.

"The doctor says that the radium is essential," said Anna.

"Does he?"

"The doctor says you have no alternative."

"Don't I? Listen, Anna, my darling. It is cowardice that causes people to wait to die by the doctor's hand. I am bestowing it upon myself. Bleeding to death is painless. It is a death reserved for the righteous. How much worse had I outlived him, if he had been killed in an accident, or he had rejected me, then I should have died of shame. No, this is best. Only, those nearby . . . you, Anna . . . ought not to soil yourselves with it. That is what would not be natural. Besides, how lucky I am. That death came to me in the guise of love. To how many is that given?" She leaned forward and looked deep into Anna's eyes. "You must know that I want him now as much as ever."

When Anna had left the room, Rosalie sank back upon the pillows. The effort she had made for Anna had drained her of strength. It was true, her longing had lost none of its virulence. Again and again her thoughts returned to that day in the park. Never, never had there been so sweet a day, when, giddy to the point of fainting, she had buried her face in his shoulder and clung to him as much, if the truth be known, to keep herself from falling as to hold him in her desperate grasp. And she had babbled so. Her very words had all but carried her away. "You do not think me too old, then?" She could not speak, and yet she was speaking. Be still, he had said. Not so loud. The others will hear. And he had pressed her to him, hushing. *Sssh,* he had said. *Ssssh,* until she had felt no further need for words. And when the laugh rose from low in his chest, she had at first mistrusted. Was it the mockery she had dreaded? But when she saw him radiant and smiling, she knew that he had accepted her.

Ken had not visited her at the hospital. At first, she had hoped against all reason that he would, that he would come and take her up in his arms and stroke her back to health. But she knew that he would not come, and she was satisfied with that, forgave him. Why should he come? she thought. He has the innocence of the well. Such innocence must be preserved for as long as possible. There would be plenty of time for death. There always is. And just as she had decided that, there was the nurse telling her that a young man was waiting in the lobby to see her and should she show him up? Yes! Yes! she said in a voice full of longing. The nurse helped her into her bed jacket. Rosalie brushed back her hair with three strokes of a transparent hand. So he has come, she thought. And waited for the nurse to return with Ken. Oh, God, the dark seam of her lips, her yellow skin?

My earrings, she thought. I must wear them. She reached for the drawer of her nightstand. The effort—or was it the pain she kept hidden beneath the sheets?—made her dizzy. At last, fumbling, she had them. Long pendants of gold that hung almost to her shoulders. Her husband had given them to her before Edward was born. She had always thought them a bit indiscreet for a married woman and had not worn them in years. All at once, it seemed the most urgent thing for her to wear them when he entered her room. She must hurry. He would be there within minutes. Rosalie raised one earring to her neck, groping shakily for the lobe of her ear. Supporting the working arm with the opposite hand, she grimaced with the effort. At last, she found the little hole and passed the wire through. Now the other. But try as she might, holding her head to the side, pulling her earlobe down to searching exhausted fingers, she could do no more than poke the skin with the cold metal. Again and again she jabbed blindly for the hole, all of her strength and will engaged in this act of adornment. At last, she sank back helplessly and gave it up. Her eyes closed on tears of disappointment. She had wanted so much to be wearing them. So that at first she did not see him standing in the doorway. When she opened her eyes and saw, saw not only Ken, but what had settled there on his face, she could not speak. She thought she must look to Ken like some submarine creature that had been thrown onto dry land and lay gasping.

Ken walked slowly toward the bed.

"Here," he said, taking the earring from her hand. "Allow me." His tone was more than solicitous; it was gallant. And, holding her earlobe steady with one hand, he passed the wire through her flesh with a single quick movement. Rosalie felt the casual dexterity of his touch spread from her ear to her neck, then across her cheek until her whole body shivered in the warmth of it. At the same time she saw his large shadow fall across her body. The weight of it made her gasp.

The visit was virtually mute, as though the passage of the earring had left them spent, in no need of speech. Ken sat stiffly upright in a ladder-back chair he had drawn up to the bedside. Rosalie watched him in silence for a few minutes before submerging into sleep. Now and then her pupils would appear beneath half-open lids. Ken watched them struggle to focus upon him, then rove upward behind half-drawn lids, leaving only the white lunar rims of blindness. At last, he rose, steadying the chair lest it scrape against the floor and awaken her. Then turned, and without a backward glance, left the room. Rosalie did not awaken.

When, later, Anna arrived, it was to find her mother deep in coma. From the corridor, she had heard a moist bubbling sound. What she saw when she opened the door was a tiny snout poking through an abandoned nest of gray hair. With each shudder of the chest, gold earrings shook off a tiny brave flash. Anna sat in the chair that Ken had earlier that day occupied. An hour later she saw her mother take the last of many deep breaths, deeper than all the others, and slowly deflate into death. A nurse entered, closed her mother's eyes with her fingers and bound up the fallen jaw with a gauze bandage. To Anna, who watched, it seemed that in that pinched mouth and closed lids, the passion expressed itself all the more; sealed now within her mother's body, it would live on long after she had died.

"Poor woman," said the nurse.

"No," said Anna. "You are quite, quite mistaken."

Tom and Lily

In the ancient city of Troy (upstate New York, not Asia Minor) in June of the year 1934, a god descended to earth in the guise of a magnificent stallion. Had the people of the town known the true nature of the horse, surely the purpose of His coming would have been beyond their understanding. A banishment, perhaps? A penance? Or to discharge some heavenly errand? But who can know the intentions of the gods? As it was, only one, a sixteen-year-old boy, knew what the horse really was. Of all the Trojans, some fifty thousand of them, it was to Tom Fogarty alone that the truth had been revealed. That is the way with miracles, even those that happen in the midst of a crowd. Perhaps only one person has been made ready to see. Sometimes it is merely a dog that beholds and will wag its tail. Tom himself could not have said what gave it away, what clue. He just knew, that's all.

∽

Since it is not good for even a god to have nothing to do all day, the horse got himself hired to pull one of the bread wagons for Freihofer's Bakery. In those days, bread was delivered. Only the lazy, frivolous, or disorganized went to the grocery store where a loaf of bread cost four cents more than if it was brought to your doorstep. The bread wagons had all been painted red-and-orange. The wooden wheels were black with bright yellow spokes. All of which might have been gaudy except for the word FREIHOFER'S in large black script on either side.

FREIHOFER'S was simply not a gaudy word. In Troy, New York, it meant bread.

But in order for there to be a job, there had to be a vacancy. And so it happened that one day Nutty, the dispirited old horse that serviced Fifth Avenue between Jacob and Federal Streets where Tom lived, took one last, noisy gulp of water from the trough at the corner of Fifth Avenue and Jacob Street and crumpled to the cobblestones. No amount of nudging, whistling, or clicking of the tongue on the part of Hank, the delivery man, could get the old horse to rise again. Like a Mohammedan who has made up his mind to die, Nutty lay with his head on the pedestal of the trough, uncaring what the world did while his back was turned. Three hours later he died. A sanitation truck came with a winch and a pulley and a large canvas harness. Before long, the deceased was swinging in the air behind the truck, all hooves, ears, and tail. No sooner had the truck started up Jacob Street hill toward the dump when Nutty slid free of the halter and thumped down with a dead echoless sound. "Machinery," said Tom's mother. "Wouldn't you know. I wish they'd hurry up about it. In this heat . . ."

"What's the weather got to do with it?"

"Nothing. I was just saying . . ."

But Tom knew. The year before, he and his brother, Billy, had watched them fish a man's body out of the river after a week.

In any case, it was Nutty's place that the horse-god took.

Irene Fogarty had had a deep-seated distrust of engines and machinery ever since the old 1921 Hudson broke down on the way from Montreal to New York City and stranded her "for the rest of my natural life" in this "godforsaken hole." Just so had she begun her life of "exile." Her husband, Nathan, who had only the week before graduated from McGill Medical School, had taken it as a sign. "We'll stay right here," he had announced. There was hardly any choice since they hadn't one dollar between them to get the car fixed and finish the trip. That very day, he had hung out his shingle at 103 Fifth Avenue between Jacob and Federal where, according to Irene, she had to live upstairs from the office and refrain from using the vacuum cleaner from one o'clock to three in the afternoon and six to eight in the evening, the office hours announced on the two milk-glass signs in the first-floor windows. What the Doctor, as she referred to Tom's father, hadn't bothered to do, she said, was to take her feelings into consideration, and she had been married to him for barely a week! By what slender threads we hang, she told everyone who would stand still long enough, as though she had to explain why a person like her from a city like Montreal, Quebec, as she put it, ended up in a place like Troy. She never should have done it. And *he,* she motioned to the office downstairs where *he* was sitting in his empty office, *he* had absolutely no right. But then, what did she know? A young girl with no experience. Just *deposited* in this no-hope town that was jammed with Irish, all of whom were stone-sucking poor and half of whom had TB. Not even the car had been able to pass through Troy without coughing out its last. So that gave you some idea. From then on, she swore, she would never count on an automobile or any other mechanical conveyance but would go on her own two feet wherever they took her and no farther.

Furthermore, it was every bit of two weeks before the first patient walked into that office, and what was *she* supposed to do in the meantime about groceries and toilet paper? The patient turned out to be Gertie Rafferty, and you know what she was. Sixth Avenue with a vengeance. Not that she didn't pity the poor creatures who had to do *it* for a living, but it just showed you what life was going to be like in this rotten town. "What's that woman got?" she had asked the Doctor. She felt she had a right. A rash, he had told her. Judas Priest, she'd said, and that was that.

∞

Day after day, except Sunday, at about ten-thirty in the morning, Freihofer's new horse would turn the corner from Federal Street and start down the block. From his stoop Tom could hear the sound of wooden wheels turning on stone and the spanking of hooves. *Clip-clop, clip-clop.* Two notes only, always the same but never monotonous. And then the long pause while he waited at the curb. His pace was slow as though he had all eternity to make his rounds. With each stop his load was lightened by a loaf of bread, a dozen poppy seed rolls, and, on birthdays, two or three chocolate éclairs. Jacob Street was the end of the line. After the last delivery Hank would click his tongue twice and holler, "Giddap," whereupon the horse would break into a canter for the barn, striking a spark when hoof met stone just so.

Wherever he stepped, birds followed. From the distance, his legs were bangled with sparrows, all cheeping for the manure which they knew was there, just within that dark pucker beneath the tail. Back and forth they flew weaving a basket of light and shadow in which to catch the prize. Until, with a ceremonial lift of his tail, he would lay the splendid braided loaf before them. Pandemonium! as they left him to drill into the steaming pile that was not unlike the bread he delivered, golden, and with the grainy scent of meadows. To the birds it was less manure than manna. On those days when he withheld the banquet the bundles of hunger grew reckless and brushed his fetlocks with their wings. Occasionally, a little ball of bone and feather launched itself upward to ride the rump. But that was going too far. One whisk of the tail and . . . back down where he belonged. Little shitpeckers, said Billy, Tom's brother. Once, a marsh hawk, like a flake of soot from a chimney, drifted in from the river, shadowing the sparrows. Suddenly the big bird stooped but the horse had gathered his worshippers beneath his sheltering belly just in time. In a moment the hawk was gone and the refugees were discharged.

Tom could have watched the horse for hours—the way he walked on tiptoe, kicking up mud, dust, leaves, but remaining somehow unstained, how he stood motionless at the curb with hooves posed daintily on the cobbles and wearing his head like a trophy or bending to browse among the weeds that flourished in the pavement cracks. Now and then an ear flicked to vent an excess of energy. Once, as he gazed, Tom saw the flesh at one place on the flank twitch to fend off a fly. Once, as he watched, a shiver caressed Tom's belly and he felt his penis grow hard. He sat down quickly and crossed his legs to hide himself. At precisely that moment the horse lowered his own long penis, startling the girlish sparrows who went twittering off.

∞

About a week after His coming, Tom waited until Hank had disappeared into an alleyway with his arms full of loaves, then he walked up to the horse and held out a lump of sugar. There was the soft trembling in his palm, the heat of the breath, those lips that were the velvetiest of his life. He ran his hand down the horse's neck and saw the skin light up the way a carpet will if it is brushed the wrong way. When the horse reared its head and shuddered, Tom was startled. That night, Tom dreamed that he was riding the horse bareback down the block, stopping at each house to toss loaves of bread like alms into doorways. In his dream he arrived at the little square with the horse trough where Nutty had died. The stallion bent to drink. There was a sudden flexing of the hind legs, a powerful thrust and they were aloft. Only then did the horse reveal his great dove-gray wings. Far below lay sooty Troy, coughing in its sleep, with only here and there a reddish light, like a drop of blood. There was the whole night of pasturing among the stars with the back of the horse between his knees and against his buttocks. And at daybreak, the gentle descent to wakefulness.

⟋

Tom Fogarty was by far the tallest boy in his class, almost six feet and still only sixteen. His Adam's apple stood forth from his skinny neck like a prow. Erupted, said Irene Fogarty, tearing yet another pair of outgrown pants into dustrags. Why won't he grow out for a change instead of up?

"Can't you find someplace else to park instead of squatting on the front stoop like a gargoyle? Scare the patients to death. That is, if there were any who could pay."

But there wasn't anyplace else to go in Troy in the summer or anything else to do, what with the Depression in full swing. The shirt factory had closed down, and the Watervliet Arsenal. The only thing still going was the coke plant, the drift from which was the reason Irene Fogarty needed so many dustrags. So, in the morning Tom sat on the stoop either alone or with his brother, Billy, just taking things in. In the afternoons Tom walked down Jacob Street to the riverbank. About two hundred yards away through tall grass he came to a small clearing he had made simply by trampling the reeds. It was his secret hideaway. Sometimes he would fish for eels, sometimes peel down and jump in for a swim after which he would lie on his back flattening the reeds still further with his body. The small clearing was partially shaded by a large willow tree that trailed its tendrils in the stream. About twenty-five feet away stood an old pear tree on its last roots. Tom counted six yellow pears scattered among the gnarled and tumorous branches. From where he lay the pear tree resembled a broken chandelier with most of its working parts missing. In the evening the six pears seemed to retain the light long after the sun had gone down. In the growing darkness they looked for all the world like half-trimmed lamps.

It was the twenty-fourth of June. Summer vacation had started three days earlier. Tom, sitting on the stoop of 103 Fifth Avenue, saw, or thought he saw, the curtains moving in the second-story bay window of 104 Fifth Avenue across the street. And behind them, something—a shadow. But that was odd. The only person living there was Maisie Kinnicut and she was at the coke plant. Tom had seen her leave the house himself. The next instant the movement stopped. Whoever it was, if it was anybody at all, had gone, and then Tom wasn't sure. What he had seen was just a pale shape, something wrapped in a sheet, more like a sheet itself with nothing inside. An hour later, when he saw the girl propped up on pillows in the window, it was a moment or two before he grasped that this was, in fact, a person. He asked his mother.

"That's Lily, Mae's niece from Cohoes. She's got TB. Her mother and father are already both at the San. The girl's going too, as soon as they find room for her, poor thing. Has to stay all by herself till Mae gets home from the plant. I think it's terrible. That Maisie Kinnicut, honestly."

"How old is she?"

"I don't know. Fourteen."

"How long she been here? I didn't even see her come."

"A few days is all. She came at night. They carried her upstairs."

"Oh, yeah?" said Tom. "Is she bad?"

"With TB there's no such thing as good. You keep away from there, you hear?" She glared out the window. "I don't know what that horse has got against us. He does it right in front of our house every time. Why us, anyway?"

∽

At precisely ten-thirty the next day (it was the hour of the horse), the manure dropped in front of 103 Fifth Avenue where Tom was sitting on the stoop. At just that moment he looked up to see the girl standing in the window of 104. Tom could not have known that for three days Lily had been watching him from behind the curtains, that at ten o'clock each morning she lay in her bed in the bay window listening for the sound of hoofbeats, straining to realize them out of the clatter of the street. When the manure fell, he looked up to see her leaning between the curtains. For a moment their gaze met. When suddenly she laughed and covered her mouth with her hand, Tom felt his face heat up and his chest fill with something he could not hold back until he, too, laughed and was relieved.

Hank got out of the wagon with three loaves of bread for 104.

"Can I take it up?"

"You want to take it up?"

Tom nodded. "Can I?" Hank gave a quick glance at the bay window but there was no one to be seen.

"Well, sure, okay. You can if you want to. Thanks. I'll do the first floor."

∽

The door at the head of the landing was half open. Tom knocked softly and entered. There seemed to be no one at home. But he knew that she was there.

He walked through the parlor to the small front room with the bay window. All the houses on the block were laid out exactly the same. It was the pallor of the room that struck him. He had never seen so white a place. A white wicker chair sat by the bed, the posts of which had been painted white. The flowers in the vase were white paper peonies. On the wall, a Japanese mask. The face was chalk-white, the hair and lips black. A glass of milk stood on the nightstand. A half-finished puzzle lay on a card table. Completed, it would depict Perseus unchaining Andromeda from the rock. The girl in the bed had a moony ashen look. Her long colorless hair lost itself in the folds of the pillowcase. Even her eyes had been taken possession of by the morning sun. They were crystals of it so that he could not read them. To Tom this room seemed a world of whiteness and silence, a snowstorm. And like a blizzard it was both alluring and inhospitable. It was a room held outside of time, far away from life. Standing just inside the doorway, he felt the menace of the germ-laden air and remembered his mother's words: "You keep away from there, you hear?" It was his first real contact with the disease. Oh, he had known when a neighbor had disappeared or one of the kids at school had failed to show up, he knew where they had gone, that they wouldn't be coming back. He had learned, too, from his father's talk of patients that he heard at the dinner table. But not like this. Untutored in the ways of illness, he felt dazed and slightly giddy. When, suddenly, she leaned forward and gave a delicate soft bark and he saw the spot of blood on the tissue, he was shocked. All the violence in the world seemed concentrated in that red.

The girl raised the glass of milk to her lips and took a tiny sip.

"Here's your bread," he said lamely. "Hank, the bread man, he said I could bring it."

"No one's here," she said. "My aunt Mae's at work. She won't get home till five-thirty." Then, remembering. "He's a beautiful horse, isn't he, just the same. I mean even if he does make a mess right in front of the house every day. I couldn't help laughing."

"My mother said he's got a grudge against us. 'Why us?' she says every time." When the girl smiled, he could have fainted.

"My name's Lily."

"I know. I'm Tom."

"What's his name?"

Tom shrugged. "Just Freihofer's horse, I guess."

She sat up suddenly and gave another flannel cough into a tissue, her head turned away from him. He saw that she had been taught to be careful about the direction of her coughing. It was the etiquette of tuberculosis. He recognized it from things his mother had said.

"You're not supposed to be here," she said. "My sputum is positive."

"Hank," he lied. "He said to bring up the bread."

"Still and all you shouldn't. I'm only here until there's a place for me at the Pawling Sanitarium. My mother and father are already there. We all got it. I have to go to the children's ward. I'll be able to see them twice a week. But right now . . ." She gave a sign. "There aren't any beds. I have to wait."

To Tom she was something less substantial than solid flesh. Beneath her eyes, on the prominences of her cheekbones, a circle of dusky red gave evidence of something hectic and ardent. He had never seen anyone so beautiful.

"I have a cavity on the right side," she went on. Tom had no need to ask. Everyone in Troy knew that word. "They tried pneumo on me three times but it didn't work. Pneumo," she said, pronouncing the *p,* "is no pfun. Now I have to have the thoracoplasty." He saw that she was taking three breaths for every one of his. The spots in her cheeks had brightened.

"I better go."

"Will you bring the bread tomorrow?"

Tom shrugged and didn't answer. But he knew that he would.

∞

At dinner Tom asked his father:

"What does it mean when the pneumo doesn't work and they have to do a thoracoplasty?"

"Fine talk at the table," said his mother. "If you don't mind."

"Pneumo means air," said his father. "Thorax means chest. If there is a cavity you inject the air in the space around the lung. This makes the lung collapse so that the cavity will fill up with scar tissue and heal. The idea is to put the lung to rest. But sometimes it doesn't work. Adhesions or whatever. Then you have to take out half a dozen ribs over the place where the cavity is. Then maybe the lung will collapse."

"Will you please?" said his mother.

"What do you look like without those ribs?"

"Caved in. Here." He reached out and touched Tom's chest. The boy flinched as though he had been punched.

"Oh," said Tom and sucked in his saliva. He had an image of her hammered, like a fender.

"Eat your dinner," said his mother. But Tom was already up and gone from the table. He felt their eyes following him out of the kitchen.

∽

The next day Tom came upon Lily sleeping. He stood in the doorway, ill at ease, wondering whether he should stay. Just then the sun slid across the street, probed the wall of the building, searching, and plunged a single ray through the bay window, coloring the face and hands of the girl. At that moment she awakened. It seemed to Tom a resurrection.

From then on he came straight to her every day, to that room where Lily, too, had been waiting for the simple sound of wooden wheels on uneven stone, and the hoofbeats. She would hear Tom's footsteps on the stairs, taking two, sometimes three steps at a time. And always the delicious pause before the click of the door being shut behind him. Sometimes in that long silence while he stood on the landing, when Lily knew he was there, and even afterward when she felt him gazing down at her, she would keep her eyes closed and just listen to the sound of his breathing, the regular slow exquisite sound of warm air passing in and out of him. Each time, she marveled at it. And to Tom, who stood there stricken mute and nerveless, her closed lids and parted lips were an expression of passion so powerful that he would feel a moment or two of dizziness when he would not dare to make a move. He marveled that anyone so free of wounds, so unblemished, so smooth and perfect could be damaged inside where it could not be seen. He didn't believe it.

"You should see my room," he said. "It's a mess. Yours is so neat and tidy, everything in its right place." He thought of the slovenly den he shared with his brother, all their anguished paraphernalia lying wher-ever it had been kicked or thrown. By all rights it should be his room that was contaminated, not hers.

Tom could not have said when it was that he fell in love with Lily. Perhaps it was the day a ray of sun poked through the gauze of the curtain and roved across her throat. Perhaps it was the time she flirted some crumbs off the coverlet with her long pale fingers.

∽

Day after day he was drawn to that room that only he had the power to set in motion, if only he could find the way to do it, find the part of his body that was the ignition. In the late afternoon, when he saw the red spots appear on her cheeks and her eyes brighten with fever, he would leave her and go down to the river.

One day, about the middle of August, he noticed that there was only one pear left on the tree. He searched the ground for the others, but they were not to be found. Something took them, thought Tom. A raccoon, probably.

"Brought you a pear," he announced. The night before, he had climbed up and picked it. He polished it on his thigh and presented it with a flourish. Lily raised the pear to her mouth, showing her teeth to it and at the same time glancing up quickly to make sure he was watching. When she bit into the pear, Tom shivered and had to look away.

"Let's do the puzzle," she said. "You work on Andromeda. I'll finish Perseus." They sat together at the card table, their heads bending close but never touching.

"Hah! Found her knee," said Tom, and tapped the piece into place. "That feel better, lady?" he said to the half-naked Andromeda still chained to the rock. "Don't mention it, ma'am." Tom could not have known that all the while he was searching among the scattered pieces, Lily, sidelong, had become absorbed in the moisture of his lips, the tiny bubbles of saliva on his teeth that she caught sight of. Once, for an instant, she glimpsed the miracle of his tongue. She made up her mind that it was in his Adam's apple that his soul resided. When he swallowed, the whole mass of cartilage bobbed up to the top, then dropped down abruptly until the next time. Lily half expected to hear a muffled clunk as it hit bottom. It looked painful. Fascinated, she waited for him to swallow so that she could see it happen again.

"You're not really trying," he said. "Do I have to do it all?" His gaze followed the pear now decorated with the indentations of her teeth to the nightstand where it rested. At that moment, he could have savaged the rest of it to the seeds.

∽

"You taking Kinnicut's?" Hank would ask and toss him the loaf of bread. And Tom would climb the narrow curved staircase to the second floor. Sometimes, in the moments before he opened the door, he would hear her singing. It was always so unexpected; and always on those days, she appeared sicker. She seemed to him then like some small nervous creature that emits sounds the echo of which place it in the world. Perhaps, he thought, it was only when the fever rose and she would feel herself floating, only then did she have to sing to keep herself from drifting away for good. Each time, the song ended in a cough.

"You have a pretty voice," he told her.

"I get short of breath."

Tom pulled a harmonica from his back pocket, wiped it back and forth between his lips. "What do you want to hear?" he asked.

"Oh, anything. You pick it." And she settled back upon the pillows to listen, but really she was watching the saddle of freckles across his nose and the way his lips held and brushed the harmonica. She had to close her eyes to hide what threatened to show there.

" 'Santa Lucia,' then, okay?" And he worked the harmonica with his mouth, pulling the melody out of it with all the raspy earnestness he could muster, all the while acutely aware of her nipples through her nightgown. Because of that he did not notice the tears on her face until later.

"I always cry when I hear that one," said Lily. "Isn't that stupid? We used to sing it in school every day." But he was not consoled, and cursed himself for making her cry. Nothing works out, he thought.

"Does it hurt?" he asked her.

"Does what hurt?"

"TB."

"Not really. I don't have any pain. But I can feel it moving inside— like a river."

∽

"I know you're goin' over there all the time," said Billy. "You're gonna catch it in more ways than one."

"You mind your own goddamn business," said Tom.

"Don't say I never warned you."

Irene Fogarty heard through the bedroom door and went downstairs to the office which she never did unless it was something she considered an emergency. She always said that it was in the worst possible taste for a doctor's wife to hang around her husband's office.

"Speak to that boy," she told him. "He's sneaking up to visit that girl at Kinnicut's. She's raising positive sputum."

"Send him down," said the doctor wearily. "I'll talk to him."

"And maybe you should go across the street and have a look at her. It's a scandal the way that child with galloping consumption is left alone all day until Mae Kinnicut gets home from the coke plant. I have half a mind to notify the Board of Health."

Tom stood in front of the desk where his father sat twirling a pencil.

"That is a stupid thing to do," the doctor began. "I thought you were smarter than that. Do you want to end up at the San too?"

The eyes of father and son met. But it was the father who, making discoveries, lowered his gaze first.

"In any case, don't," he said into an ashtray overflowing with cigarette butts.

From then on Tom walked up Federal to Sixth Avenue, then through the alleyway between two houses so he wouldn't be seen. The gate to Kinnicut's backyard was unlocked. He could get to the front hall by climbing into a window. A row of whorehouses occupied one side of Sixth Avenue. Troy was famous for them. The other side of the street was the train station. Every Saturday men came from as far as Hudson and Poughkeepsie to "get their ashes hauled," as Billy put it.

There came the night when Tom, emerging from the alleyway into Sixth Avenue, saw his father come out of one of these houses. Father and son were no more than fifteen feet apart. His father was wearing his gray fedora. A Lucky Strike dangled from his lips. They both stopped dead in their tracks. Nathan Fogarty recovered first.

"Making a house call," he said. "One of the ladies has pneumonia." He saw Tom's gaze lower to his hand where the little black bag should have been but wasn't.

"What are *you* doing on Sixth Avenue?" said his father. "Get back where you belong."

I won't tell, Tom thought. I'll never tell on you.

∽

"Lily?" he called into the room. "It's me, Doctor Fogarty from across the street."

Lily studied the man's face, searching for Tom. All the while he tapped and listened to her chest, she was peeling off the layers of his gray skin, the toothbrush mustache, defleshing the nose, whitening the eyes and teeth, smoothing out the loose folds of the neck that bulged above the collar. But she could find no trace of Tom in this carbon-lipped puffy man. No matter how hard she looked for that bony, lion-haired, hay-scented boy she could not see him. Maybe he takes after his mother, she thought. What she did see in the doctor's face, no matter that he kept it as still as the Japanese mask on the wall, was what she already knew.

∞

"She doesn't stand a chance," said the doctor at the dinner table. "There's no good lung left. It's the worst kind. Miliary. Spreads through the bloodstream. I don't know what's keeping her going."

"You're crazy," shouted Tom. "Goddamn you!" He was up and out of the house before his mother was sure she had heard what she did.

∞

Now it was the first of September. So soon! School would start the next day. What would happen then? Tom dared not think of it. From the landing he heard her singing, just a few notes at a time separated by long pauses during which she coughed softly. He stood outside the door palming the still-warm loaf of bread. A wave of fear took him. Oh God! What if his father had been right? When at last he opened the door, he was shocked by her appearance. He had never seen her working so hard. Pale as death she lay, one hand trailing over the side of the bed in what might have been languor. With each breath her nostrils flared to open wider the apertures through which air could be drawn. Even the muscles of her neck had joined the battle, sucking in the small hollows there that were wet with perspiration. The muffled coughs were not enough to clear the rattling that slid to and fro deep within her chest.

"Lily?" But she did not turn to see. Tom felt his own chest filling up, congesting. He could hardly breathe himself. He cleared his throat. Twice she closed her mouth to speak, her chin lifting to force a word. "Tom," she managed. He darted to the bed and knelt beside it.

"What?" he begged her. "What is it? What's happening to you?" And he strained to hear, placing his ear next to her mouth. When he touched her, she was like a smooth stone that had spent all day in the sun. Tom had often seen how, after a fit of coughing, her breathing eased and she would be quite composed until the secretions rose again.

"Cough harder," he said. "You got to get it up, Lily. Please cough, Lily. Please." Dropping the bread he seized her floating hand, seized it almost brutally, surely with too much force, and raised it to his lips. That hand, every detail of which he knew, even to the moons of her nails which he had committed to memory. Even now he longed for the private history of each of her fingers, no one of them the same as any other—where they slept, what and whom they had touched. He could have spent his life recording such data.

"I love you," he said. "I love you." It was all he could think to say. Not "with all my heart" or "forever and ever" or any of the tumultuous phrases that swirled inside his mouth. Only "I love you." Those were the only words he knew. He had forgotten all the rest of the language. "I love you," he said again and relished the freedom that the words gave him, the release from all these weeks of restraint. From then on he did not so much bend over her as revolve about her like the sun.

It was his name with which she pulled herself to the surface.

"Tom," she said, her voice whitened by fatigue. "Oh, Tom, raise me up." He knew then that above the tempest of her respirations she had heard him. She had never asked him to do anything for her before, to tend or minister, even on those days when she had been too weak to move from the bed to get something that she needed. Now her asking him to raise her up seemed the most natural thing in the world. They might have been married for years.

He stood then, bending over her, and slid his arm beneath her, feeling for the first time the bones of her back like the wings of a small bird. His own awkward hand was a large and clumsy shovel scooping the girl against his chest. Her hair fell over his arm. For a long time he held her just so, feeling through the thin nightgown the rattling that by all rights should have made the windows shake, the pictures on the walls fall from their hooks.

His arm was heated with her fever. Holding her with her head extended, he watched the wavelike pulse beneath her ear. With every cough she became more beautiful to him. When at last the trace of a smile broke the surface like some rare and beautiful fish, he lowered his mouth to hers. Again and again he wiped the spongy fullness of her lips, playing her with his mouth. There was no going back. Once he had set out in this direction he was unable to stop. They would have one common mouth. He would lick the pain away, suck it from her, find the way to do it, this thing that he had never done before. And so he followed her, breath for breath, drawing in as she exhaled, blowing into her his sweet cool air, pulling out the fever and siphoning off the terrible heat with his own chest. Doctoring her. And himself, too. For this was what he needed in order to survive. And all the while listening to his body ripening, learning what love really was, a contagion. All at once a long soft noise came from her throat, a moaning, entirely distinct from those other terrible sounds. It drove everything else out of range of his hearing and he could only hear that low intoxicated groan into which he plunged and submerged himself.

He was like a conspirator who had at last found the one human being in the world to whom he could pass on his secret, and here he was, whispering it to her, hurrying, desperate lest she leave before he had finished telling her.

Suddenly her breathing quieted, became almost normal. The muscles of her face and neck relaxed, ceased to participate in the violence. He held his own breath in mingled fear and elation. What had happened? Had it passed? Then there would still be time. Oh, please, he thought. Please! Her body which had shaken like a bundle of sticks grew still. All this while Tom continued to fence in her body with his, to cover her with thatch. He would allow nothing in. Let whatever hail or hot ashes fall upon his back, scald or freeze as it would, this, in his arms, would be safe. He inclined his head a fraction down and away from her. When he looked back again he was struck by her calmness. She could not have appeared more composed had she been on her way to church instead of dying, which, all at once, Tom knew she was.

"I'll get my father," he said. And lowered her toward the pillows.

"No," she whispered. "Stay with me. Stay." Her fingertips rose to his face. "You cannot . . ." she began, then faltered. "You cannot love me

. . . more than I love you." Her eyes filmed with moisture, grew preternaturally bright.

"I never wanted to go to the San," she whispered, "and have that awful operation. It wouldn't have helped anyway. I'd rather have had you."

"No," cried Tom in a hoarse voice that broke on the single syllable. "No. Don't. Please don't." He shook her against him.

As abruptly as it had let up, the struggle resumed. Already the fleeting momentary smile had drifted from her face. She lay with her eyes closed, not asleep, of course. Acutely awake. Still, he felt excluded. She was dwelling in a place behind her closed lids to which he could not go, nor was he welcome there.

Suddenly she roused herself once more and tried to lift her head in alarm. Had she remembered something that she must tell him?

"Go," she cried in a surprisingly strong voice. "Go away. You must. Don't stay here. Please. Don't watch me. Open the window. Lay me down. Oh . . . go . . . God." Then came the blankness of coma in which the body works long after the mind closes down.

He could not know that what she did not want was for him to see her die. He had never seen anyone die before. He had told her so himself, once when she had asked. And she had imagined it so many times, the going slack, mouth falling, eyes staring, and worse she was sure, although she didn't really know. Tom lowered Lily to the bed, walked to the door, closed it behind him and crouched on the landing in the posture of vigil that humans assume instinctively, hunkered and with his arms folded about his knees. And he listened to the grating noises that came from the other room, each of which pulled her farther and farther out of his time, his place. She had, with her last words, banished him. He could not go back into that white room into which she had retreated to die. But she had recognized love. He had seen to that. Now when what she asked for was privacy . . . well, he would give her that too.

At five-thirty the noises from the room stopped. At twenty minutes to six, Mae Kinnicut came home from the coke plant. As she rounded the curve in the darkened staircase, she stopped, one foot on the next stair, her hand on the bannister, and stood perfectly still, for she saw him crouched on the landing, and she knew.

"Tom Fogarty," she said quietly, and raced past him into the room. Then Tom heard her wail. "Jesus! Mary! Saint Anthony!" And that awful sobbing. Tom stood and bolted down the stairs and across the street.

"Where've you been all afternoon?" said his mother. "I've needed you to do the garbage cans. Been hollering for you. Can't you hear?" But she stopped when she caught sight of his face and saw the great bereft dumb thing padding across it.

"She's gone, then," said his mother, tying her apron and patting the sides of her hair. "I knew it. I knew it. Oh God, I'm sorry for her and you and everybody in this damn, damn town. I'll be across the street. Don't you dare show up there, you hear? Tom? Tommy?"

She walked to the front door. "May God rest her soul," she said. "The poor little thing never had a chance to live."

Tom said nothing, because he knew that just wasn't so.

∾

Later he saw Lily at Bryce's Funeral Parlor, tiny and mute and drained, a white ash that keeps for a time the shape of the coals from which it has been reduced. He made it out the door of Bryce's and around to the alley before bursting into tears.

The morning after the funeral Tom climbed through the back window of 104 Fifth Avenue as he had done so many times. He had to visit once more that room that all summer long had watched and waited. Every object was there, keeping still its mystery. On the wall at the foot of the bed, the Noh mask, chalk-white and with a cowl of straight black hair, shaved eyebrows and open smiling black lips; on the nightstand, the ivory crucifix which time and again he had seen inching toward her fingers, and of which he had been envious, because it, and not he, had enjoyed the stroking of her hand; the vase of paper flowers. Everything watching and waiting as before. Tom thought of Lily's gaze imprisoned within the white walls with only these things for company until the day he had come into the room with love in the shape of a loaf of bread. Even with their terrible permanence, the objects had failed, as he had failed, to hold back dissolution. He would never come to this place again. Tom turned to leave.

Just before he did, he lifted Andromeda's knee from the puzzle and slipped it into his pocket.

The next day was Sunday. It had begun to rain—a cold Irish Catholic rain, remorseless and punitive. At exactly ten o'clock Tom heard the bells of St. Patrick's knifing through the streets. A wreath of lilies and gardenias had been nailed to the door of 104 Fifth Avenue. "That's the least she could do," said Irene, referring, Tom supposed, to Mae Kinnicut, whom she felt was somehow to blame. The smell of the flowers permeated the block, infiltrating the alleyways between the houses, coiling and drifting along the gutters, perfuming the brown rainwater that twined downhill toward the river. Tom closed the bay window to barricade himself against the smell; it made him sick, but there was no keeping it out. The sweet odor came through the glass and settled into the lace curtains. He wondered what happened to her germs, whether they died with her, or whether, like fleas that leave the carcass of a newly dead animal, they were now roaming the town in search of fresh lung, his own, perhaps, to which with all his heart he had lured them.

"Get dressed, Tom," said his mother, "and shake a leg or we'll be late for Mass. I'm really surprised at you."

"I'm not going," said Tom softly. And thought, I'm never going again.

"If you think for one moment . . ." she began, but it was that softness in his voice, she had never heard it before, that kept her from insisting.

"You've grown out of that shirt," she said. "I'll be using it for a dustrag."

A minute later, Tom watched his father, mother, and Billy moving through the rain toward St. Patrick's. When he saw them turn right at Jacob Street, he slid down the bannister, took his slicker out of the front-hall closet and slipped into it. At the corner he turned left toward the river. The rain was slanting down harder now. In a minute his hair was saturated. He walked three blocks along River Street until he came to the narrow path that descended to the water's edge, and stood in the little clearing among the cattails that was his place, and his only. This at least had not changed. The same three ducks sat in the water rigid as soldiers. The same willow shed its hair in the stream, carrying in its leaves the same maidenly singing. All at once a wind of its own making flaked the surface of the water. The ducks, disturbed, rose gawkily, flew twenty yards and then came down again, not with any confidence but tripping over the water like skimmed stones, lifting again before settling for good. For a long time Tom stood watching the rain add itself to the river, feeling that it was raining inside his body. Lily, he thought, then said aloud: "Lily, Lily." A single crack of thunder turned up the intensity of the storm, and shutting his eyes against the rain's driving, he headed back home.

By afternoon the rain was smoking all around, an unwholesome gray water that sucked whatever color there was from the town, turning brown as it thickened in the gutters to run down toward the river. But the fall itself was singularly devoid of energy. There was no rebound from the sidewalks, no variation in intensity. It neither waxed nor waned but was of that desolate sameness that wears away the defenses of the mind. It's never going to stop, thought Tom; and he stared down at the street purged of debris and at the rain-beaten cobblestones, each one the blistered face of someone old and crazy.

In the morning he awoke to the drums of rain. Occasionally it would stop to see how much it had already accomplished, then, dissatisfied, would renew itself. During these respites there was a deathly silence while the people waited.

"This town's got nuthin' but weather," said Hank. He was an hour late from having to wrap each loaf in oiled brown paper. "The next thing you know that river'll be givin' us hello right up here on Fifth Avenue. You watch."

Let it, thought Tom. And all at once it was what he wanted more than anything else. By evening the streetlamps illuminated only their own halos. The pace changed. Where before there had been monotony there was now a hectic unpredictability. The wind rose, flinging the rain about. To open the door or window was to breast an element. In the street a bulky shape passed, hidden under a slicker and with an umbrella pulled down about its head, a strange amphibian that neither walked nor swam. Throughout the night and all the next day, Troy sulked. The men got drunker and the women slid further into melancholy. It would never end, they said, never. "Gonna be a flood," they said. And they sat down and waited for it. Even as they spoke, the Hudson River, taking them at their word, heaved itself over its banks.

On the morning of the seventh day, when Tom looked out the bay window, he saw the silver snout of the flood sniffing Reardon's stoop at the end of the block. Moments later the water was dashing to swallow the whole street. One by one the other stoops were lapped. He stared down with momentary excitement. At last, he thought. At last. And he raced downstairs and out into the street. He would go down and greet the flood, usher it in so that it would cleanse the town of false promises, tuberculosis, and all the other incurable diseases, the worst of which was his own life without Lily. The rain itself was hard and quiet, no longer punishing the pavement but falling down into itself. There was a new sound, the distant, alluring roar of the river. All around his feet, masses of water, newborn waterfalls, instant whirlpools. A trash can freed of its mooring floated toward him. He pushed it away and watched it go tilting down the stream. His heart pounding, Tom slogged ahead, rejoicing in this water that left no path behind him, no footsteps to retrace. At the corner, he turned left to face the broad expanse of the flood. The water was deeper here. It rose from his ankles to within inches of his knees. He paused and lifted his face upward to the rain, wanting to be even wetter than he was. No amount of it would slake his thirst. For drenched as he was, his heart was still dry.

The noise of the river grew louder. He descended toward the wooden footbridge that crossed into Watervliet. He had to see the flood from the bridge. His mother would be missing him. She would be at the bay window, holding back the lace curtains, peering into the rain for a sign. But he could not think of that. His was an act of repudiation of caution. He had tried with his kiss to stop her from dying, but it hadn't worked. This came next.

He grasped the handrail of the footbridge and made his way to the center where the bridge arched before descending to Watervliet. He stood there, gazing down into the torrent below. He could feel the heartbeat of the river thumping against the floor of the bridge. It had the same rhythm as his own! He was fully aroused, expectant, like someone wanting to make love.

The water was rising rapidly. Already the bridge throbbed and groaned under the pummeling. What if it broke? Tom had never felt so keenly alive. Every part of him relished toying with this danger, this venturing so far that he might be irretrievable. He raised his head, taking the rain in his teeth, shouting into it with whoops of joy. "I love you, Lily," he shouted, above the roar of the river. "I love you!" But he could not climb the rigging of his still-breaking voice.

I'm going to leave this place, he thought. Get out of Troy. His mother was right. It is a godforsaken hole. He gazed down. The wild current at his feet was like something let out of its cage for the first time. All at once, that portion of the railing that he held was whisked from his grasp. Tom backed away from the naked edge of the bridge. A moment later he heard a crack and a groan as the bridge bent upon itself and sank. Only the single beam to which Tom clung protruded from the flood. He felt the water hit him on the shoulder; he was in the river, in pain, holding to the beam with his good arm. The river reached out and slapped him in the face, driving water into his throat. Coughing, gagging, Tom pulled himself higher on the beam. His lungs, already full of water, seemed to have no room for air. He struggled for breath. So this is what it is like, he thought, not being able to breathe, just holding on until you die. A powerful punch of water upon his back knocked loose the cough he needed to raise the fluid from his lungs. And he could breathe once more. Still another wallop broke his hold on the beam, and he was being carried along in the current, now submerged, now surfacing, his arms and legs strewn about him. He would not struggle. He would be like any of the helpless shapes that swept by him. He would offer himself. Besides, there wasn't any use in struggling.

In a week or so, when the flood was over, he would be found floating somewhere downstream. They would fish him out with a chain and a rope like that man Billy and he had seen. He thought of that sodden bloated corpse. And at once, his outflung hand filled with leaves. He closed it and held on, feeling himself jerked back from the current. Turning he saw that he had hold of a branch of the willow tree that was trailing in the stream. Steeling himself against the pain in his shoulder, he pulled himself hand over hand until his feet felt the solid bed of the river. He pulled himself erect, then toppled over into the shallow mud. He was out of the current. Safe.

✤

"Why did you do it, Tom? Just tell me that, why?" It was his mother, peeling off his wet clothes. "Judas Priest! There's a bone sticking through your skin. Now see what you've done. Why? I asked you. You'd better tell me, you foolish boy."

"It's only the collarbone," said his father. "Billy, pull his shoulders back as hard as you can, like this. There, you see? That reduces the bone back inside. Hold him there while I clean it up and stitch the wound."

He watched his father's face as he rolled the warm wet plaster in a figure-of-eight around his chest, under his arm, then over and back again. Over and over until the splint was thick, molded with infinite gentleness. It had been years since he had felt his father's touch. He thought of him coming out of the whorehouse wearing his gray fedora and with a Lucky Strike hanging from his lip. A wave of affection overtook him for this gray, carbon-lipped man who all these years had faithfully sutured winter to spring, summer to fall in this cheerless town and never once berated himself for having chosen misery as the color of his life. He doesn't have long to live, thought Tom. He is dying too.

When the plaster splint had dried, the doctor spoke:

"Your mother asked you a question, Tom. Why did you do it?"

But Tom did not answer. He didn't really know why himself, only that he had to go down to the river. He needed to dare, to be valorous, for Lily and not just have her die and that's that. He had to mark her passing with some deed of his own, even his own death. He hadn't counted on the river refusing, insisting that he go back to Troy where he belonged. But he couldn't tell them any of that.

"It was that girl, wasn't it?" said his mother. "It was Lily. I knew the minute they brought her here, something awful would happen."

During the night the rain petered out and stopped. The sudden absence of the sound of its falling woke Tom up. He sat and listened to the silence that extended outward from his bed to fill the whole town.

Once before he had heard such a silence when, from the landing at the head of the stairs, he could no longer hear Lily breathing.

He lay back in bed, thinking of Lily and of the sound of the river which was her sound too, murmuring, whispering, breathing, coughing, saying his name in a hundred different ways.

❧

The next morning, the air was still, the sun came out. Almost at once the floodwaters receded from Troy. From beneath the brawling water the inert city stirred and, baffled, mute, embarrassed, began to extricate itself. One by one the doors and windows opened. People peered out, stepped into the filthy street, full of mud and stones. They called to one another, poked among the debris. Tom sat in the bay window and looked out over the city. I'm going to get out of here, he thought again. But even then he knew that flight or exile was a kind of dying. Living meant always coming back to Troy.

Like everyone else on the block, Doctor Fogarty and his wife were out on the front stoop surveying the wreckage. Here and there quiet puddles reflected the blue sky.

"I'm worried about that boy," Irene said to her husband. "He's looking pale. You don't suppose . . . ?"

The doctor scanned the sky. "There's no rainbow," he said. "The least we deserve is a rainbow."

"A rainbow over Troy would be Heaven getting sarcastic," she replied.

He smiled. The remark reminded him why he had married her.

❧

It started snowing early in November before the Trojans had gathered themselves together to sweep up and hose down the city. The low-lying streets were still littered with branches of trees, mud and penitent stones.

When the snow fell and covered the debris, Tom's mother was relieved. She'd face up to it in the spring.

Just about then the bakery switched over to trucks. They were painted in the same old Freihofer colors—red, orange, yellow, and black. They looked like toys.

"What happened to the horse?" Tom asked. "What did they do to him?"

"What horse?" said Hank. "Ooh, *that* horse," finally remembering something that had happened a long time ago. "The one that used to pull my old wagon?" Hank threw back his head, clicked his tongue twice, and turned on the ignition.

"Giddap," he hollered, and drove away.

∞

The first week in December, Doctor Fogarty sawed through the plaster splint and took it off.

"The bone's not straight," he told Tom. "The splint didn't hold it. You're going to have a bump."

In the mirror Tom saw the mass on the left side between his neck and shoulder. It was the size of a plum, and the overlying skin was bluish red and shiny. Like a badge, it seemed to draw light to itself. He touched it with his fingertips.

"Don't fool with it," said his father. "If you let it be, maybe it'll go down some."

But as the weeks went by and the lump remained the same size, Tom knew that the deformity was permanent. Sometimes, without thinking, he would press the bony hard mass and experience a deep aching sensation which, far from causing him distress, pleased him strangely.

∞

By Christmas, Tom no longer believed in the horse-god. Perhaps it had just been something he had made up to tell Lily, to make her laugh or keep her alive and he had talked himself into it, the way you do when you invent things.

But he would never stop believing that it was the manure, that golden vaporous Grace coming with its sweet message, that made Lily and him turn toward each other at precisely the same instant; Lily looking downward and to the right from the bay window of 104; him, down there in the street, looking upward and to the right, over his shoulder. And that it had been the manure that caused them, after the moment of surprise, to laugh, him in embarrassment, Lily with her hand covering her mouth. Sometimes, months later, when his window was open and he heard laughter or singing, he would race down the street to see a white curtain stirring in a bay window and feel the flaring of that brightness.

In the years that followed, Tom did leave Troy, but never for good. Everywhere he went, he found a strange vacancy that only this sour, unsmiling Troy did not have.

Whenever he got off the train at Sixth Avenue and Federal, he would carry his suitcase straight down to that river into which he had once plunged and which had rejected him, and out of which he had emerged purged of his childhood, wounded, and with the awful knowledge of what could happen to a man, but not why. And with the understanding that love makes grief, and grief, love. For, if anything, he loved Lily more.

And so he would return to rummage in that city of soot and Swiss-cheese lungs, leaning his ear toward echoes, looking in the luminous shadows for evidence of that summer when he had been trapped in the elaborate webs of love.

A Worm from My Notebook

Were I a professor of the art of writing, I would coax my students to eschew all great and noble concepts—politics, women's liberation or any of the matters that affect society as a whole. There are no "great" subjects for the creative writer; there are only the singular details of a single human life. Just as there are no great subjects, there are no limits to the imagination. Send it off, I would urge my students, to wander into the side trails, the humblest burrows to seek out the exceptional and the mysterious. A doctor/writer is especially blessed in that he walks about all day in the middle of a short story. There comes that moment when he is driven to snatch up a pencil and jot it down. Only, he must take care that the pencil be in flames and that his fingers be burnt in the act. Fine writing can spring from the most surprising sources. Take parasitology, for instance. There is no more compelling drama than the life cycle of *Dracunculus medinensis*, the Guinea worm. Only to tell the story of its life and death is to peel away layers of obscurity, to shed light upon the earth and all of its creatures. That some fifty million of us are even now infested with this worm is of no literary interest whatsoever. Always, it is the affliction of one human being that captures the imagination. So it was with the passion of Jesus Christ; so it is with the infestation of a single African man. Shall we write the story together? A Romance of Parasitology? Let me tell you how it goes thus far. I will give you a peek into my notebook where you will see me struggling to set words down on a blank piece of paper. At first whimsically, capriciously, even insincerely. Later, in dead earnest. You will see at precisely what moment the writer ceases to think of his character as an instrument to be manipulated and think of him as someone with whom he has fallen in love. For it is always, must always be, a matter of love.

∽

Let us begin with a man leading his cattle to a watering hole at the edge of the desert. We shall call him Ibrahim. Shall we locate him in Chad? No, Zaire, I think. For the beauty of the name. Such a word . . . Zaire . . . plays to the savor of the silent reader's speaking tongue. Such a word can, all by itself, sink one into a kind of reverie. Writers must think of such seemingly unimportant attributes as the sound of a written word.

∽

Ibrahim is barefoot and wears a loose earth-colored tunic that flows to his knees. Thin, black, solitary, he walks behind his small herd of cows. Seven. Eight, if you count the calf. For counterpoise, he carries a crook taller than himself with which he poles the sand as he paces. His very stride is ceremonious. Mostly, he is solemn, silent. But at times he sings to the cows until their ears begin to move, the better to catch his voice. He knows that they need song to keep going. It is clear that he loves them. Two years ago his wife died in childbirth. Her hands are what he remembers best—what they did to his body: sorted among his hair for lice which they slew between thumb and fingernail with a delicious little click, cleaned out his ears with a piece of straw, smeared him with ornamental paint, and, on the floor of their hut, crept all over him like small playful animals.

∽

At last Ibrahim reaches the watering hole. Only when his beasts have begun to drink, only then does he think to slake his own thirst. Wading into the pond, he bends to scoop handfuls of water to his mouth. It is a fated moment. For this is no mere water, but water inhabited by the tiny crustacean Cyclops, a microscopic crab with a large and median eye.

∽

Unbeknownst to Ibrahim, Cyclops is harboring within its tiny body the larva of *Dracunculus medinensis*. No sooner does the little worm recognize that it has entered the intestine of a man than it casts off the Cyclops which has been for it foster parent, pantry, and taxi, and it migrates into the soft tissues of the man. Shortly thereafter, somewhere inside the flesh of Ibrahim, two worms mate; immediately afterward the male dies.

∽

Time goes by during which the worm within Ibrahim grows to a length of more than two feet and the thickness of a piece of twine. One day, while Ibrahim is squatting by his resting herd, his idle finger perceives the worm as a long undulating ridge just beneath the skin of his abdomen. Again and again he runs his finger up and down the awful ridge, feeling the creature respond with slow pruritic vermiculation. And the face of the man takes on the far-off look of someone deeply, obsessively, in love. With just that magnitude of attention does Ibrahim dote upon the worm. Look at his face! Of what can he be thinking? Of his mother? His childhood? His village? Of the forest spirits with whom he must each day, and many times each day, deal, and whom cajole? At last the spell is broken; sighing, Ibrahim takes up a small twig and, with his knife, carves a notch in one end.

∽

At the end of a year, the intestine of the worm has shrunk away, and the uterus enlarged to occupy its entire body. It has become a tube filled with embryos. Then comes the day when an instinct, more, a diabolical urge, tells Dracunculus that the hour of its destiny has arrived; it must migrate to the foot of the man. Once having wriggled down the lateral aspect of Ibrahim's left foot midway between the malleolus and the head of the fifth metatarsal bone, the saboteur worm chews a hole from the inside out. Ibrahim feels the pain of the chewing and, peering into the hole, he sees for the first time the head of the worm advance and retreat in accordance with some occult Dracuncular rhythm. And he shudders, for it is with horror that you acknowledge the presence within your body of another creature that has a purpose and a will all its own, that eats your flesh, that you can feel. Feel moving!

∾

Ibrahim does not know that the worm is waiting for water, that only when water covers the hole in his foot will the worm stick out its head and spew the liquid that contains the many hundreds of its get. The worm knows that it would not do to spit its precious upon the dry sand to die a-borning. And so it comes to pass that once again Ibrahim has brought his cattle to the watering hole at the edge of the desert. No sooner has he followed them into the pond than the head of the worm emerges and discharges its milky fluid from the submerged foot. Again the thirsty man stoops to slurp his palmsful of Cyclops and larvae. The cycle begins again.

∾

But now a look of stealth and craft sidles across the otherwise impassive face of Ibrahim. His nostrils dilate, and his face, beneath the high and brilliant sun, seems to generate a kind of black sunshine of its own. Reaching into the folds of his tunic, he brings forth the little notched twig that he had fashioned those many weeks ago. Up till now, he has had the patience of the desert; now he will have the heroism of the leopard. If he has prayed to the Gods, propitiated the Spirits, we do not know it. No amulet swings at his neck. There is only the twig. Hunkering by the side of the pond, one foot in the water, Ibrahim waits. He would wait here for hours, for days, if need be. All, all has been swept aside. Even his beloved cattle are forgotten. There is in the universe only Ibrahim and his Worm. He stares down at his foot as though it were not his own, but a foreign brutish appendage that had been left lying on the desert and that had somehow been woven onto his body, attached there. At last he sees that an inch or two of the preoccupied worm is protruding from his still submerged foot. Darting, he grasps with thumb and forefinger, capturing, and, with all the grace and deftness of a surgeon ligating an artery, he ties the head of the worm in a knot around the notched end of the twig, ties it so that the worm cannot wriggle free.

Very, very slowly, a little each day and for many days, Ibrahim turns the twig which he wears at his ankle like a hideous jewel, winding the worm upon it out of a wisdom that has been passed down to him from the earliest time of mankind, through the voices of nameless ancestors, telling that the truly dangerous is not hard or stony, but soft and wet and delicate. There is no room for rashness. Ibrahim cannot be hasty. Turn the twig too quickly and the worm will break; the retained segment retracts to cause infection, gangrene, death. How dignified the man looks. Each time he squats to turn the twig, then stands up, his full height comes as a fresh surprise to the cattle who lift their horns so that the sun can gild them in celebration. In just this way, fifteen days go by. At last the whole of the worm is wrapped around the twig. It is dead. Ibrahim is healed.

Now Ibrahim turns his cattle on the long trek toward home. It is hot, hot. The world longs for a breeze, but the winds are all asleep. He feels the desert little by little envelop his solitary body. A vast sand grows even vaster. There is less and less for the cattle to eat. Each year he has had to walk them farther. See how they bob their heads with every step as if they were using them to drag along their bodies. It is true—the desert is spreading—Ibrahim thinks. At the watering hole the men were speaking of famine. But that is far away, he says. Not here, not in the villages of Zaire. In due time, in due time, the older ones say. Ibrahim feels a vague restlessness, a longing. In three days there will be a feast in his village—the rite of circumcision when the young boys are taken into the adult life of the tribe. An animal will be slaughtered; there will be meat. Should he walk fast or slow? All at once, Ibrahim quickens his pace, calling out to the cattle to move along, hearing already the drums and the singing of the women. He has been away for three full moons. The smells of his village come out to the desert to grab him by the nose, to pull him toward home. Hurry, hurry, Ibrahim! On and on he walks, and all the while the space within him where the worm had been was filling up with the music of the feast until now Ibrahim is brimful of it. And he has a moment of intoxication during which he feels the sun pounding him like a drum, and he feels his blood seeping out of the still unhealed hole in his foot to dance about his footsteps in the sand. Then, something stirs in Ibrahim, something, like a sunken branch long trapped beneath the water, bobs to the surface with considerable force. At that moment, Ibrahim decides to take a wife.

∞

Such, such are the plots of parasitology. Ah, but now you are hooked, aren't you? I have caught you, then? You want me to go on, to write the story of Ibrahim? Well. Where should the story go from here? First to the village, I think, where Ibrahim would join the feast, find a woman with good hands and abundant breasts and make love to her. They would be married. I should like very much to describe the ritual circumcision, the ordeal of the young boys in the jungle, how they are wrapped in the skins of three animals and put in a pit for nine days from which they emerge reborn as men. I should like to render for you the passion of Ibrahim for Ntanga, his new wife, who each night lifts her throat to him for whatever he might wish to do to it; then tell of how, in time, he must once again take his little herd away from the village in search of forage. But now the terrible drought *has* come, the famine as predicted by the men at the watering hole the year before. The desert itself is undulant, looking most like the water it craves. Ibrahim's skin and hair are soon white with the dust kicked up by the starving cows. He watches the cloud of sand rise and slowly descend. Even the desert wants to leave this place, he thinks. The knives of the sun have split one of his cows in two so that it falls apart before his eyes. Another, the sun has turned into metal. Ibrahim's fingers burst into flames as he grasps a bronze horn to ease the creature's last stumble. Still, on the scabby backs of the others, the white scavenger bird rides. Even that is almost too much for the cattle to carry. He tries singing to them, to offer them syllables of rain, a melody of cool grass, but his tongue is dry. Sand clings to the roof of his mouth. He tries to spit but he cannot. Instead he closes his lips. The last of the cattle dies within three hundred yards of the watering hole at the edge of the desert. The faithful beast leans against something to break its fall but there is only the air into which it slumps. Ibrahim watches the dying animal collect sand in its mouth, watches death cloud the eyes in which only a short while ago he had delighted to see himself reflected. Now his own body is a knife blade across which, again and again, he draws himself, each time feeling the precise exquisite incision with undiminished pain. Ibrahim staggers on to the watering hole—three hundred yards, yet a whole day's trek. It is a dry ditch, the bottom fissured. Sinking to his knees, he lowers his head like a cow and licks the clay. Kneeling there alone, his tongue stuck to the baked basin of the hole, Ibrahim hears a muffled clamoring as of a herd far off. A lamentation of hoofbeats and mooing swirls about him. Then all is still. The life cycle of the parasite is broken at last.

Witness

There are human beings who spend their infancy in pain. One, perhaps, is born lacking, and must be completed, or a pot of hot coffee
is spilled and another must be grafted and grafted again, first with the
skin of strangers and then, if any, his own. Still another becomes the
toothsome morsel of a tumor. This baby must be cut and suffer and
even die. What is one to think of that? When an old person dies, it is
of his own achievements. But here was a body to which nothing had
happened until this pain. If this body had lived, you say, it would have
known no pleasure, remembered no comfort. It would have had only
a heritage of pain upon which to base its life. It is for the best, you say!
Then what of this?

The boy in the bed is the length of a six-year-old. But something
about him is much younger than that. It is the floppiness, I think. His
head lolls as though it were floating in syrup. Now and then he unfurls his legs like a squid. He has pale yellow hair and pale blue eyes.
His eyes will have none of me, but gaze as though into a mirror. He
is blind. The right cheek and temple are deeply discolored. At first I
think it is a birthmark. Then I see that it is a bruise.

"Does he walk?" I ask.

"No."

"Crawl?"

"He rolls. His left side is weak," the mother tells me.

"But he has a strong right arm," says the father. I touch the dark bruise that covers the right side of the child's face where he has again and again punched himself.

"Yes, I see that he is strong."

"That's how he tells us that he wants something or that something hurts. That, and grinding his teeth."

"He doesn't talk, then?"

"He has never been heard to utter a word," says the mother, as though repeating a statement from a written case history.

I unpin the diaper and lay it open. A red lump boils at the child's groin. The lump is the size of a walnut. The tissues around it slope off into pinkness. Under the pressure of my fingers, the redness blanches. I let up and the redness returns. I press again. Abruptly the right arm of the child flails upward and his fist bumps against his bruised cheek.

"You're hurting him," says the father.

The eyes of the child are terrible in their sapphiric emptiness. Is there not one tiny seed of vision in them? I know that there is not. The optic nerves have failed to develop, the pediatrician has told me. Such blindness goes all the way back to the brain.

"It is an incarcerated hernia," I tell him. "An emergency operation will be necessary to examine the intestine that is trapped in the sac. If the bowel is not already gangrenous, it will be replaced inside the peritoneal cavity, and then we will fix the hernia. If the circulation of the bowel has already been compromised, we will remove that section and stitch the ends together."

"Will there be . . . ?"

"No," I say, "there will be no need for a colostomy." All this they understand at once. The young woman nods.

"My sister's boy had the same thing," she says.

I telephone the operating room to schedule the surgery, then sit at the desk to write the preoperative orders on the chart. An orderly arrives with a stretcher for the boy. The father fends off my assistance and lifts the child onto the stretcher himself.

"Is there any danger?"

"There is always danger. But we will do everything to prevent trouble." The stretcher is already moving down the corridor. The father hurries to accompany it.

"Wait here," I say to him at the elevator. "I will come as soon as we are done." The man looks long and deep at the child, gulping him down in a single radiant gaze.

"Take good care of my son," he says. I see that he loves the boy as one can only love his greatest extravagance, the thing that will impoverish him totally, will give him cold and hunger and pain in return for his love. As the door to the elevator closes I see the father standing in the darkening corridor, his arms still making a cradle in which the smoke of twilight is gathering. I wheel the stretcher into the operating room from which the father has been banished. I think of how he must dwell for now in a dark hallway across which, from darker doorways, the blinding cries of sick children streak and crackle. What is his food, that man out there? Upon what shall he live but the remembered smiles of this boy?

On the operating table the child flutters and tilts like a moth burnt by the beams of the great overhead lamp. I move the lamp away from him until he is not so precisely caught. In this room where everything is green, the child is green as ice. Translucent, a fish seen through murk, and dappled. I hold him upon the table while the anesthetist inserts a needle into a vein on the back of the child's left hand, the one that is weak. Bending above, I can feel the boy's breath upon my neck. It is clean and hay-scented as the breath of a calf. If I knew how, I would lick the silence from his lips. What malice made this? Surely not God! Perhaps he is a changeling—an imperfect child put in place of another, a normal one who had been stolen by the fairies. Yes, I think. It is the malice of the fairies.

Now the boy holds his head perfectly still, cocked to one side. He seems to be listening. I know that he is . . . listening for the sound of his father's voice. I speak to the boy, murmur to him. But I know it is not the same. Take good care of my son, the father had said. Why must he brandish his love at me? I am enough beset. But I know that he must. I think of the immensity of love and I see for a moment what the father must see—the soul that lay in the body of the child like a chest of jewels in a sunken ship. Through the fathoms it glows. I cup the child's feet in one hand. How cold they are! I should like to lend him my cat to drape over them. I am happiest in winter with my cat for a foot pillow. No human has ever been so kind, so voluptuous, as my cat. Now the child is asleep. Under anesthesia he looks completely normal. So! It is only wakefulness that diminishes him.

The skin has been painted with antiseptic and draped. I make the incision across the apex of the protuberance. Almost at once I know that this is no incarcerated hernia but a testicle that had failed to descend into the scrotum. Its energy for the long descent had given out. Harmlessly it hung in midcanal until now, when it twisted on its little cord and cut off its own blood supply. The testicle is no longer viable. The black color of it tells me so. I cut into the substance of the testicle to see if it will bleed. It does not. It will have to be removed.

"You'll have to take it out, won't you?" It is the anesthesiologist speaking. "It won't do him any good now. Anyway, why does he need it?"

"Yes, yes, I know. . . . Wait." And I stand at the table filled with loathing for my task. Precisely because he has so little left, because it is of no use to him . . . I know. A moment later I tie the spermatic cord with a silk suture, and I cut off the testicle. Lying upon a white gauze square, it no longer appears mad, threatening, but an irrefutable witness to these events, a testament. I close the wound.

∽

I am back in the solarium of the pediatric ward. It is empty save for the young couple and myself.

"He is fine," I tell them. "He will be in the recovery room for an hour and then they will bring him back here. He is waking up now."

"What did you do to my son?" The father's eyes have the glare of black olives.

"It wasn't a hernia," I explain. "I was wrong. It was an undescended testicle that had become twisted on its cord. I had to remove it." The mother nods minutely. Her eyes are the same blue gem from which the boy's have been struck. There is something pure about the woman out of whose womb this child had blundered to knock over their lives. As though the mothering of such a child had returned her to a state of virginity. The father slumps in his chair, his body doubled as though it were he who had been cut in the groin. There in the solarium he seems to be aging visibly, the arteries in his body silting up. Yellow sacs of flesh appear beneath his eyes. His eyes themselves are peopled with red ants. I imagine his own slack scrotum. And the hump on his back—flapping, dithering, drooling, reaching up to hit itself on the cheek, and listening, always listening, for the huffing of the man's breath.

Just then the room is plunged into darkness.

"Don't worry," I say. "A power failure. There is an accessory generator. The lights will go on in a moment." We are silent, as though the darkness has robbed us of speech as well. I cannot see the father, but like the blind child in the recovery room, I listen for the sound of his voice.

The lights go on. Abruptly, the father rises from his chair.

"Then, he is all right?"

"Yes," I nod. Relief snaps open upon his face. He reaches for his wife's hand. They stand there together, smiling. And all at once I know that this man's love for his child is a passion. It is a rapids roiling within him. It has nothing to do with pleasure, this kind of love. It is a deep, black joy.

Chatterbox

Homage to Saint Catherine of Siena

*I*t is not always the doctor who heals. Sometimes it is another patient.

The following is taken verbatim from the diary of a woman who was a patient of mine some years ago. It is in the form of a letter to her brother Raymond. The diary was mailed to me by her brother some months after her death.

Catherine Goodhouse had been what in high-school yearbooks is called a "chatterbox," and in textbooks of psychiatry is called a "compulsive talker." Catherine was a talker the way other people are writers or actors. Talking vouchsafed her life. "Do you hear me?" she seemed to be saying. "Then I am alive." It satisfied her as sucking satisfies the baby who likes the feel of his lips and tongue working.

Talking was an affliction of which life had made her painfully aware. One day, her husband Joe had stood up in the middle of Sunday dinner and walked out of the house. She never saw him again. When he was sixteen, her son Warren had said to her, "Why the hell don't you shut up?" Then he was gone—enlisted in the Navy. For four years Catherine lived alone, talking to whoever would hold still long enough, or to herself. She couldn't help it.

When I first went into practice, I used to work part-time at Golden Gardens to make ends meet. The nursing home was far enough outside town to enable the owners to describe it in the brochure as "rustic" and "rural." What the people in Golden Gardens needed was not so much country air as someone to talk to. Company. All day long they sat encased in silence, unable to find a way out of it.

"You ought to sign up at Golden Gardens," I told Catherine. "Go out once or twice a week to visit with the patients. They're lonesome, and you have what it takes." The next day Catherine called to say she could go every Tuesday and Friday from two to three in the afternoon.

Catherine Goodhouse was one of those petite, doll-like women given to lavender sachets and dresses made of organdy or dotted swiss. Every time she came to Golden Gardens she looked and smelled like spring itself. The patients adored her. She was assigned five of them, the same five each time, so that they would come to look upon her as family. There were four women and a man. Two of the women were in wheelchairs. When she arrived at five minutes to two, they would already have been assembled in the "parlor," and had been drawn up into a little semicircle in front of which Catherine would stand babbling on about what she was wearing, where she learned to bake, what she was going to plant in her garden. The weather. It was only fair, she told an attendant at the home, to start with what she was wearing because Mr. Freitas and Mrs. Celli were blind. As far as anyone knew, none of the five was ever heard to utter a word in reply. It didn't matter. They just sat there for the hour, rapt and adoring, as though she were the most beautiful, most charming, the freshest thing in the world. As time went on, it was plain to see that the five old people were stronger and more alert than they had been before. They certainly looked better. Their faces were pink, their lips moist. Pretty soon, Catherine was going to the home five days a week.

"Well now," she would say at the close of each of her visits, "we've had a lovely time, haven't we?" And she would walk slowly toward the door. All five, including the two blind ones, would turn to follow her right up to the last second. About a year later, I stopped working at the home, and lost touch with Catherine. Three years later I heard that she had died. And then there was this diary.

My dear brother Raymond,

For some time I have been going out to a convalescent home to talk with the patients. They don't have much company, you know. I cannot believe now that when I first saw them I was horrified. That first day and for a while afterwards, they seemed not only grotesque but dangerous. Were they contagious? I wondered. Or violent? And with all their bodily functions—salivation, excretion—unpredictable, sort of wild. If one of them touches me, I thought, I'll die. There was Mrs. Greenwald, with her wet chin and that cackle that just welled up out of her every little while. And Mr. Freitas, with those boiled swollen hands that looked like *Blutwurst*. His fist on the handle of his cane was like a just-born infant's face, engorged, angry. His hands seemed always to be hot. He would reach for things to cool them on, like the armrest of his chair or the knob of his cane.

But right from the beginning there was something about them that drew me. It was their pathetic confidence that they were human. I saw bravery in their very act of coming to listen to me. And they never missed a visit. I knew that they needed me as much as I needed them.

One day there were only four of them. Mrs. Greenwald was missing. "Where is Mrs. Greenwald?" I asked. Of course, they didn't answer.

"A massive hemorrhage from the stomach," one of the nurses explained. "She was dead in an hour." A hemorrhage, I thought. As though the old woman's blood somehow knew it was dwelling in a doomed body, and had hurried to escape it. I swear it seemed that the other four were embarrassed that I should have to find out and be upset by something that one of them had done. All at once I felt bereft, deprived of something, like an old coat that, without knowing it, I had been wearing to keep myself warm; and now that it was gone I was chilled to the bone. From that moment I never had any doubt that I would be going to Golden Gardens for the rest of my life.

And now, Raymond, I want to tell you as well as I can what happened. On the day of the event, I bathed and dressed carefully. I had bought a new white dress, and I was wearing it for the first time. White is so virginal, the clerk in the dress shop had said, and she had smiled knowingly. And she was right. It did make me feel . . . well . . . cleansed to put it on. I don't know why I am telling you about that except that now it does seem important to me somehow. It was such a good visit. I told them so many things. You should have seen how they were nourished by my talking. I like to think that they would have been dead long ago if I didn't talk to them like that. I had been told to limit my visits to one hour so as not to tire them, but on this day about which I am writing, they didn't seem a bit tired at the end of an hour, and truthfully, I hadn't had enough either. I just went right on for another hour, while the four old people sat there and listened.

At the end of the second hour, I stood up. "Well," I said as usual, "we've had another lovely visit." First I brought the two women in wheelchairs out to their rooms. The third woman followed on her own. When I returned to our meeting place, I saw that Mr. Freitas had stood up but had made no move to leave. "So, Mr. Freitas," I said, "it's time for me to go home." Still, the old man made no move to leave. Instead he took one step closer to me so that he could almost have reached out and touched me. Another step brought him still closer. We were standing facing each other. All at once I was aware of a strange, warm sensation. As though my body were darkening, and even my dress were pink. I could have heated the building with my presence. Thus we stood for a long moment. I studied the old man. Every bit of his clothing took on an immense importance, just as my dress had seemed to me important before—his stained vest, the yellowed armpits of his shirt, the crumpled stovepipe trousers. It seemed to me special raiment. Even the angle of inclination of his head had meaning.

Then slowly the old man raised his arms and held them out. If I were a clock, he would have been pointing to ten minutes before and ten minutes after the hour of twelve, which was my throat. My gaze was lashed to the dance of the calcified artery at his wrist, which beat at the same rhythm as the pulse clapping in my ear. As though our blood had hurled itself across the distance between us, receding from me to flow into him, then back again. Even so, I had the most ordinary thoughts. I wondered, for instance, what direction I faced. Was it north? No, impossible. It was east. Yes, I was facing east. I remembered something that had happened a long time ago when I was a young girl. A boy at school had approached me. His hand had been made into a cage. Through the aperture formed by the curled index finger and the web of his thumb, I could see the head of a little bird. A purple finch, it was. The bird lay still in the firm grasp of the boy. Beneath the row of fingers which dipped into his palm, I caught sight of three tiny talons and a tiny foot.

"Would you like to hold it?" he asked me. I felt desire and revulsion at one and the same time. I *wanted* to hold that bird more than anything else in the world. And I did *not* want to hold it with exactly the same intensity.

"Here," said the boy, "take it." I held out my two hands, covering his fist with both of mine, and I received the little bird. In the quick movement of departure of the boy's hand from mine, I felt the fluttering of the bird's wings. All of a sudden, I became terrified, and I screamed.

"Take it back. Please take it back!" He did, relieving me of it as gently as possible.

Now I stood in front of the old man, feeling the same confusion of desire and dread. My blood was tumbling. I felt that I must leave at once, or die.

"I must go," I managed to say. But I made no move to leave. He was like the stub of a white candle melted, run over, but with the flame undiminished. With each intake of my breath, that flame bowed toward me, designating me, electing me. I could feel its heat upon my cheek.

Suddenly, I was afraid. Perhaps he meant to throttle me. Do it! I thought. Do it! Whatever it is you are going to do, for God's sake, do it! Slowly his hands enfolded my neck, closing upon it with a perfect balance of lightness and firmness, as though it were a small bird. And when, at last, his fingers reached me (they were so long in coming), I slipped into them, was caught, lay still, quieted, the way a bird, once caught, ceases its frantic efforts to escape and embraces captivity, understanding at last that captivity was what it had wanted all along.

His opaque blue eyes, all scarred and milky, were fixed upon me. They took in no sight, I knew, but seemed now to give forth a light of their own, as though far behind them they kept an everlasting source of it which needed no ignition from the outside. And just as a sailor *confides* in a lighthouse, so did I confide in this light, certain that long after he left me, his eyes would glow on. His eyes contained the world. They conjured me. I existed in those eyes.

What a feeling of utter renunciation I had! I would not have held anything back from him, would have surrendered blood, breath, and whatever else he would have. I remained still, listening to the singing fingers about my neck, and my heart dwelt in a snug cottage. For his touch was hushing, the way a finger to the lips is hushing. With just such infinite gentleness the old man bade me be quiet. And I was quiet, silenced, healed.

For a long moment the old man held me between his palms. At last his grasp lightened and he withdrew. The shuffling of his feet and the tapping of his cane told me that he had gone. I did not dare to turn and look. Alone, I had the feeling that something had at long last been set right, as though a room full of awkward, ungainly furniture had been rearranged by someone with style and good taste. Long after the old man had left me, I stood honoring the event, letting comfort fill me up, expand in me the way dough expands into bread or sleep swells a lover's face into softness. Had he really touched me? I wondered. Had it really been his flesh upon mine? Or merely a close proximity, something that had come careening from a great distance to swipe within a hair of me, then dash away? But I knew that he had.

I still go to Golden Gardens to visit. But it is different now. Sometimes, I don't talk at all. Sometimes I just sit with them. I bring flowers and arrange them, or cookies that I have made. These things they receive with the same pleasure as my talking. Now and then, one of them will smile happily at me the way a mother does whose child has been ill and has recovered.

Impostor

There is a certain region of Asia, not far from the Arctic Circle, where the villages are scanty and remote, and where the customs and pace have not changed for three hundred years. Because of the poverty of the soil, the landscape, the stinginess of the sun, the wolves, for whatever reason, the rest of the human race has not rushed to visit this place. Even Genghis Khan had given it a wide berth. There were czars who had never heard of it. The sole occupation of the people is the felling of trees for timber. But if there is no wealth, neither are there any beggars. Their only nod in the direction of government is the existence of a village chief, who is the eldest son of the oldest man in each village, a person of middle years and with a venerable heritage, for old age is venerated here. The only recreation through the long glacial winter is to study the sky and to repeat the tales of their ancestors. Now only bureaucrats come to take the census, levy taxes, and to enforce regulations. And once a year, the Health Inspector.

Even after N. had been in the village for a year, it still amazed him that no one here had ever beheld the sea. It made the inhabitants seem drier, heavier, more solid than he. Not less, only different. The way a sturdy black clot differs from the coursing liquid form of blood. In the absence of a sea, the people hunkered and stared up at the sky for hours at a time. It seemed to satisfy them the way the sea satisfies those who dwell upon its shores. Perhaps, he thought, there was once, eons ago, a sea that covered this place, and this village then lay

on the edge of a great ocean which long ago had turned to vapor and
been gathered into the sky, and which now the people studied as
though it were the sea. It was a village without church or priest, a
pagan place that had gotten separated over the centuries from its
Christianity. In the absence of faith, he thought, superstition did them
very well.

The time of his coming was still what passes for autumn in these
parts, and the woods were in waning leaf. Just at sunset he broke
from the matted forest upon a field that had been planted with potatoes. He paused there, legs apart and wobbling. The sound of his
breath scraped at his ears. Shielding his eyes with one hand, he gazed
beyond the field at the village which glowed and undulated like a
molten core. Was it real, or another hallucinated place? He had seen
so many mirages. Near the far side of the field two men squatted,
working potatoes out of the ground. Had they glanced up at that moment, to one he might have resembled a newborn colt making its
first boneless stand. To the other, he could have been a wild creature
caught in the last agonal lurch of its life. But they did not look up to
see him.

With his coat flying wildly about his legs, N. staggered across the
open country and into the streets of the village itself. Before long he
came upon a small, cobblestoned square from which the rest of the
town radiated. In the middle of the square was a stone horse trough,
or so it seemed to the dazed and delirious stranger. He bent over the
trough. Again and again, he scooped water and dashed it into his
face, anointing his head, ladling it into his upturned mouth. It was
sunset, and the empty square was heated to a deep red. The water in
the trough, too, was red and thick as temple oil. N. straightened and
stared at the sun, which seemed to him a coin that had been fixed and
minted at that spot. All at once a crow flew across the sun at its very
middle, bisecting it with its flight, then emerged into the honeyed sky.
N. felt a sudden sharp pain in his temple, and something else—a
fluttering as though the flight of the bird had entered his own blood.
An irresistible giddiness came over him, and he fell unconscious to the
cobblestones. But not before he knew that he had found his place, that
here, in this tiny square, he would end his flight.

✑

N. awoke foaming and with all of his muscles having brawled among themselves. He was in a bed. A woman was standing over him. At his first stirring, the woman leaned nearer. He saw that she had a harelip that completely bisected her upper lip to the nose. Through the rent he could see the moist red darkness of her mouth. It was like a fresh wound. Because of this, and because she was wearing a kerchief around her head, he could not judge her age.

"How long have I been here?" He wanted only to know how long he had been at the mercy of strangers. He did not think to ask where he was.

"Three days." The voice sloshed in and out of her nose.

"What is your name?" he asked.

"Mona." She began to question him.

"Where did you come from? What are you doing here?"

He closed his eyes. After a long silence he spoke. "I am a doctor."

From the finality of his voice she knew he would tell her nothing more. He took the soup she fed him from a spoon, with the obedience of a child. When he had finished, the woman left the room, and he slept again.

Heavy bootsteps on the wooden floor awakened him. Again he saw the woman and a heavyset, bearded man wearing a fur cap.

"Ah, so you are awake. Good. I am Seth, the chief of this village. Not that a chief is needed here. Like the others, I work in the woods." He fell silent as though there was nothing further to say. At last he spoke.

"You are a doctor." He stated this as a fact that he had always known. "We have had no doctor here for as long as anyone can remember. Many of the people are sick. The phlegm in the streets is red. The people say that you have been sent to them. They promise that if you stay here they will build a cottage with a table and chairs and a bed. There will be a garden. This woman will serve you. . . ."

N. was silent. The man continued.

"You must remain, anyway, for the winter. There is nowhere to go. Soon it will begin to snow. It is beginning already, and the road will be impassable."

"I will stay," said N. "Only . . ."

Seth waited. "Yes? What is it?"

"I do not wish to answer any questions. Nothing. I am . . . who I am. That is all."

Seth nodded. "I will tell the others."

Alone with the woman, N. gazed up at her in silence. Mona dropped her glance from him as though to hide something which might have been revealed there. The truth was that N.'s coming had been foretold to Mona in a dream. In her dream, she was a child again and had been sent by her father on an errand. She did not know what it was she had been sent for, only that she must retrace a trail of footprints in the forest where no vegetation grew, and where the grass had been burnt by the steps of whoever had walked there. The path led to a clearing at the center of the woods, a place as bright as childhood. Here the light poured through the trees from a source high above. In her dream, Mona approached the bright place as though beckoned. She held out her hands for whatever she was to receive. All at once the light softened and dimmed. Mona opened her eyes. In her hand was a single drop of pearly fluid.

When she awoke, Mona felt reassured in some deep sense. She dressed and ran to the fountain in the square, understanding only that the time and place of the rendezvous mattered so. From the edge of the square she had watched him tremble and fall. In the few seconds it took her to reach his body, the sun dropped from the sky like a stone.

∾

From the beginning, the people came to his cottage seeking relief from their pain and cough, and for the repair of their wounds. Early each morning, Mona came, bringing food and clean linen. All day she worked with him among the patients. He taught her which herbs to gather, and how to grind them in a mortar and pestle, how to measure out and mix the ingredients of a medicine, how to bathe and dress a wound, how to care for the instruments that he whittled and carved from the bones of squirrels and mice. Each new task she accepted eagerly, but with virtually no speech. She had learned early not to inflict her nasal wheeze on others. Almost at once, N. seemed to know the villagers in some profound and ancient way; not their names as yet, nor their temperaments, nor the facts of their small histories, but their bodies, both individually and collectively. At times, he thought of the village as a single body that had been given him to tend, so that when, here and there, a part of it fractured or burst or wilted, he would turn it over and over in his hands until the damaged spot became visible to him, and he would repair it. In the weeks that followed, what had seemed a village of freaks into which he had stumbled became a village of friends to whom he was bound by a thousand cords of trust. These people would risk everything to save him; he saw it in the faint smiles they let play upon him when he passed.

To the villagers, N.'s diagnoses and treatments were infallible. What he said was the matter with someone became the matter with someone. As though all disease hastened to mold itself to corroborate his intuitions. To bathe the wounds of his patients, N. used freshly melted snow from the center of virgin drifts. The knives he chipped out of slate were sharp and gray as the edge of a pigeon's wing. Once, to suture the thigh of a man who had been clawed by a bear, he used Mona's long black hair, twisted and waxed. There was a woman whose husband had been covered with boils. Before her eyes, he cut open each one of the abscesses and expressed the pus. Then he applied an unguent on a cloth. A week later, the wounds were healed. Nor was there later any sign on his body where they had been. Later, the woman would tell how he had plucked the red sores from her husband's body one by one as though they were flowers. Often, he would coax a patient into sleep, and heal him through dreaming. Before long, the village was like his clothing that he wore next to his skin. Here and there, there would be a tear in his shirt, or the stain of berries. Then he would wash and mend the injured shirt, and put it back on as before.

He had trained himself to gaze at his patients as though he were Adam and each patient were the second human being created. One morning from the doorway of his cottage N. watched three men emerge from the forest. They came across the open field and headed for the village. An old man walked between the two younger men. The old man was bent forward and to the right, as though pulled in that direction by an invisible rope. With his left hand, he gripped his right wrist, supporting it at a fixed distance from his body. The right arm was not allowed to move. The old man's legs were not injured. His step was sure. His head, too, was carried without pain. The men entered the cottage and told their story. Old Rolf had lost his footing on a muddy slope, and had fallen on the outstretched arm with which he had meant to break his fall. There had been a sudden pain in his right shoulder. He was unable to move it.

N. took the right wrist in his own hand, supporting it at the same angle, and he helped remove the old man's jacket and shirt. Then he gave back the injured arm to Rolf, who held it once more, rigid, listing. Now N. could see the difference in the two shoulders, the right being hollow above, and with a lower bulge where the head of the bone had slipped out of its socket. N. motioned Rolf to lie down upon the table. The old man did so, never letting go of his wrist. Now N. knelt to remove his own right boot and sock. Once again he took the wrist of the injured arm in his own hands. This Rolf relinquished in silence. N. raised his leg and gently inserted his bare heel into the old man's armpit. Bracing the body of the man with his heel, he drew down on the arm at the same time, turning it outward. Gradually he increased his pull, until there was a sudden muffled sound as though an apple had fallen from a tree into wet earth. At the sound, the two men, Rolf and N., looked at each other and smiled. N. moved the shoulder through a gentle range of motion, then returned it carefully to the side of the old man. Weeks later, he came upon Rolf chopping wood in front of his cottage.

N. seemed always to be available to the villagers. They had only to seek him out, and with rare exceptions, his whereabouts were predictable. Anyone who was injured or ill knew exactly where to find him. When he was not needed, N.'s existence was not obvious in the village. He faded from the consciousness of the people, remaining as a vague continued presence among them. Only the loss of him from their midst could have informed them of the extent of their calamity.

Far from resenting the indifference of the villagers, N. enjoyed the solitude afforded him to fashion his instruments and create his medicines. Sometimes, it seemed, he cultivated his strangeness. He was not one of them, nor did he wish to be. Only to dwell in the shadow of the village, ready to be summoned or withdraw. Now and then in the evening Seth came to sit with him, bringing a wooden figure that he would set about carving, while N. sharpened his own tools. Mostly, there was no talk, only the silent working in each other's company. Each visit was closed with a glass of brandy. Gradually N. came to count upon Seth's visits, his quiet companionship. Once, when Seth had remained away in the forest for days, N. felt something akin to loneliness.

To the rest, N. was nameless as light. Why had he come there? How? From the very beginning, they assumed that he had *fallen*, in some mysterious way, and they received him with the largeheartedness of people who suspect that someone has already suffered quite enough. Still, they wondered what it was he had done. One old woman, with the audacity of the aged, asked him point-blank what crime had driven him to this "godforsaken place." Had it to do with a woman? He had been sanding down the calluses on the old woman's feet with a rough stone. He smiled, and without pausing at his task, he told her with mock seriousness that he regretted only those sins that he had not had the time or strength to commit. The old woman shrieked and cackled. Mona was outraged at the woman's familiarity. She clamped her hand over the toothless old mouth, and whispered something fierce into her eyes, after which the old woman gasped and sat perfectly still. But N. knew that these people would have forgiven him everything. Murder, even. Such an act could only have been a momentary lapse, not anything to be weighed against him. And without doubt, it would have been justified. If someone should suggest that N. was secretive, someone else would counter by saying that he didn't like wasting his breath. When he looked back at his fugitive months and years, N. was unable to quite remember the pain in his lungs, nor the thorny feet upon which he tottered from city to city, from forest to cave, nor what sustained him, what food, what drink. Only that he had fled and escaped to this place, at this time, and that, without any guidance or help, he had kept a rendezvous.

∽

Every morning at dawn N. returned to the trough in the square to bathe and drink and feel the reflected moon take shelter in his body. The trough itself was of stone and made like the plainest, most ancient fountain. It was bare of ornament. Only that beasts be led there to drink. But surely, he thought, this was more than a mere trough which holds standing, unfed water. This water flowed! It refreshed itself. The more N. gazed into its depths, the more he saw that the trough was, in fact, a small bridge of stone spanning a stream that ran beneath the village. Only a small portion of the running water was led into the catch basin which was the trough. The rest flowed on as a heavy tide. Whatever dark cold energy he drew from the stream was reconstituted into something he could use to heal himself and others. He was learning ancient laws. This stream that he tapped had been flowing since the dawn of mankind. Not even the sound of the cobblestones crying out: Move on! Move on! Not even that warning could have broken his fated sense of homecoming.

∽

In this manner three years went by. One evening, after serving him his meal, Mona tidied up and made as if to leave for the night. But she did not go. Instead, she paused at the table where he still sat, and stood above him in silence. He understood that there was something that she wanted to say. He looked up at her, questioning. At last she spoke.

"My lip. I want you to fix my lip." The suddenness of her request shocked him. All at once, he was trembling.

"That I cannot do," he said quietly. "It is too difficult for me."

"I need you to do it." Her voice, even with the leaking air, was precise and strong. The clarity of it surprised him.

"No. I cannot do it." N. could not have said why. He only knew that he could not. All at once her manner changed. Her voice rose.

"Why? Why? You must help me. You must!" She turned her face and wept into her hair until it was heavy with tears. The breath tore up out of her throat. She doubled over in anguish. He watched the heaving-up and the swallowing-back-down of her disappointment, how it gave and tightened and gave again in her chest. All at once, N. saw that it had been a hope that she had held close to her heart from the moment he had arrived. And hope was something she had never felt before. Had she not attached herself to him like a serf? He waited for her sobbing to subside.

"It is just a small tear," she whispered, "a torn piece."

N. made no answer. Again she was weeping, like a child, with no restraint, as though a whole part of her mouth had been eaten away. N. sat at the table, his head inclined away from her, fending off her sounds. All at once, she fell upon him in fury, punching his head and shoulders and chest with her powerful fists. Seizing him by both arms, she shook him as though to shake out the sutures that she needed, that *must* be lying there like coins in his pocket. What she could not tell him, speaking with her fists, was that there was no way to hide it, that only the night covered her shame, that she had lived like a bat until he, N., had come and led her forth into the light of day. It was he who had done this to her, given her hope. And now, he must. He must!

For a few minutes, N. submitted, then rose to his feet. He put his arms around her, steadying and imprisoning her. Suddenly, she was still, like an animal that slumps into torpor in the jaws of its predator so as not to feel the killing. Carefully and with great precision, the way one fits together the two parts of a broken dish, N. covered her mouth with his own, so that the harelip of the woman was held between his own lips. To the woman it was like a branding. His refusal! And now this! She struggled to free herself, rearing backward, whipping her head from side to side. Her nails dug and raked his back. She bit his lips. She felt herself dying. Blood was coming through his shirt where she had raked him. She tasted his blood in her mouth. In their struggle, the table skidded, a chair overturned. And still he held her. Then, with a quick movement, he bent her backward to the floor. He lay on top of her, pressing against her soft belly between waving, frantic legs. Again he placed his mouth on hers. His tongue was a wasp, stinging the edges of her cleft lip first one way, then the other. Exhausted, she gasped into his open mouth, then pulled his breath back into her lungs, and felt the warmth of it inflating her body, floating it. . . .

Holding her pinned, the ripped and twisted face so close to his own, for a moment N. himself was afraid. The ferocity turned her features into the very jungle through which he had fled for so long. But now N., too, let the kiss take over, submitting to it, he as well as she, stoppering their mouths, stopping up her anguish and his helplessness, sensing somehow that the deed would speak the truth for them both to hear. And he, for his part, when he sank his hands into her long and powerful hair, encountered a braid so thick it satisfied his whole fist. And he, for his part, drank from her as though he were a sunbaked rock at the edge of the sea, and she were the cool foam of the incoming tide all trimmed with bubbles. Now his tongue was like a cunning knife; her mouth was bathed in his medicinal saliva. Mona felt her lips heating, growing hotter and hotter, until her whole mouth turned molten and fluid. There was a flowing, a fusion. Something, a process that had been interrupted long ago, was now being completed. She had a moment of rapture in which healing and ecstasy were indistinguishable.

For a long time they lay still, as though sleeping. At last N. disengaged himself from her and rose. He gazed down at her and his eyes filled with tears. Before he had seen her as whole; now she was wounded in a way that no man could heal. Poor woman, he thought, now you have caught the wound you have longed for all your life. From that day, Mona lived with him in the cottage.

✖

It was spring when the Inspector arrived from the capital. It had been a long journey, first by riverboat, then on horseback. There had been no warning in the village of his visit. Only, perhaps, a slight graying of the sky, which might have been enough to warn the older people, but this year it did not. The Inspector was a short, thick man wearing a long black coat. With the seal of office around his neck, he could have been mistaken for nothing else. About his mouth there lay the lax fatigue of an overtired child.

The Inspector seated himself at the table in N.'s cottage, and took a pack of playing cards out of his coat pocket. He shuffled the cards elaborately and for a long time, then began to deal them out. Each card was served with a small, sharp slap upon the table. Only when the game had been fully set did he begin to speak.

"It seems to me that we have met before?"

"That is always possible." N. was trembling, but willed the muscles of his face to freeze.

"Have you served in the military?"

"I do not like to speak of it."

"Were we together for a time in a hospital during the southern campaign? I think we were. It seems that something happened. I cannot recall it for the moment. Never mind. I shall, in time." The Inspector had the same smile as a scarecrow, and of the same sincerity.

"May I see your credentials? It is a mere formality, you understand." N. made no answer. The Inspector gathered in the cards and riffled them once loudly. "Your diploma, your license to practice medicine."

"I have no credentials."

"What! Nothing to prove that you are what you say you are?"

"I have no papers."

"But this is impossible! What if I say that I do not believe that you are a doctor? Perhaps you are an impostor." The scarecrow smiled again. "Don't take offense, please. One has a right to ask, hasn't one? After all, the people are not sheep to be led to pasture each day by some mysterious shepherd. Come, come, I must have your credentials."

"I have no papers. Doctoring is my work." The words were pronounced quietly and with no trace of outward defiance. He was merely offering an explanation to someone unfamiliar with the customs of a foreign land. Above all, N. wanted to explain to this man that it was not diagnosing that he did, but deciphering. He was, it was true, no doctor. He had merely been given the secret of a code.

The Inspector rose from his chair so abruptly that the table slid and one of the cards fell to the floor at his feet. N. knelt to pick it up, then held the card up to the Inspector, who towered over him. N.'s outstretched arm and upturned face were suppliant. At that moment, N. felt no fear. Only the sudden immense and painful onset of old age.

"It is of no use," said the Inspector. "I remember everything. Who you are, what you have done. An epileptic! How is it that you presume to cure others when you have not the least idea how to help yourself? But this doesn't matter any longer. You are under arrest. You are to remain here under guard until transportation to the capital can be arranged."

In the house of Seth, the Inspector did not smile. "That man, your 'doctor,' is nonesuch. He is a fake, a liar, a criminal. He is wanted for murder."

Even at that moment, word was spreading from mouth to mouth.

The village took on the nature of a town that has been seized and occupied by an enemy. The few survivors of the siege were now being interrogated. They would like to resist; they did not know how. Seth sucked in his saliva.

"How do you know . . . ?"

"I knew him at once, of course. We were stationed at the same military hospital fifteen years ago. In the south. I was in charge of medical supplies; he was an orderly in the surgical wing. It was a famous case. Even then he was a stranger, kept himself apart from the others. Efficient, I'll grant you that. And dependable, or so it was thought until the truth came out. This man is an epileptic. He is subject to violent fits and fits of violence." In answer to Seth's astonishment, the Inspector went on. "So! He has managed to conceal it here also. He is clever enough about it, knows in plenty of time when a seizure is coming on, and he keeps out of sight. It all came out in the court-martial."

"But epilepsy . . . it's no crime."

"One day he had a seizure without any warning. It took place in the middle of a ward full of freshly wounded soldiers. For the first time his convulsion was witnessed. Just before he fell unconscious to the floor of the ward, he leaped upon one of the injured soldiers and strangled him. The man died. When he awoke, your 'doctor' professed no memory of the event, of course. It was later learned that the dead soldier had lent him money. Your man was arrested. A court-martial convicted him of the murder. He was sentenced to be executed by the firing squad. On the eve of his execution, the man broke from his guard and disappeared into the jungle. He was never seen after that." The Inspector bit off the end of a cigar and spat it into his palm. "They tracked him with dogs. Each time they came close, he would slip away. But now . . ." He gave a tiny smile.

"What will happen to him?"

"I leave for the capital in an hour. You are to arrest and guard him day and night until the police arrive to take him off your hands. It will be a matter of six or seven days. If he is not here when they arrive, this entire village will be rounded up and treated as prisoners. I promise you that."

"Arrest! Guard! As though he were a thief! Listen, Excellency . . ."

The Inspector had turned to go.

Seth ran to catch up with the striding man, calling out to him, "What are certificates to us? For three years he has lived among us. He had brought us nothing but comfort. He is a good man. And so many have been cured! Old Rolf, the Abban childbirth . . . you have heard the stories yourself."

"Coincidences. I am not ignorant of these matters. Come now. The truth is that most things will cure themselves if left alone by doctors. The less meddling, the better. The human body knows how to take care of itself. You insist that this man meant well? So be it. Motives are not my concern. Credentials are." The Inspector had already untethered his horse, and mounted. From the height of the saddle, his voice took on a warmer tone. "I am interested in the truth. I do not settle for illusion, no matter how sweet. Why, I believe you people don't care a bit that he is in fact an impostor."

Seth did not answer, but glanced quickly up and down the street as though to commit some act that must not be witnessed. But he made no move. The Inspector smiled.

"Tell me something. Why are you so intent upon protecting him?" His voice was quieter now, insinuating, almost musical.

Beneath the cold smile of the Inspector, Seth shivered.

"Because . . . I love him." But his words never carried to the Inspector over the quick sound of the hoofbeats.

❧

Once again the two men sat at the table in N.'s cottage, as they had so many evenings for three years. Seth spoke softly, behind his hands as though fearing to be heard.

"Why did you do it? Why did you lie and pretend? I must know."

"It was what I expected of myself."

"Weren't you afraid to fail?"

"There are worse terrors. I knew that I could do this work, would not shrink from it. Nor did I imagine it very difficult. And I was right. It is in largest part a matter of craft and intuition. I had only to make and use objects, and to retain the clarity of childhood."

"The people will not accept it. We will never submit. We will rise up."

N. shook his head. "No. You must not resist. In the end it would all be the same."

"But this time you are wrong. There is the small matter of the human spirit."

"No," said N. "I forbid it."

Seth rose from his seat, and came around the table to face N., who had remained seated. In a moment, Seth was on his knees looking up at N. "Please," he said. "We will find a way. What is different today from yesterday?"

"Everything is different."

"But we are all impostors of one sort or another. The worst thing is not to know you are one. That is the real pity. And falseness can collapse under the weight of good work. You have shown that. Please." Seth threw his arms around the seated man's knees, pinning him firmly, as if at that very moment he intended to walk away.

∽

From the beginning Mona had known of his seizures. On that first day, had she not watched him awaken chewing his saliva? Had she not, on that first day, examined his body, looking for inscriptions on it? Once, when they had gone into the forest together to gather herbs for medicine, they had become separated for a bit. All at once she had heard a terrible cry like the scream of a parrot. She had run then in the direction of the sound, calling out for him. She had come upon him lying on the ground in a deep, unrousable sleep. All about him, the stalks of the underbrush had been trampled and bent as in a violent struggle. She had decided then never to speak of it. Nor did she speak of it now. Such a thing was private, unshareable.

N. could tell, often days ahead of time, that an attack was coming. Evidence would begin to accumulate in his body. Feelings of strangeness, dreams, a sudden jerking of his left leg, palpitations, giddiness, unrestrainable laughter, a bunched-up pressure. Above all, that trembling in the pit of his stomach, as though his blood contained the flight of a bird. When the time came near, there were other signs—flashes of light, a hissing as of a great serpent. Long ago, as a youth, he had tried to stifle that hissing with his hands pressed over his ears. But it was of no use. Whatever it was that made that noise lay coiled somewhere within him. At the last, there was a jolting blow to the side of the head that knocked the world aslant. Then, nothing.

Always, on the day after a seizure, he was able to see more clearly than had before. As though the convulsion had somehow blown off a haze that had settled across his mind. At these times, he knew a rapt penetration into things.

∽

From the day of the Inspector's appearance, N. had discontinued his morning visits to the trough in the square. The accusation of the Inspector seemed to forbid it. The very words of the man had rendered him unworthy. Even in his own mind, N. felt himself humiliated. For the first time, his door was barred to the villagers. Hidden, and alone except for Mona, he awaited the police. On the third day, there was a knocking at the door. Mona opened it to Seth, who entered carrying in his arms the body of a small boy, about ten years of age. A glance informed Mona that the child was dying. She motioned Seth to lay the child on the cot. She waited for the man to leave, then closed the door after him.

"It is a child from the next village," she told N. "The father has been walking for two days to bring him here. His name is Mikhail."

N. rose from the chair with great effort. He seemed ancient, ossified. His movements were ponderous. He stood by the side of the cot and reached for the boy's pulse. He found it and trapped it between his fingers. What he felt there was no more than a twine of falling water that wavers in and out of existence. Each time he thought he had it, the pulse darted away. The eyes of the boy were sunken and glazed. They roved aimlessly, now and then disappearing behind the upper lids. The thin nostrils flared with each breath. He breathed in quick, shallow drafts, his mouth open to gulp each bit of air. About the mouth, a pallor. The hollows there were whitened. The mouth was without the least moisture, the teeth coated with a paste of brown and dirty saliva. Inside, the tongue had wilted. N. removed the boy's clothing and exposed the shiny, mounding abdomen. How ashamed it looked! The light pressure of N.'s palm on the abdomen aroused the boy. The roving eyes slowly found their focus, and he saw the man standing over him. All at once the thin little snout crinkled in beggary, and with each quick breath came the mewing of a cat. The abdomen was hot and tight.

Mona watched him standing over the body of the child, watched his fingers playing the belly lightly, counting, receiving. To her, his fingers were like the growing tips of a plant reaching into the unknown. There was something prophetic about those fingers, willing the events here to happen. Now and then she saw him look away into the distance, as though he had left the room, descended into a furrow on his own brow. And all the while his hands never left the body of the young boy. To do so would be to surrender himself to the uprooting of a fierce wind. Only the clean heat of the boy's flesh kept him from being whipped off into a wild air.

"Make ready," he spoke over his shoulder.

The boy was weightless in his arms, a wraith. He laid him upon the table and straightened the thin legs, slid a pillow beneath the head. He might have been arranging a corpse. Taking soap and water, N. bathed the child's belly with solicitude, taking care not to press. The child's small penis stirred in answer to some uninterpretable memory. The veins in the child's skin were green. For a long time he washed the child, repeating the same movements over and over, rubbing in a circular pattern, beginning at the navel and ever increasing the size of the circle until the whole belly was covered. N. could feel the sweat blistering his forehead. He was trembling. I cannot do it, he thought, as though the announcement of his imposture had robbed him of the way to heal this boy. Better for him to die without me as his executioner. It would be another murder. Just then N. felt the handle of a knife slip into his hand. Had it leaped there? His fingers closed around the instrument, each one falling comfortably into rank.

N. laid the belly of the knife against the belly of the child between that pouting navel and the flare of the right hip. He pressed and drew, feeling the exquisite sharpness of the cut in his own flank. Again and again he sliced, each time descending deeper into the body of the child. He knew the landmarks—fat, muscle and the last, the glistening peritoneum. What he sought would be just beneath this.

Mona soaked up the blood with her cloths, and held the incision apart for him to see. Another pass with the knife, and . . . pus. Up and out it billowed and rolled. N.'s hands were covered with it. It ran across the boy's unbearded pubis to fill his groin. It slipped from the sides of the table to the floor. The boy's belly seemed to deflate before his eyes. The breathing eased. The pulse at the groin was rapid and strong. N. propped open the wound with long wicks of waxed cloth, and stepped back from the table. It was done. Mona covered the wound with cloths and tied it around. When she had finished, she turned to see that N. had slumped into a chair. His whole body shook, as though he had become infected with the pus from the child's abdomen. The woman saw that the eyes of the man were caged foxes prowling in slatted light. And she was afraid. She took a pitcher and started out for the square. She knew that she must bring back some water from the trough. She ran all the way, filled her pitcher, and raced back to the cottage. The door was open. The child lay sleeping peacefully on the bed. N. was gone. The empty chair told her that he would never come back.

❧

N. turned abruptly from the path and stepped into the darkness. He felt the forest enter him the way night enters a cottage, through the window, the door, the chimney. Or the way the sea enters a sinking ship. He was absolutely calm, taking upon himself the patience and renunciation of the trees. Out there, in the village, he had given what he had; what had, on that panting, rabid day three years before, been given to him. He remembered Mona flogging him with her howls, himself struggling to create her with his tongue. He had no more of it left. The surgery he had just performed on the boy was the last of it, the final act of incision and drainage. Somehow he had always known that it would be here in the forest. As a child he had been both terrified and charmed by the tracklessness of it. Every blade and twig wanted him. The leaves waited to lick him clean. From far away he heard the sound of men shouting to each other. There was the barking of dogs. Once again, he was a fugitive. He crashed ahead through the underbrush, weaving among the trees. The muddy, reluctant floor gave back each of his footsteps. From this mud his boots sucked up phantoms. No sooner were these freed from the wet earth than they, too, joined in his pursuit. On and on he slogged. He would not choose the exact place; he would know it when he arrived. He had only, when the moment came, to turn and face it without imposture. At the end point of life was honesty. The low branch of a beech tree swept across his chest, pressing him gently to the ground. There, caught and flickering in a thicket of his own planting, N. turned and lay on his back, letting his fingers enjoy the shallow mud. High above, specks of blue sky, fragments of another world from which he was already receding.

He remembered the cobblestones of the square dancing about his feet. He remembered leaning over the trough, dipping out the secrets of the river and listening to the heavy drag of water far below. It had the solidity of ice. He remembered it streaming through his body until he himself was transparent and permeable, like a fish. He had felt then that he was in the process of *becoming*—exactly what, he did not know, something between the golden sun and the dark river, something like the moon, a midmost thing that hides itself in the light of the day. Now N. turned to lie facedown, pressing his cheek into the wetness. The cool mud was a healing poultice. He had never known such a sense of well-being, so exultant a physical health. All at once he became aware of a sound at his ear, repeating and repeating. It had exactly the soft, muffled click of old Rolf's dislocated shoulder as it snapped back into place. He held himself to that sound for a long minute as though it were a plank that had been cast to him in a raging sea, then relinquished it with all the rest. N. smiled. Who would have thought it would be old Rolf who would make the sound that would usher him away. And make it not with his mouth, but with the capsule and cartilage of his shoulder? It seemed to him a sound for which he had been listening all his life, and that had always eluded him, but that now at last he had heard.

Now N. turned his head and pressed his face into the floor of the forest. Deeply he inhaled, drawing the mud in, feeling it slide at the back of his throat. There was no pain, no choking, as though water were passing over the gills of a fish. Nothing but immense and endless comfort, a sense of being reclaimed. No pain! But this was the death of a righteous man. He had not earned it! Pushing in, he filled his lungs with the benevolence.

∽

For three days they searched, crashing through the woods, following each flutter and wave, sniffing every wind, scanning the sky for smoke, bounding up toward some movement and finding only each other. The dogs never caught his scent. As well hound the moon across the sky, the people said later. At last they gave up. They left him to the forest.

From the day of his disappearance, the stories began. That day, it was said, all the pigeons of the square twined and wove through the streets of the village, then flew away. Nor had they returned. A town without pigeons is a dead town, the old women said, and consoled themselves with weeping together. The villagers whom N. had treated were envied and deferred to. Whenever people gathered, someone was persuaded (without much difficulty) to tell once more the story of his healing. Come on, Rolf. It's your turn. Tell how he put your arm back in its socket. And Rolf would step forward a bit and tell again how N. had taken off his boot and his sock, how he himself had waited as a child waits to be tickled until he felt (ah!) that heel snuggling into his armpit. The pressure of N.'s bare flesh against the hollow of his own was snug and more perfect than anything his old body had ever known; then there was the pulling, until the little click at the end. And as he remembered, Rolf's left hand would rise to the place where N.'s heel had rested, as though to recapture the touch.

A woman told how he had plucked the red sores from her husband's body as though he were gathering flowers. Each one tried to recall the things he had said, his words that should console them through the lives they must now live without him. But they could only remember his deeds; there were no words, nor any writings. Only the remembered pressure of his palm, the rapt penetration of his gaze, the notion that where he had walked, it became brighter.

Wherever he walked, a sweet smell lingered, they said. When he coughed, every door in the village swung open, they said. One man, a hunter, remembered his footprints, and the lingering steam of his breath. The boy, Mikhail, the last of them to be touched by him, remembered his own head falling against N.'s chest as he carried him to the table, remembered his own open mouth, and the feel against his cheek of N.'s nipple through the cotton shirt. To another child, who had been healed by dreaming, he was a shapeless vision, with no words or pictures to represent it, yet past all forgetting. And all together they remembered the time that a bear shambled into the village and right into the square. There was the ring of its claws on the frozen stones. The frightened cottage doors had never seen anything like it. And how N. was not afraid, and had gone to it, smiling to see the bear mounding over the trough, dipping its paw into the water, fishing.

What first were recollections became legends. A wind of prophecy blew through the village. There were rumors. Soon N. had entered their dreams, not only the dreams of each one separately, but the dreams of the whole village, in the same guise. No sooner had a woman lain down in her bed than she would see N. bending over the horse trough, or squatting near the road, whittling toward sharpness. Mostly they saw him touching them. It was like a slow contagion of sleep that spread from cottage to cottage until the dreams of every man, woman, and child were infested. They reported their dreams to each other. An old woman told of walking along the edge of the forest behind his cottage. She heard a flapping noise as though a blanket were being shaken. And then she had seen him rising in the air to the topmost branches of a tree. Just folded his arms across his chest, like this, she said. And she would show them. And cried out, "Oh!" in a loud clear voice. Then up he went. Oh, yes, it's true, Lubov's cat had gotten stranded. Which is Lubov's? The gray-and-white with six toes. Shut up and let her tell the rest. What does it matter which is Lubov's cat? You want to know, go to Lubov, he'll show you. Come, Granny, tell the rest. And the old woman would fold her arms across her vanished bosom to show how he came down in the same way, holding the cat on his shoulder.

A man lay in the forest with blood pillaring from a wound in his flesh. From his cottage, N. had called over to the column of blood, "Stop!" And it had stopped, frozen. Then he walked to where the man lay and knelt to break off the solid spurt from the clean healed skin.

And this from a young man who had been born a little foolish: He had been setting his traps in the woods just north of the fields when he caught sight of N. standing alone in the middle of a meadow. The youth drew near to greet N., who had not long before stitched up a deep gash in his thigh. But when he drew near, N. was nowhere to be seen. Instead there was a pool of clear water spreading on the meadow where he had been. The water was both transparent and reflecting. Fish and lilies and clouds were contained within it. And the moon. The young man felt a great yearning to enter the pool. He closed his eyes for a moment. When he opened them and gazed again into the pool, the moon was gone, and where it had been there was the pale and luminous face of N. Just as the youth might have entered the water, he saw N.'s head rise from the center of the pool, then his neck and chest, his whole body, and even as he emerged, the pool shrank until it was only the shirt and sleeves the man wore. Then N. turned and saw the young man, and he smiled as though he had just been surprised in an act of play. Think of it! It had all happened within the space of one breath. Up and out came his head, then his shoulders, arms, legs. Then he drew the water upon himself like a robe with flowing sleeves, until there was no pool at all, only N. standing there smiling, and shaking the last drops from his head.

∽

And Mona, too, lay in her bed, her head filled with the consequences of the kiss that she could never express, when, like a bat, she had fastened on his warm blood and drank him in and in, parting and searching the hair on her lover's chest, becoming absorbed in the mystery of his nipples. She saw him trembling in the grass, all about him shadows lying curled like great beasts. Needles of light pricked his body. And she tasted again his blood in her mouth where she had bitten him.

For her now, the kiss was a thing that existed by itself. Somehow, between his giving of it, and her receiving it, the kiss had sprung into real substance, something made of flesh, that knew her entirely. And Mona remembered and kept secret the body of N. the way she had kept secret his epilepsy, as though she were a priestess whose charge it was to guard a sacred flame. But the others wondered about it and whispered. After all, it was no secret that she had shared his bed. What must it have been like to lie with such a man? And so N. entered the fantasies of the women. They would lie awake in the dark and try to imagine his body, which must have been the most beautiful in the world. They would try to picture long white limbs, not too fleshy or thin, a blend of strength and languor. Oh, what must it have been like? The men, too, dreamt of it, and their pulses speeded up. Had anyone dared to ask her, Mona would never have said what she had known of his body, known with her eyes, her hands, her teeth even; would not have said that even in his nakedness he had been shielded from her, as though he had been fully clothed; that, even naked, he had seemed to her to wear his own body as raiment.

Mona continued to live in the cottage she had shared with N. For a while the villagers came seeking medicine, but Mona offered none, and soon they stopped coming. As time went by, she withdrew further and further from the life of the village. She left the cottage only to tend her garden, or to get water. On the street, after dusk, she was a shadowy figure with scarves and shawls flapping about her head. It seemed to the others that she had lived in another age, when myths were made, and heroes and gods walked among men. Somehow she had survived, and was here amongst them now, a bit of evidence.

"Ahhhhh! . . . Look!" A woman would see her on the street and she would stand aside to let her pass. Later the woman would send her child to leave a basket of food on the steps of Mona's cottage. But don't knock, she would instruct the child. Just put the food there, and run home. A few of the oldest people remembered her as she had been. They remembered that there had been something wrong with her, and that she had been healed by N. None could quite recall what it had been . . . something about her face . . . but to anyone who caught a glimpse of her, half hidden in scarves, there was nothing to be seen.

∽

In this manner, sixty years went by. Seth had died a year after N.'s disappearance, calling out, it was said, in a voice full of terrible longing. Mona had long since been buried in the garden at the back of N.'s cottage. Some say that she had taken her own life, had thrown herself into the great river on the anniversary of his coming. Early the next year, just before the thaw, a fisherman caught sight of something gleaming just beneath the transparent ice. He chipped away the crust and saw an upturned face. It was Mona, her frozen body intact. But the face was that of a beautiful young woman.

On the anniversary of his coming, the shrine was opened to the public. Visitors came from far and wide. From the capital, even. By carriage and sled and riverboat, they came to dip their cups into the horse trough. Their sips were self-conscious and reluctant. Was the water safe for drinking? The Fountain of Healing, it was called. From there, the pilgrims crossed the well-worn (and often-replaced) cobblestones to the village street on which N.'s cottage still stood. Inside, they would ogle the glass cases of polished mouse bones, the strands of hair, braided and waxed, the mortar and pestle, the bed where he had slept, his chair. They were silent, save for the loud clomping of their boots on the bare planking of the floor. The noise irritated Mikhail, who would scold them rudely.

"Pick them up, Princess Heavyfoot. Come, come, Twinkle-toes. This is a shrine. Show some respect."

Mikhail's ill temper was famous. A favorite blasphemy among the pilgrims was to whisper that N. had left some putrid humors inside the old fellow's belly, and that only now were they working their way to the opposite. But then they would gaze at the handmade oak table upon which the cranky old man had lain as a child, waiting for N. to lay open his body. Then their eyes would be drawn to the sacristan in awe, and they would forgive him. At precisely that moment Mikhail would lift the hem of his shirt, and pull down on his belt to show the scar. The women would draw in their breath, and the men would reach for another coin. It was a good living.

Semiprivate, Female

Room 324 is at the end of the corridor. It has four beds, each separated from the others by a curtain which can be drawn to achieve that status listed in the admissions office as Semiprivate, Female. In this room, at this time, it is less the presence of the curtains between the beds than the shrouded minds of the women that secure for each her territory. In any case, they lie hidden from each other. Only their dreams cannot be kept separate. These issue forth in sallies from the beds to mingle aloft. Opposite the door is a bank of windows coverd by slatted blinds. The roses are cruel that line the ledge in front. From the outside ledge comes the low, watery trill of roosting pigeons. The nurse in charge of this ward will strive by her presence to bind the patients together. She cannot bear their isolation. All day she will use her strong body, stepping from one bed to the other, spinning threads of cheerful talk. Her hands will touch them each in turn, her voice urge them into a community, coax. But in the end, neither she nor they will be persuaded.

All night the women have fed the sick moisture with their lungs. The curtains belly and collapse with each breath. Palpable wisps are a gauntlet through which the nurse must pass. She sets her bowed head against the air and barges in. Then goes quickly to raise the blinds. The windows are flung open, discharging the pigeons and bringing into focus the litter of the night. This nurse depends upon the magic of air and sunlight. For a long moment she stands in the center of the room and sighs for her task. Somehow she must scour it clean, make of the dark, infectious squalor a neat thatched cottage. But even then she knows that in spite of everything it would remain a stumpy, cockeyed hovel. She could hope only for the simple dignity of shiny floors and plumped pillows.

The hush of the night is still present, made even more hushed by the noises that come from the beds, as though small deer are stamping among dry leaves. It cannot be done, the nurse thinks. Although God knows she has hummed hymns often enough as she mopped and swabbed and polished. Precisely because she has tended and pitied, the desolation is hers as well. Soon she is joined by another woman, an aide. They smile and draw resolve from each other's bosoms and arms. The aide steps to one bedside and gently shakes a vanished shoulder.

"Wake up, dear," she calls into the heap of cinders and other hard particulars. "Time to get up. How do you feel today?"

A purse string is tugged, and a dusty mouth that had hung open all night is slowly gathered in.

"How do you feel this morning?" she calls out again. The woman in the bed stirs. A pair of gulls is pulling at the carcass of sleep. At last she speaks.

"How do I feel? Dead. And it ain't half bad. So go away and let me be."

"We'll have a nice bath. Don't you want a bath?" says the aide. And the two nurses begin with pans of water. Together they soap armpits and legs, taking some pleasure themselves in the warm lather, then wiping dry with towels. No crease so hidden, no bag of skin so empty, that they will not bathe and powder and cream. They turn the woman from side to side to extricate wet yellow sheets and lay new resentful ones, pulling them tight. Old dry hair that at any given cough might be dislodged from her head is brushed and braided. Now and then a groan reproaches good intentions. All the while the hungry bed curtain reaches for the backs of the nurses, mad for attention. The nurses move quickly now, emptying pans, bringing fresh water, crooning. Their uniforms stir up the smells of alcohol, tincture of benzoin, oil of cloves—sincerer smells than the cajolery of the flowers on the ledge. At last, creamed and oiled with rich vowels, the woman settles back in the bed, sighs and takes root. Who can withstand the battering? Just so, these nurses repeat over and over the simplest tasks, faithfully trimming toenails, and wiping the matter from eyes, never voicing their love, but storing it up in the bodies of these others until, one by one, they should burst into flower.

"Give us a chance, ladies," they call out to the other drawn curtains. "You'll get yours soon enough." Even before they have finished tidying, the first bed is soiled by the woman's whimpers.

∽

But now the doctor has arrived. It is like a rock falling into moist earth. He is a big man, a surgeon after all, with a clumsy face rescued by pale green eyes and by a mahogany voice which any number of nurses have said is a powerful therapy in itself. Years ago, he had not hesitated to lower his voice even further at the bedside of a patient he had diagnosed as being susceptible. But no more. The green eyes have long since been weakened, made more permeable by the sights they have seen. He has lost an entire dimension. He has forgotten himself. Now he listens to presences. On rounds the imperious placement of his feet has softened into a kind of lumbering. In his youth he had played football. Still, at the first sound of his footsteps the room trembles, then recovers itself.

Again and again the doctor has tried to cast his net about the secrets of this room. But he cannot. All he can do is gaze and listen. There are times when he is in a tomb ministering to phantoms. Perhaps if he were to make a diagram of this room, everything drawn to scale, if he were to count and measure every object, perhaps he would come upon the one piece that did not fit, a blunder in the design. He would study this mistake until it revealed the mystery of this place. Then it would be given to him to know. He envies the nurses to whom the patients will offer fragments of their lives, small illuminations from which by his gender or his position, whatever, he is excluded. He must divine. It is never so reliable as revelation. Once, while standing at the bedside of someone who had just slipped into coma, he had had an urge to bend close to that face, which was like a blank sheet of paper, and tell his own secrets, which he knew would be safe there and nowhere else. But he had not uttered a word to that muteness where sleep and waking take no turn, where nothing is born and nothing dies. The bed is still empty where she had lain for months blind and bandaged like an ear of unshucked corn. Coma—who can elect it? Who renounce? Her age could not have been told, existing as she had on some vestigial, osmotic plane which required only an occasional breath, only the slowest crawl of the blood. One night, even these sluggish tides had stopped. The change was imperceptible, the way rain slowly sifts through the trees long after a storm. So that when the nurse had discovered her, lapsed at the end of a long sigh, for a few moments she had not been sure.

⁐

The patient in the next bed is an emaciated woman, a Filipina in the sixth month of a pregnancy. There is a frost of ashes about her mouth. Each night she is swept clean by a fever that has burnt up every bit that is not essential—blood, saliva, tears, tissue. Only the mighty fetus, raving to be born, is not touched. Even as the child buds and splits and specializes, the woman grows daily less differentiated until she is something rudimentary, a finger of flesh, unfulfilled, unformed, that will surely die of its one achievement. She resembles a snake that has swallowed a rabbit and is exhausted by her digestion. Through the translucent, dark-veined belly, the legs of her meal, moving.

She has had no visitors, the nurse informs. One morning the sun was sparking the blinds. A breeze from the open window blew aside the smoky curtain around the Filipino woman's bed, and he had a glimpse of her lying with her robe half apart. And the flickering, radiant abdomen swollen like dough under a damp cloth. Waves of heat rose from it, distorting his vision. He was shocked to find her so young, a child, really, with eyebrows thin and arched like a moth's. And tiny inquisitive fingers probing her pouting navel. On that morning, behind the untrustworthy curtain, alone save for the ghost of pleasure she was bearing, she had been smiling! The last of it was still upon her inconsolable mouth. She had seemed then beyond the reach of anyone. He had an impulse to step through the curtains and examine her body for the imprint of a hand, teeth marks, some proof that once a man had bent there to kindle a fire and warm himself.

∽

The doctor goes to the bed next to the one where the nurses are working. When the occupant sees him standing there, her thin neck strives to rise from the pillow, but cannot lift the heavy fruit it carries. He has often been able to tell by a woman's neck that she will not last long. The woman watches him the way a dog eats his master's face while waiting for table scraps. A flame of hope blazes up. It leaps out of her blue eyes and singes him. He finds a reason to step back from the bed. During the night a red rubber tube had crept into her nose and wound through the swollen coils of her intestine. Ever since, it has fed with long, wet sucks, until now the bottle on the floor is half filled with suds and stagnant slime. The doctor draws down the sheet to percuss and auscultate her chest. Through the stethoscope, a feeble crackling. Beneath the skin, the ribs swirl and wallow with each breath. He remembers how two weeks ago she had walked into the hospital dressed in green, which he had taken as an ominous sign. When he was a young boy he had seen the ripped lawn of artificial grass that had been thrown over a new grave to hide the rawness, but which could not conceal his embalmed father beneath it. Oh, yes, green was the color of foreboding. Life had taught him to look for these little clues. She was a timid, powdery woman who seemed to perch alongside her body lest she be overly identified with something that might not really be hers. Then, she had answered his questions vaguely, disremembering events, losing track, evading, because what she feared more than anything else was becoming trapped in this capsizing body and never being able to get out. She much preferred to hover like a ghost. When he pressed her abdomen, he knew it was her thoughts more than the pain that made her wince. Still, he saw, timidity had not robbed her of grace. Now and then, when she reached out to move something two inches to the left, her long pale fingers stirred him.

The doctor removes his white coat and rolls up his sleeves to change the dressing over the colostomy he has made in her abdomen. Her hands, trying to keep out of the way, become hopelessly lost. Beyond all intent her eyes rove the mound of her entrails. She had not meant to look. She who has always rejected all mysteries is forced to unravel this one. Not so long ago in the orange groves of Florida she had loved a man with all her heart. From the day he had left her, without a single word, she never dared to utter his name. Now, when she sees the intestine arching thick and raw from her body, she is somehow reminded. In the risen coil of bowel nailed to the surface and broiled by the unaccustomed sunlight, she sees her lover in a scum of glazed fat. The scent of oranges drifts into the room and creeps into the openings of her body.

"It is time to open the colostomy," the doctor says. "There will be no pain. There are no nerve fibers in the bowel." And he plugs in the electric cautery. It is a gun that he holds. He presses the trigger and she watches the wire loop brighten. When it is red-hot, he presses it to the bowel. There is a hiss, crackling. Smoke rises. She smells herself cooking. Then the long brown smell of feces. The doctor has long since trained himself to remain aloof from the smell of burning flesh, and presses on with his task. Still, it happens that while operating late in the evening and having missed his dinner, he, too, smells the meat cooking. Then, it can't be helped, saliva gathers.

"In a few weeks it will shrink down to a rosebud," the doctor tells her. "You will only have to wear a little bag." In the harsh light the belly gasps. A fit of retching takes it. Up comes blood.

"What . . . ?" she asks him. And waits. She has the petaled look of something in a vase.

"Cancer," he says. The word blisters his lips. And he thinks of an ox trampling a pasture, transforming the grass into its own thudding excrement. And he wonders with what she would be able to persuade herself now that he has set her mind adrift in this room. He does not approve of lying to patients to encourage them falsely. But, it is possible, as every gardener knows, to fool flowers into blooming by keeping a light on all night. In the leaden bafflement that follows, he is aware of his naked forearms, the black hair on his wrists, the ropy veins. There had been trouble drawing her blood for the laboratory. She had been stuck so many times. The veins were broken, thrombosed. He himself had tried without success.

"Open and close your fist," he had told her. "It's time to feed the vampire. That's it. Pump up a good one." Her fingers bunched, but it was very far from a fist. Nor were her veins to be seen or felt—shy little lizards' tails that sensed the needle drawing near, and laid themselves flat among the hummocks of fat, changing color even. He wished he could have lent her one of his own. It was as close as he had ever dared come to taking upon himself the pain of someone else. He himself has yet to be sick. By what seems to him a miracle, considering the possibilities, his parts have continued to mesh and revolve smoothly for fifty years despite the beating he has given himself in this work. Only now and then, lately, he finds himself listening for the faint sound of turbulence in his blood, the grating of cartilage over a bony spur. That the patients did not enjoy the same physical ease, well, once in a while it did make him self-conscious, but never to the point of guilt. No one, he reminded himself, could refuse the gifts of health or disease. Still, he would gladly have opened one of his veins for her.

Now, he sees, without looking about, the crack in one of the windows, the large water stain on the ceiling, the peeling radiator. Already new blood was darkening the fresh dressing he had just done. All these things expressing themselves. Even the mop and pail, the rampant mantling curtains. He longs for his carpentry bench. The smell of the wood soothes him as he cut it to size, planes it smooth. This room is like the belly pocket of his overalls into which once he had reached for a nail and pulled out a still-fluttering brown moth.

At last the woman's lips part and the tip of her tongue surfaces. Her mouth is crammed with words that she does not know how to speak. Only the sunlight passing through the crack in the drawn curtains gives any reason to hope.

"What is the cause of it? Why did it happen?"

"It is one of those things," he tells her. And thinks of how, two days before, he had payed out the length of her intestines with his hands until he had come to the blockage, had seen, then, the peritoneum cauliflowered with growths that mounted each other wildly. Ever since her admission to the hospital she had been dosing herself with bits of the past, feeling that she had to remember it all, must not leave anything unrecollected. As though her life were a silver path that she had secreted, and in order to survive she had to retrace every step of it. Now, all at once, she knows that she will go no further than this, that she will stop here at this hole in her abdomen.

Mistakes, like copper bands, tighten around the doctor's temples. What kind of honest work leaves scabs on someone else's knuckles at the end of the day? How he hated this room—the dubious promise of the place, the duplicity of it. Toying with the hopeful, singling out the weaknesses of the downcast, until their hearts were broken. When, finally, the woman opens to scream, it is he who claps a hand over her mouth to hold it back. What comes from her is the sound of a horse blowing out its nostrils. The ceiling, having heard it all before, has grown deaf, and is intent only upon extending its watermark that has no shape or image. At last he leaves her alone with her hands that lay at either side of her head to form a fragile basket for her eyeballs.

The solarium is at the opposite end of the corridor. It is another sorrow of a room. Here, the doctor watches as a man wearing a brow of thorns waters the artificial plants with real tears. He is the woman's husband. His name is Tom.

From then on, the woman never stops. To and fro her flesh swims in quarter circles, paddling for all she is worth to reach a shore. But sinking deeper and deeper. Now and then she will rise to the surface, take a few swallows of air, squawk, then down again to whatever murk. On her last day, at that red hour of evening when Grace, if it will come at all, is most likely to make an appearance, the doctor, laying himself open, returns to her bedside. The thorned man is there, holding the curtains away with his broad back to keep them from reaching for whatever is left still quivering upon the bed. A pot of yellow tulips sits on the nightstand and voices assurance that nothing bad is taking place. All at once, the woman pauses in her work, turns her head as though to listen. A breach of clarity opens, and with it, immense pain. Her eyes are crystals of it.

"Eddie! Eddie!" she cries out. "For God's sake, Eddie!"

But the husband's name is Tom!

"Shh . . . shh," he says. "I'm here."

"Eddie! Oh, love!" she calls out again. She is running wildly through streets of confusion, thinking to tag a footstep, making a last run for it.

"Yes," says the man simply. "It's all right. I've come. I'm here." And takes her hand. But the hand will not be deceived and flicks away an imaginary insect. So that the man, Tom, knows that she has kept a secret. He wrenches his gaze to a distant place somewhere above the bed, looking after something slippery that he had once held but that had suddenly spurted from his hands.

A young boy, too, leans against the gassy curtain. Dazzled, the boy cannot pry his gaze from his mother's face. Nor ever would be rid of it. Years later, in these deep breaths, one after the other, rolling in, rolling out like the sea, in the deepest of them, he would locate his own most painful memories.

✑

Much later, the doctor hurries up the steps to his house. He turns the key in the lock, opening the door only wide enough to let himself in. But it is no use. Like an unwanted homeless dog the room follows him into the house, demanding that he step into it and *do something*.

Brute

You must never again set your anger upon a patient. You were tired, you said, and therefore it happened. Now that you have excused yourself, there is no need for me to do it for you.

Imagine that you yourself go to a doctor because you have chest pain. You are worried that there is something the matter with your heart. Chest pain is your Chief Complaint. It happens that your doctor has been awake all night with a patient who has been bleeding from a peptic ulcer of his stomach. He is tired. That is your doctor's Chief Complaint. I have chest pain, you tell him. I am tired, he says.

Still I confess to some sympathy for you. I know what tired is.

Listen: It is twenty-five years ago in the emergency room. It is two o'clock in the morning. There has been a day and night of stabbings, heart attacks, and automobile accidents. A commotion at the door: A huge black man is escorted by four policemen into the emergency room. He is handcuffed. At the door, the man rears as though to shake off the men who cling to his arms and press him from the rear. Across the full length of his forehead is a laceration. It is deep to the bone. I know it even without probing its depths. The split in his black flesh is like the white wound of an ax in the trunk of a tree. Again and again he throws his head and shoulders forward, then back, rearing, roaring. The policemen ride him like parasites. Had he horns, he would gore them. Blind and trussed, the man shakes them about, rattles them. But if one of them loses his grip, the others are still fixed

386

and sucking. The man is hugely drunk—toxic, fuming, murderous—
a great mythic beast broken loose in the city, surprised in his night
raid by a phalanx of legionnaires armed with clubs and revolvers.

I do not know the blow that struck him on the brow. Or was there
any blow? Here is a brow that might have burst on its own, spilling
out its excess of rage, bleeding itself toward ease. Perhaps it was done
by a jealous lover, a woman, or a man who will not pay him the ten
dollars he won on a bet, or still another who has hurled the one insult that he cannot bear to hear. Perhaps it was done by the police
themselves. From the distance of many years and from the safety of
my little study, I choose to see it thus:

The helmeted corps rounds the street corner. A shout. "There he
is!" And they clatter toward him. He stands there for a moment, lurching. Something upon which he had been feeding falls from his open
mouth. He turns to face the policemen. For him it is not a new challenge. He is scarred as a Zulu from his many battles. Almost from
habit he ascends to the combat. One or more of them falls under his
flailing arms until—there is the swing of a truncheon, a sound as
though a melon has been dropped from a great height. The white
wedge appears upon the sweating brow of the black man, a waving
fall of blood pours across his eyes and cheeks.

The man is blinded by it; he is stunned. Still he reaches forth to
make contact with the enemy, to do one more piece of damage. More
blows to the back, the chest, and again to the face. Bloody spume flies
from his head as though lifted by a great wind. The police are spat-
tered with it. They stare at each other with an abstract horror and disgust. One last blow, and, blind as Samson, the black man undulates,
rolling in a splayfooted circle. But he does not go down. The police
are upon him then, pinning him, cuffing his wrists, kneeing him toward the van. Through the back window of the wagon—a netted
panther.

In the emergency room he is led to the treatment area and to me.
There is a vast dignity about him. He keeps his own counsel. What is
he thinking? I wonder. The police urge him up on the table. They put
him down. They restrain his arms with straps. I examine the wound,
and my heart sinks. It is twelve centimeters long, irregular, jagged
and, as I knew, to the skull. It will take at least two hours.

I am tired. Also to the bone. But something else. . . . Oh, let me not deny it. I am ravished by the sight of him, the raw, untreated flesh, his very wildness which suggests less a human than a great and beautiful animal. As though by the addition of the wound, his body is more than it was, more of a body. I begin to cleanse and debride the wound. At my touch, he stirs and groans. "Lie still," I tell him. But now he rolls his head from side to side so that I cannot work. Again and again he lifts his pelvis from the table, strains against his bonds, then falls heavily. He roars something, not quite language. "Hold still," I say. "I cannot stitch your forehead unless you hold still."

Perhaps it is the petulance in my voice that makes him resume his struggle against all odds to be free. Perhaps he understands that it is only a cold, thin official voice such as mine, and not the billy clubs of half a dozen cops, that can rob him of his dignity. And so he strains and screams. But why can he not sense that I am tired? He spits and curses and rolls his head to escape from my fingers. It is quarter to three in the morning. I have not yet begun to stitch. I lean close to him; his steam fills my nostrils. "Hold still," I say.

"*You* fuckin' hold still," he says to me in a clear, fierce voice. Suddenly, I am in the fury with him. Somehow he has managed to capture me, to pull me inside his cage. Now we are two brutes hissing and batting at each other. But I do not fight fairly.

I go to the cupboard and get from it two packets of heavy, braided silk suture and a large curved needle. I pass one of the heavy silk sutures through the eye of the needle. I take the needle in the jaws of a needle holder, and I pass the needle through the center of his right earlobe. Then I pass the needle through the mattress of the stretcher. And I tie the thread tightly so that his head is pulled to the right. I do exactly the same to his left earlobe, and again I tie the thread tightly so that his head is facing directly upward.

"I have sewn your ears to the stretcher," I say. "Move, and you'll rip 'em off." And leaning close, I say in a whisper, "Now *you* fuckin' hold still."

I do more. I wipe the gelatinous clots from his eyes so that he can see. And I lean over him from the head of the table, so that my face is directly above his, upside down. And I grin. It is the cruelest grin of my life. Torturers must grin like that, beheaders and operators of racks.

But now he does hold still. Surely it is not just fear of tearing his earlobes. He is too deep into his passion for that. It is more likely some beastly wisdom that tells him that at last he has no hope of winning. That it is time to cut his losses, to slink off into high grass. Or is it some sober thought that pierces his wild brain, lacerating him in such a way that a hundred nightsticks could not? The thought of a woman who is waiting for him, perhaps? Or a child who, the next day and the week after that, will stare up at his terrible scars with a silent wonder that will shame him? For whatever reason, he is perfectly still.

It is four o'clock in the morning as I take the first stitch in his wound. At five-thirty, I snip each of the silks in his earlobes. He is released from his leg restrainers and pulled to a sitting position. The bandage on his head is a white turban. A single drop of blood in each earlobe, like a ruby. He is a maharajah.

The police return. All this time they have been drinking coffee with the nurses, the orderlies, other policemen, whomever. For over three hours the man and I have been alone in our devotion to the wound. "I have finished," I tell them. Roughly, they haul him from the stretcher and prod him toward the door. "Easy, easy," I call after them. And, to myself, if you hit him again . . .

∽

Even now, so many years later, this ancient rage of mine returns to peck among my dreams. I have only to close my eyes to see him again wielding his head and jaws, to hear once more those words at which the whole of his trussed body came hurtling toward me. How sorry I will always be. Not being able to make it up to him for that grin.